TRIAL OF FIRE:
Elf Queen of Kiirajanna (volume 4)

STEPHEN H. KING

(TOSK)

CONTENTS

ACKNOWLEDGMENTS

It's not easy to write a novel. Sometimes it takes months, and sometimes it takes – well, years.

This one in particular was born in a time when I wasn't in my best novel-writing mental space. It was very difficult to move from extremely rough draft to a novel I felt was befitting the final legacy of the Elf Queen of Kiirajanna. Thankfully, my beloved Heide never gave up on me or the novel.

To my fans who kept pushing me to get this one done – thank you.

To Pam Manning, the amazing leader of the best project based course in graphic design I've ever seen, thank you.

To Zowie Griffith, Pam's student – you took my idea and created an amazing cover. Thank you.

To those who explicitly doubted my ability to get this book completed and out – huh. Here it is.

To my loyal readers who've been waiting on the climax of the series – huh, here it is. I'm so glad to be able to present you with this, and I'm even more glad you've hung on so long.

War is On

The day I *became* queen in my own head is also the day the whole elf monarchy quite nearly came crashing down.

First, though, the story of how the day shaped itself around me.

I stood in the middle of the clearing in the heart of Kiirajanna, a naive eighteen-year-old girl from Mississippi, surrounded by my few allies: my father the elf king, his queen, the powerful high priestess, and a much-too-small group of retainers and warriors and priests. At my side stood Aerona, my faithful bodyguard, Sephaline, my cousin and partner in crime, and Prince Keion, the dashing elf warrior with soft, mesmerizing lips who could probably in solo combat take on an entire company of those who stood in riotous anger against us—against me, personally, and also against my rise to the throne of Kiirajanna.

I don't think I'd ever done much to upset them, at least not on purpose. I'd arrived fairly ignorant of their ways, sure, but I'd gotten to know the elves of Cysegredig, the central palace area, and their customs, as well as those in the north. There was only the one minor instance of library-burning to put down as a negative. And, maybe, once I'd punched the high priestess in her stern nose. Well, that, and the minor war between Dad and the north, but that was because I'd found one of the bad guys—girls—whatever—hiding in plain sight and...well, that was an old story by this point.

Not too bad, right?

There was also the matter of the prophecy. It *had* predicted I'd burn the library down, to be honest, and since I hadn't intended to start that fire I still chalked that one up to – well, I guess prophecy. The rest of it all didn't sound a whole lot better for my case, granted, but I thought I should at least be given the chance to prove it wrong.

The group of elves gathered against us didn't think so.

Anger and contempt swirled around the clearing, the energies plain and palpable. I felt like a pillar of self-doubt buffeted back and forth by the raging storm of chaos that surrounded me. The elves, the nice, peaceful folk I'd encountered not quite a single year before, were shouting, actually raising their voices, and I...just stood there, confused.

If I had to paint a picture of "Exactly The Opposite Of What A Queen Should Look Like" it would have been me, at that moment, in that clearing.

"You said you would banish the demon child!" Swadda screamed. The other side's ringleader was called Swadda of the Serpent Veils because nobody ever saw her actual skin; most blamed it on the intense sun of the continent's western region. Everything she wore sparkled like the iridescent scales of a great viper while still hugging her well-shaped form so that every curve she was blessed with was opaquely visible.

I'd noticed Keion appreciating those curves a time or two, but this time he loomed like a statue at my side, his jaw clenched angrily at the insult she'd hurled at me. She was the *penna*, the leader, of the massive, warlike clan of elves of the Western Desert, and so her words were powerful, but he was the son of the queen, a magnificent warrior who could take on pretty much anybody in a fair fight, and I treasured his presence.

It wasn't looking to be a fair fight, though. The king had brought an honor guard of a couple hundred, which was actually plenty more than the situation demanded on its surface. If he'd brought more, the message it would have sent could have triggered an immediate battle. Swadda's honor guard was about the same size, to be honest, but beside them stood an equal number of tall, sleek Amazonian warriors from the south, led by Glenys the Learned, and another numerically similar force from the eastern mountains led by their own hulking Hefin.

Against them arrayed the black-clad king's troops as well as a couple hundred elves of the Northern Reaches who answered to Padrig the Hulking, Dad's staunchest, and, it appeared sole, ally. I hoped that they were all on my side, and I was pretty sure Dad thought the same, but I was learning pretty quickly that nothing was ever as simple as it seemed on the surface.

I stood in the middle of the brewing, roiling mess. Me, just me, Alyssa of the Small-town Mississippi. Nowhere in my high school courses or the training I'd received after did they cover what to do in situations where several hundred well-armed warriors wanted you dead. I had to figure it out, which, I guess, was only fair since I was on track to become queen of the elves, the prophesied Dragon Queen, the destroyer of tradition, the breaker of society, the scourge of the wyrm, the so forth and so on—some day.

Maybe, anyway. Prophecy, prophecy, prophecy – whatever.

If I survived that long, a statement that stands in opposition to the concept of a prophecy, but then again, the odds weren't very much in my favor.

Speaking of odds, I had Keion to my right, my cousin Sephaline and her familiar wolverine Booboo to my left, and well-muscled and battle-scarred Aerona just over my shoulder. We'd made a formidable team before, hacking our way through blight-sickened monsters to reach the library and battling at Padrig's side to defeat his enemies. There was no way to know whether the same team would be formidable enough to even the skewed odds present in the clearing, but I was confident that they'd give it their all if it came to that.

"No!" Dad's voice rang out. He raised his hands in a calming gesture, leaving his sword passively sheathed, and stepped out a little farther ahead of us. The raging energies abated ever so slightly. My father was, by all accounts, the most popular king ever to rule Kiirajanna. It was obvious why; not only was he well-toned and athletic, one of the best wrestlers in the realm, but he was also charming and affable nearly all the time.

Now, not so much, but he was trying. Arms spread peacefully, he continued, "We agreed to table the discussion until after she completed her coming-of-age ritual. Now, in light of news of—"

"News of what? A dragon? You expect us to believe that story?" Hefin challenged. Chortles followed from the ranks of his retainer, a thick, swarthy bunch. "That is ridiculous at best, is it not?"

"Convenient, is what it is," Swadda shouted, drawing out the syllables. "What a magnificent way to scare us into submission, make us follow along blindly thanks to this dreamed-up threat to our safety. We're so terrified now that we can't think for ourselves. Aren't we?"

"I am not!" Hefin bellowed, and suddenly the swirls of angry chaos were back.

"None of us are," Glynis's voice pealed into the storm. "Surely you're not, are you, Padrig?"

All eyes focused behind me on the northern elves, and I turned my body toward them. Grigor, standing just behind his *bennaeth* in a position of respect, shot me a dismayed look and shook his head slowly. *Get your magic ready,* his eyes said, flickering meaningfully down to the ancient pendant and powerful relic that dangled from a chain around my neck. *This won't end well.*

I shrugged, smiled as confidently as I could, and turned back around. Draignerthol, the source of my questioned power, warmed against my breast, and I could sense the blue glow flickering to life.

I trusted Grigor. At least, I did now. At first he'd seemed overly paternal, but later he'd explained it as a matter of being Dad's uncle, secretly working in service to Padrig and anchoring Dad's northern flank. He'd seen a lot in his many years, so I was glad he, at least, was on my side. I wondered how his bennaeth would respond.

"Come now," the barrel-chested northern commander growled, his rich baritone voice carrying through the maelstrom. "I have not even had an opportunity to speak with the girl yet. Give it time—"

"Bah!" Hefin bellowed, cutting his peer off about as rudely as possible. "We have given the king, his whelp, and his sycophant from the north too much time as it is!" A loud cheer from his honor guard followed, sinking my heart.

Padrig's face colored red at the spray of insults.

"We will have a decision this day!" Hefin cried.

"You—we—shall all have a decision, and on this day," the king said calmly, stepping forward one more pace, still holding his arms up and out. Behind them as I was, I couldn't see the queen's and the high priestess's faces, but both of them clenched their fists and radiated anger.

This isn't going to end well at all, I thought.

In spite of the angry muttering, my father, the mighty and formerly popular elf king, continued forcefully, "Now, let us retire to the comfort of the throne room to calmly discuss the matter—"

"No!" Swadda shrieked, her voice slicing through the tumult. "We pulled you out to this neutral ground for a reason, Cadfael. We will tolerate no further delay. What will it be, your daughter or your crown?"

With the lilt she gave his assumed first name came a grave insult, not just to him but to the crown he wore and all that it symbolized. My gasp was echoed by several of those beside and behind me.

I am needed. I come, a voice rang in the back of my head.

No, Kluzhka. Your presence will only make things worse, I sent back to my new familiar. She's...well, she's a wyvern, which is unusual enough since they're really only ever depicted as the antagonist in elf stories. A good creature, much less a familiar to an elf crown princess, is unthinkable. Still, she'd helped me out of the dragon's lair, and we'd bonded in spite of both of our efforts to the contrary, as well as our rather solid underpinning of dislike for one another, so—well, it is what it is.

I see what you see, remember? Steel will soon be drawn, and elves will kill elves. I can stop this now before it begins.

Or you can make it worse, I argued, forming and sending mental images of a massive army of elves fighting, and killing, a wyvern. As it was, nobody but my closest circle knew I'd come back from the hunhymgais, my coming-of-age ceremony, with a wyvern familiar. Any familiar at all was rare; only rangers get those. The type depends on the ranger, it appears—some get birds, others dogs, and some, like my cousin, creatures of fury like a wolverine. That mine was a wyvern, the creature just behind dragons on the overall food chain, had caused a stir of consternation so far within my family and friends.

If the wyvern were to suddenly show up, and on my side, it would result in an all-out war against her, and worse, even Dad's and Padrig's troops would be unprepared for the intervention and probably join in.

It would be messy, and I'd seen what happened to wyverns when a large group of elves banded together against one. I wasn't certain, but I'd learned enough of my fledgling bond to figure that it would hurt me deeply if something happened to her.

You should have warned the troops on your side.

Ya think? I was happy to have found that sarcasm traveled quite well across the mental link of our ranger bond. *There's nothing to warn them about, though. You can't come. It's a bad, bad, horribly bad idea.*

"You would have us destroy centuries of peaceful tradition over your fears?" Sternyface asked. Her voice was calm but rebuking as she stepped forward to stand beside my father. Talaith, the magnificently beautiful queen, stepped up to form a unified line of the ruling triumvirate. It didn't seem to change the other tribes' attitudes, but the show of unity stiffened our own backs.

Some day I must teach my familiar to address serious situations without flippant sarcasm, Kluzhka observed wrily.

I'm not your familiar, I spat back. We'd had the argument before, several times. She, being the wyvern and a sentient being higher on the food chain than an elf, assumed that she must be superior, while I'd argued that elves had always been and always would be the rangers, thus making her the familiar.

Obviously, it wasn't settled yet.

"Our fears are coming true as it is, a result of your bringing the witch to the castle," Hefin spat. All three to my front cringed, as did I, at the term the eastern ruler had used. "Witch" meant "magic," and that was a bad, bad word.

Magic, witchcraft, had been despised by the elves for hundreds of years, thanks to the blame they put on it for causing most of the violence in their history. I had other ideas, of course, and I'd tried, more or less unsuccessfully, to make Dad and the others see as I did regarding the similarity between their powers of healing, nature-craft, and so on, and my own. But the simple fact was that I'd returned a pendant Momma gave me to Kiirajanna. It was an heirloom of our family line, and unbeknownst to me it held a significant, terrible, and terror-inducing place in their lore. Once I'd arrived in the realm where magic was real, Draignerthol had flared to life and proved itself capable of incredible feats with a minimum of prompting from its wearer. That, by itself, made me both feared and despised. Heck, it even scared me in the beginning. The fact that I'd grown accustomed to it and was actually willing to use it when circumstances required, as I'd shown in saving my friends a couple of times here and there, made it much worse.

All things considered, it wasn't actually surprising that the elves of the east, south, and west all wanted to see me go back to Mississippi. The elves of the north had, too, in spite of their leader's bond to my father, but after the battle with me standing by Padrig's side their opinions had shifted. Only a little, maybe, but it was enough.

Hefin advanced toward my father, just enough to make his hostile intentions clear, calling out, "Cadfael, I must command you to step down and allow wiser leaders to take charge." He drew steel for the first time, pulling about six inches of his blade out of its scabbard.

Dad's shoulders sank momentarily; he'd apparently just realized that he couldn't talk his way out of this one. Within a single heartbeat, though, he recovered and drew himself back up to his full height. He responded to Hefin's threat by pulling his own sword out by the same amount.

The challenge was met.

I come.

No! We can handle this! Somehow.

Uh huh. I can see that. No, clearly, you cannot. You do not even possess conviction in your own words. But do not fear; I shall protect my familiar.

"You—would—" Sadness, resignation, and disbelief colored Dad's voice, but he stepped forward anyway, sword partly drawn, ready to meet the eastern elf leader's steel with his own.

"I. Am. Not. Your. Familiar!" a frustrated, angry voice rang out. Shocked silence followed. As all eyes turned on me, I realized with a start that I'd just yelled that out loud.

I am not your familiar, Kluzhka, I repeated mentally. *I am your friend, your partner. We face this together as equals.*

Equals, then. Prepare for our arrival.

Our?

There wasn't a lot of time to process her strange use of the plural, though. Keion and Seph both understood what my yell had implied and started moving. Eyes widening, Seph stepped in closer to me, Booboo by her side. She levered her bow into a defensive posture and smoothly nocked an arrow.

The prince, meanwhile, spun about waving both hands wildly at Padrig's and my father's troops. "Take cover, take cover!" he yelled.

The confusion on the soldiers' faces turned to terror as a *pop* sounded overhead. I groaned; I'd forgotten that Kluzhka could teleport. Any chance we had of preparing our own forces for the sudden appearance of a monstrous creature in the sky above melted in that instant.

The opposing forces didn't need any preparation, it seemed. They released several hundred arrows nearly simultaneously. I'd already perfected my shield spell, though, so I wrapped Kluzhka in a hazy blue sphere just as the volley arrived.

"Witch!" the cry rose as the soldiers watched their arrows fall uselessly, most of them broken, to the ground. The next volley appeared to be aimed at me, so I quickly pulled the energy through Draignerthol to put up another shield, this time protecting Seph and me. I thought about trying for three, with the third about the ruling trio, but by this point Dad already had his broadsword, magnificently engraved in beautiful knotwork down both sides, drawn and ready. He stood protectively in front of the queen and the high priestess, though I couldn't help wondering whether the high priestess would be all that bad at protecting herself if needed. She could, after all, be quite a powerful magician if she just let her hair down.

Dad's honor guard, meanwhile, moved toward their lord. There was no way they'd make it in time; all the opposing elves were already drawing arrows.

The high priestess, who could have helped in time, didn't. Instead, she glared impotently but furiously upward.

Drop your spell, Alyssa. I am quite competent at protecting you and do not require any reciprocation.

They would've skewered you.

You might not have realized this yet, but my body is quite well armored. Your arrows are—laughable.

She sent me the last after a quick pause while she darted downward and out of the protective shell that I hadn't yet figured out how to move. The second volley of arrows, this one apparently all aimed for me, clattered against her hide and joined their broken fellows in the heap on the ground.

"Never mind that. Charge them, warriors of the east!" Hefin bellowed, waving his broadsword toward my father. The eastern elves in the front line took off at a pace that would cover the hundred or so yards between them all too quickly.

I searched my memory for a spell, any spell, that might help. I'd read plenty of great ideas, thanks to the magic text from the library as well as the one I'd taken from the dragon's lair. None of them seemed appropriate, though. Panicking, I gave up on being clever and started to conjure another windstorm, which I already knew I could use against a large number of people.

Pop.

Pop pop pop.

Pop pop pop pop pop pop pop pop pop.

It sounded like we were underneath a popcorn bag in a giant microwave.

The sky overhead filled with hundreds of dark shapes. The sun disappeared behind a massive wave of multicolored (and, I noticed absently, quite beautiful) wyverns while Kluzhka and the first few landed in front of Dad, talons reaching toward the charging elves who, suddenly, were no longer charging. They probably calculated the same odds I did, bless their hearts. At the library, we had fled in fear from a single wyvern. It had taken Dad's entire honor guard plus the rest of his army, a few thousand well-armed and well-armored elves, to drive the thing away. Even then, they hadn't done any significant damage to the creature.

At this point, the wyverns in the air outnumbered the elves on the ground, and the powerful creatures were still popping into position in a dome above us.

Some flew to the rear of the opposing elves, needing only a few beats of their powerful wings to surround them completely.

The popping stopped. Other than the steady whooshing sound of thousands of pairs of wyvern wings, the battlefield stood completely silent, the wyverns protecting – us, I hoped?

How many should we kill, Princess?

Kill? No! The thought horrified me.

Dad, sword down and facing me now, must have read my expression. "Alyssa, a word before your—your wyvern force—attacks, please?"

You are foolish. They need to die. They would have killed you. They were charging to do just that, in fact.

They are scared. They need to be made to see that I am not the foe. If I kill all of them, who will stand against Xlixi when he comes?

You have a point, she grudgingly returned. Xlixi is the dragon, by the way, who'd promised to return to Kiirajanna to eat my people. If it took an entire elf army to turn away a single wyvern, I couldn't contemplate what it might take to dissuade a dragon that was easily ten times larger than Kluzhka and oozed magic from its very being. He had a massive superiority complex to boot, I should add. I needed everybody I could get, armed and uneaten by wyverns.

"Alyssa?" Keion asked, stepping in to command my field of vision. He continued quietly, "Your lips are moving again, but it's us you need to be talking to. Look, we've won. Please don't let them kill any elves."

Some need to die, to teach them a lesson, or else they'll try it again.

Elves are smarter than that.

No, you're not.

Funny. Give me a chance to talk to my king and queen, though.

"So, Your Majesty, what does protocol suggest that we do?" I asked as matter-of-factly as I could. It was the wrong thing to do, apparently, if Padrig's and Grigor's snorts from behind were any clue.

"Crown Princess," Dad replied somberly, silencing the two with a glare. "Our—tradition—does not lend itself well to describing protocol in…a situation such as this, but I would suggest that the elf who commands the greatest force makes the decisions. I doubt anyone would argue against my assertion that that elf is you, my daughter."

"Me? Could I get some advice, please?" I pleaded. I lowered my voice so that only the closest circle could hear. "I didn't call for this, Dad. I'm still in shock as to what happened. I'm really at a bit of a loss here."

Make a decision! Kluzhka fired at me.

"You should make a decision," Dad stated. "I would, however, advise that, while ordering the massacre of your fellow elves from the other regions of the continent might feel right and justified given their approach to this day's—council—I have often found tremendous success in enacting less permanent responses. You might, at least for this first offense, consider—um, mercy."

"Agreed," Padrig rumbled from behind while the queen nodded.

I rounded on the northern bennaeth. "You were going to kill Ben Merfyn for rising against you."

"Well, yes, but you yourself talked me out of that, remember? And that was one, and a leader. This is hundreds of followers."

Alyssa, my people wish to eat. You need to make a decision soon, for they must either fill their bellies here, or elsewhere.

Have them remain for just one more moment.

Okay. Or you can, if you would prefer. It is a simple matter to communicate amongst my kind, and your words might calm them somewhat more than mine.

I don't want to. I'm having enough trouble communicating well with my own kind right now.

Well, your kind can be difficult to communicate some fairly basic matters with.

Oh, well, bless your cold little lizard heart.

Heart-blessing is noted. You do need to make a decision, though.

I know. It's hard.

Being a queen will be hard, so now's as good a time as any to get used to it.

"Alyssa, your lips are moving again," Keion said.

"I know that! Just—get out of my way." Frustrated, I came to grips with what I had to do and stepped around both him and my father to face the elven horde. Kluzhka stepped aside for my benefit, her hulking waddle almost humorous enough to break my dark mood. I walked directly up to Hefin, his gaze held solidly by my own, and stuck my hand straight out, palm up expectantly.

I was careful not to show my relief when, without argument, he turned his sword to place its hilt in my outstretched palm. His face might have been curled up in undisguised contempt, but at least the huge man was willing to admit defeat when the reality was in his face.

"People of the East, of the West, of the South," I started, reaching through Draignerthol for the power to magnify my own voice. At this point, I didn't care what they thought of my "witchcraft." Turning, I included Padrig's army, "and of the North. It has been prophesied that I will one day be your queen. In that same prophecy I am foretold to break my people, to shatter tradition, to destroy much of the society that has

14

been built. It is also written that my leadership, and my power, will be necessary in the coming age for our race to survive. I know you fear me and the powers I bear. I understand that. I respect it. Even I must respect the power that flows through my veins. But your fear is unfounded. I mean you no harm, not today, and not in the future. There has been and will be no elf blood spilled on this day, and for that I am grateful. Tomorrow, we may not be so lucky. For now, return home. If my request to you to return peacefully is not enough, let it be my command. My wyverns will follow you to ensure your obedience as well as your safety. You will take the most direct route available, and once there, you will hug those close to you and tell them how much you love them. You will do this because tomorrow you may not have the opportunity. Rest, and love, for when I need your assistance in facing the coming darkness I will call upon the strength of your arms, and when I call you must come. You *will* come. Until that day, go. Go!"

Nicely said, my wyvern approved at the same time as my father mouthed similar words.

"Not you," I released Draignerthol's amplifying power and called to the elf leaders nearby, and still feeling free to do as I wished magically, reached out with tendrils of blue energy to lasso Hefin, Swadda, and Glynis. "You three are coming back to the castle with me."

Part of me wanted to crumble when I saw the terror in their eyes, but the smarter, now slightly more experienced, part of me that knew I had to remain in charge. At least, I'm hoping it was that part of me. That part won out, in any event. I turned to face Kluzhka.

"Thank you for your assistance this day. Please pass my appreciation on to your fellows, and ask them to dine on creatures, not on elves, along the way."

Elves are *creatures,* she grumbled, and before I had a chance to argue she took flight to follow the rest of her kind into the sky.

Tasty creatures, at that.

Kluzhka!

War is Off

"They didn't follow their first oath of fealty. Why would they follow a second?" Padrig growled, his voice echoing around the throne room but not directed at anyone in particular.

I looked around for help figuring out what to do next. Padrig and Grigor both stood to one side, with Keion and a very uncomfortable Seph on the other, with the ruling duo seated on their thrones and a very stern-faced Sternyface standing behind and between the high raised backs of the beautiful ornately gilded seats.

I stood right in the middle, facing them all down, or so it seemed. If Dad could sense my discomfort he showed no desire to step in and help, though, his own face even sterner than the high priestess's. The queen shared the look—neither angry nor disapproving, not even very upset. Just—stern, in a very "you got yourself into this, so you get yourself out" sort of way.

"Would you have preferred that I hold them prisoner?" I asked. We'd walked more or less silently the couple of hours back to Cysegredig, and upon the castle steps I'd made all three of the treasonous leaders kneel and take vows to follow my Dad, their king, and the queen for all their remaining days, no questions asked. Period. It was a little more stringent than the standard oath of fealty, Sternyface explained, but only in the prohibition against questioning the leadership. Elves were very proud of their spirited independence, and I'd just made them promise to set that aside.

"It would be largely the same as the oath you extracted from them," Dad injected.

"You behaved wisely today, Crown Princess," the queen said, pausing before adding, "until the oath. I fear you have put the three of them—leaders of a large majority of our population—into a corner. Some day they may be in a situation where that oath might cost their people lives "

"That's something that just—might happen, though. It didn't seem wise to act on a hypothetical when the leaders were right there and the matter was hot."

"It is not merely hypothetical to them."

"Fine. Can you tell me a better way that I should've handled it, then?" I challenged, getting tired of the third degree I was receiving. I was, after all, the winner of the confrontation, even if I'd had to win with a wyvern army. The point I wanted to scream was that we had won, and elf blood was not spilled.

"No," she admitted. Then, after a long breath, she continued, "but that does not mean you should have extracted the oath you did when you did it. Sometimes it is best to wait, to consider all options before taking action."

I held my sigh in as I presided over an internal debate over whether to blurt my immediate thought out. The "you should definitely blurt," side won, which won't be a surprise to anyone who knows me and my fondness for saying whatever's on my mind without much, if any, regard for the wisdom of doing so.

"On the field, I was pushed to make a decision quickly. I was—still in that mode, I suppose." I avoided looking at Dad; he was, after all, the one who'd pushed me into it. Well, he and Kluzhka, but she wasn't there to shame.

It apparently was the wrong move. Dad cleared his throat and quietly, with steel in his tone, said, "Crown Princess, you must learn when to take decisive action—a situation that occurs with a surprisingly vanishing frequency, I have found—and when to consider your words and actions carefully. The oath would have been a good time for the latter course of action."

An uncomfortable silence stretched out from his rebuke, filling the room. Finally I figured it was best to just acknowledge what he'd said.

"Well, okay. Point taken. I can't take it back, though."

I could go eat them, though. That would resolve any internal dispute they may have, now or in the future, and would also resolve my internal hunger.

No, Kluzhka. No eating elves, not even bad ones.

The bad ones are the tastiest.

Hush, you.

"It is talking with you, is it not?" Dad asked. When I nodded, he said, "It is easy to tell. Too easy, perhaps. You look off into the distance, and often your lips tremble. I have seen similar in new rangers, including your cousin, and.... While a ranger communicating with her familiar is an accepted practice, a queen communicating with a wyvern is—a—different case, entirely. I would recommend, Crown Princess, that you work harder to squelch the physical motions that give you away."

"Yes, Your Majesty," I replied, poking back at his tone.

I could eat him, instead.

No! Kluzhka! That's my father! I focused on keeping my expression neutral, which was particularly hard considering how horrified her comment made me.

"Did you see anything just then?" I asked, turning my attention from the horror of the thought back to the throne room. Dad shook his head with a confused look, and I smiled inwardly. That was, at least, one small success for the day.

"You did, however, broadcast it loudly. I suspect every ranger within several leagues of the castle heard your mental shriek," Seph offered. She grinned and said, "Cousin," when I turned to shoot her an angry glare, wondering where she'd learned such dripping snark at the same time.

I mean, I knew for a fact where she'd learned it, bless her heart. Still....

Hah! Broadcasting, see? Some familiar you're turning out to be.

How many times do I have to tell you? The elf is the ranger. You are the familiar, bless your heart.

Say whatever you wish about my heart, but you know that I am correct.

Whatever.

"So, since I cannot go back to undo the oath, what is next?"

Keion stepped forward, finally raising his voice. "We are going to have to keep a good eye on our neighbors, that is what is next. Your oath, wise or no, left holes, Alyssa."

"Holes?"

"Yes. You didn't require them to promise anything about their armies or their chief lieutenants. Nor..." he sighed. "There was more left out than there was covered, is all. We must be ready for invasion, and with a much larger army, from any side. Any side but the north, of course, Padrig."

"Of course," Padrig answered.

"While we make ready for a dragon attack," I observed.

"That may be years, decades, even centuries in the future," Dad mused.

"Why would the dragon give us that long to prepare?"

He shrugged my question away. "Why would he not? He considers himself superior to us in every way, I would assume, from the little you've told us of his...interviews. Tactically it makes sense for him to attack swiftly, but will his ego demand that?"

"Maybe. Maybe not. So we don't know what's in a dragon's mind. Nor can we tell for certain what the other elf clans will do. We must—wait, then, I guess," I said drily. "I do waiting so well. What do you suggest we do in the meanwhile?"

"Meanwhile, we continue with your ascension training, Crown Princess," Sternyface said just as drily.

"Yes, I suppose we must," the queen said with a smirk.

I looked around to see what was funny, but nobody else was smirking to match. Instead, Dad and Padrig were looking at me thoughtfully, Sternyface just glared as usual, and Keion and Seph looked as confused as I felt.

She's going to be in charge of your training now.

How do you know? You're a wyvern, not an elf.

The queen interjected, "I shall be in charge of your training from here forward, my young princess. It is the queen's right and responsibility to train her successor, in any event, and I believe it to be prudent at this point."

See? I told you so.

Bless your familiar heart, thank you so much.

Any more insight I can offer on elf ways, you have but to ask.

Just hush.

Unfortunately, as much as I would probably enjoy that, I cannot. You will not be able to get me out of your mind any more than I can get you out of mine.

"So, what does that involve, Your Majesty?" I asked, wincing as Kluzhka sent me an image of a beautiful buck she was zeroing in on for her next kill.

"Learning to school your expression, among other things." She gave me a look that told me she knew exactly where my mind had been. "You will spend most of your waking hours with me for the next several weeks, if not months, during which time I hope to be able to hone the leadership abilities you have, which I must compliment you on, into true royal presence."

"And while you do all that, what of the rebels at our borders?" Padrig demanded, his voice overly heated for the small confines of the throne room. Everyone stopped and glared.

"What of them?" Dad asked. His voice was calm, but his eyes flashed.

"You know, Cadfael, that had I rebelled like that, you would have my head."

"I recall that we were actually at war not too long ago." I and Padrig both colored at Dad's reminder. "You still seem to be quite well in possession of that grizzly appendage."

There is an awful lot of hair on that head. It would make it unpalatable, I must say. Now, that young prince over there....

Hush, you.

"That was quite a different matter, mostly procedural. You had to capture Blodwyn the Grey, and I had to object, but once you had secured the young lady and removed your force from my clan's territory we've gone back to being friends. Speaking of, though, how is the young lady doing?"

"Unknown. She apparently caught wind of our approach and vanished into the snow." Dad shrugged, not seeming to care much.

"That is a harsh part of the realm to vanish into, especially on one's own," Grigor said. His voice was low, but everything was easy to hear in the throne room.

"That is a harsh part of the realm to fully explore," Dad corrected. "She could have gone nearly anywhere, and from what I have heard, she has quite a few benefactors and supporters in that region."

I could explore it quickly.

Hush, you, I repeated.

Did you know I can see heat, also?

I look through your eyes way too much to not know that. Now hush. Please.

"You may not know yet that our crown princess brought back from the dragon's lair a book chronicling the Cult's activities," Sternyface added. "My team is busy poring over its contents to find information that might help."

"A chronicle of the Cult? How—unusual. Why, that is an extraordinarily good find. May I look at it while I am here?" Grigor asked.

"I would suggest, my old friend, that we leave that to the priests," Padrig said. "Or does my presence bore you?"

"Not at all, Padrig. It is just that they have been plaguing our land for so long now. But you are correct in your assertion that it is best left to the experts."

"You should return to your people," Dad said to his long-time supporter. "They will need your calm presence, particularly if our ancient foe chooses to return to our realm in the northlands. I will send emissaries of peace to the other clan headquarters in hopes of mending the situation. There is no good to be had in leaving the matter to fester, and besides, it would be wise to have agents present should this dragon choose to reappear...wherever it chooses."

Dragons prefer warmth. I bet he'll reappear in the south or west.

Shush, Kluzhka. I am trying to listen.

Me, too. What is that you say, bless your heart?

Hush, you.

"Speaking of agents, I will ask Grigor to remain behind, here at the castle, so that he and I may communicate. And yes, my old friend, so that you can scour over whatever books you choose, whichever ones the high priestess's minions will allow you to touch." Padrig said with a grin.

"I take it that cylchoedd season is now officially off," Keion interjected.

We all looked over at him in surprise. My jaw nearly dropped before I caught it and held my expression neutral. Prince Charming was actually pouting!

"Don't pout, son. It is not becoming of the lord prince of the realm," the queen admonished, tempering it with a half-smile.

He snapped back, his own expression leveling out. "Pout? Not at all. It is simply that we were in the lead to another trophy," he explained with a shrug. Seph snorted her derision, and he shot her a glare in response.

"Maybe we shouldn't call off the season, though. Don't the people need a diversion from their worries over the darkness that is likely coming?" My question earned a nod from Dad, an appraising look from the queen, and a very non-pouty look from Keion.

"If the teams from the outlying clans refuse to come play, the season will be awfully short, regardless," Seph observed.

"Why would they refuse to come play? My team would not refuse such a challenge."

"You are not at war with the territory you would be entering, for one thing, Prince Keion." Dad said.

"They aren't either, but—I see your point. And there is danger, of course. Still, I would have my own team around me, and we cylchoedd players always treat each other with honor."

"When you're not shooting *mwswgl* at each other," I added, earning another snort from Seph. The game I'd watched had been won in large part through successful mwswgl—moss-tipped arrows—shots on the opposing team. The point was to get a hoop over a stake in the middle, of course, but there were other ways of scoring points.

"Even then, Alyssa. Honor, remember? Remember the gentlemanly greeting after the game? We would do no harm to each other."

I see these teams in your mind's memory. They all look quite tasty to me.

Hush, you. Go eat something. Not an elf! Quietly. Don't broadcast it.

"You would be gentlemanly, but what about the fans? Especially ones who recognize that the First Prince of the Realm would make a great hostage."

"No..." the prince started to argue, but the argument died away as it appeared he had no counter.

"It is unfortunate, my son, but prudence is key. We must put this season on hold until I and the king return the realm to peace."

Keion didn't like his mother's pronouncement at all, but he just nodded, his face etched in stone.

I tried shifting the topic. "So, anyway—but what about the dark-skinned elves? We need them, and their magical powers, now more than ever."

"They do not exist," Dad, Sternyface, and the queen answered, all at once.

"Yes, they do. You admitted to me that you knew of them. Seph, you know they exist, right?"

My cousin leveled a questioning expression Dad's way, and then shook her head. "Alyssa, what I know is of no concern at the moment."

"Oh, come on!" I exploded. My angry outburst earned me a surprised sense through the link I shared with Kluzhka, but that was okay. "Look, I know it's not politically correct to acknowledge that—the other group—is out there. I get that. It's wrong, but I get it. I also know, for their part, they'll be more than a little hesitant to speak of or to you. But they're out there, and they're still practicing the powerful magic that we'll need to – how do I say this most plainly? -- to keep from being eaten, by a dragon. We need them as badly as they need us. You saw how ineffective our arrows were against a single wyvern—just one!—and how everybody gave in and stopped fighting when a group of them showed up. How do you think our archers will do against a dragon? Ten times the size of Kluzhka, and way more powerful magically. Xlixi was even able to control me for a while."

"Speaking of wyverns, where did that horde come from? It was rather spectacular," Keion asked.

"You're changing the subject."

"Yes," the prince said, his leveled gaze unapologetic.

"The priests will examine the lore related to all we know of— the others," the high priestess said, shrugging, after entering the conversation with a loud grunt. "It will be a fast study, I assure you, Crown Princess. And then we will advise the crown accordingly."

I let out a loud, long, expressive sigh, then gave up, knowing I couldn't erase centuries of racism and division in a single meeting. At least Sternyface had acknowledged them, sort of.

"The horde of wyverns, Alyssa? We really would like to know."

I'd asked Kluzhka that question on the way back, so I already knew the full, detailed answer. "They came from all over Kiira-janna. They communicate with one another much as Seph and Booboo, and as Kluzhka and I, communicate, in the way all rangers and their familiars do – um, whether or not they can decide which is the familiar. And they can teleport, by the way. They don't do it very often, but she was roosting a couple hundred miles away up in the mountains to the east one minute, and then she was right overhead the next. She decided, entirely separate from any conversation she and I had, to send out a call for help, and her—um, friends? Colleagues? Associates? I'm not sure the right word, but you saw the hundreds that teleported in as well. She relayed commands to them during the battle, and they used that link to 'escort' the elves back toward their own homes as appropriate."

"Well, that solves it, then."

"What solves what?" I asked. Everyone else shot Keion an approving look; apparently I was the only one confused by his comment.

"The problem. You know, how to kill a dragon, at least without losing thousands of elf lives. You control the wyvern, who in turn controls a thousand more of her kind. We wait for the dragon to be sighted—heck, we can use the wyverns as lookouts—and then they crush him under their power. There's no way a dragon could stand up to a thousand wyverns, so this is easy."

"Oh, sure. Easy. Very easy," I nodded, my voice dripping in sarcasm. "It won't work, but it sure does sound good. And—easy."

He sighed. "Why won't it work?"

"Well, first, I don't *control* the wyvern. I believe that she considers me the controlled one, in fact. At best, the two of us are peers. Matter of fact, I told her not to come, which is when she told me off as her familiar."

"She is being ridiculous," Seph stated, shrugging dismissively. "The elf is always the elf, and the creature is always the familiar."

"You tell that yourself to a creature that, before the bond, made a regular feast out of elves. I wasn't exaggerating when I said that we were the livestock on Pazhbojanna. No, trust me on this; I've seen the world literally through her eyes. To her, we are small, frail, crunchy, and taste good with ketchup."

"What is this ketchup?" Sternyface asked, her face deeply creased in concern.

"It is not worth explaining," Dad answered. "Continue, Alyssa."

"Well, like I said, I don't control her. She helps me. And she doesn't control her fellow wyverns. They work loosely together when asked, but only when it is important to all. Kluzhka called them to the aid of the Dragon Queen, she told me, and that meant something to her kind. Something significant—something she hasn't even been able to express to me yet. Whatever it is, though, it was big enough that every single wyvern in the bunch—in the world, maybe? Her vision was unspecific on that, so I couldn't tell whether that was all the wyverns in Kiirajanna or just all the ones she knows, but they all came immediately to my aid without asking for anything in return. Which, by the way, she tells me is rare."

"So we rephrase the prince's suggestion and ask her to help by calling in her kind to help the Dragon Queen in defeating the dragon. That still seems to be a much simpler solution than—than any of the others recommended." I noticed Dad avoided mentioning the dark-skinned elves, and I'm sure by his expression that he noticed me noticing.

"Still won't work."

"Why not?"

"Well, I—let's just say it this way. When Xlixi comes through to this world, Kluzhka is going to get as far away from both him and me as possible, for my own protection."

"Don't be coy, girl. Explain, please," Padrig snapped. Then he shot me a grin that dulled the sting. His words interrupted a confused silence, though, and so everyone echoed his command.

"I don't know how it works, Padrig. I don't know whether I can explain it well. I only know what Kluzhka has told me. Her fear, and now mine too, is rooted in one of the many powerful abilities dragons have."

"And this ability is...?" Padrig prompted.

"They can control others. People, for one. Remember how I said I almost fell under his mental control at first?"

"But you found a way to block it. Is that not what you said?" Dad asked.

I nodded. "I did. I blocked it through strength of will, but she doesn't believe a wyvern can. Something about shared genetic makeup. No wyvern has ever opposed a draconic order, though, and she mentally shudders every time I suggest it."

"But has a wyvern ever tried?"

"Not that I know of."

"So the wyvern might be afraid of shadows that do not really exist?" Keion asked, prompting a shake of my head.

"No. I mean, yes, I suppose. But no."

"That does not make sense."

"Look, the reason it hasn't been attempted is that the penalty for failure is too great. We have the same problem here. If we call a thousand wyverns to us, and Xlixi manages to gain control of them all, as Kluzhka is pretty certain he can do, what chance will we have with a dragon *and* a thousand wyverns trying to skin us alive? Look, I don't know a lot of the strategy that we must eventually accept, but I'll promise you this—without the dark elves, we can't win. We might as well just send a peace emissary to Xlixi asking him to eat as few of us as—"

"Alyssa, we have beaten dragons before," Keion, who'd stepped back a little when I exploded, stepped up again and assured me.

I shook my head. "Only with the help of the dark skinned elves. Is that not correct, High Priestess Naissa?"

She shook her head. "We cannot, Alyssa. We cannot—"

"What, acknowledge their magic? Yes, we can, especially after you've stood there and supported mine." I glared at her, but then it switched to my father.

"We cannot violate that separation, Alyssa. It is—just too complicated."

"Maybe too complicated for you, Dad, but not for me. Like it or not, I'm going to seek their help." I met his look with an angry one of my own.

"We are all tired," Grigor stepped into the silence that followed my pronouncement. "Perhaps we should all get some rest for the evening and reconvene tomorrow. Your Majesties?"

"That would be fine," Dad said, breaking eye contact and slumping just a little. For the first time I'd seen, he looked defeated.

"First light tomorrow, Crown Princess, you will report to my chambers," the queen said. Her voice carried a hint of sadness and resignation, but she looked nowhere near as down as my father did, and her order carried enough strength that I wouldn't have disobeyed if I'd wanted. "If you are to be making queenly decisions, it is past time that you are trained to do so. We shall begin tomorrow, first thing."

"Your Majesty," I said, heat still evident in my voice. I gave her, and only her, a gesture of respect, spun on my heel, and left the room, leaving a shocked Keion and Seph in my wake.

Queenly Lesson

The next morning, I rose from bed at what had become a fairly normal time. Ordinarily, I would've dressed and run straight out to the archery range. The prince had, after all, gotten me into shooting a hundred arrows a day, every day before breakfast, and it was a habit I'd learned to enjoy, with the steady *thwack thwack* of the arrows against the target and the mental ease of the repetitive motion. This morning was different, though; I had an appointment. Instead of running out, down the king's end of the top floor hall, and then down the stairs, I stood by the window and waited for the first initial rays of dawn to peek into my vision, singing softly to my little tree to pass the time.

The sun's entry seen, I leapt into motion and jogged down the hall to the opposite end where a door with a raven's head carved into it stood. I knocked once, and immediately Lady Meredydd answered the door. I was glad to see her; the queen's Lady of the Bedchamber, her main personal servant, had always treated me pleasantly, and so she represented the perfect, pleasant way to begin what promised to be a pleasant, perfect morning.

I was, after all, going to be trained on being a queen, by the queen. Her daughters had been managing it pretty awfully, so I looked forward to the promotion.

"Princess," she acknowledged as she let me in. "I trust your evening was restful?"

"It was!" I said. I meant every ounce of joy in my tone, too. Aerona, who was apparently impressed by the stand I'd made, started acting more an equal than someone with a charge to oversee, and she'd actually spoken to me a little.

"Have you eaten?"

"No, the queen asked me to come at first light." I was proud of the fact that I'd managed to knock on the door within moments of seeing the first rays through my window.

"Well, that was dumb. The queen, whom you should address as Her Royal Majesty even when she is not present, expects you to be prepared for her lessons as soon as you arrive, and to be ready to go the full morning. You must go get food immediately."

"But I'll be late if I—"

"Quiet. Go!"

I returned to the raven-carved door not five minutes later, having dashed down to the kitchen, grabbed a few pieces of fruit and cheese and stuffed them all in my mouth as fast as I could, and sprinted back upstairs.

"Princess," the Lady acknowledged as she let me in the second time. "You are late."

"You told me—"

"What I told you is of no import. You must never make excuses. While you are in the chambers of Her Royal Majesty, unless she tells you otherwise, you may only respond to queries with a 'Yes, Your Majesty,' a 'No, Your Majesty,' or a 'No excuse, Your Majesty.' Should you not understand her instruction, you may include a fourth response: 'Your Majesty, I do not understand.' Do you understand?"

"Why are you being so mean to me all of a sudden?"

"Do you understand?"

"I asked a question."

"So did I. Are you ready to learn to be a queen, or will you remain a brat your whole life? That was rhetorical. Do. You. Understand?"

Eat her.

I don't eat elves.

She deserves it, if you did.

Hush, you.

"Yes." I glowered at her. She deserved it.

She ignored it. "Yes, what?"

"Yes, Your Majesty? But you're not the queen."

"Bzzt," she shushed me with a buzz. "My identity matters not at all when you are responding in one of your four responses. Do you understand?"

"Yes, Your Majesty." I replied with as much venom as I could squeeze into those last two words. I followed it up with a heated glare, but she was unfazed.

"Wait here, then. Her Majesty will be with you in time." She disappeared into an inner room, leaving me and my heated glare behind.

Why are you accepting this treatment?

She's the queen.

Oh. I thought the other, fluffier, one was the queen.

Fluffier? Huh. Well, the other one is the queen. This one is the queen's first maiden.

So the Dragon Princess is scraping to a servant now.

Not a servant. She's the queen's right hand.

Every time I've seen her through your eyes, the queen has had two hands of her own.

I didn't mean literally, silly. I meant she does everything for the queen.

So, a servant.

Not a servant. She just...

Serves.

Yes. I guess.

You elves are strange creatures. One should expect such of inferior beings, I suppose.

Thanks, you. Hey, how about you checking out of this channel and, without showing me what you're doing, hunting down a nice big buck and ripping it to shreds?

I am a little hungry, indeed. But this is more entertaining.

I don't need you in my head when I deal with the queen.

I am not certain I agree with that assertion. Still, I will do as you ask, my familiar.

I am not your familiar.

And yet you will bow and scrape to a walking right hand that I would be pleased to eat in two gulps. I see how it is.

She doesn't consider me an inferior race, anyway.

I do not see much difference in how you are being treated, but I shall honor your wishes anyway. My stomach rumbles. But Alyssa? Seriously? Stop letting them treat you like this. It is unbecoming for one of your station.

I need the training.

No, you do not. You already know most of what you need to act as queen. You have proven that. You need to accept that.

Whatever.

I am the one being you cannot lie to, Alyssa, and vice versa. You know that I am correct.

So what would you have me do? Bite her head off?

As tasty of a sensation as that would be, I do not believe your weak lower jaw could encompass her entire skull. No, I would have you meet her as equal, at least an equal in training. And now, I go.

Happy hunting, Kluzhka.

Same to you.

I disconnected and slowly came back to my own eyes, my own skin, my own spidey-senses—and then jumped in surprise. The queen sat calmly in a beautifully carved wingback chair a dozen feet to the side. Her right knee was crossed gracefully over her left, hands clasped on top of that, posture erect and leaning forward, her face regarding me in an unreadable expression. Most surprising was that she wore regular, unadorned clothes, a green tunic over beige pants. It was the first time I'd seen her without sequins and beads and shiny metal, either in her hair or on a formal gown.

I forced myself to recover quickly and then met her eyes.

"Speaking to your winged friend, were you?"

"Yes, Your Majesty."

"You two certainly do share a unique relationship."

"Yes, Your Majesty."

"Stop it."

"I—I do not understand, Your Majesty."

With a sigh, she rose, eyes never leaving mine. She glided slowly across the floor—she was pretty in her regular formal gown, but stunning in the simpler clothes—and stopped right in front of me. Her porcelain hand with perfectly manicured red nails reached out and stroked my cheek, her expression softening.

I noticed that it was her right hand she used, and grinned.

"Kluzhka, is it not? Was she regaling you with stories of her hunting to have your expressions bouncing so much between moods?"

"Yes, Your Majesty, her name is Kluzhka. But no, Your

Majesty, she was—she was talking about leadership and training."

"Oh? Do tell." Her hand dropped to her side, but she retained her warm, curious expression. I realized suddenly that I could finally describe the quality I'd found so enchanting in her before, and still did now: presence. She was Queen Talaith, responsible for all of Kiirajanna, and yet here, now, she was completely engaged in whatever I was about to tell her.

I wanted to learn how to do that.

"Your Majesty, she asked me earlier why I took instruction from Lady Meredydd. I explained that she acted as your right hand, and the wyvern took me literally. It was a humorous conversation."

"I imagine it must have been," she replied. She turned, glided back to her seat, and regained her regal sitting pose. It was all so graceful, so elegant.

"She eats people, does she not?"

"No, Your Majesty. Well, wyverns do, and she used to. She has often kidded me about elves being a tasty snack. But she has promised to eat only beasts of the forest while..."

"While what, dear?"

"While we are bonded, which I guess is forever. I had not thought much of it before."

"We had better see that she remains well-fed, then."

"Yes, Your Majesty," I laughed. It was hard to take offense at her flippant tone.

The tone went back to serious. "So why do you?" she asked in her smooth and calming voice.

"Why do I what, Your Majesty? I do not understand the question."

"Clearly. Why do you take instruction from my Lady of the Bedchamber?"

"She's your agent, Your Majesty."

"So? You are the Crown Princess." Her inflection made it easy to hear the capitalization of my title.

"But she speaks with your authority, I thought." I quickly added, "Your Majesty."

"You would accept such treatment from me?"

"Well—I—you are the queen, right?"

She smiled a gentle and genuine warmth across the room. "The last I checked, yes, dear, I am the queen. Have you seen me treat any of my subjects so strictly?"

"No," I admitted.

"Why would you believe I should treat you so?"

I shrugged, lost. "Because I need the training?"

"Training for what purpose? To learn to scrape your knees?"

"To—to become you. I thought you were training me to become your replacement."

"Ah. How would being subservient train one to become a queen?"

"Well, I'm not sure." She had a point. I was stumped.

"Guess."

"I—I can't. I've never trained anyone to be queen before."

"You seem to imply that I have?"

"At least you were trained."

"You make many assumptions, young lady. Very much as I did, I must admit. You are smart, and headstrong, and likely to make a very good queen if you just let go of your apparent desire to act silly."

"Just as you have made a very good queen?" I wasn't sucking up, but I wasn't being sarcastic either. I hoped my sincerity came through my voice.

"Well, let us not compare too hastily. My reign has been marked by peace and a large degree of happiness, so yes, I believe your comment is appropriate. While not—"

"I—I'm sorry to interrupt, Your Majesty, but I am curious whether you and your predecessor had a similar discussion. Was her reign as successful as yours has been?"

"I believe so, yes. We have had quite a run of successful reigns in Kiirajanna, I must say. Did your history lessons not tell you so?"

"They do, but I realize that I should be concerned over what might not be in the history. How difficult was your transition?"

Her smile shifted slightly, subtly, from genuinely pleasant to genuinely pleased. Elves have this beautiful way of smiling with their whole faces, and she had been and continued to let her smile through her eyes as well as the muscles. It just became—happier, if that was possible.

"My transition was quite difficult. More difficult than anything else I have ever attempted, before or later. And yet I fear it was nothing compared to the challenge that you are facing, my dear. I hope to assist in guiding you through your transition, but I suspect that the prophecy has much more in store for you."

"I bet." The grimace I felt made its way onto my face as well as into my voice. So far, the prophecy hadn't treated me very nicely at all.

"No, it is not entirely negative. I mean it, Alyssa. You have already been tried and tested, and the most difficult tests are likely still in your future. But do you know what makes the difference between pot metal and the fine steel used in our blades?"

"Um, carbon? I think I heard something about that back in chemistry class."

"I doubt there is all that much difference, chemically, between the two types of steel. But ask my son. The blade steel is repeatedly worked—heated, and beaten, and heated, and beaten, over and over again until it becomes hard yet flexible. This is what you must become, my dear. I hear that your archery skills are now second to none, and my son is quite proud of that fact, but you did not start out that way. The challenges ahead of you are, I believe, put there to temper you into the strong leader you must become, the strong leader this realm needs and deserves after centuries of softness."

"You think we've become too happy, don't you, Your Majesty?"

"You missed my point earlier, didn't you, Alyssa?"

I thought for a long moment, going back over what we'd talked about. I was confused at first; we'd covered swords, and troubled times, and transitions, and assumptions, and the training—then it hit me.

"Oh. I did."

"Where did the Your Majesty go?"

"Away with the lesson you were trying to teach me."

"Which is?"

"You know," I argued. She did know, and we both knew she knew, but I was being coy on purpose.

Her frown clued me in that it was a bad move.

Her voice dipped into a hard irony to match her face. "Humor me, please."

"You wanted to teach me how to take someone who assumed a position of authority a little less seriously in that position than they expect me to."

"Go on." A ghost of a smile returned to her face.

"Your Lady of the Bedchamber was a perfect choice, having been my teacher before, and one whose knowledge and expertise led me to grant her a great degree of natural respect. Naturally, when she informed me that the rules had changed drastically, I accepted the message she brought rather than questioning it as I should have."

"Should you have questioned it to her?"

"Um, no. Maybe. It depends?" I tried to read her expression to figure out what I needed to say, but failed. She was too good at the poker face thing, bless her heart. Finally I took a deep breath and continued on instinct. "It depends, I think, on what I stand to gain from playing along versus countering her immediately. In most cases a queen would stand very little to gain in allowing someone to speak down to her, but a queen should be both sensitive enough to determine the proper reaction and courageous enough to display it."

"Bravo!" Lady Meredydd said, coming into the room. "Alyssa, you have now passed your first test."

"Hardly my first test."

"Right," she said, apparently reading the darkness in my face. "You have been through quite a lot. I would apologize, but as Talaith argued, it takes quite a great deal of heat and hammering to make steel. That said, I was referring to your first test in this phase of your training, here with Talaith."

"Is the Lady of the Bedchamber always on a first-name basis with the queen?" I asked.

"When it is Her Royal Majesty, Queen Talaith's desire, yes," the Lady replied with a disapproving glare.

I turned to the queen to be clear who I was asking. "No, I wasn't being smart. I'm really curious. I've been taught a great deal of elf customs, by the priests as well as by your children, but bless their hearts, all of that was related solely to public courtly behavior. Is this sort of thing—acceptable—in private?"

The queen smiled, a kindly expression, and asked, "Acceptable, to whom?"

"Well, to—oh!" I started answering the question before I realized that it had actually been an answer in itself. "That's up to me, isn't it?"

"It will be, yes."

My mind did a sudden right-hand turn on the topics high-
way. "How does a queen find her staff? There aren't any job-
hunting web sites or classified pages here."

The queen nodded; I'd asked a good question, it appeared.
"When—I should say if, but we all know at this point that you
will be queen no matter what the other clans, or I myself, think
of it—no, that is not a negative thing. I believe you will make a
fine queen. You have a rough reign ahead of you, one I would
not wish on anyone, and while your success is not by any
means guaranteed I will admit to placing better odds in your
lane than in anyone else's. But back to the original point. When
you rise to the crown, yourself, you will inherit all of my staff
who choose to stay on. In my case that included all of them. In
your case, who knows? We all see tough years ahead, and most
of my staff have earned a peaceful retirement in spite of what I
assume will be a desire to continue their noble service to the
realm. In any event, if the world truly does not end in the initial period of your reign, as I do not believe it will, you will end
up replacing them all through natural retirements. Meredydd's
predecessor left to return to her family in my second year as
queen, and she herself was the next in line for the position. I
replaced her in the ladies-in-waiting list with a lovely lass who
has since returned home after a remarkable, if short, period of
honorable service to the crown. Turnover is natural, but you
will find that a desire to serve is widespread. Do not forget that
you will also have a wonderful selection of—temporary castle
workers to choose from."

"Slaves, you mean." I'd been repulsed by the idea that
Padrig took slaves from villages he'd beaten, but only until he
explained that Cysegredig did it, too. Then I'd been repulsed by
Dad's flippant acceptance of the practice once I confirmed that
many of the castle workers were actually working off slavery
contracts they'd been taken under. It was barbaric, to me, but a

way of life to the elves. It was a way of life I'd promised to end, to be certain, but I'd sort of forgotten about it when the racism toward the dark-skinned elves reared its head.

"Slaves, yes. Meredydd was a so-called slave, were you not?" We both peered at the Lady, who nodded. Her expression told me how little it mattered, but Talaith continued, "She was brought to the castle not long after her own hunhymgais. She was raised to the ladies-in-waiting by my predecessor, and she spent a great deal of time traveling in her entourage around the countryside. Her term ended not long ago, but she has elected to remain in my service. Others choose to return home, and it is their right to do so. Once my term is over, her choices will be to return to her home—"

"Which is not likely, since I would point out to the crown princess and remind my queen that has not been my home for many years," the lady interjected. "I am much more likely to stay on to try to keep you from eating your own foot, and then only once you no longer need my experience, to return to Talaith's home to continue more or less in our current relationship."

"Are you—two—*gyrywgydiwr*?" Though the queen had kids, it was a fair question, I figured, since I never heard or saw anything of a male figure in her life. It certainly wasn't my father, who was clearly smitten with my mother. It was probably none of my business, I realized as the words slipped out, but I asked anyway. After all, I wasn't known for discreet subtlety, nor was I likely to gain that reputation anytime soon.

I was rewarded by a humorously surprised expression from the queen and a scandalized look which quickly morphed into the same that the queen was wearing from the lady.

"You do ask the silliest questions sometimes, Alyssa," the queen mused.

"I never see you with a guy," I shrugged. "Either of you, really. It was a fair question."

"Fair, perhaps, but incorrect. You never see me with a man because you never see me on Sadoorn. Similarly, Meredydd is always doing her duty to the crown when you catch sight of her, is she not?"

"It is time for Talaith to prepare for court," the lady interjected. "Alyssa, I must ask you to leave now, but you will be expected to join Her Majesty every morning, and when asked, for tea. You may have passed the first test, but you still have a great deal to learn."

I rose, nodded quietly, and left.

GWERS

Literally, "lesson"

Something I had been receiving

for more than my fair share

of time in Kiirajanna.

A Fight

thwack *thwack* *thwack*

The arrows followed one after another into the small dark dot in the center of the farthest archery target. I couldn't help curling the ends of my lips up into a feral grin at the display. My fear had been that I'd lost my skill—a skill developed over hundreds of hours of practice shooting at least a hundred arrows each morning—in captivity with the dragon. I'd actually missed with the first few arrows, too, but then my brain let go and the muscle memory came back and I started relaxing, allowing and even willing my subconscious to guide each shot. Immediately the arrows started following that will, each one landing right next to its fellow in the center.

"Nice job, Princess," a voice rang out from behind me. I calmly sent another arrow into the bulls-eye and then turned around to show Keion that I hadn't been surprised. It was a childish move, of course. Nobody could surprise me any longer—nobody except my father, that is, and sometimes Ranger Master Owain—and Prince Charming certainly could not, no matter how hard he might try. But it was still Prince Charming, and I still had a crush on him, so I sometimes act a little—differently. Just for him. Because—well, because I'm just kind of dumb that way sometimes, I guess.

"I was taught by the best," I said, lowering my bow to rest the point on the ground.

"To put your bow in the dirt? I see that."

"I'm a maverick that way, I guess." I wasn't backing down or apologizing. I'd learned the queen's first lesson well, so I internally congratulated myself.

"A maverick?" He glared at me, warring emotions crossing his brooding face.

"So, now that you have more time thanks to the cancellation of the cylchoedd season, can I hope for your tutelage to start up again out here?" I realized I'd brought up the wrong topic as his face darkened even further.

"It is a disgrace. My team was off to a strong lead, quite likely to win the season. It is—gah!"

"I know how you feel," I said, grabbing hold of whatever phrase I could use to commiserate.

He turned his dark mood my direction, focusing it directly on me. "Do you? Do you really? How could you? You've never had to strain and strive with a team toward a common goal in your life."

"What? What do you call the run to the library?"

"I call it a princess en route to a childish goal, being defended and assisted by two noble and capable companions."

I was caught for a moment between wanting to thank him for the first compliment he'd ever paid my cousin and wanting to verbally assault him for the rest of his statement.

The anger won.

"Princess? Childish goal? You didn't say that when we took off."

"I wasn't with you when you took off, remember? I had to follow your path. Your father came to me that morning, worried that his dear sweet naive daughter might get hurt out there, and would I please take off at a gallop to watch over her."

"I saved you from the poison!"

"It was a poison I would not have been subjected to had I not been sent after you on your foolish quest."

"You're a jerk, you know that?"

"A well-bred jerk, at least."

"What's that supposed to mean? My father is the king."

"And what he saw in a simple Mississippi woman is beyond most of us. At least my mother's parents were wealthy Londoners. They came from class, without all this blessing of hearts silliness."

Anger flooded my face. I couldn't believe he'd said that. "Look, you, last time someone spoke about Momma, I punched her."

"Well, here you go, if you think you can." He jutted his chin out my direction, looking exactly like a glaring peacock.

I didn't take him up on it. I couldn't. Somewhere in the back of my mind the crown princess spoke up, urging peace and discernment. The rest of me was having none of that, though, as I very quickly arrived back in my own room in the castle, chest heaving from the sprint. I finally allowed tears to flow, once the door was firmly shut to keep the rest of the world out.

"Men are, in my opinion, most assuredly not worth the torment," a stony voice sounded from the corner. I jumped, a little, and tried unsuccessfully to hide it mid-air. I'd gotten plenty used to Aerona being there, but her speaking up was a new thing.

"How did you know?" I asked, hauling my sobs back in with an effort and blowing my nose on a basin rag. I glanced at the mirror, didn't like what I saw, and turned away.

"How did I know about men? Oh, I have some history in that department," Aerona said with a rare gentle smile.

"No, how did you know it was Keion who..." I left the sentence unfinished, unwilling to use my voice to reason out who had been right and who wrong in the argument we'd just had. It was, I figured, easier to just hold to a vague notion of being wronged, at least inside my own head.

Besides, I was suddenly curious about her admission.

"The wall you have built, Alyssa. In the few months I have known you, I have seen a supple, strong-willed, somewhat naive girl turn into a strong woman, at times through no fault of her own. Along the way you have done as we all do, building walls around your heart and your soul to prevent the world from teaching you the same lesson twice. The one area we are slowest, or in some cases unable, to erect walls has to do with our brushes with men, no matter how painful they are."

"You are...so wise. It's hard to imagine a woman as tough as you, someone who literally bristles daggers when she wants, who can do that little thing with daggers dancing across your knuckles, would have ever been wronged by a man."

She chortled, her face twisting into an ironic grin, and all of a sudden Aerona the Linebacker vanished. As the toughness fell away, her shoulders relaxed, her eyes stopped challenging the darkness in the corners of the room. With a few silent steps she arrived at my bed and sat down beside me, reaching down to grab my hand as she did.

"What's this, a newer, tender Aerona?" I poked, pushing my smile up even higher than it needed to be to make sure she'd know I was joking.

"Don't push it, Princess. However, yes, I can see that at the moment there aren't any physical threats to your wellbeing, so I feel it right to address the non-physical ones."

"Keion's not a threat to my well-being, physical or otherwise. He's just a jerk who can fight. I'll get over him."

"The prince may not be a threat, but your reaction is. I know, I know, you are young and loving and full to those beautiful sandy-brown eyebrows of yours of a desire to heal and help and love the world, and your heart leaps at the chance to find a mate who will do the same. And the prince is quite a monolithic star, seemingly uniquely able to face that world at your side. And, you have to admit, if it weren't him, it would likely be someone else. I was your age, once, too, remember?"

"Did you know any actual—um, prehistoric creatures?" There wasn't a word for dinosaurs in elf, as their history didn't mention any. Plus, there didn't seem to be a prehistory, which was why Aerona just looked a question at me and shook her head. "Sorry, it was an age joke, and a dumb one, so I'm glad I messed up the punch line. But if I may ask, how old are you, Aerona?"

The guardian my father had assigned to watch over my safety day and night, six days a week—in a realm where there were only six days in a week—had never opened up to me about her past before. I'd gotten little snippets here and there in short conversations, but I'd never really had a chance to get to know her, so you can't blame me for trying.

"Old enough, dear. It is not my place to have a past, only to ensure that you have a future."

Well, I suppose I deserved that. Still, I kept trying.

"No, really. You've watched over my safety tirelessly every day for months, yet I don't even know where you grew up. You mention having had brushes with manhood, yet you seem so strong, yourself. Have you always been this strong?"

"No, of course not. Okay, so you ask me now, when I have let my own walls down and am at my weakest, so I shall tell you truthfully. But what I tell you must remain within these walls forever, yes? Not even your father can know what I will tell you. Promise me this?"

"I promise," I said and sealed it with a solemn nod and a squeeze of the hand she held. It was an easy promise to make, I figured, and I looked forward to the resulting confession to get my mind off of my own comic tragedy.

"I was born in a village not far from here, one much like every other village you have seen. My father raised goats, and everyone assumed that I, his only child, would do the same, while my mother worked the resulting milk into cheeses and butter of a quality that people came from far away to trade for. We were not rich, but we were not poor, either. Father saw that I wanted for nothing. I was the apple of his eye."

"And—the boy?"

She nodded slowly, her eyes looking off into the corner of the room and, for once, not threatening the shadows there. Instead, it looked like she was peering through time itself. "I am getting to him. But it bears pointing out that I have never had the comeliest of female figures to attract the young men. It was, thus, quite a surprise when a very desirable young man, a champion from a neighboring village, selected me as his mate."

I shook my head in disbelief. Aerona wasn't supermodel material, certainly, but there was a rugged attractiveness to her that was stunning in its own way. She maybe had small-ish breasts, but that just accentuated strong, broad shoulders and sinewy arms that could spend all day working and never tire. Her hips weren't sleek and angular like those of most elf girls, but they were solid, blocky, and some would say they were perfect for motherly needs. Regardless, they perfectly matched the rest of her body in strength and stockiness. Thick leg muscles that most girls could only dream of bulged out no matter how loose Aerona's pants were. Granted, the scars on her arms and face marred the perfect elf lady beauty, but I had to assume they hadn't always been there.

"I think you're very attractive." Her body, thick and roped in muscles as it was, made the perfectly opposing counterpoint to my own tall, gawky form.

"Thank you, but your opinion matters little. I mean that not in a harsh way, Alyssa. You are young, though, and from different worlds as well as different eras, so we see things in somewhat different light."

"So, the boy?"

"Yes, the boy," she said, her exhale becoming a wistful sigh. "He was strong, and brave. The strongest, in fact, which was a trait my father valued in him as my future mate. Which was why he approved, pushed me to court the boy. I remember the gleam I saw in his eyes when the boy won a wrestling tournament, in fact. 'That, Aerona, is the man for you. He is strong, and walks with a solid presence. He will make you a fine home, and you will make him fine children,' he said. Things were different, much more patriarchal, back then, you see. You young kids have no idea how rigidly we used to see the roles of the woman, and the man."

"Now you're starting to sound like my mother, talking about growing up in Mississippi."

"It is, perhaps, the way of things generally, then."

"Perhaps. So did you love him?"

Aerona didn't answer at first, instead fixing the corner with a soft, dew-eyed stare. She chortled softly, a happier sound than I'd ever heard her make. Finally she broke her own spell, nodded, and replied.

"Yes." Her voice was quiet, barely more than a whisper, her stare to a place far away.

"So what happened?"

"What happened? Which happening are you referring to? Do you wish to hear the long version of the flowery romance we had, the Sadoorn days spent by the creek, laughing and talking of the brilliance of our future together? How in spite of our villages being a long half-hour run apart, he brought a single wildflower to my door every evening? How we embraced in love, whispering to each other of the family we would be? Is that what you wish to hear, or are you more interested in the tragedy portion?" She trained wistful eyes on mine.

"Wow. I—I couldn't have imagined, Aerona. That is amazing. So what happened?"

"He broke my heart," she said with a simple shrug, corner of her lips turning up into an ironic grin. "He stopped bringing me flowers one day. The next Sadoorn he did not come to meet me by the river. When I went to confront him, at my father's urging, he told me simply that life had turned, that he no longer felt for me as he had, that he could not see me again."

"What did you do?"

She shrugged as though it were a water glass broken instead of her heart. "What did I do? What could I do? Nothing, Princess. I sat, unable to comprehend life, love, or much else for a long series of crushing moments. Finally I regained the strength to return to my own village, though it took another several days to build the courage to tell my father the news."

"Did he go to tell the boy off? Kill him, even?"

"He went to challenge him, yes. He returned shortly after, bleeding on one cheek, mumbling something about duty and requirements and life, and how love must take a back seat to reality. I could see through his eyes that he had no conviction in his heart. It broke his heart, too."

"So how did you and your father recover?"

"We just did. It made me stronger, to be honest. You do know what they do to make a sword blade stronger, yes? Heat and hammering?"

I nodded, having heard the same thing from the queen only hours before.

"Not long after, I got my first dagger by trading some of the cheese I'd made. I learned as much as I could figure out on my own, and then went to seek out an expert. He was a knife master named Aron, and he lived to the north and far to the east of here. He took me in and trained me for several years."

"I've seen the result. He's obviously excellent at training."

"Yes," she replied simply, the sudden ice in her voice surprising me.

"Maybe I should look to him for lessons?"

"I would not—recommend it."

"Oh? What happened to him?"

"He—went too far one day."

"Too far? I don't understand." I used my weakest voice, trying to draw the iron back out of her face. Her walls seemed to be rapidly setting back in thanks to the memories.

"Payment, Alyssa. He would not teach and feed me for free. It started as chores, simple help with gardening and so on. But then that was not enough."

"And you—oh." I blanched, realizing what she meant. "I—I'm sorry. I can't imagine...."

"It is easier than you are thinking," she said, returning to the present to give me a wry smile. "It was merely a physical act, a joining of flesh with no sensation required. That part of me was dead, anyway. I killed it, vowing never to allow a man to get into my soul, not ever again. It took many ice baths, and a fair amount of these," she stopped to show me the inside of her wrist, where faint white scars told an ugly tale. "But I came out of that much stronger, more resilient than anyone. I left the mountains, journeying to Cysegredig to seek employment. I impressed the officers and joined the king's guard, and have been his loyal servant ever since."

"My goodness, you've.... I...." I shook my head, unable to come to terms with what she'd told me, much less come up with any other meaningful conversation. "So what was his name?"

"The boy? Yes, I have already told you the trainer's name, have I not? I believe this is when you would bless his heart, yes? I—no. That, I will not confide. To give it voice is to unlock too much ugliness from the past. It must remain here," she said, pointing to her heart, "buried inside layers of iron and ice, for the remainder of my days."

She rose, disconnecting our hands perfunctorily. She resumed her position, eyes once again glaring at the shadows as the tears they'd held dried rapidly. Her walls slammed back down, and Aerona the Linebacker was back.

To Handle Keion

Sitting on my bed feeling sorry for myself only works for a little while, especially with a little potted elm annoyingly dancing in place trying and failing to cheer me up. Before long I was ready for something new, so I grabbed my bow and headed downstairs, asking Aerona to leave me to my own devices for the afternoon. Seph got the same request when she met me on my way out of the castle.

Soon I was back at my place at the archery range. My original bucket of a hundred arrows had been replenished in my absence, the couple dozen I'd shot removed from the target. They weren't ever just cycled back, because as Keion had taught me, they needed inspecting by the range master, a grizzled old bowman with incredible knowledge in both archery and arrow makeup. He wouldn't let an arrow be fired if it had even the slightest hints of a crack started; those he stripped the finishing from and put into a pile to be burned later.

"Couldn't stay away, could you?" Keion asked as I took up a firing position and sighted down the first arrow.

thwack

Both of our arrows hit their respective bulls-eyes at the same time. Rapidly I reloaded, and the prince kept pace. I enjoyed the practice, to be honest: the constant repetition of motion, the taut strength involved in the pull, the precision of the aim, and the calm detachment of the archer's frame of mind. Soon I was lost in the rhythm of my shots, and the prince's smoothly matched pacing served only to soothe me further.

Before long I came out of the spell to realize that I was the only one shooting. I glanced over in spite of my desire for detached solitude and saw Prince Charming standing with an appraising expression. His bowl of arrows was empty, his target bristling with all hundred arrows. He'd been well into it when I arrived, so it didn't surprise me that he was done first. It was pleasing, though, to see that my own shots were every bit as accurate as his. Then, as I sank another arrow into the middle, I reminded myself that it was as correct to say that his shots were every bit as accurate as mine.

I finished as smoothly as I'd begun, the last arrow sailing into the forest of shafts that sprouted from my target. I lowered my bow and waited, refusing to look his way. It was, after all, his turn.

I didn't have to wait long. "Not bad, for a ranger," he said softly. The haughtiness in his voice was gone, replaced by a certain light-hearted softness. For once, he'd given me a compliment rather than a sarcastic insult.

I stifled my initial response, to ask whether I could check the boy for a fever, and instead muttered, "Thanks. Not bad, yourself, for a warrior."

"Thanks," he replied, and then, finally, after a lengthy silence, he continued, "Alyssa, may I have a word?"

"I believe you just did," I teased with a grin.

"Another, perhaps," he returned, his nod and smile showing that he was at least minimally enjoying the banter.

"That was two. How many words are you going to use in asking me for a word?"

"As many as it takes."

"Fair enough. Word away, yon prince."

"Walk with me," he commanded, and immediately softened it with a "please?" He turned and ambled out the other direction from the castle, toward the horse barns and the galloping archery range I'd enjoyed with Seph. I couldn't turn down such a plaintive request from Prince Charming, so I ambled along behind, and then beside as I caught up. The pair of us walked in silence for quite a distance into the woods.

"It amazes me how clean the rangers keep the forest, even in the deepest days of winter," I said, as much to break the spell as to communicate anything. It did amaze me, though. I'd grown up in forests that were wildly overgrown with kudzu, towering pine and oak trees overpowering anything that might try to break through the forest floor below, shutting out the daylight only to have portals opened once the winter took the oak tree leaves from their branches. In elf land, though, everything was neat, and all was planned. The bushes grew where they were supposed to, and the trees tolerated their presence with a brotherly affection. The grass died back a bit, losing the manicured shapes that had amazed me in the summer. Meanwhile, the days were starting to lengthen, but the sun was still already nearly down to the tops of the trees.

"They do. It is quite a feat of—magic," Keion murmured. It shocked me to hear him actually acknowledge that it was magical; before, he'd sung along to the standard gospel that ranger powers with the trees and priest powers with healing were different from magical powers. Now that he'd stood by my side as the people called me a witch, he seemed to be okay with a different tune, but I still watched his face in silence.

"I—sometimes—wish I—sometimes wish that I could see the magical flows as you do, Alyssa. The blue tinge to everything must be beautiful."

"Not everything. In fact, it's kind of rare, to be honest. I remember seeing the blue-tinged walls that surrounded Ganolog, wondering what it could possibly mean. Once I'd realized it indicated magic, I wondered what sort of magic anybody would apply to walls made from vertical logs."

"Garrison walls," Keion corrected me, his tone sincere and gentle. "That's what they're called."

"Garrison walls. Thank you."

"You are welcome."

The conversation lapsed for a while longer. Our breath came out in little tufts of mist as the sun set and the air cooled around us. Our steps beat a crisp rhythm along the forest floor. It lulled me into a sense of comfort, of rightness.

Then the *tylwyth teg* appeared. The little faerie folk flitted around and over our heads, darting and giggling. Keion glanced upward, eyes glaring with fear in anticipation of the trickery that the little creatures usually brought. They were always there, of course, but only sometimes did they elect to make their presence visible. They seemed to have a thing for me—a positive thing, anyway, one far different from the thing they had for the prince, whom they loved to mock.

I laughed, and kept the laugh going for a little longer than usual as I enjoyed the tinkling sound that the chill air gave it. The tylwyth teg reacted as well, raising their own high-pitched laughter. They hovered over us, their iridescent wings difficult to see as they beat rapidly against the winter wind's gentle gusts.

"Go away, my friends. This is a private moment. Let's play tomorrow!" I called.

One of the tylwyth teg, a male who looked like the ringleader of the bunch, darted down to just in front of Keion's face. Thumbs met his cheeks and fingers waggled in an obscene gesture punctuated by a messy raspberry. Keion chortled good-naturedly, surprising me. He had always acted hostile to the creatures before, but something about this evening made him seem different in so many ways.

The tylwyth teg noticed, too, darting upward as a group to disappear among the tree branches above.

"They're actually following your direction," Keion mused. He turned a surprised look my way.

"Will wonders never cease?"

"Probably not," he said, decisiveness coming into his voice. He stopped walking and turned toward me, reaching out for my hand. I stopped, too, and let him take it. Carefully, slowly, he pulled me in toward him. Soon the warmth of our bodies mingled together, and I could smell the musky aroma that always made my knees weak.

"So, Prince, what's the word?" I asked, teasing. Our faces were mere inches apart, and my eyes looked directly into his where, once again, I saw emotions at war with one another.

"I will start, I believe, with 'I apologize.'"

"That's two words."

"So it is. You deserve more words than that, Alyssa. I am so sorry that I snapped at you earlier today. I—I have been disappointed, distraught even, with the canceling of the season I had been looking forward to so eagerly. That is certainly not an excuse, but it is the only, best, explanation I have available."

"That's okay. I—said some things I shouldn't have, too. I'm sorry."

Don't you dare kiss him.

Get out of my head, Kluzhka.

Can't do that, Princess. Bonded, remember?

Well, at least shut up about it.

But....

Shut up!

Fine. But you'll be sorry.

I know I will. Shut up, you!

Hmmph.

"You're talking to your wyvern—friend—aren't you?"

"I have got to learn how to do that without it wrapping across my face. Yes, she's convinced she knows more than I do about my social life. I told her to shut up."

"Your familiar speaks against me?"

"She speaks against everyone, me included sometimes. Don't take it personally."

"She counsels against—liaison. With me."

"Liaison. That's—yes," I admitted, not sure I liked his way of putting it, but figuring that he was probably as confused as I was about the whole mess we'd created. I let it go. "She says I'll regret it."

"What do you believe?"

"I—I'm not certain. I don't know what the future will hold, or—or...." My intoxication rose as more and more of his essence suffused each breath. Soon it seemed like I could smell nothing but Prince, and suddenly I wanted nothing but to be wrapped up in him, to be protected by his strong arms.

Our lips found each other in the dim twilight. He shivered, and I willed energy into Draignerthol. Slowly the air around us heated even more than our shared passion required, his shivers abating in the dim blue light of my power.

"I can feel it, even when I cannot see the power," he murmured into my ear, and then he started kissing his way downward from there toward my collarbone. "It is incredible," he breathed once his lips arrived at their destination.

"The power, or the collarbone?"

"Your power. It is intoxicating," he said, looking me in the eyes, and then he latched onto my lips with his once again. "Your collarbone is pretty nice, too."

Then it happened. It just...did. Suddenly the whole thing melted away, intoxication dissolving into spittle swap. He stopped at the same time I did, disconnecting curiously.

We stood silently for a long, long moment, our eyes meeting and then flashing about.

He reached out and tentatively gripped my hands with his own. This time, though, there was no hunger, no desire. It was just...peace. Togetherness, in a strange way.

"What just happened?"

"I don't know."

"Maybe we need more time?"

"Maybe it just wasn't meant to be?"

"Your guess is as good as mine."

"It feels like kissing my—"

Both of us finished the statement at the same time: "brother," and "sister." Both of us laughed.

The spell was broken, apparently. Keion was still Prince Charming, every bit as handsome as the day I'd met him. But now I had him, all to myself in the middle of the forest, nobody around to say yes or no, nobody to judge. Now he had me, under the same circumstances. We had each other, right where we wanted ourselves, and once that happened, it was done.

Yes, I accepted, at the same time I saw a similar acceptance wrap itself across his face.

It was done.

We trudged back to the castle in silence, at least outwardly. I was treated to Kluzhka's laughter keening in my head the whole way.

MARWOLAETH

*Death, in Elf tongue. They make it hard to say,
but that's sort of expected, right?
The Elves have been a long-lived folk, so death
would be a special sort of thing to them.*

The First Casualty

Seph intercepted me on the stairs. "You look—different," she mused.

I stopped. "Do I? How do I look different?"

"More relaxed. You just look lighter, like a weight is off of your shoulders. Like you've finally figured something out. Your face is more relaxed than it has been since you got here. And you know what else is funny?"

"I—didn't realize my appearing to have lost some stress would be funny in the first place, Seph, but no, what else is funny?"

She brushed off my objection with a gesture and continued, "I just saw Prince Keion pass through and, if we'd been better friends, I would've said the exact same thing to him."

"Oh. Well, yes, that is funny. Ha ha," I deflected, wanting to get up to tell Aerona about my—what did Seph say? The weight now off my shoulders?

"Sarcasm, Cousin?"

"No, I just—well, okay, yes. This afternoon Aerona kind of straightened me out in terms of men, and I just wanted to tell her the result and how great I feel because of it. Strange, too, like the weight that was lifted was a chunk of my soul, but not really. Does that make sense?"

"Not in the slightest." She wrinkled her face up in concentration, thinking about it.

I almost laughed at her. It wasn't funny, but it sort of was, as embarrassed as I was to admit it. She'd never been much into boys, so her naivete was—cute, refreshing, and nearly brought me to giggling. But I felt like I needed to get up to my room to tell Aerona first.

It was, after all, mainly her words that had brought me there.

"I'll go up there with you and listen," Seph offered as she fell into step beside me on the stairs. "Maybe it will make sense then."

I shrugged and continued. I hadn't set out to bring Seph into what had started out as a very private conversation, but I had to admit that I didn't mind too much. She was, after all, aware of my weird relationship with Charming, and she often seemed even more scared of Aerona's gruff sternness than I was.

Still, it was a private thing, I thought as I turned into the hallway that connected the king's suites. It had been my home for nearly a year, my safe space away from all, or at least most, of the intrigue and machinations of the Cult. I normally began to relax starting from the top of the stairs.

But not today.

Something was wrong.

I stopped, my body going rigid as I tried to interpret the weird sense of wrongness I felt. Seph didn't make it very far, her momentum carrying her almost to the first set of doors before she noticed and turned back to me.

"What's wrong?" she asked, a perplexed look on her face.

"Something. I don't know. Maybe nothing. It's—weird. I just feel—something. Something wrong, something bad. Remember that feeling I got in Blodwyn's house?"

She crinkled her nose up, obviously thinking back to when we'd been taken in by the Cult leader up in the frozen tundra of Padrig's area. Blodwyn had welcomed us with all the hospitality and charm of a Southern belle, but something was off then, as it was now.

"You're whispering," Seph said.

"Yeah. Hang on a sec."

I reached through the glowing pendant at my neckline and pressed out tendrils of power. I really had no idea what I was doing, and I knew I had no idea, and that was frustrating. Still, I'd managed similar feats before.

This time, though, there was nothing. It was wrong, and it felt wrong, but I'll be darned if I could point to why.

I shrugged. "I…I may be wrong."

"Booboo may be a *pwca*, too."

I grinned in spite of the overwhelming sense of wrongness that permeated the hall. Poocas were little sprites that elf mothers scared their kids with, the more troublesome cousins of the tylwyth teg. I'd never actually seen one, but given their reputation I'd not gone looking for them either. Skilled shapeshifters, they were, and for all I knew they could probably pretend to be a wolverine if they wanted to. I shoved that back for my next scary dream.

I could see that my door was left open a crack, which bothered me even more than the weird prickles I sensed. I never left the door open, period. Meanwhile, the still silence that drifted out through that crack was deafening. Little Treebeard always let me know he knew I was there, but instead there was nothing.

Terrified, I placed my hand on Draignerthol, feeling the warmth and the power through my thin blouse. I felt the reservoir of magical force on the other side fill me, and then, once I felt "full," I kicked the door.

Ethereal bands of blue stretched across the room. I took them in immediately and reached across with my own power, severing the ones that held L.T. rigid. Immediately the little potted elm reacted, thrashing about angrily. I'd never seen it so agitated. Its little limbs bashed repeatedly against the wall, leaving little brown streaks where the tree was using so much force the paint was gouged.

I realized that none of us could hear the flailing, though.

As an automatic reaction I started crooning a wordless song of peace and relaxation, trying to get my little buddy to calm down, but I couldn't hear that either. The silence spell was harder to see, running about the corners as it was, but once I saw it I realized that it enveloped the whole room. It was cleverly formed, but I'd seen the spell in the dragon's book.

The counter spell was actually far easier than the silence spell itself.

As soon as I twisted the energies back and let them fall away, L.T.'s frenetic shaking and banging sounded through the entire hall, the ferocity apparently bringing several people running, from all the pounding footfalls I could hear. I didn't pay attention, though. Instead, I worked harder at quietening the tree down, singing my little calming song louder, over and over.

"Alyssa," I heard from the other side of the room, but I ignored it. L.T. needed me.

"Cousin!" the voice sounded louder.

"Not now," I muttered and went right back to singing.

I felt hands grab me roughly by the shoulders. I started to object, but I could tell that they were Seph's. "*Cousin!*" she yelled into my ear, jerking me out of the little calming song-world I'd created for L.T.'s purpose as she physically spun me around toward the corner behind the door.

It was Aerona's corner.

The burly woman who'd been my guardian and companion still stood, slumped. She was held up by blue bands of power, though, and not by her own strength, as I could tell as I took the magical version of a sledgehammer to the spell. Tendrils shattered and flew about, and she slowly toppled to the floor.

Paralyzed, I stood and watched Aerona fall. She was tough, the toughest person I'd ever known, in fact. There's no way someone got to her. No way she wouldn't come to, catch herself, and be right back up. She was fine, just needed freeing, I knew. I just...knew. The blue tinge at her lips, the graying of the tip of her nose that I could somehow see from far across the room—those were just nothing. Temporary. Nothing could or would happen to Aerona.

People charged through the door. I noticed several in the black uniform of my father's personal guard. I thought I saw the king's pendant, itself, dangling from the neck of a tall, strong figure that closed in on me.

This wasn't happening, I tried to convince myself.

Brown robes of the priesthood joined the black warrior attire. People were moving. Some stepped between me and Aerona, and I tried to yell at them. *Move! I can't see! I can help, somehow, if only I could—why can't I move, speak, do anything?*

I come.

No, Kluzhka. There's—there's nothing you can do indoors, and there's no danger right now. Stay.

You can't say for certain that there is no danger.

You can't help. Stay where you are.

Fine. I shall stay where I am, but I worry over your tone. I will come immediately if anything changes.

I heard Sternyface's voice drift over from the chaos in the other corner. Aerona's corner. It was unmistakable, the tenor and the power that only the high priestess of Kiirajanna could muster.

I heard her say, "She's gone," and then blackness overcame me.

Magical Murder

I came to with a jerk, the strange lineup of events of the day flashing through my mind's eye. I sprang out of bed, looking around—my room, check. Now, if my memories were in any way accurate, a murder site. I glanced over at the now-empty corner: nothing. Nothing except a faint hint of magic, that is. I made a mental note to check the residue further later.

"Alyssa," my father's voice called from across the room. It didn't startle me; I'd noticed him sitting there when I'd glanced around. But he was the rock, and I trusted he was okay, and so I was more worried about Aerona and about Little Treebeard.

"How are you, little guy?" I intoned in the sing-song I used to communicate with the elm. I got a gentle shake of the limbs in response. Somehow I always knew what the limb-shakes meant. I'd doubted my ability to interpret at first, but the day I'd connected with the trees of the realm, and through them to the soul that was L.T., I realized how right I had been to trust my instincts.

"Shaken, not stirred. Sad, and a little scared, but okay in general. Good," I said. I rose from the crouch I'd taken on.

"Dad, what happened? Where's Aerona?" I turned my eyes toward him, then, and saw his grief-stricken face for the first time.

"She is gone, Alyssa. We held Council while you recovered. Naissa says it was foul play. Magic," he added, his voice wrapping the word up in centuries of distrust and fear, and then after a pause for effect he continued. "Asphyxiation. Whoever did it managed to stop up her airway long enough to stop her breathing."

"Here, Dad," I said, handing him a basin rag and then taking one for myself. We both had rivers running down our faces, rivers we each mopped at for a few long, silent moments.

"Any idea—where is she being kept?" I felt myself start questioning like one of those television show detectives, but my mind wanted to know other stuff, answers that I knew he couldn't possibly have.

"In the inner chapel of the cathedral."

"Where is her family?"

"She doesn't—didn't...." He sighed, deeply, and then continued. "Here. Her family is here. The guard she has served so well through the years. You. Me. We are the only family she has, Alyssa. Her parents died years ago, and she had no siblings or children. She will be remembered here."

His language choices struck me as a little off; he never, ever used contractions. Probing, I asked, "Did you know her parents?"

Dad shot me a strangely guarded expression, one I couldn't read, and then after a long period of thought, he nodded. "I did. Not well, but I had the occasion to know them. A fine pair, and a fine man her father was. He raised goats. A simple goat herder, he was, but one who was well known throughout the region for the quality of his efforts and the honesty of his word. I hated.... I—I miss them. Terribly. And now...." He sobbed again, basin rag held tightly to his face.

Something clicked. I stared in disbelief, at first, and then I shook my head.

"You were the boy."

"What?" he asked, bringing his tear-laden face up out of the rag to meet my eyes for the moment. "What boy?"

"Aerona—told me a story today. It was when I came back from a raging argument with Keion. She let her guard down, and actually talked to me. First time, really. Made me promise to keep her words between these four walls, and now—now look at me telling them. But I don't think they'll surprise you, somehow. She told me about growing up the only child of a goat-farmer. Told me about finding the love of her life, about cheering him on when he won—a wrestling tournament. You were—you were known for wrestling, weren't you?" I plunged ahead, not waiting for his solemn nod. "And then she told me about losing him. How it ripped her heart out through her chest, made her never want another man again. She wouldn't tell me the name, but—that was *you*, wasn't it, Father?"

His face remained calm, expression unreadable for several long moments. I'd shocked him out of his grief, it appeared. Finally his face collapsed and he nodded slowly, slightly, as though the truth was going to grudgingly come out in spite of his desire to keep it back.

"Yes. It was I. But that takes away nothing from your mother and me."

I thought about that, about how I felt now that I knew. He was right, I supposed. That wasn't really my point, though.

I shrugged. "I didn't say it would, Dad. You were young, and alive, and in your prime, and she was, too. I presume that the sudden shift in — interest — was when you learned you were to be king?" He nodded, and I continued, "So tradition did a little number on your relationship, and you did your duty. Just like...."

71

I let the obvious comparison slip without granting it air time. "And you and she stood side by side all these years, didn't you?"

"We did. Alyssa, she was—she was so beautiful in her youth. In her older age, too, but...."

"I get it, Dad. It's a lot to take in, I admit, but I get it. Your secret is safe with me, too. I've seen the way you are with Momma, and I don't doubt that you love her very much. Our first loves don't always turn out like we expect them to, do they?"

He got a suspicious look on his face. "There is something you are not telling me, is there not?"

"What do you mean?"

"Your tone, when you issued that wise proclamation about first loves. What is going on, Alyssa?"

I gave in and told him all about Keion, how we'd snuck off from the castle and made out under the twilight silence. He started to look angry, but he wistfully smiled and nodded when I reached the conclusion of the story. Eventually the wistful smile made it up to his eyes, blossoming into a real smile, and he even chortled a couple of times.

"You could have listened to me when I said that it was not meant to be, but I suppose that would have left you always wondering, my daughter. My dear, you are destined for a wonderful young man one day, of that I am certain, but our tradition holds fast to the fact that Keion is quite likely to become my successor, and in doing so, he and you cannot be a couple. You—yes, you do know that, and fully." He waited for my nod, and then continued, "Over and beyond that, though, I must say that I always thought you made a really horrible pair. You would very likely have killed each other within your first year."

"I guess—I have to agree, Dad. It's just that he's so—"

"Yes, I am aware of how smashingly handsome the crown prince is. I will also point out, however, that you have not yet hit your own nineteenth birthday. I am willing to assure you, my own breath as surety, that what you consider handsome will change quite a few times over the next several years, so if that was the prince's main attraction for you, then rest assured that any pain you feel will dissipate over time, more likely rapidly than not."

"I don't feel any pain."

"Well, um.... Good. That's—that's good. There will be other, better potential mates—"

"Dad, enough, please."

Tell him I will eat any who are unsuitable.

I will not. Bless your heart, you need to get out of my head, Kluzhka.

It is good to see you alert again, my familiar.

Fine. Go.

"So now I must get to the effort of finding you another suitable guardian," Dad said. I was cheered that he hadn't noticed the conversation in my head, but then again, he wasn't entirely there at the moment anyway thanks in part to his own grief.

"I'm fine. I'll find my own, how about that?"

"Alyssa—"

"No, Dad. I will find my own."

"Alyssa, no. Listen. There was just, this afternoon, a murder in this very room. I will *not* entrust my daughter's safety to the hands of any but the best."

"Dad, I agree, but how was Aerona killed?"

"Asphyxiation."

"Right, but asphyxiation how?"

"With magic. I already told you that."

"Right, you did. But I was making a point. Whoever killed her walked in, probably under the cover of a magical spell, tossed up a silence sphere around Little Treebeard, and then strangled one of the toughest guards in the land, all without lifting a finger physically. Right? So tell me, what are your other guards going to be able to do against that when it happens again?"

"I shall ask Naissa for priests to share in the guard duty."

"Sternyface doesn't have enough priests at her disposal to cover everyone who needs covering, and besides, they've been denying the existence of magic for so long they have no idea what they're doing."

Dad's face was stormy as he considered the potential objections, but it finally fell away and he shrugged. "So, what do you propose?"

"The dark—"

"*No.*"

"Yes, Dad. *Yes.* I have to fight fire with fire. I have to go find a magician among the dark-skinned elves."

"So let us say you find one. Why would that magician be any more trustworthy than the murderer?"

"Dad, did I not tell you all about what I learned that night when I met the tribe? No, I guess I didn't, because you never asked. Did you? Believe it or not, they're on our side, Dad. They want to help. You just keep pushing them away."

"Well, that is fine. I shall—I suppose—let us open a parlance with them, once I can figure out a way to do so without gross upheaval in the realm."

"A parlance? Oh, how open minded of you. Bless your open-minded heart, Your Majesty."

"Alyssa—"

"No! Dad, no. You can't push them away into a parlance."

"I shall agree to talk to their leaders, I promise, Alyssa. It is—one does not undo thousands of years of history in an afternoon no matter how shocking the events of that afternoon might be. In the meantime, you're going to get a platoon of my soldiers and a trio of Sternyf—Naissa's—priests. And that, my daughter, is that." he added when I started to object again.

"Fine," I said, though it really wasn't. I stalked out of the room, intent on finding something to eat in the dining room.

I didn't turn into the dining room, though. Instead, I bolted out the front door and went for another run.

AMDDIFFYN

Protector. Or protection. Either one is okay, I guess, when you're under attack.

Legolas

I ran.

It wasn't a fast run, more of a jog. But it was a ground-eating lope, and I covered a lot of distance quickly. It was dark, but with the moon's help I was able to see just fine. I tried following the same rough path I'd covered the last time I'd gone on a jog, when I'd run into the dark-skinned elves in the first place, but that proved impossible. The night I'd taken off, not long after what passed among elves for New Years Eve, there were a whole passel of unfriendly elves encamped around the castle. I'd had to pick my way very carefully, paying more attention to staying away from roving bands who might want to strangle me than to following a repeatable course.

As I got farther away from the castle and from other elves, I felt the same magic coursing through me that I had sensed that night. Everything—the sky, the air, the trees, even the grass—seemed to come alive and want to interact with me. I had a mission, though, so I kept jogging, loping along instead of stopping to talk to the trees as I had before.

I slowed to a halt after what seemed like a couple of hours on the trail without seeing anything familiar. I'd only run for an hour or so the other night, so it was pretty obvious that I'd already passed the camp of the dark elves. Then, as I thought more about it, I realized that running around the woods probably wouldn't get me to where I needed anyway. The dark elves were masters of blending in with their surroundings, of using magic to obscure the magic they used to obscure their lives. I'd been certain that night that even Master Owain would have a hard time figuring out there was a camp there.

What chance did I have in randomly running around?

But I did know *someone* who could find them.

Kluzhka.

I'm sleeping.

She sent me a series of images of a beautiful young buck, a strong meaty male that had only recently fallen to her talons. She'd ripped its head off, drinking the life blood that poured from its neck, and then set to picking the skeleton clean of flesh, and she proudly showed me how the hunt and subsequent kill and feast had happened. Then she sent sensations, a fullness and a wellness that did not wish to be disturbed by flight.

Look, I'm sorry, but I need you.

To do what? I am tired.

You can see heat signatures, right?

Is that a trick question, Princess? You have seen this in person. It is how I hunt at night. Would you like for me to show you the memories once again?

No, no thank you. Once was quite enough, especially when it came to—ew. How can you drink that blood?

It is quite easy, and delicious as well. Perhaps if you have a while to evolve sufficiently, you too will—

No, I won't. No. Now look. I need your help. My guardian died—was murdered—tonight. I sent her mental images of the scene, and then one of my father's grief.

I suppose I can be your guardian for a while, then. But unless your kind evolves your opinion of mine, and fairly rapidly, you will have to find someone else.

I want to find someone else, yes. Can you imagine what might happen if you are beside me when Xlixi comes through? I need your help in finding them, though, since they use magic to cover up their existence.

I explained more of what I meant, sending images from memories I had of the camp.

Ah, yes, I know of these people. They are difficult to hunt, and quite challenging for us to track down and kill. There is one problem, however. If I help you find a camp of these elves, they will not react well to the sight of me.

If we find the right group, I can figure that part out.

And if we find the wrong group?

I—I guess I can figure that part out, too.

We shall see.

You gonna help me?

...Fine. I come.

With a pop and then a whoosh, the wyvern appeared above me. Wide, graceful wings blotted out the moon as she sailed gently down onto a perch on the ground.

Well, get on. You will have to ride me to make this happen.

I know.

I sense trepidation in your voice.

Ya think? Last time I got on for a ride, you almost killed me in a free-fall.

Last time you got on for a ride, we were fleeing a dragon. I take your safety very seriously, Princess, and when it comes to making you scream a little in fright versus seeing a dragon chomp on your face, guess which one I will always select?

That doesn't make it feel any better.

I don't care. Get on so we can get this over with so I can get back to my digestive rest.

Okay, fine. And...Kluzhka?

Yes?

I...appreciate it.

I climbed carefully up her foreleg and swung my leg over her back, landing in what felt like a safe spot behind her shoulder blades. It was harder in the dark than it had been in the dragon's tower, but I managed it without cutting myself on her sharp scales.

Ready, Princess?

Without waiting for an answer, Kluzhka shot upward through the trees, leaving me hanging on for dear life.

I have to get a saddle and bridle for you. I sent her mental images of fancy examples.

Good luck getting me to wear such restraints, Princess. After all, I am, and it is disturbing, and perhaps somewhat indicative of our relative intellectual gap, that I must keep repeating myself on this count, but I am not your servant nor your pack horse nor your beast of burden.

Fine, I said, happy that for once she hadn't added that, to her opinion, I was her familiar.

She banked slowly over the trees, head sweeping to one side and back in search of the mound structure I remembered seeing. It was different, looking from the air, but she had enough practice at it to make it work. She flew back toward the castle at first, since I figured I'd passed the point by, and then she started diagonal N patterns toward the east.

After a while, I signaled that we'd probably gone the wrong direction. She nodded and doubled back, finding the spot she'd landed quickly from the dissipating heat signature of my own feet and hers. Then she started the same type of search pattern toward the west, flying slowly just high enough above the tree tops to allow us a good vantage to see down through them.

There.

It was tricky, turning the input from her vision to mine on and off, but with some effort I was able to look through her eyes and then overlay that with what an elf, or human, or even a mixed-blood princess like me, could see. Granted, I could see magic, and so once I was keyed in on that to look for, the subtly-woven blanket spell that was meant to cover the other concealment magic was actually a glowing blue bulls-eye when seen from above. At the same time, the wyvern's heat-sensitive vision picked out several dozen little elf-forms, all scurrying this way and that as they apparently realized that a fearsome predator was approaching.

Maybe we should set down at a safe, nonthreatening distance.

I am not afraid of them. They look tasty.

You said, yourself, that they're hard to kill. Does that mean they're more dangerous to you, in return?

A bit. Their spells can be powerful. Certainly not enough to fear, with a band this small. Still, you are—correct, this once, as our goal is not to kill them, or to scare them, but rather to make contact.

I nearly flipped over her head and fell to my death as she suddenly flipped her wings toward the front in a full stop, and then surged to the right as she found a clearing and landed gracefully in its middle.

I slid clunkily down, stumbling and nearly falling onto my face as my feet touched the ground.

Thanks. Some warning before you bank like that might be nice in the future.

Sorry. Someone was warming up a spell for me, so I needed to act quickly.

You can see that?

Of course. Can't you? Now get up; they approach. They move stealthily, but not enough so.

I rose and held my arms outward in a traditional elf greeting. Belatedly realizing that the older woman who led the tribe had never actually told me her name, I put my plan to call for her aside and settled on merely saying, "Hello!"

A light pop sounded on the opposite side of the tree to my front, and a pair of white eyes peered around it at me. "Princess?" a voice asked tentatively.

"Yes, it is I, Princess Alyssa."

"What are you doing here?"

"I come to meet you again and to ask for a favor."

"You have a strange approach for one seeking a favor, young one," the older lady's voice carried from the darkness.

"I am Alyssa. This is Kluzhka, my...my familiar."

Quiet, you. I don't need you in my head right now.

"I seek your assistance in what may very well be the end times. Will you come out and talk to me openly? I give you my word that my companion will not harm you."

Slowly the dark-skinned matriarch crept into the clearing, passing by me to approach Kluzhka. She reached up and touched the wyvern's pointed snout, held still for a moment, and then whirled about to face me.

"You obviously have a strange tale to tell us, coming as you do now with such a powerful beast as your familiar. Please, follow me to the safety of our camp, but also please aid me in comforting my own people by asking your wyvern to—look peaceful. Her expression says she wishes to eat me."

"I shall."

You heard her.

I don't want to eat her. She's too old and stringy.

Well, stop looking like you do.

I don't look like I do! I look perfectly normal.

Normal for a wyvern. Look—peaceful.

I assure you that I have no idea how to do that, nor would I ever wish to learn.

"The two speak in the ancient manner," an old man said as he crept out into the clearing to stand beside the woman. "This is unheard of. A miracle, perhaps."

"Yes, and every elf ranger in the vicinity is going to zero in on your wyvern—friend—here. We must return to the safety of our campsite quickly," she muttered, glaring from me to the wyvern and back.

The dark elves teleported with a pop. Shrugging, I followed, arriving at the campsite in a few hops.

Why aren't you teleporting to follow?

I don't need to. My legs work just fine, and besides, I do not want to threaten them, or to seem threatening. Your legs work just fine, too, by the way.

Fine, I'll follow you the hard way, Kluzhka grumbled in my head. She landed on the edge of camp and waddled in, her long tail brushing a path behind her. As she walked, little black-skinned children gathered to the side, eyes wondrous and terrified. A few reached out tentatively to touch her hide, and when she did not flinch back, a couple of brave ones actually reached in and squealed with delight.

Oh, this is so much fun. Are you sure I can't just eat them?

I gave them my word. And be nice; no telling who here can listen in on our conversation.

No one can. Being able to tell we're talking is different from eavesdropping. One is hearing the babble of a creek, while the other requires a powerful being to immerse themselves into the torrent.

"So, what brings you to our camp once again, my young princess, if not merely to scare the wits away from us? You must be an adult now, if you are coming with a—familiar," she said, shooting a concerned glance toward Kluzhka. The wyvern somehow managed to smile and nod in return.

"I need a guardian," I said, figuring there wasn't much to be gained by beating around the bush.

"Well. Okay, so now I have to ask what happened to your former guardian. I assume you had one, yes?"

"I did. Her name was Aerona." I told the tale of Aerona's toughness, how she'd fought by my side up in Ganolog. Then I told the tale of her death at the hands of a magician, how we had discovered her strangled, murdered, in my room.

"You sound like an exceptionally difficult person to guard, Princess," the old man said.

"I don't try to be."

"Nobody tries to be. But you have your own wit, your own will, and both are strong. On top of that, you have powerful enemies. Very powerful ones, if they can slip into the castle, silence your tree with magic, kill the unkillable using undetectable magic, and then escape with none the wiser. So that leaves me with one question."

"Which is?"

"What made you believe that we would be at all interested in providing you with such a guardian?"

"Well, you liked me, I thought—no, you didn't?" The snickers that had come to the clearing died off rapidly, and I pressed on, "at least, you are on my side, and I thought you wanted to return to your place beside your light-skinned brethren. Besides, you know what will happen if a dragon takes over the land."

"Well, my young princess, that is a lot of presumption. I mean no offense, but your youth blinds you, it seems. Oh, it is safe enough to assume that some of us enjoyed your presence. You are a likable person—not that that means much of any positive value to one who would be a ruler. To assume we are on your side is incorrect, however. We are, of course, as we have always been, on our own side. As long as your path marches in the same direction as ours we will march along, but at the point where they diverge, we will most likely do nothing but disappoint you. As for our 'place,' that is here, in our communities, away from all of your castle's foolishness. I have as much desire to leave our home in the trees as you do to see your own head taken off by—a dragon, you said? Please, tell us more of this dragon."

I did as he asked, telling the story of the hunhymgais gone horribly wrong, how I'd ended up on a realm no one had heard of, met an elf who was the exact twin of my cousin here, come to bond with Kluzhka, and fled from the dragon. I spent extra time telling of the dragon's fierce terror, how it had been able to control me. Then I told of how it had wanted my oath of subordination in order to peacefully come in and use Kiirajanna as—a farm, essentially, with elves being the livestock.

"Why would a dragon need your approval if he's as powerful as you say?" the old man asked.

"I wonder...." The older lady looked keenly at my chest, her gaze boring through the shirt to the pendant it hid, thoughts running plainly across her face in the flickering light of the fire. "Have you tried asking your pendant?"

"Asking? My pendant? No, Draignerthol is...just a pendant. A powerful one, at that, but...."

"I wonder...."

"What is it that you wonder?" I asked impatiently after her pause had left too great a gap in the conversation.

"Nothing," she said, shaking her head with a dour expression. "No point wondering silly things, is there? But that is a good question—why would a dragon need your approval? Does your wyvern friend know the answer to that?"

"She does not. We are scrambling for everything we have, and the priests are working on that as well."

"Oh. Well, if your priests are working on it, then why come to us? We can all just take a vacation," the old man said drily.

"Look, I know you don't respect them, and that is your call. But they are all I have, especially if you will not help me find a competent guardian."

"Princess, have you thought much about what this competent guardian might look like? What traits are you looking for?"

"I don't care about the color of her skin."

"Clearly, or you would not have come to us. That is not what I was talking about, though. You have mentioned needing someone with magical capabilities. Which magical specialization did you have in mind?"

"Which what? There's—there's specializations?"

I was dismayed by the barks of laughter that broke out around the campfire, all of them seemingly at my expense. Apparently I'd just asked a really dumb question.

"Of course there are specializations, dear," the old lady said after quietening them down. "Just as in the world you are used to. The girl we see you walking with, the one with the powerful wolverine at her side, is a ranger, no? And the boy you kissed today, a warrior? That does not mean they cannot do each others' activities, merely that they prefer duties in a ranger's or a warrior's scope. Do not look so embarrassed, girl. You shared a beautiful kiss out in the forest, and there is nothing to be ashamed of for that. But another example—your priests at Cysegredig. While it is certain they can take up a bow and fight if they wish—"

"They could probably do that every bit as poorly as they bumble around with their misuse of the gifts of Gaia," a man, sleek and powerfully built, grumbled from the side. He was gently shushed by the matron, but I noticed that there was no correction in her quieting gesture. I couldn't help noticing as several others nodded approval.

"Teeri, here, is strong in battle and in offensive spells. You would not want to get him angry, I tell you this with surety. I am a healer. Masu," she indicated the older man who had been speaking beside her, "is a weather watcher. We all, or most of us, anyway, can perform work with all of Gaia's gifts, but we all prefer certain aspects of those gifts, and it is in our preference that we build our strength. Those, then, are specializations."

"Do you have any rangers?" I asked. I hadn't seen any familiars.

"You already have a ranger companion, dear."

"No, not for me. I was just curious. Are they one of your specializations?"

"Yes, but no. That is an option, but none of us would take it. There are plenty of rangers among the others. Plus, these days, wild ones are coming forth at a rapid rate. I do not believe even your Master Ranger knows how many tree-lovers there are."

"Shaping the grass is a somewhat useless exercise, is it not?" the one she'd called Terri blurted, and I shrugged. As much as I didn't like the direction the conversation was taking, I couldn't really argue against the sentiment.

"So—for me," I said, trying to move the conversation away from the jab at my cousin's field of expertise. "I haven't really thought that far. Now, and later on as queen, I'll need to surround myself with smart people."

"Who all agree with you," Masu slipped in, a huge grin on his face. The elder lady nodded.

I also nodded at first, but then I thought about it more and recognized the trap for what it was. "No. It is tempting, certainly, but my father already covered that with me in one of our discussions, and I agree with him. As queen I won't need agreement. I will need competence. In fact, he tells me that sometimes disagreement is the foundation for the best decisions."

"A wise man, your father is," the old lady purred.

"Who has set himself up beside the high priestess, a woman as disagreeable as they come," Masu slid in. The lady rolled her eyes, but again did not correct the younger man.

"Perhaps the future queen should return to her castle and consider the question of which specialization she most needs to work with," Masu said, but the lady shook her head.

"While I agree that the princess should consider more closely the qualities in the people she would choose to surround herself with, I am not going to have her go back to the castle with a wrong idea, a hope that will never be fulfilled. No, Princess Alyssa, as noble as your request is on its surface, I cannot—I will not—put one of my people in a position to have to fight off both enemies and allies. You know the division between your people and mine. I see it in your eyes. You know the castle would erupt in anger should you bring one of my people back even just to wash your dishes. Bringing one of my sons into the stone edifice to stand beside you would be uncomfortable to him and unforgivable in many of both of our own people's eyes. You already broached the idea with your father, yes?"

I nodded.

"He did not approve, yes?"

I shrugged. Not approving was a little bit of an understatement for how he'd reacted.

"And he loves you much more than anyone else at the castle, yes?"

"Yes." I was tired, it had been a very long, very bad day, and I couldn't hold the facade of regal bearing up much longer. The loss of Aerona felt like a weight around my neck, and duty or no duty, I needed to deal with it. "Look, okay, I get it. You would, if you could, but you can't, so you won't."

She looked amused, which just drove my blood pressure higher. "No, you are incorrect. I am not saying that I would, if I could, my dear. That decision would require a conference of all the matriarchs, and then I would send none but a true, willing volunteer into such a dragon's maw. By then, you could be dead. You should look within your own people, focus on—"

"Excuse me, Grandmother, but I would willingly perform this duty," a voice interrupted, bringing a scowl to the old woman's face.

I turned and nearly fell off of the log I was sitting on.

It was Legolas.

CWTCH

This one doesn't directly translate to English
because there's no real correlation.
In Elf, a cwtch (pronounced 'kooch')
is a protective embrace, a very safe
place to be.

Arguments

He wasn't actually Legolas, of course. Legolas is a fictional character, a hunky elf archer and warrior played by an equally hunky actor back on Earth.

This Legolas, the elf boy I'd met soon after my arrival in Kiirajanna, was neither fictional nor probably all that epic in skill as an archer or a warrior. But he was present, at least. He stood uneasily to the side of the circle that had gathered to watch the matriarch and the princess talk. As he shifted his weight from one leg to the other, he chewed on his lower lip. His eyes, though, bored right into mine, bearing a weighty plea that seemed nearly as important as life and death itself.

"Gwyn," the old lady started, reminding me of his actual name. I'd taken to calling him Legolas due to his rangy good looks, long blonde hair, and confident air. He looked, and acted, exactly like the character, so it was an obvious choice for nicknames. But he was a troublemaker, according to my father, and he'd run away from his village soon after we'd met.

And he is white. Pale, anyway, as much as any of the elves I'd come to know, which sets him way off against the blackness of the skin of those in the camp I'd come to visit.

"Teeri, go straighten Gwyn out," Masu ordered, but I stopped him.

"No. Let me at least hear him out. Please, Grandmother?" I used the same title and tone of deference that Legolas had used, hoping it might make a difference. It was an interesting idea. Dad had forbidden me to see Gwyn, true, but that was because he'd gotten in with bad people. Now, of course, I recognized that these were the "bad" people—people I'd come to ask help from—and that probably meant he could use magic. Had he been exiled properly—whatever "properly" meant? Or had he just run away? Either way, it was an interesting proposition.

She made a show of considering my words, and then nodded. Some day, when I became queen, I figured I'd have to consider whether deference to the dark elves was a good idea, but I put that thought away immediately. Now was not that time or day, and we were still in the "if I became queen" phase rather than the "when" one. Regardless, she'd given in, and so as long as I was getting what I wanted, that was okay, right?

I will eat her if you wish, no matter how tendony and ropy her flesh would be.

No, Kluzhka.

The boy is too attractive to you.

Shut up, Kluzhka.

I am just saying.

Gwyn, meanwhile, strode out into the circle of light. He was tall—not as tall as either my father or Keion, but tall enough to match my own height. His long blond hair was pulled back and braided. Bright, pretty blue eyes glistened in the firelight. Muscular arms ground his hands together at his front in what would be a submissive posture if not for the worried rubbing. It made his chest muscles move under a fairly light tunic, though, and that was nice. He was well-built, to be certain, if not nearly as well-built as Prince Charming. Still, angular and sleek weren't things I'd mind looking at over the long run.

You're selecting a guardian, not a companion, Princess.
Shut up, Kluzhka.

"Make your case, boy," the matriarch grumbled.

"Well, as much as I have come to love each and every one of you as a sister—or a grandmother," Gwyn started, smiling toward the old woman, then continued, "I do not share your skin tone. While none of you has ever held this against me, and I do not feel different from any of you around your fires, I have the advantage of physical similarity and can thus meet the godless ones on their own terms." He was speaking to his peers, I knew, and not to me, but the reference to sisters, not brothers, made me curious about the culture, while the godless ones comment got me just a little bit angry.

"That you have the appropriate skin coloration does not make you a good choice for the guardian for the queen," Masu pointed out.

"Correct, but my specialization does."

Gwyn's assertiveness earned him a hoot from Masu, who blurted, "Boy, you have not had time to even have chosen a specialization, much less honed it."

"I am the only true protection mage in the camp," Gwyn objected, a glare forming on his face. His defiance toward the elder was comforting, and a little scary too.

"We do not know that yet," the older lady said, gently.

"I do. You know what I saw on my vision quest. You have seen what I can do around camp already for tracking the trackers, and for reinforcing our hiding spells. You have praised me many times for my knowledge, my quick study, and my power. What more would you ask of one who guards?"

"A few years more of experience, I would say," Masu said.

"A few more years, and the princess could be dead," Gwyn said, holding his ground. It was gruesome, but effective. "It is her choice."

A tense silence followed, finally broken when the elder cleared her throat meaningfully and turned to me. "Gwyn is correct. It is your choice, Princess. Be advised that he is still very much a boy, not even close to his full potential yet. But he is strong, and by all evidence I have seen, he is devoted, and he is also smart and quite cunning with the spells he has learned to cast. He will need to return to us occasionally, and for that I must extract your word that his journeys will remain untracked by your own rangers. Not that I am saying he could not defeat them, but instead I suggest that there would be no true winner in such a battle. It is against my better judgment that I pass the recommend on to you, but such a recommendation is, in fact, up to you to take or to reject."

When I paused, Teeri whispered, "He would certainly be better than nothing. Not by much, mind you, Princess, but by some at any rate."

You're not really going to—

"I accept," I stated loudly, then shot a glare toward Kluzhka, who just looked back, her armored features impassive. I think I imagined seeing her shrug her huge shoulders.

"Not very bright, is she?" I heard Teeri say to a nearby friend. Acting on impulse, I reached out with a tendril of magic and whipped the warrior's feet out from under him, an action that provoked a cacophony of hoots from the watching people.

"Teeri, apologize," the older lady said, and the young man did, sincerely, not even rising from a kneel till he'd finished and I'd accepted.

"So, we should probably be on our way," I said, for lack of anything more queenly to utter. I turned toward Kluzhka, who unfolded her mighty wings with a single flip. I turned back, though, when I sensed Gwyn's hesitation. He was making eye contact with the older lady when I caught him, and then he turned back to me.

"Your wyvern can teleport, can't she?"

"Yes, she can. How did you know, Gwyn?"

He's pretty smart, I tell you. And probably very tasty.

Hush, you.

"My people have a wide variety of wyvern lore available to us. But to avoid your people's trackers finding my people's village, she should teleport out. Then you and I can walk out, safely. I can protect us and cover our trail, but if we were to blast up out of here we'd light up every ranger's view in the area. Plus, I had to work extra hard last time you were here to conceal our presence from those who saw you running."

"Oh. I'm sorry. I didn't realize."

"Nobody expects you to realize such things, Princess." He grinned at the use of the term, a very boyish, very eye-catching, grin. "That is why you now have me as a protector."

I caught the older lady flash Gwyn a proud look in the corner of my eye, and then I relayed the instructions to Kluzhka.

I shall leave you in the hands of your capable—protector.

He is capable, Kluzhka.

And cute, too, I believe you meant to add.

Hush, you.

I'm going to go sleep now. Let me know if there is a true emergency—you know, an apocalypse or anything of that magnitude.

I will. Rest well.

She blasted up, clearing to the tops of the trees before she vanished with a loud pop. Everybody in the camp had stopped to watch her leave, I noticed, and they all breathed a sigh of relief after she was gone. I figured that I'd have to talk to her about her kind's relationship to the dark elves, some day.

"Time to go, Princess."

As we walked away from the camp, I got to watch Gwyn work his magic. His gentle, deft touch was amazing. We broke into a jog that both of us felt comfortable with, and I thrilled in watching tiny blue tendrils flowing from his hands backward to the trail behind, each airy azure blossom working at removing scents and scuffs and every other mark of our passing.

"So what is a protection mage?" I asked once we slowed down. There wasn't much point in hurrying back, after all.

"A magic user who specializes in protection-type magic."

"Well, duh. Why is it such a big deal?"

"In your case, because you happen to need protection."

"Can you give any answers that weren't already obvious?"

"Why, yes, I can."

My glare caught his smirk in the moonlight, but it was difficult to really get irritated at him. It was nice, not being called Princess with every other word and either being talked up to, or down to, by someone.

"A protection mage," he started after a deeply-drawn breath, "is quite rare among the people—my people, I should say, now. Oh, there are plenty of mages who can cover tracks and camouflage campsites, but a protection mage is so much more than that. I have been trained to detect magic weavings, and to weave their counter faster than the other mage can complete them."

"You're trained in all that? That's impressive. It certainly seems useful. And—hard. How much time did it take?"

"I'm—not quite there yet, I must confess. More practice will suit, as Grandmother says."

"Ah. Well, we'll have to get you more practice. What else does Grandmother say?"

"She says it would be better if I were a girl."

I wondered at that—he was pretty handsome as a boy, but part of that was due to his delicate, almost feminine, features. It made him not just handsome, but quite beautiful. Statuesque, even. "Yep, I can see that."

He caught me looking speculatively and shook his head forcefully. "No, not like that. Protectors are supposed to be women. All of the most powerful mages are women. All our leaders are women. I was born with all the powers of a woman, in a man's body."

Oh, great, I thought. The two best-looking guys in the entire world would be right near me, in my daily presence, and one was no longer attracted to me—and vice versa—while the other wanted to be a girl.

"It's not like that, either," he corrected, correctly interpreting my expression in the moonlight. "I'm perfectly happy with my gender. I just would have made a great leader if I had been born female."

"And black."

"That is but a skin tone. A minor happenstance of birth genetics."

"To you, maybe. And to me, I will admit. But they were right that the people of the castle wouldn't consider it so, and I would suggest, based on what I saw in the encounters now, that maybe your friends wouldn't actually consider it so if you delved deeply enough."

"They're my family, not merely my friends."

"Friends, family, whatever. The castle is right up there. We should probably go find Dad right away."

He swallowed a little harder than usual. "Can we wait till tomorrow to bring it to His Majesty's attention? Maybe have him drink a little first? Or maybe we could approach Her Majesty first and seek her—assistance?"

I glanced over; his face was whiter than the moon above. He met my eyes with a terrified stare.

"So what's a proud protection mage got to fear from the honorable and gentle king?"

"Oh, nothing. Pain. Torture. Death, maybe. Not anything significant, really."

"Pain? Torture?" I shook my head; the king he was referring to and the king I knew as Daddy were two very different men.

"He threatened me, Alyssa. Said he would run me through, personally, if I ever laid eyes or hands on you again. He—he didn't tell you, did he? Of course not; what father would? But he knew the rumors of my playing around with magic, and he also knew of your propensity toward it, especially insofar as the prophecy was concerned, and so he pulled me to the side at that party and said I'd better never see you again. Never. If I did, he described in great detail how he'd pull my fingernails out one by one, make me eat them for my last meal, and then slowly run his sword through my bellybutton up into—"

"I got it."

"Okay, well, you could say that it left a lasting impression on me."

"I bet. And you didn't think to tell me all this before we left your new people?"

"I—forgot."

"You *forgot*? How do you forget a threat of torture and running through from your bellybutton up? Especially one coming as it did from the king of all Kiirajanna?"

"I was staring into your eyes, Crown Princess, marveling at your beauty, amazed at the opportunity to serve your need in these crucial times."

"Oh, shut it. Look, I have an idea. We're going to go tell my father *first*. He'll agree, or he won't, but that won't matter."

"It won't matter? How won't it matter?"

"It won't matter much. I'll figure it out. Trust me," I said as I launched confidently onward toward the castle.

"Ohh kayyy," he said, his voice tentative as he leaped to follow me.

"You have *got* to be kidding," Dad said after I'd physically pressed his hand down to keep him from drawing a sword on Gwyn. "Tell me you are just joking, Alyssa."

I was impressed, in a way. We'd pulled him out of bed, and so Gwyn had to stand in the king's antechamber while Dad pulled on a shirt and trousers. His guard had told him it was me, so he'd come out unarmed, but as soon as he saw my new guardian he'd swooped the sword up off of its stand in the corner in a single motion. He still held it in its sheath, but his knuckles tightened around it menacingly.

"I am not joking, Father. Gwyn is particularly well suited to watch over my back, since he's trained and seasoned as a protection mage."

"A protection *what?*" Dad made a point of looking him up and down and scowling over the thinness of his frame. "Forgetting for the moment that you just said 'mage'…no. The boy does not look like he can protect much of anybody."

Gwyn's head dropped a little at that, so I decided to go on the offensive. "Swords can't protect me against what I am to face. You know that, Father. If Aerona couldn't, how could anybody? She was killed by magic, not by might, and that is how I need to be protected from now on."

The king looked Gwyn straight in the eyes. "You ran away from your village, boy. What are the odds you will run away from my daughter, too?"

"There is no chance I will do that, Your Majesty," Gwyn argued, meeting Dad's eye firmly. I was glad to see that he was getting his courage back after the very tall, very angry king had rattled a sword in a sheath in front of him.

"No chance? Even if I try extremely hard?" Dad moved forward to where Gwyn had to crane his neck back to continue meeting the king's gaze. He didn't pull his sword, but by the whiteness of his knuckles as well as the quiet menace in his voice I knew it wouldn't be long.

Gwyn met his gaze solidly, rooted in place. I was impressed at the boy's courage, but enough was enough.

"Dad!" I yelled, punctuating the word with a touch of force from Draignerthol that literally made the pictures on the wall bounce. It caused both men to stop their little posing and look, surprised, at me, which was, I guess, the intent. I plowed ahead. "Now, you just stop that right now! No, I mean it!" I yelled again when he opened his mouth to object, and was rewarded with a deep but silent frown.

"Now, look, Father, I'm just about fed up with this. I need to be a ruler, and everybody else needs to accept your daughter's intelligence and wisdom, and I'll be a fine queen and all, and then when it comes to me making a decision for myself, you, yourself, don't trust me. What sense does that possibly make? Now, you didn't train me to be a fool, and you need to acknowledge that and let me do what I think is right."

"I do not know—"

"Well, I sure as heck do. On this, at least, I know. I know better than anybody, in fact. I've seen the dragon. You haven't. I know what I'm gonna face. You don't. Am I clear?"

My father's shoulders relaxed from the stiffness they'd held, and he nodded, once, just barely. I was relieved to see his hand relax its grip on the sword hilt, and it looked like Gwyn was, too. His face bounced through several expressions before he turned a glum one toward Gwyn.

"If you ever consider having a daughter, take this advice if you will take none other from me. Do not. No daughters. They are entirely, completely, wonderfully impossible. And you, young lady—" he swiveled his head and spoke directly at me with a neutral expression, "I shall most assuredly resume this discussion later on, but I need to get back to sleep now."

"So he can stay?" I asked, trying and failing to remain in charge of the conversation.

"For now. Not that I have much to say about that, it would seem. Only, not—well, oh, never mind. Go to bed, as I will return to mine. Good night."

Dad turned abruptly, waved backward at us, dropped the sword back into its basket with a thud, and returned to his own inner chamber.

I shrugged and led Legolas back to my own room. "Aerona stood..." I started, and then my voice cracked when I realized what I'd been about to say. Suddenly my new guardian was at my side, holding me up as I inexplicably found myself wracked with sobs.

"I can't—I don't—I wasn't—we didn't even know each other," I burbled out finally.

"Yet you did know her. She was a fine warrior. Even the people of the earth knew of her, and spoke highly when they mentioned her name. You must let yourself grieve, Alyssa. You have been holding it in, and you cannot do that."

"Sure, I can," I whimpered, my own voice betraying me.

Finally the uncontrolled torrent let up and I was able to detach from his support enough to fix him with what must have been a very fake-looking smile. "I'm fine."

"Sure, you are. Go change for bed. I will ward your room properly and then—you don't have an antechamber, do you? I will sleep on the floor, then."

"You can't—" I started to object, but he stopped me with a finger on my lips.

"Merely sleeping in this room is scandal enough. I should, honestly, sleep in the hall, but that would be a black eye in His Majesty's face in the morning."

He was right, but I hadn't thought that far. I made a mental note to fix it in the morning.

The crying bout seemed to have sapped all the remaining strength from me, so I wearily ambled to the changing screen in the corner, pointing as I did. "Dad's guard force, before Aerona, was posted in a hidden alcove there. There's probably something more comfortable than the floor."

"It will do nicely," I heard him agree through the divider.

By the time I emerged in a nightgown, the room appeared empty save the blue tendrils of spells that were woven about its walls. I said good night to L.T., and as the little tree somehow radiated happiness, its little branches swishing gently around, I climbed in to bed.

Massacre

I don't know which actually woke me the next morning. As I came to, Kluzhka's keening ricocheted off the insides of my temples and rolled through my inner ears while L.T. loudly thrashed all its little limbs angrily against the wall. It was a terrible din to come awake to, and I stumbled out of bed and only barely caught myself before sprawling across the rug.

I wondered how the whole castle wasn't awake with the noise. Then I realized that half of the noise was in my head.

Oh, it hurt.

QUIET!

I confess, I screamed that a little too loud—maybe—across the mental link. For once, Kluzhka obeyed, coming abruptly silent, which suddenly worried me more than her enraged keening had.

What is going on? I asked, allowing the frustration I felt to come across in my thoughts. It probably sounded nearly as rude in the way I "phrased" it, mentally, as my scream had just prior, but at the moment I didn't care a whole lot. I pulled a curtain aside to peek through the window; it was still the deep dark of night. From where the moon's sliver stood I figured the sun would make its appearance within less than an hour, but we were still in the thickness of pre-dawn. I'd been asleep for only a couple of hours.

Oh. So may I speak now, Princess? The iciness of the response was apparently intended to hurt, but I just shrugged it off.

By all means, go ahead.

High King Xlixi is killing your people as we speak, Your Highness. I thought you might like to know, but if you'd prefer to return to sleep, I—

Wait! What? Xlixi? Where? I froze, my skin prickling at the mere name of the dragon. I'd feared his entry into Kiirajanna ever since my escape, and the fact that it was coming to pass, now, sooner than I'd thought it could, electrified my nerves in terror.

Off to the east. She dropped her icy tone and grew forlorn. *My kind from that region have been forced to join him in attacking, though their reports to me indicate that they are certainly not needed. The elves fight ferociously and die by the score. The one you call Grigor is, I believe, already dead.*

Grigor? You mean Hefin?

Whatever. They are all the same to me. The clan chieftain is dead, according to my sources.

Sources?

They talk, even when controlled by the dragon. But we cannot be certain of their words.

Whatever. There's trouble! You—we—should go! Come to me now!

A silence lingered for just a moment longer than was comfortable, and then she replied in a subdued tone. *No. I will not go, Princess, and neither should you. Xlixi cares naught for these elves. He seeks only to draw you out. You realized that already, I see.*

Yes, I guess I did. I need to go find my father.

Yes. The elf king will know what to do. You might also consider soothing your little tree pet. I can hear its agony through the link.

Oh, right, I...lost track of it.

It is hardly surprising, Princess, but you should learn to keep better track of your surroundings even when we are speaking.

I didn't grace her jibe with an answer.

Instead, I ignored Gwyn's appearance behind me and knelt before a crazily active Little Treebeard. Singing a few notes usually had it—her—him—whatever—reacting almost immediately, calming and relaxing into my song. This time it didn't, so I went farther. Placing a hand on the soil in the pot, I murmured nonsense in a sing-song voice while I started to open myself up to the tree community.

I'm never really prepared for that "community." The first time I'd bumped into it by accident I was amazed at the vastness, the richness. It's like being dropped into a city would feel, I think, if you could read everybody's mind. Only, there's no panhandlers in the tree community. It's a vibrant quilt of voices, some carrying the booming authority of ancient oaks and others the eager youth of the scrub pines and, like my little L.T., elm saplings, a quilt that stretches for as far as the mental eye can see, or imagine.

Today, the whole quilt joined together in one voice:

Panic! The global sense picked me up and slammed me as I entered the mental world. Stately trees of Kiirajanna that had lived together for thousands of years had suffered together through blight, drought, and other hardship, but nothing was as painful as the marauding monster to the east ripping and burning down swaths of brethren.

I sought out and quickly found L.T.'s being among the others. The young elm was shivering, shrieking, terrified for his fellows. Mentally, spiritually, I wrapped myself calmly around the tiny soul, and it calmed.

"All will be okay. I must leave and take action now, but all will be okay," I said in my sing-song. Then I sprang to my feet.

"What is going on, Princess?" Gwyn asked, concern creasing his features. "Is it normal for the tree to—"

"No. No time to explain. Follow me," I ordered and hurried to the door, satisfied as the thrashing of branches calmed and ceased.

My door, being the last in the hall prior to His Majesty's door itself, opened just behind a contingent of excited priests talking rapidly to an equally-excited contingent of black-clad kingsmen, in front of whom my father loomed with wavy bed hair and furious eyes.

"There's been an attack," a priest whispered.

"I know," I said, letting my voice carry. Suddenly the voices in the hall stopped and everyone swiveled their gaze toward me.

"What do you know, my daughter?" The king swept his men as well as the priests out of the way to bring himself to me. His eyes focused a little more, and he started looking less crazy berserker and more king of the realm.

"It's the dragon. The one I told you about. The one they said didn't exist. King Xlixi. He's come, and he's in the east killing members of Hefin's clan, burning trees, and laying waste to the area. We must go, now."

"How do you know this?"

I wanted to scream *what difference does it make? A dragon is eating people! Let's go!* but instead I just took a long, deep, calming breath. "Kluzhka told me first. She has connections to other wyvern in the area, and they are being forced through Xlixi's will to participate in the slaughter. That's why she isn't—can't—go. Then I connected through L.T. to the forest and saw the destruction being wrought for myself."

"You—you connected to the forest?" Sternyface's voice carried through and her face appeared over Dad's shoulder. "You can—

that's—unbelievable." Her eyes unfocused for a brief moment, but then her attention abruptly snapped back to the present. "We must speak on this later, my dear. Cadfael, what your daughter says is accurate according to the reports of the priesthood. We must—"

The High Priestess of Kiirajanna was interrupted rudely as a brown shaggy beast, a waist-high blob of furious death in combat, nearly knocked her over. It stopped at my feet and turned, waiting for the ranger it belonged to to catch up. Seph did quickly, her feet pounding down the hall making enough noise to wake the dead—of whom I feared there would soon be far too many.

"Sorry, High Priestess. Booboo roused me and wouldn't stop clawing at the door till I opened it," my wide-eyed cousin said, quick breaths filling the space between her words. "Then he ran up here, me doing my best to tag along behind. Cousin, what's going on?"

I looked from cousin to king to priestess, each pair of eyes trained on mine and heavy with expectations. I decided to try the simplest answer. "The dragon I escaped from has come to Kiirajanna. He is killing the elves of the east."

Everybody but Dad and Sternyface gasped in horror, and the gasps apparently reminded Dad that the priests and kingsmen were still arrayed in the hall behind him. He rounded on them with a shooing motion. "Off to your duties! We have much to discuss," he added, turning to include us in that statement. "To the throne room, then."

"Dad, we need to go. Not sure about the rest of you, but Kluzhka can have me there in moments."

Gwyn, Dad, Sternyface, and Seph all snorted in unison. Apparently when I have a bad idea, I have a universally bad one. "So that you can do what, Alyssa?" Dad replied gently. "Die? Have your familiar come under mental control like his brethren? Or be forced to swear fealty to a dragon? I am not even fully aware of the entire situation, and yet I can still grasp that is the primary reason for the dragon's appearance. Unless it is just a strange coincidence that a dragon chose now as the first time in thousands of years to visit and challenge us."

"Maybe. Maybe not. But we have to do something."

"Your spirit is noted, and applauded, my daughter, but...." He let his voice trail off as his face embraced sadness. He shook his head. "Sometimes there is nothing to be done. We must move this discussion to the throne room. Someone should awaken Talaith."

"Who can sleep with all this noise?" the queen's voice cut in from the end of the gathered crowd nearest to her own quarters, and then she turned and silently led the way down the two flights of stairs.

"What is the situation?" the queen snapped, all business, once the door was shut, even before her back side made contact with the throne. Dad sat down slower, his own grogginess in stark contrast with the queen's alert and commanding aura. Seph and Naissa stepped in to either side of me, the high priestess standing before the thrones instead of behind for once.

Gwyn, meanwhile, slid along the wall to the side and stood passively. The queen glanced sharply his way, a whole buffet of thoughts—many of them clearly negative—crossing her face in plain view, and then she returned her gaze to me.

Each set of eyes turned toward me with a waiting expression. I wasn't certain where or how to begin, or even how frantically to get the truth out so we could start doing something to aid the eastern clan.

I decided on the most direct path. "The elves of the east are being attacked by the dragon Xlixi, the one that briefly imprisoned me. Kluzhka says that Hefin is already dead and that many other deaths are happening as we speak. Through the link with the forest, I saw acres upon acres of trees consumed in flame."

The last was a little bit of a wild guess; I really didn't have any idea how big an acre was, but I didn't figure it mattered much.

Sternyface nodded her support. "Majesties, the reports from the priesthood confirm what the crown princess has stated. A dragon has entered the realm."

A thought struck me suddenly, and I voiced it even though it didn't have much to do with the dragon. "You priests have a telepathic link, too, don't you?"

The high priestess shrugged. "Of course we do, Alyssa. It is only since your demonstration in the forest that I have begun to consider that it might be accurately called magic. But yes, those of us with the gift do have a limited means of communication with one another. Just as do the rangers, I should add."

It was Seph's turn to shrug. "Well, sure, we do. It's just part of the training."

"Does everybody have a telepathic link I don't know about?" I asked, and then instantly regretted the peevish tone. The queen and Sternyface just snorted, while Dad's face clouded over.

"Look, we're wasting time," I brought it back to topic. "Kluzhka doesn't want to, but she can get me there within seconds."

"We already discussed how bad an idea that is, my daughter. You have told us of the wondrous powers of this dragon king of your nightmares, and I would not have our future Dragon Queen head off to fight a battle by herself that the solid elves of the east cannot win as a group. No, we must first marshal our army, and then we will march that direction. You may come with us, but we will go as a single force."

"Great. Marshall our army. How long does that take? An hour? Two?" I challenged him.

"Quite long if you keep pouting."

"Not funny, Dad."

A gentle, understanding smile covered his face. "The whole of this is not funny, not at all. But it will not take long. We have been preparing for battle for days, though, since the uprising of the bens, so we should be prepared to march well before midday. Hefin's city is a solid five-day march from here, but we can shorten the transit substantially by taking a ley-gate a half-day's ride from the castle."

"It is inadvisable to take the ley-gate, Cadfael," the queen argued. "Alyssa's experience proved that the dragon exerts some degree of control over them. Until we know how much, we should avoid them."

"I agree, Talaith, but my daughter frets for speed for good reason. No matter how badly they and their leader may have behaved when last we met, Hefin is still our subject, and we must come to his aid by the quickest path possible, advisable or no. Perhaps we could ask a couple of your brethren, Naissa, to test the channel ahead of us to avoid a trap of the main force? Do you have anyone so skilled?"

"I do. It is dangerous."

"We do not march to tea, but to war, and that against one of our most fearsome, powerful, and ancient of foes," Dad reminded the room. His groggy shadow had let loose of him, and he was looking like a king again.

"The world would be so much nicer if we all did march to tea," the queen observed drily.

"Perhaps we should petition the dragon such when we finally meet him," Dad shot back, a grim smile taking the sting out of his words.

"If we don't hurry, he may not be there to meet."

I crossed my arms defiantly as everyone turned a glare at my impatience.

"If the legends are accurate, and your experience suggests that they are, the one we hurry to meet is flying death. Hurrying the preparations will do no one any good, my daughter. Not us, and certainly not those we go to defend."

"But they'll die."

"They may. They will," Dad amended as he saw Seph's and Sternyface's shadowed looks. "Their lot is cast, though, and we should take care to not join them in defeat but rather celebrate in victory. Gwyn, a word?"

My young guardian jumped at his name, but regained his composure quickly and then stumbled into place in front of the thrones. "Your Majesty?"

"Will your people join in the attack?"

"My people?" Gwyn's face colored briefly. He and I had talked about how he felt kinship with all the elves, not just the dark skinned ones. Still, he apparently recognized that it wasn't a good time to press the fine points. He shook his head. "No, Your Majesty. They will fight to defend themselves, or to defend me, or, I am fairly certain, to defend your daughter, as they have accepted her into their—our—ranks. But I do not believe, in all honesty, that they will leap in to challenge a mighty wyrm on behalf of those who have scorned them."

Dad let the dig go, nodding. "So. Should she ask in the future, when and if the crown princess needs them, will they fight alongside us?"

"You would fight alongside them?" Gwyn's tone was as shocked as the queen's expression.

"I am a practical man. For my daughter's safety, I would fight alongside anyone."

"I will ensure that the people of the earth know of your sentiments."

"So. We must prepare. Sephaline, call to Master Owain. I would ride with a thousand rangers if I could, but I will be pleased for as many as are available. Naissa, we need your priests in their best battle armor, and while they prepare have your librarian bring a brief for Alyssa, Keion, Padrig, and me on what she knows of dragons. I know, she has discussed the topic before, but there may still be an advantage, no matter how small, that has gone overlooked. Talaith, your own guard needs to take tight control over the castle, for in our force's absence you become a ripe target. Gwyn, find Padrig and have him ready his troops and then report to the throne room. Let us be deliberate yet expeditious, people. We march to war before the sun reaches its peak."

Eastern Elves

"Before the sun reaches its peak" turned out to be accurate. Padrig arrived almost magically, striding up to martially salute and declare his force's readiness to march on command. Keion arrived on Padrig's tail, grumbling about "noisy damn trees" but stepping quickly with a bright warrior radiance in his eyes. Both proclaimed that they were ready to face the dragon in single combat after having heard how the dragon treated me.

Remembering the dragon's sheer might, I just grimaced and nodded, the gravity of what we were marching into settling on my shoulders. I wondered which of these men, my brave father included, I was seeing for the last day ever. It was a dark thought, but I couldn't quite shake it. But looking around at the assembled warriors I saw not a single hint of the same trepidation I felt. It was all battle lust and more battle lust.

Is it a man versus woman thing, I wondered? Or is it a fundamental difference between elves and humans?

I didn't have much time to ponder that, thankfully. The cathedral's head librarian arrived and ran through everything he knew about wyrm lore, which wasn't a whole lot beyond what

I'd already told them. Huge, check. Armored, check. Insane level of arcane prowess, check. Evil as Satan's older brother, check. Oh, and in possession of a long, hot, wet tongue, I added, and I couldn't help grinning when the librarian hadn't heard about that. The grin turned into a shudder as the memory brought the revulsion of the dragon tongue licking sweat droplets off my face.

The fools looked even brighter and more battle-lustful when I explained that last, bless their hearts.

L.T. wasn't happy at all about my departure, but I got a strange sort of acceptance from the little elm once I explained that I was headed off to defend his brethren. That was sort of a new thing, too. I'd communicated with the potted tree before, roughly and sort of stilted in a sing-song way, but this time by planting my palm against the soil in the pot I managed to express a fairly complex idea and receive a surprisingly nuanced response.

Before the sun was halfway up we began putting together our formation for the march. For the trip to the "neutral ground" Dad had only brought a couple hundred of his best men, but now that we were headed to war the black-clad cavalry stretched in ranks eight across and as far back as I could see. Dad told me proudly, quietly, that his column alone numbered more than two thousand elf warriors on horseback. Each sat calmly on a steed's back, black armor shining and cloak billowing. They weren't big on heavy armor, I saw; most of them wore formed leather that I could almost see melting under the dragon's fiery breath. They were the image of discipline, though, with full quivers, strung bows, and sheathed swords.

They were ready to battle.

They were ready to die, but I forced that thought back before it could appear on my face.

The priests of Cysegredig also wore black. There were a hundred or so of those, and what they lacked in warrioresque steadiness they made up for in blue auras of magical ability. They'd each been issued an amulet that mimicked Draignerthol in shape, if not in raw power. It was smaller, and didn't glow nearly as brightly, but I could sense a touch of energy in each. The terror in their eyes made it clear, though, that they had never imagined being in this position. I felt for them.

Padrig's militant force was lined up next to Dad's. What they lacked in discipline and martial blackness they made up for in pure projected power. In the short time they'd had to gather, they'd donned dark war paint and skins, and the two hundred who had initially come with Padrig had swelled to nearly a thousand fierce nordic savages who grumbled and rumbled beside Dad's crack troops, beating primitive but scary weapons against hide and wooden shields.

The treeline shimmered in activity as Seph and Owain's rangers gathered. Before long she and Booboo bounded out of the woods toward me, an excited grin covering her face. "We've got your thousand, plus some, Your Majesty!" she exclaimed. Many of the northern rangers had followed their warrior brethren, she explained, and now all were itching for a fight against their most ancient of enemies.

Booboo growled its assent, bless the foul little killing beast's heart.

A shriek overhead announced Kluzhka's arrival, her winged form shadowing over the forces arrayed in front of the castle. She circled once, and then dropped to a soft but grandiose flapping landing to our front, her sudden presence frightening Awel, my normally-steady mare, nearly to a heart attack.

"Nothing like a grand entrance, right?" Dad hissed once he'd gotten his riders to calm down and put away their bows.

"I don't believe she has any choices for an entrance other than grand," I argued. I reached out as best I could through Draignerthol and connected with Awel, soothing the poor beast and pushing her toward the wyvern. Soon we stood eye to eye, human/elf and wyvern, and we both inclined our heads at the same time.

I have lost connection with reports from the east, she told me. *My kind have gone into hiding.*

That is not surprising. Can you fly ahead and scout for us?

That is—dangerous. Xlixi is far more powerful than you can know, Princess.

So people keep telling me. But riding in blind is even more dangerous, right?

That is the difficult position we are in, indeed. I will fly ahead, but should I stop responding or behave erratically, please quickly search for cover.

Go, then, and…. Well, whatever you are supposed to do. Good luck. Stay safe. Vaya con dios, mi amigo. All the above, bless Xlixi's foul heart.

Your soft sentimentality will kill you some day, Princess, but for now it is—appreciated. With that snipe, Kluzhka spread her wings with a snap and launched her bulk into the air. Her form rose rapidly to the level of the tops of the trees, and then she suddenly disappeared.

I turned to find a sea of eyes appraising me, most of them positively. Dad nodded, so I raised my voice and asked, "So, Your Majesty, the wyvern scouts ahead. Shall we march to save our brethren?"

He nodded again, and I only barely heard him mutter, "Such as can be saved." A single forward gesture from the elf king, and the entire massive army lurched into action fully two hours before midday.

It didn't take us too long to reach the ley-gate, though my worry over the last thing I'd heard my father say made its length seem excruciating. Finally, though, we took a moment to bunch around the little circle of stones, and then two priests strode resolutely into the circle.

Moments passed; I couldn't help my mind treating me to the imagined horror of an angry red dragon leaping into the two unlucky men of the cloth, catching them unaware from above, rending both into tiny pieces of flesh.

Before too long, what could only really have been a couple of minutes, Sternyface turned to Dad. "The way seems clear, Cadfael, if not entirely pleasant."

Two of Dad's black-clad guards were followed immediately by two rangers, and the army crouched in wait again. This time the answer came quicker as one stepped back through and signaled: still clear. A dozen more kingsmen stepped bravely through the portal, and then it was time for the royal party ourselves.

Dad glanced over at me before he and I stepped into the portal together, his expression unreadable. "I love you, my daughter, and am proud of you," he stated as his foot stepped through.

I'm not sure what either of us was expecting. I'd told them all how the weird hinky-jink journey to Pazbojanna, the dragon's world, had felt, and Sternyface's priests said it was evidence of the pathway's corruption by the dragon's power. I'd asked if the dragon could've had any way of knowing it was me in the passage rather than any other elf traveling to hunhymgais, and there'd been no answer to that, so I wouldn't have been too surprised, at that moment, for a rapid jerk to the side or, really, just about anything else.

None of what I feared, happened. Instead, it was the normal lurch of my stomach, the wrenching feeling and then the release.

I glanced over at Dad, who was opening his eyes from the travel. "What was that supposed to mean?"

He raised his eyebrows in surprise. "What—would you think it to mean, if not what I said? Oh, let us move away. Others will come through quickly now."

He was right; the warriors of his own and of Padrig's armies started streaming through the portal, held open by a priest's staff on this end. Keion, Seph, and Gwyn all leaped to my side immediately.

"It was just strange timing," I muttered, trying to keep the whole army from hearing the conversation.

Dad stopped walking and held my eyes in a gaze. "Alyssa, I have been a warrior all my life. A king, some also, but a warrior more of it. If something needs to be said, and the time in which I exist may be the last opportunity for the saying, then I have learned to say it."

"Oh. Well, um, thank you. I love you too, Dad," I stammered. The words were much easier to respond to, I realized, than the sentiment behind them.

Dad raised his voice. "Let us keep moving forward. We have a large perimeter to establish before we move on." He pressed us forward, dozens and then hundreds of yards past the circle of stones.

Soon boys with the king's stag and raven insignia embroidered on their breasts caught up to us, handing us the reins to our horses before fading back toward the circle. Awel seemed terrified, but I got her to relax by humming softly, while the king's war charger was, as always, the king's war charger in attitude as well as name. More horses streamed out to the troops around us, and the entire army's movement seemed to pick up some steam.

I'd been glad to hear we could take our horses. Before, up in the north lands, they'd told me that horses could not pass through the ley-gates. That was why we'd left one of Dad's guards behind, and it was also why we'd been on foot when I'd had to save the party—most of the party, anyway—from death-by-falling.

It turned out, the priests of Cysegredig had told me, you could take horses through a ley-gate. Just—not with a rider. Their mass was already at the upper limits of the magical forces involved in the transport, and adding a rider made it impossible, unless both horse and rider were—well, whatever. It was practically impossible to do both at the same time. So we'd planned on the kids of Dad's junior force, a bunch of feisty ragamuffins who were already looking pretty fierce swinging a sword, to bring the horses through and then retreat until time to return.

It was a big deal, it turned out, to get two thousand war horses through a ley-gate. Men formed ranks and mounted and waited what seemed an interminable time.

"We need to move on toward Tirfllannerch, Majesty," Keion said, barely-restrained impatience in his voice.

"What did your martial studies on Earth teach you about allowing your army to arrive spread out, Prince Keion?" Dad chided, and Keion flushed. It was the harshest I'd seen Dad get onto Keion, but I could tell it was just Dad's worry over what we'd find at the end of the march. "What does your wyvern say of our path, Crown Princess?"

"Destruction. Not much else. Some warm bodies are still alive and stirring, she says, but she's not certain whether it's elves or large deer. She's been keeping a good distance, but she's seen no sign of the dragon."

"Yet there is no guarantee that he has gone."

"If Kluzhka cannot see him—"

"We have discussed this already, Alyssa. How much do you know about the powers of a dragon?"

"Not much," I admitted quietly, surprised by the fierceness he now turned toward me.

"And so how many of my soldiers' lives are you willing to risk on the assumption that your wyvern can be guaranteed to sight an incoming dragon in time?"

"None. Sorry, Dad." It was a little weird seeing him pivot from blustery military man, sure of his own battle prowess, to cautious battle commander, from what appeared to be underestimating the dragon's abilities to overestimating them.

Are you all right? Kluzhka shot, picking up on my distress.

Fine. Just getting a difficult lesson on tactics.

An important topic, I must say.

Yes, yes, it is, bless your heart. So you still don't see any sign of Xlixi?

I see plenty of sign of him and his destructive capacity, enough that you should shield your heart before you arrive. But indication of his immediate presence, none.

And if he were there, you'd see it, right?

He is a wyrm, Princess. I am but a wyrmling. You would do better asking one of those horses what they know of a unicorn's capabilities.

"Speaking with your wyvern again?" Dad asked.

"Yes," I answered glumly, letting the irritation I felt into my voice.

"And what does she say?"

"She says you're right. A wyvern has no idea what a dragon is capable of, and cannot know whether we're in for a surprise. But she also advised me to enter the area around Tirfllannerch with a shield over my heart. Apparently it's pretty bad."

I'd been dreading it even without Kluzhka's warning. Tirfllannerch, which literally means verdant glade in elf, was, by all accounts, a stunningly beautiful town, if you could call it town. It was constructed around and above a massive forest clearing that Hefyn's people used for gatherings, and the towering cedar, pine, and oaks that ringed the clearing doubled as central beams and supports for hundreds of tree houses. I had looked forward to visiting Hefyn after my trip to Padrig, partly to see the soaring levels of Tirfllannerch.

That wasn't going to happen, apparently.

I wrestled the dismay, fear, and dread out of my mind and plunged along. Soon the smell of woodsmoke hung around us, and then the smoke itself made its presence known. Before long we were all breathing through special cloths the rangers provided for both elf and horse and our eyes started to sting.

I repeated Kluzhka's words over and over again inside my head: *Shield your heart. Shield your heart.* It was difficult, but even as the smoke grew denser and the sound of still-crackling brush hinted at the devastation ahead, I did everything I could to brace myself for whatever we might find.

It wasn't enough.

The change from green to blackened timber was abrupt, but the smells were the worst part. Mixed in with the wood smoke was another aroma, one I'd never experienced before. Its source was unmistakable, though—it was the pungent aura of death on a massive scale, the olfactory evidence of thousands of charred, lifeless bodies of the glade's would-be defenders mixed in with those of its once-happy residents. A very few survivors, their own bodies blackened and torn, brown congealed blood mixing with black soot in matting hair and shredded clothing, struggled to collect and organize the corpses in the center of the bare area in front of us. As the king's vanguard entered, a couple of them glanced our way and then returned to their somber duties.

In the distance, blue flashes of magical energy and occasional patters of chanting attested to the surviving eastern rangers' attempts to control the blazes that continued to consume patches of forest around them. Seph and Master Owain both glanced Dad's way at the same time. A nod from the king released them, and both set off at a sprint to lend their assistance, a thousand Cyseg-redig and northern rangers following.

Dad was off his horse and bounding toward the center quickly, and I followed. The sights and smells combined with a ghastly quiet to make the scene mind-numbingly surreal. Following Dad was all my brain could come up with to do.

With a firm, silent gesture, the king ordered his private retinue to join in the efforts of collecting the dead. A few of them looked doubtful, their charges of protecting His Majesty heavy on their shoulders, but they all obeyed crisply.

Their reaction made me curious, so I looked back at the king's army, into their faces and their eyes. I realized they had just passed into the same sort of mental daze I'd entered, a fog that could only be dealt with through direct action. The silence was harshly broken as somebody started barking orders—I recognized the barker as one of Dad's chief commanders—and black-clad soldiers leaped to set up defensive perimeters and lookout stations and all that military stuff.

Dad, meanwhile, crept silently through the rows of bodies in the middle. Soon enough, he found what he'd been looking for—Hefin, the eastern chieftain, now an eviscerated corpse that would have been unrecognizable save its tremendous bulk and flowing mane.

Dad wept.

As I watched my father, one of the strongest men I'd ever known, openly weep, the scene overtook me. The grief clashed raucously with the clanging activity of the king's army surrounding us. The obvious grim determination of the survivors, who worked steadily and yet continued to ignore the reinforcements that rushed in to help, bore into my soul as the putrid smells of seared, dead elves assaulted my senses.

I felt my head spinning, but couldn't do anything to stop it.

Kluzhka's mind snapped me back from the impending crash. *Princess, your grief does you credit, but it does no other good at the moment. Your father and his followers need you.*

What—what do I do? What can I do?

A large winged shape soared across the opening in the canopy, blocking the sun momentarily as its shadow coursed across the field of death. Dad's men jumped in shock, a thousand arrows nocked, a thousand bows trained, only to all relax as they realized what I'd already known. Kluzhka was with us, not even trying to hide her presence, instead filling her own role as guardian from above.

Surprisingly, the survivors of Xlixi's attack didn't even flinch.

Those who survived the attack—join them. Help them, and do so directly, by hand, joining in their efforts. Can you not see their need in their breasts?

I see—something. I don't—know. I don't.

Don't know. Now is not the time to know, Princess. Now is the time to do.

The last sentence echoing in my head, I nodded and wiped my own tears away. She was right. I hadn't lost anything, really. I had no business standing, sobbing. The people needed me.

I picked the smallest one to help. As I closed, she glanced up and I saw a young girl, no more than thirteen or fourteen, probably only just returned from her own quest for adulthood. I saw, in her face, a grim, solidly furious determination that no child that age should ever experience.

I felt it, too.

What had drawn me to her was her struggle with dragging a much larger elf's body toward the center. She didn't seem weak, but the man she was trying to pull by one leg was at least twice her weight. I nodded silently, reached down, and grabbed the other leg. She nodded in return, which I realized suddenly was the first acknowledgment any of the survivors had given our arrival, and we both heaved.

It took us a few minutes, but we managed the task by pulling together. Finally the corpse was lined up with all the others, and the little girl tenderly arranged his mangled arms across his chest and closed the one eyelid that remained. She took just a moment, and then stood, wiped what might have been either sweat or tears from her face, and nodded to me again.

"My pa," she said simply. I looked carefully over her young features, trying to read her emotional state, but there was too much there: grief, resignation, rage, shock...a potent cocktail of emotions held back only by there being something important to be done.

"I'm sorry," was all I could say.

She turned without a response. "More," she said, and walked stiffly back toward the edge of the clearing.

We all worked till the sun dropped from the sky, building the field of corpses into a series of long lines. In the woods to the west the supply wagons caught up, set up, and made a dinner that we all ate silently, morbidly. The rangers joined us, having successfully extinguished all the remaining flames, and then after eating they filtered out into the woods once again.

Dad brooded, the darkness of the moonless night matched by the expression on his face. The gloom spilled across the king's assembly, setting Gwyn, Seph, Keion, Padrig, Owain, and even Sternyface each into our own private pools of despair.

"At first light we must return to Cysegredig," the king finally growled. "No telling where the danger will be next, and we must be ready to fight wherever we are needed."

"Some of my followers will remain and assist any survivors," the high priestess offered.

Nobody said anything else. I glanced around and, in the faces that weren't closely shielded, saw the same emotions I was feeling, the same thoughts I was thinking. Even if the king's men all gathered in force at Cysegredig, a dragon that could wreak this much destruction would be unmatchable. Oh, we could fight. We *would* fight, but there just wasn't any way we could win.

Finally we all turned in, cots creaking under our weight. Tomorrow would be a busy day, another long march, and this one with a heavy burden on our minds as well as our souls.

Suddenly I realized I hadn't even asked the little girl's name, or that of her late father. Sleep evaded me as I turned that fact over and over, examining it ruthlessly for what it meant about me, about us, and about the future ahead.

It only made it worse that I could tell from my own father's rapid breathing in the cot next to mine that he was having the same problem.

TRISTWCH

Doesn't even come close to what I was
feeling after this episode.
Sadness, sorrow.
But sometimes a keening wail,
such as from a wyvern,
is the most fitting song

Aftermath

"The good news, I suppose, is that Your Majesty will now have the full allegiance of the clans." Grigor's voice broke into the somber gloom, adding to the steady plodding sound of horses' hooves.

"What?" Dad asked, obviously startled. He'd been brooding for the whole ride, which he'd insisted on starting well before sunup, surprising even his own cooks as they had rushed to feed the army that was on the move again.

The weight he carried on his royal shoulders was visible in his posture.

"The clans to the south and west have no choice now but to join forces to fight the now-all-too-real threat of the living dragon," Grigor pointed out, his reedy voice sounding as dry as the branches on the ground.

"That allegiance comes at a terrible price," Padrig's voice rumbled. The massive bennaeth of the northern tribes rode just ahead of his liege lord, his own shoulders hunched in misery at what we'd seen.

"And yet, that price has been paid," Grigor argued, but was silenced by the king's hand rising sharply, a gesture visible even in the dark shadows of pre-dawn light.

"We have left over ten thousand bodies, bodies that were once our brothers and sisters, our friends and, even in spite of the current political challenges, our allies, lying in the fields to be disposed of," he observed. It was true; by the time we'd gathered what we could the rows had extended to close to fourteen thousand men, women, and children massacred by the powerful wyrm, according to the estimates of the priest who'd been given the grisly mission of counting. Now, the few that were left of the eastern clan would spend several long, arduous days burning the bodies, spreading the ashes about in the hopes of fertilizing a new glade, and only then could they get to the actual emotional grief part.

And I still didn't know the little girl's name. It had haunted me all night, but there hadn't been any time that morning as we broke our fast in our saddles.

"Let us not speak of prices or of allegiance today," Dad continued. "It is well, instead, that we let our hearts remember our fallen brethren. There will be plenty of time for political and war counsels after—just, after. Today, though, shall be a day of mourning."

It was. We arrived back at Cysegredig at around noon, unhurried as we were in spite of the invisible danger that loomed just over the horizon. Dad had prodded us up in the name of getting back quickly to assume a protective front, but once we were marching nobody had displayed the gumption to push us faster than a slow, miserable, defeated lumber.

The queen met us on the entry steps to the grand palace, her ashen face making it clear she already knew what we had run into. Her daughters flanked her, their own faces purged of all their normal haughtiness.

The elves had surprised me when I first arrived with their ability to smile with their entire face, lighting up whole rooms. It wasn't surprising, then, that they could also mourn with their complete beings. The silence itself was solid, a mournful force that was present everywhere. Servants and slaves—I still was having a hard time coming to grips with that last aspect of life on Kiirajanna, but I had to acknowledge it first—yes, even slaves met us with a drooping face and bowed shoulders.

News travels fast, apparently. I'd known that, of course, but I had no idea how fast. Everybody in the castle seemed to be on the verge of breaking down, in spite of there having been nothing in the way of an announcement. Neither Dad nor anyone else said anything. He retired directly to his room, as did Keion. Padrig and a darkly quiet Grigor and the rest of the northern clans retired to their camp near the castle. Everybody else just—dispersed.

Gwyn and Seph joined me in my room. I would add "to talk" but if that had been our goal, we failed miserably. We sat on my bed, with Seph at the foot and me at the head and my protection mage over to the side. Nobody even tried. L.T., who at least was usually good for comic relief, could have been just any old potted plant for all the positivity that flowed from that corner of the room. Booboo curled up at Seph's one foot still on the floor, covered its face glumly, and watched us not talk.

After what seemed like hours of awkward, tortured silence, Seph cleared her throat. She shot me an apologetic look and then left wordlessly. Gwyn watched her go, shrugged, and just as silently stepped through the hidden door into his own chamber, leaving me alone inside my own head.

If it'd been up to me, I would have stayed in my room all day, and probably even longer. I'd known, in my head, what Xlixi could be—would be—must be capable of. But knowing it and seeing, smelling, feeling it are very different things. Part of me, the part still right up inside my head, wanted to consider how the other clans would try to blame the attack on me, how the aftermath might shape itself. That part wondered what we, the "we" being those of us ensconced happily in a mighty stone castle, might do to fortify our positions, not just against the dragon but even against our own kind.

The part of me in my breast, the manifestation of the living, breathing heartbeat I knew was in there somewhere, felt differently. Who cares what the aftermath is, when I'd just seen thousands of my own kind slaughtered? That evil still lurked out there, and it terrified me, but the sense of sorrow, shock, and horror at the carnage I'd just seen overwhelmed any fear I might have felt.

I wondered how real leaders from back in Earth's history deal with all that. History classes had taught us all about the horrors of Pearl Harbor and most of the rest of the second world war. I vividly recalled some of the lectures, in fact, since Miss Taylor's lectures were known throughout the school to be epic. She'd taught us all about the war, and about the human toll.... Still, somehow in all the numbers and dates and places the books had left out how the leaders had felt, how they'd dealt with the knowledge of the massive toll in human lives on their watch.

Turns out history class wasn't much help, I supposed.

All that dark musing was interrupted by a surprisingly timid knock on the door. I managed a somber "Come," and the servant opened the door, informed me of the mourning that evening, and vanished before I was done acknowledging him.

"Oh, great. Group mourning. I'm sure that'll help me feel better," I muttered to the now-closed door.

"Princess?" Gwyn's voice came from the guardian cove.

"Nothing. Just...me, being me. Oh, and we're invited to a group mourning ceremony tonight. Right after dinner, rain or shine!"

"Yes, that is...thank you for the notice, Princess," he said, clearly starting something and then switching tunes mid-sentence. I let it slide as he asked, "But why do you point out that it is rain or hot?"

I shrugged. The elf language had no word that I knew for lack of rain, so I'd had a hard time putting that idiom together in the first place, but it was beside the point anyway.

"No particular reason. I don't see any point in getting together to express a huge boatload of sadness, is all."

"It is what we do."

"So is kicking people out of society when they want to use magic."

The silence dragged on from my comment. I could feel the wound I'd dug into even if no words were expressing it.

"Gwyn, I'm sorry. That was low."

He emerged from the guardroom cubbyhole, his face somber. "No need for apology. It took a moment for me to process, but you are right. Our traditions—we are nothing without them, but I wonder whether they serve us as well as we believe. I am certainly not one to ask," he added with a self-conscious little bark of a laugh as punctuation. "But this is not a tradition you should buck, Crown Princess. Formal attire, be there, show sadness along with all of your current and future subjects."

"Sounds like a blast," I said, my sarcasm ringing through the room. "You'll be there, though, right? To guard me, I mean."

He shook his head. "You'll have plenty of guards in the room, and I will most certainly not be welcome there. Your father—is a wonderful ruler, and that is all I should say."

I decided against pushing him out of his moment of being politically correct. My room in the castle, to be honest, wasn't a good place to be talking about anybody, and with everything else swirling around my head I had to admit I wasn't ready to hear negative comments about Dad.

I shrugged it away. "I suppose I should get dressed."

"You might consider getting some rest first. It's still a few hours away, and...it has been a long day, has it not?"

That evening we, the ruling nobility of the elves—though I briefly allowed myself a cynical reminder that I wasn't truly one of them yet—gathered in the castle's cavernous ballroom. Instead of the gaily-colored tunics of the celebrations before, everyone wore dark, earthy colors, and their faces were gloomy enough to match. They got down to the actual mourning part quickly, the orchestra launching into a slow, painful dirge that only got more depressing as it went. Solemn voices joined in, keening in an ancient elf tongue that many had actually spent most of the afternoon re-learning. The need for a full day of mourning, the librarian had quietly explained, hadn't presented itself for hundreds of years, after all.

I couldn't take it for long, so I slipped out and found my old favorite spot in the dark corner of the front entryway of the castle. It was a weird spot made weirder by the wails that carried through the walls and windows and blanketed me in sorrow with the power of their sound. I sat, alone, on the cold stone and thought of all the things I'd read about, all the horrors that filled the typical history book. None of those had made much sense or even prepared me even slightly for facing the scene we'd entered the day before.

"Hiya, Princess," Gwyn's voice shot out of the gloom to the side, startling me.

I turned toward him, internally chastising myself for not sensing his approach. Those spidey-senses I bragged about were terrific when they worked, but they only seemed to work when I didn't need them.

"Hiya."

He bent down and reached out a hand and gently wiped away a tear that I hadn't even realized was perched on my cheek. Then he sat quietly beside me, taking my hand in his in a comforting gesture.

"Rough day," he said, his gaze traveling out to the dark depths of the night beyond.

"Rough day," I echoed.

"How're you doing?" he asked, his voice obviously forced into a pleasant tone.

"Oh, you know, hanging in there," I said, forcing the same into my own voice. Then I caught his weird sideways glance and thought about what I'd just said. Hanging in there wasn't an idiom in the elf language, and unlike nearly everybody else in my company Gwyn had never been taught to speak English. I quickly explained.

"Ah. So no actual hanging. So you know, there's nothing you could have done to prevent—what happened," he said, easily swiping the conversation back to the monster in front of us.

"Of course I know that. I just don't—know that," I admitted, coming to grips with the battle between my brain and my heart. "Sometimes I wonder, if I'd only found some way to make Hefin see—"

"See what? A dragon? Alyssa, if you'd accomplished the impossible and gotten all three to agree to join your father's forces immediately, the dragon would still have been able to ravage the eastern elves. There's no way they, alone, could have done anything about it, no matter whose side they were on. Or was what you have told us of the power you saw in Xlixi not the truth?"

"No, it was true, every bit. And you're right. It's just that—I never even asked her name," I said, coming around to what still hung over my own head, my own shame in the affair.

"You helped her do what was most needed at the time," he reasoned, surprising me at how quickly he understood what I meant. "That is more important than asking someone their—their label."

I sighed, looking out into the distance, myself, as I weighed his words. Finally I shook my head. "No, Gwyn, it's more than just a label. Our name is part of who we are, and I didn't ask."

"Well, beat yourself up for that one all you wish, Princess. Your choice, and all. I hear a dark corner upstairs calling out to be guarded. I'm going back inside now." With that, my new protector rose and slid back through the castle's main doors.

I followed soon, first nodding to where my now-active spidey-senses guided my eyes to Seph among the trees watching me. She smiled, ruefully, and then she nodded silently.

I arrived back at the mourning just as the queen and her kids made to depart. She stopped in front of me, drawing me up to my full height with the strength of her gaze and then seeming to measure me. Finally she nodded, apparently at least a little bit pleased with what she saw. I had no idea what it was, but I made a mental note to some day be able to do that, myself.

"First light tomorrow, Crown Princess Alyssa, I believe the time has come for another lesson."

I nodded and bowed my respect. "I will be there, Your Majesty."

She glided through the doors, her daughters following, the pair surprising me with a complete lack of daggers in their matching expressions as they paraded past their mother's future replacement.

Second Lesson

"Good morning, Your Majesty," I said, offering a polite curtsy to the queen as I entered her apartment.

She returned the gesture with a gentle smile, and then said, "I see that your new guardian is not with you. Gwyn, his name is, yes? Why do you walk so far from your guard given—recent events?"

I fought to maintain my smile. She had to be testing me. She wouldn't waste her own time without a test, even if I couldn't figure out what it was.

I responded as casually as I could manage, "I trust the security of your room."

She nodded. "My chambers are quite secure, indeed. That said, I would suggest that you should not trust the security of any place, here in the castle or otherwise. It has been an alarming series of days, and you should take care with your precautions at all times."

"Should I go and get him?"

"No, you are here now, and I do not believe that there is a need for concern. On another topic, I take it from your response style that we are to continue speaking as equals?"

"I would prefer it if it does not discomfort you." I had to hold myself off from finishing the line with "Your Majesty," but I did want to make a point. "As a recent—discussion—with my father showed, I need to start acting and thinking more like you if I am to ever have a chance of succeeding in the shoes I inherit from you. Do you agree?"

Her face remained neutral as she slowly considered the matter, and then she asked, "So why did you approach with some formality at first?"

I'd prepared myself for that question. "Respect. Even if I already held the crown upon my head, and you and I were formally equals in everyone's eyes, I would still owe you a deep and abiding respect for your leadership of the people through the years. As I have thought about the interactions between elves at the different levels of our society, I've realized that some of the gestures of salutation are intended as simply that—something the people do upon meeting someone above them in rank in order to—well, not get into trouble. I confess, I was in that particular mode in the beginning, having never been around true royalty before. But a second, more fundamental, reason for those gestures is a matter of expressing honest respect, as I have watched my father receive when we visited villages. The people there obviously genuinely like him personally and appreciate his leadership, and so their gestures are a little bit different."

"Ah. A wise perception. Which is better?"

"Which is better what?"

Her Majesty smiled gently over my sudden discomfort and explained, "Which gesture is better, that of social requirement or that of honest respect and appreciation?"

I sensed a trap in how she asked the question, and saw it in the subtle narrowing of her eyes, so I thought about my response, sorting it around before taking in a deep breath to give it. "I—would have to say neither. I don't believe either is better, really."

"Explain."

Well, darn, I thought, I sure could use a few more minutes, or maybe weeks, to make a sense out of the jumbled thoughts.

Her expression told me I didn't have a few more minutes, much less weeks. I blurted, "Both have their place. I mean, the sincere appreciation and honest respect are important to a ruler, because the people will follow someone they appreciate and respect. Most of the time, anyway," I added, remembering the near-riot Kluzhka's horde had gotten us out of. "But I was taught the importance of the symbolic gesture when I was taught the gestures themselves, and they are what regulate society. I—would think that even when a person does not respect the ruler, nor doesn't even like him or her, the symbolism of the gesture is what keeps our society moving forward."

"Good," she said, nodding decisively, and then added a little pleasantly, "Good. I see you are still struggling a little with these concepts, and that is to be expected with one so new to the concept of one's own seat upon a throne. You are traveling down the correct path, however. Meredydd, would you please fetch us some tea?"

The lady, who'd been standing quietly behind and only barely registered as a blip on my spidey-senses, departed instantly. The queen asked as soon as the door shut, "Do you believe that the Lady of the Bedchamber has always liked and appreciated me?"

The question, casually tossed out as it had been, still struck me as another one that needed a careful approach. "Well, no. I mean, I can't imagine you would have ever done anything to make her dislike you, but—well, forgive me. You're asking the question that way for a reason. I am just not certain what that reason is."

Talaith chortled and shook her head. "Please, let us just be open and communicative, in as direct a manner as is possible. Gaming my questions will only lead you into confusion, my dear Alyssa. You are correct this time, I should add. While I have not ever gone out of my way to cause disagreement, we have had some. It would be impossible for that not to be the case, in fact. As—as you will no doubt learn for yourself some day. She is quite wise in many ways, knowledgeable of nearly everything and everywhere, and very, very strong in her opinions. Yet she, at the same time, respects me more for the fact that I have my own strongly-held opinions as well. I doubt, though the topic has never come up, that she would hold any respect for me if I did not. I am certain that you can guess what the result of those two strongly opinionated people in the same room for so much of our time must be."

"Arguments."

"Indeed. Wild ones, in fact, especially when I was younger. They have always been private, of course. The arguments you have with your Lady must remain so as well, for a united front is vital. But she and I have had some good ones over the years, both of us quite passionate about what needed to be done for the good of the people. Each time, once we walk into public, she has shown me proper respect in word and gesture. Because, as you said, that is vital to the structure and continuance of society."

The Lady of the Bedchamber entered the room carrying a tray. On it was an unadorned white porcelain teapot, two similarly plain tea cups, and a tray of pastries.

The queen gestured in a completely unregal way toward her lady and said, "Get yourself a cup, dear. This is morning tea, and there's no point in formality with Alyssa here."

While Meredydd busied herself as the queen requested, I asked, "Why such a plain tea set? It seems like the queen of Kiirajanna should be sipping out of something grand."

Talaith smiled while the Lady returned with another cup and gently filled all three with the steaming beverage. She gently added sugar and creamer and stirred silently for several long moments, staring into the mixture as it changed from three separate ingredients into a single composite, and then she continued smiling quietly while we did the same. Finally, once she'd enjoyed the first sip, she spoke again.

"You do not like my tea set?" The smile, half-concealed behind the tea cup itself, softened the question.

"I do like it. It's very nice quality porcelain." I responded quickly, too quickly. I should have added "I think." I couldn't tell quality porcelain from white glass, to be honest, but I was trying to backpedal and it seemed like a safe assumption to make. "It's just that the other tea sets I have enjoyed with you have been covered in flowers. This one is simpler, plainer, and I marvel at the difference."

"Ah. Yes. So you have made a study of fine porcelain?"

I hid my grimace; had she been in my head? That wasn't possible, I knew, but she'd found the soft spot precisely.

Honesty seemed the best answer. "No, not at all. I just figured this had to be fine quality. It feels smooth and light. Is it? Fine quality, that is?"

She nodded, apparently pleased at my honesty. "It is not, particularly. Breakfast tea is different from afternoon tea, though. Breakfast tea is—well, breakfast, while afternoon tea is much more of an affair. I generally use simpler implements for breakfast—of course, right? But in this case, well—this was my great-grandmother's first tea set, back before my family had anywhere near the wealth they have accumulated today. I was given this when I crossed over to Kiirajanna in much the same way you were given Draignerthol, from what I understand, and for much the same reason."

"Well, given its history, it is beautiful," I finished.

"Beautiful in its simplicity," the queen stated with a nod, ending the thread.

We sipped our tea for another moment, then she asked, "What do you know of duty, Alyssa?"

"Duty is—the need to do what needs to be done," I said, shrugging over the simplicity of my answer. "I guess I hadn't thought much of it."

"It is seldom a lesson we teach to our children, so that does not surprise me."

"Gee, thanks."

"I—do not understand your comment."

"Sorry, I was being sarcastic at your calling me a child. I should hold my sarcasm in better."

The queen's eyebrows shot up and the perceived temperature of the room dove. It was obvious that I'd said something wrong. She looked over at her Lady, who whispered, "Talaith was not calling you a child, Alyssa. She was only pointing out the truth, that you were a child until only very recently."

"Oh." My folly brought red spots of embarrassment to my vision, and I was certain my face was the same color. "I am sorry," I said, stifling the "Your Majesty" that wanted to come after. "I should not have assumed incorrectly."

"Nor should you use sarcasm as a single tool for all situations," the Lady continued to chide me. I shot her a glare, but she replied with a disarmingly caring smile and, "I seek only to make your eventual reign more effective and enjoyable, my dear. A good queen, as you can tell from the histories you have undoubtedly read, has any number of conversational tools she can use to make her point known. Wit and sarcasm are the sharp daggers of the tool set, useful only when sharp daggers are called for."

"I—have to confess, I haven't read all that many histories that apply to this ascension." As bad as that might be to confess, it was relieving to shift the topic away from my own faux pas.

"I shall see to it that the cathedral's librarian has some suitable material brought to your room."

"Thanks."

"Sarcasm again?" The Lady shot me a questioning look.

"No, I really meant thanks. I appreciate the offer, and look forward to reading them."

"So, duty," Talaith interjected. She'd watched the interchange between her Lady and me quietly, eyes flicking from one to the other. Her expression suggested that she was tired of listening to it. "Alyssa, I am glad you can define the word duty reasonably well, but I am curious what you know of the concept, not the definition."

"Well, duty," I said, thinking quickly. I'd rather talk about books or history, honestly. I had no idea, never having pondered the concept, but I didn't need to be that honest. "It's—important. To do your duty. A ruler—a queen should always do her duty."

Meredydd snorted softly, while the queen was obviously trying hard to hide the smirk that formed on her lips by slowly sipping another cup of tea. My face colored again with embarrassment, and the queen quickly jumped in to reassure me. "No, my dear, please relax. As I said, it is to be expected that you would not have given much thought to the concept before today. You could—perhaps—have done better than 'a queen should always do her duty,' but, well, let us just call this an advanced topic. That is why I have chosen to discuss it with you today. It is, in my opinion, one of the most important concepts for you to understand."

She let her words sink in for a moment, and then continued, "So, why is it important to do your duty as a ruler?"

I shrugged, unwilling to open myself up to being chortled at again. "I—I don't know. Besides the obvious answer, of course. But 'you should always do your duty because it is the right thing to do' seems too shallow for what you want—or for who you are."

"Correct. Continue."

"I said I don't know."

She nodded, smiling, put her tea cup down, and spread her hands. "Of course you do not know. It is, as I said, an advanced topic. Try anyway. You must, Alyssa. Duty is not a topic you can come to grips with by listening to me lecture."

"Okay," I said after another sip of my own now-tepid tea. It wasn't the taste, but the delay. I needed time to think, and I got some, but it didn't help much.

"The people need to be able to trust the queen to do her duty," I finally blurted out, relieved to be able to say something.

She shook her head. "How do the people know what the queen's duty is?"

"Well, it's the right thing to do," my mouth continued blurting. My mind realized the error, but I had to leave the words out there anyway.

"Do the people always know the right thing to do?" Her eyes glinted; she knew she had me.

"No, they clearly do not, as they proved by drawing on my father."

"Correct. So how do the people figure in a queen's observance of her duty?"

"Well, I—I think—I think there will always be some people who know the right thing to do, and it is those people who need to know the queen will do it."

"Okay. Let us shift a little. Allow me to modify my previous question somewhat. Does the queen herself always know the right thing to do?"

"I've been hoping you do."

My comment drew open, much-too-loud laughter from both of the other women.

"I would apologize, Alyssa, but surely you recognize the humor in your response. And if you do not, sometime when we are casually sitting around an alcoholic beverage or two I shall—well, I shall tell you some stories. But this is about you. Your new guardian, for example. Was that the right thing to do?"

"I think so."

Her eyebrow raised and she pointed a finger at me. "Of course you do. You did it. But is duty the requirement to always do what the queen thinks is the right thing to do, or to do what the truly right thing to do is, regardless of whether the queen recognizes it as such?"

I had to think through her roundabout phrasing for a moment, but eventually I got it. "No," I said, shaking my head decisively. "I think the queen's duty is to do what is right. But wouldn't that also equate to what the queen thinks is the right thing to do?"

"So as the queen, you will never be wrong?"

"Of course I'll be wrong. But is it my duty to assume I'm wrong on some things and to do what I don't think is the right thing to do?"

"This is me teaching you, Alyssa. I ask the questions, not you."

"I am sorry." I nodded, trying to look meek in spite of my sudden desire to whip out my sarcasm blade. "Please, go ahead."

Once again I could tell from the expression she passed to her Lady that I'd messed up. It was a challenging game I was playing. But this time she continued without passing it over to her chief reprimander.

"Thank you for permission, Alyssa."

"I, um, didn't mean it like that." I did, however, recognize her own display of sarcasm as a tool, and was impressed.

"I am certain that you did not. Still, you need to be advised when it comes out as it did so that you will learn. Yes? So, here is a question whose answer may clear the matter up a little for you. Where does duty come from?"

"Where does duty come from?"

"That is an accurate repetition of the question, yes, Alyssa."

"I—I don't understand the question. Duty doesn't come from anywhere; it just—is."

She shook her head slowly, her eyes twinkling. She really was baiting me for something. I only wished I could tell what it was. "That is incorrect, Alyssa. Duty does, in fact, come from somewhere. Think about its nature and try again."

I sat and thought while the two most powerful women in the realm watched me do it. It was painful; what I really wanted to do was to throw my hands in the air and walk out—but I knew that wouldn't be the right thing to do. So I worked it through in my head. If duty had to come from somewhere, where were the possible places it could be? It wasn't either the queen's opinion or the people's; we'd already established that. It couldn't be the law, either, since the elf society was really weird in its lack of laws. Tradition seemed too obvious of an answer, and as I thought about it I realized why. I'd been bucking tradition for my entire time here, in one way or another, and frankly, it felt to me like my duty to do so. The prophecy said I would, for one thing, but the real, simple truth was that tradition was just plain stupid sometimes, and I knew from some earlier comments that the queen actually agreed with me on that. The only other external source I could think of was an agency, like the priesthood, or something physical, like a plaque on the wall, but I'd seen no evidence of either.

All that meant that there wasn't anyplace external that duty might come from, so I turned to looking at internal sources. Logic didn't seem right; it was too—cold. And it was related closely to the knowledge of right and wrong, and that wasn't quite right either. Both were important, but neither really spoke to a reason for why duty might exist. I thought of the most dutiful people I knew—my father, and the queen, and also my mother, who had always set to doing her duty no matter what, and while they were all plenty logical, what Momma had done in the name of duty had at times completely defied logic. It also, from what I'd seen, was almost never selfish. It had to be an emotion, and it had to be strong, and suddenly I hit on what I knew was the right answer.

"Love. The source of duty is love."

A wide smile spread across the queen's face. "Love of what?"

"Love of—people. Your fellows. Whoever you owe the duty to. You do your duty to serve the elves of Kiirajanna not because you agree with them, or because they agree with you, but because you love them. My father does the same."

"Yes," she said, giving me her broadest smile. "You are quick, Alyssa. It took me several lessons to come to that answer. Can you tell me why, then, the elf queen must come from Earth rather than one of the four clans of tribes?"

That answer was easy compared to what I'd already come up with. "Yes. If she were to come from one of the clans, her love would primarily be from, or for, that clan. She could still come to love the others, but not in the same depth as she loves those from her homeland. That would alter her perception of duty at times."

"It might, yes."

"But…and so why does the elf king come from Kiirajanna rather than Earth?"

"My questions, remember?" she chided me without losing any of the warmth of her smile. I nodded, and she said, "So, Alyssa, why does the elf king come from Kiirajanna rather than Earth, as the elf queen does?"

I sighed. No point getting irritated, though; she was obviously trying to teach me something. "That's a very good question, Talaith. Let me think on it for a moment." I did, just for a moment, and then plunged forward with what I assumed the answer was. "It's the nature of the role of queen versus the role of king. I've watched you and my father handing down decisions, and you are always the one who approaches the question with feeling—with love—gently, while Dad approaches the topic from the standpoint of reason and logic." She nodded slightly, so I continued, "I thought initially that it was just a matter of your personalities, but now, knowing both of you better than I did back then, I believe that it must be a chosen persona—roles you are playing."

I suddenly realized that I was figuring something out that I hadn't understood my whole time, so I kept going, more excitedly. "The king's job is to be logical, traditional, strict, in a way, and so having a childhood and young adulthood grounded in elf custom and tradition helps him approach questions that way—no, no, not just helps. It actually gives him strong credibility with that approach, doesn't it? I've seen him mention his early adulthood in discussions, noticed the subtle reminder that he had always been one of them, and sometimes even wondered why it was needed. And you—you always connect with the supplicants, without bringing up your own early years, because it is your role to approach from the heart. Would a king and queen always need to take on those two roles, though? No, I know, that's my question to answer. It might or might not be the standard roles on Earth—I need to read more on that topic—but it is the distribution of responsibility that much of the entire tradition of Kiirajanna is built upon, so it must be."

"It took me a few months to come to that conclusion, myself," Talaith whispered.

"A fruitful series of lessons for today, then," the Lady said, moving to start collecting the tea hardware.

"No. There is something further I wish to delve into," Talaith stopped her. "So, Alyssa, how do you know what your duty is to be?"

That was easy. "Hopefully I will just know it. That is why I will surround myself with good people, though—Lady Meredydd, High Priestess Naissa, and so forth. But if I lead with my heart, I will do okay, yes?"

She shook her head. "Now you are giving in to the easy platitudes, dear. And, if prophecy is to be believed, you of all queens will not be able to get away with doing so. You must be a strong queen, set in your knowledge of duty."

"Okay," I said, letting the acknowledgment linger. I wasn't sure how I was going to be set in my knowledge of duty, honestly.

"Let me take one key example. In the throne room, when everyone stood around you questioning your legitimacy to ascend to the throne, and before you proposed the hunhymgais, you were ready to just acquiesce and leave, weren't you?"

"I was." I hadn't said it, at least not that I could recall, but somehow she had picked up on my overwhelming feeling of everyone else being right and me not being fit for the job ahead of me. It seemed silly, in hindsight, but then again, it wasn't all that silly. I still wasn't certain I was up for the queen job.

"If circumstances had allowed you to act upon your desire to leave at that moment, would that have been doing your duty?"

"To some of the people, it would certainly seem so."

"Are we back to assuming that other people define your duty for you?"

"No." I'd meant it as a joke, but it wasn't even funny to me when I said it, and I wasn't about to admit that to the queen. "It just seemed like it to me at that moment."

"Based on what?"

"Based on—nobody seemed to want me there. Except you and Dad and the high priestess, of course. At a certain point I was wondering whether I'd make a decent queen after all."

Talaith snorted with enough force that it surprised me. "Honestly, Alyssa, if fear that you aren't good enough is going to define you, make you want to run away from your duty—yes, your duty, when defined as it must be by your love of the people—then you might as well abdicate now."

"But—"

"You believe you're the first to realize it's a hard job?"

"No, but—"

"You believe that your father and I are lying to you when we say you can do it?"

"No, but—"

"Is your love for the people where it needs to be, or is it more of a love for yourself?"

"I don't know!" I answered with far too much heat in my voice for the company. I wiped the tears that were streaming down my face at being grilled, noticed that nobody was complaining about the outburst, and kept going. "I do love the people. Really, I do. And I've come to grips with the fact that my desire to just leave was wrong, for more than one reason. I—I get the idea of duty. And I'm sorry I failed. I won't fail again."

The Lady calmly handed me a tissue while the queen said, simply, "I believe that you will not." Then she rose and entered her inner chamber, her attendant behind, leaving me alone with my tears, wondering why it bothered me so much.

War Council

"This is—unprecedented," Grigor said as I entered the throne room, closing the door tightly behind me. I looked around at the faces I was coming to know all too well: Dad; the queen; Sterny-face; Keion; ancient Ranger Owain; my cousin, looking as out of place as ever; and Grigor, sitting in for Padrig. All wore deepening scowls.

"Looks like I missed something terrible," I observed, slipping into the spot left open for me between Keion and Grigor in the circle. Dad and the queen were the only ones seated, on their thrones as usual, but instead of the proud, board-backed posture the king and queen usually showed, both were slumped into their seats.

"I came as quickly as I received word," I noted, wondering as I did how the queen had made it down before me. A servant stopped me on the way back to my room, and I came immediately. There had to be a secret path from her chambers to the throne room. Meanwhile, everyone else must have received summons be-fore my training session broke up.

"Hello, Alyssa. You missed little. We just joined together, and I informed all present that the reason I have called a council is that we have received our first word back from the emissary I sent to the south," Dad said, his voice reverberating in the op-pressive silence. He and Keion both eyed my red, puffy eyes mo-mentarily, and I gave them a tiny shake of my head, hoping to get them to forget about it.

"My priests have already begun healing the lash marks." Sternyface advised. I looked at her closely; the typically high-featured, stern countenance that had earned her my nickname seemed to have melted into a worried mess of lines and pouches.

"Lash marks?" I couldn't help repeating in shock. I hadn't heard that elves even had lashes to make the marks. "Lashing? For punishment? I've—not heard of lashings applied as punish-ment."

"Lashing for punishment is extremely rare, Alyssa," Keion explained.

"This was not lashing for punishment," Dad snapped. "This was a statement aimed directly at me. At the ruling party, I should say," he amended quickly as both the queen and the high priestess shot him a surprised look.

"It was a very clear statement," the queen said. "Your father said lash marks, but the simple fact is that the envoy was beaten to within inches of his life."

I looked across the triumvirate as knowing glances were shared among them. The queen's mistake—Sternyface was who actually said lash marks—was evidence of her stress, and though the other two obviously caught the error, neither of them seemed to be in the mood to correct her.

"I am sure my lord will jump to turn his forces about and join you in the attack, Your Highness," Grigor said. "Surely, whether the wyverns are available or not—"

"We are not attacking," Dad cut his uncle off fiercely, earning a hurt and surprised look. "I am sorry, Grigor. I did not mean to speak so harshly. But I am not going to thrust this kingdom into war."

"By all appearances, Your Highness's decision has already been made," Grigor said.

"My decision is mine to make, not Glynis's. I will see to it—or Naissa will see directly to it, in any event—that our man is tended to appropriately and given suitable libation and reward for putting up with the stupidity of our friends to the south. And I will send a stronger, but *peaceful*, force to discuss the matter with her."

"She will see that as weakness, Your Majesty," Grigor argued. I could tell from the subdued nods that Keion and Owain agreed with the advisor. Dad obviously noticed it as well.

"What say you, Ranger Sephaline?" he asked, earning a little jump of surprise from my startled cousin.

"I—I am hardly the person to ask, Your Majesty."

"Do not question my wisdom, young ranger. I am asking you because I believe you are the person to ask. What say you?"

Seph paused only momentarily before visibly gathering her courage and plunging in. "I agree that war is what Glynis was clearly calling for, but everyone can see that. It surprises me that she, of all the three, even based on what little I know of her, would be the one to react so. I think there must be something, some dark force, brewing down there. I know so, in fact. Our rangers have sensed it for some time. If that can be defeated without a continental, all-out elf-against-elf war, then we should try that first. Otherwise we're just feeding our own corpses to the dragon."

"Well said," the grizzled ranger said, and Seph beamed at the praise. Dad nodded.

Grigor disagreed vehemently. "You would send troops on a fool's errand, a small contingent that will merely be cut down, on a small hope that whatever may or may not be darkening the minds of the elves down there can be defeated separately. It would be a useless gesture, Your Majesty, and worse, it would be interpreted as a show of weakness by the other two clans."

"No," the queen stated flatly. "I hear the logic, as well as the fear and worry, in your words, wise Grigor. However, I must stand opposed. Alyssa, what are your thoughts? What of duty?"

Suddenly Dad's face softened and he seemed to understand something he hadn't before. He nodded gently. He cast a sympathetic look my way, and that wordless glance in turn helped me understand a little more. I felt better about what had happened in the queen's chamber, suddenly, strangely. The sensation, the inner knowledge, made me a whole lot more confident in my authority to answer.

Still, I had to be cautious. I knew that the queen wouldn't want the word love trotted out in front of everybody, since that would just invite mockery. The answer, then, was to phrase my response to give the result, not the path to the result.

"It is your—our—duty to forestall war against your fellow elves for as long as possible, as fervently as is possible. Until war is the only clear option available, we *must* find another path to deal with our fellows."

I couldn't help glancing around at the faces in the room, gauging support, though I knew as I did it that it might be taken as a sign of weakness. That, or caring, and I wanted to show that. I was rewarded, for the most part. Grigor gave in with a begrudging shrug, though his face remained dark. Dad nodded his approval, though, as did Sternyface. Seph looked relieved, while Keion wore a thoughtful expression. Master Owain could have been watching a tree sway in the wind for all the expression in his face.

Nice job.

Hey! I wondered if you were still there.

I am always present for my familiar.

I'm not your familiar, remember?

You're getting better at filtering what comes through to me, though I did see that the queen ran you through quite the emotional flight. You seem all right now.

I am.

"Hmm. What does—Kluzhka, isn't it? What does your wyvern familiar say?" Master Owain broke in, a gentle smile shading his face. His eyes stood piercingly out of the gentle expression, though.

"Kluzhka is the correct name. She says she agrees with me."

I did not.

Did, too. Now hush.

"Mmm," Master Owain hummed, his knowing look focused on my eyes. "Some day I would treasure the opportunity of an extended meeting with this familiar of yours, to see if I can speak with her directly. Kluzhka seems—fascinating."

Tell him he looks too old to be tasty.

I will not. Hush, you.

"So...." Queen Talaith let her voice trail off, obviously trying to get back to topic while watching the interplay between the elderly ranger and me with some clear interest. Finally it was over, so she continued, "So we have decided, it seems, and fairly clearly, what we will not be doing. What we will be doing is a bit more open. Cadfael, it is yours to select a group of your finest to make their way back down to the southern clans to appeal for peace once again in a little bit stronger manner. Ranger Owain, it is yours to select rangers to shadow that team to uncover the source of the disturbance down there. Meanwhile, we wait to hear back from the other envoy to our—friends—to the west."

"It will not be good news," Grigor groused. "...I am afraid," he added quickly to get out of Dad's glare.

"I believe that we are decided," Dad said. "Now, may I ask for my daughter, and Naissa, and Talaith to remain for a few minutes of discussion upon another matter?"

Grigor, the prince, Seph, and the senior ranger departed quickly, leaving the four of us behind. Dad looked to each of us carefully and then moved to the back of the chamber, opening the door to his private reception lounge and gesturing for us to pass through.

"I'm not—supposed to," I started to object, but the queen shushed me, took me by the hand, and led me into the chamber. Sternyface glided after, and Dad shut the door quietly but firmly behind us.

"I thought none were allowed in here but the king?" I asked once we were safely inside the space.

"By tradition, that is correct. I find it strange, and to be honest, a little bit farcical, how you worry about holding fast to the most minor of tradition, given what your arrival has heralded thus far," Dad said as he moved over to his private stash of whiskey. He dropped two ice cubes into each of four tumblers and then covered the ice with whiskey, and passed them around. Sternyface took one and sipped it with relish, earning a gasp from me.

"You—you drink whiskey?"

"What did you expect me to drink, Princess?"

"Well—not whiskey."

"You think you're the only one who's been down here in the silencing area with your father? Stop looking so surprised. The king hides nothing from us, and vice versa. And that is as it should be. This room, just as the queen's private chamber that is its twin, has a very important protection charm—go ahead, call it a magical spell if you wish—laid upon it, one of the strongest in the land. Only, the energy is anchored between layers of rock so that not even you could detect it. This is where the most secret of Kiirajannan policy discussions are held. And...." She quaffed the rest of her whiskey in a single gulp and held the glass out for more, a nonverbal request my father happily fulfilled. "...always accompanied by sufficient libation."

"I—I guess—I just had no idea that priests and priestesses could drink."

Sternyface made a lie of her name as she leaned her head back and let out a mirthful howl of humor.

"But you said—" I started accusing my father, but he cut me off.

"I lied. On this matter, Alyssa, and only this. You must understand, our society is built upon open and transparent workings, except in the very rare cases when it is not. But if anyone knew of the times when it is not, then that knowledge would break down the rest of our time, so it must be very carefully guarded."

"Okay. I get it, I think. The swamp must be drained except when it is not," I answered, tossing in a reference to American politics that I was sure Dad wouldn't get.

He didn't. "Swamps. Yes, I suppose. So, we must speak," Dad said, silencing the mirth. We all looked at him, and he continued, "Alyssa was provided three books while in Xlixi's captivity. We are not certain why she was provided these books, but we must accept that they are most likely to be taken at face value. One, and the one she provided to us as the most valuable to me and my security team, is an accounting of the exploits of the Cult of the Wyrm over the years. It has become clear to us that they infiltrated many of Kiirajanna's clans, and in numbers that we did not believe possible. But with Aerona's—untimely passing—we skipped ahead in our reading. It is clear that they have infiltrated, as they say, 'to the highest level,' the royal palace. If I had known that prior to—well, I might have been able to prevent—it. As it is, we must be vigilant. I stand here with the only three in the realm whom I completely trust. Do any of you have any thoughts as to who among our castle group may be a Cult infiltrator?"

The silence spread among us. It was hard to imagine that there were people out there who wanted to see us fail, even wanted to see me dead. It was harder yet to imagine that these might include people who were closest to us.

"It is not my children," Queen Talaith said, her voice firm.

Dad gave a pretense of thought, and then he nodded. "I have watched them grow up. If the Cult has been good enough to take one of their minds for its own without me seeing it over the years, then they are probably too powerful and competent to defeat in any event. I believe Sephaline is safe as well, as she has been unknown to many right up until she was surprised with a relocation into the castle."

"What about Grigor?" Sternyface asked. "His countenance is always dark, but it seemed even darker just now when we refused to go to war."

Talaith nodded, but Dad shook his head. "No," he said. "I will vouch for Padrig's advisor. I have known him for many years, and the darkness there is understandable. I am certain that he really did believe that the best thing to do, based on what Padrig himself would do, was to go to war. He is not the first, nor will he be the last, to have his mood turn dark when his opinion is overruled."

I nodded. "When I arrived in Ganolog, I thought Grigor was too dark, also, but in the end he convinced me that he was on our side."

Talaith sipped her whiskey and then asked, "So, does anyone suspect Master Owain?"

"The eldest, most respected ranger in the realm? Who could suspect him?" I was glad Dad answered; I wasn't sure I trusted the elderly elf, myself, but I wasn't about to say that out loud.

"So all we are left with, then, are the servants," the queen observed.

Sternyface said. "And my priests, and I do not believe that they should receive an automatic exemption. Let us require all of them to go through a careful screening using lie detection."

"You have—" I started to ask, but was cut off again.

"Yes. We do. Now that you, our dear Crown Princess Alyssa, have split tradition asunder, in fact, I will just call it a magical spell of lie detection. We will undertake this effort right away, Cadfael."

"Thank you all," Dad said with a nod as he tossed back the rest of his whiskey. We followed suit, and then left the room.

WISGI

Whiskey
Duh.
Why do so many civilizations
have the same word
for fire water?

Tragedy

Sometimes my spidey-senses are not all that helpful.

The next morning it was still dark when I headed to archery practice, but I knew I had to get it in before my lessons. Otherwise there was a chance for another council and whiskey and so on. But in spite of the darkness, I could still sense, and therefore see, both of the boys hovering behind me.

It felt weird, having not one but two boys watch over me as I performed the repetitive motions involved in shooting arrows at a target. They both said that it was important, though. Keion wanted to watch my practice, or so he said, while Gwyn wanted to watch my safety. Or—so he said. By the way they stood glaring at one another, Keion with muscles popping out of his other muscles and Gwyn with his magical blue aura roiling around him held at the ready, I'd guess each one was there mainly to watch the other. Neither elf trusted the other, it was clear. Keion had whispered something to me once about Gwyn being a wild, magical freak who couldn't be assumed to be on our side, so his distrust was both something I could understand and nothing I could change. I figured it irked Keion especially much that the protection mage was allowed to spend the night in my room, while a noble elf of grand character would not have even thought of violating a fair maiden such as me.

Gwyn, on the other hand, didn't trust anybody where my safety was concerned. I'd had to talk him out of coming to my third lesson that morning with the queen, just as I'd had to with the two previous, using the logic that if I couldn't trust her, then my time with her was pretty much useless anyway. He'd also gotten onto me for heading on down to Dad's hastily-called war council the day before without coming to get him first, even though I explained how the whole timing thing went when the king summoned. But he was right in a general sense, I had to admit.

I happened to be glancing his way when Gwyn's entire countenance changed. Suddenly he stopped glaring at Keion, whipping his head about toward the castle instead.

"Princess, there is a problem."

"I didn't hear anything," Keion challenged.

"Not a sound. An emotion. Didn't you sense it, Princess?"

I worked hard at reaching my own energies toward the castle, even grabbing for Draignerthol to be on the safe side. I plunged and poked around and through the stones as well as I could figure out how, finally deciding there wasn't anything I would be able to sense.

"No, I don't get anything."

"Well, I'm going to—"

"You're not going to do anything. I'm done for today. I can't get any real practice done with both of you watching each other watch me, anyway. You're going to follow me back to the castle."

You should probably listen to—

Not you, too. Hush.

Okay, suit yourself.

The walk to the castle was perfectly silent. The argument with Gwyn once we got there was less so.

"I am coming with you to your lesson."

"You are not going to come with me to my lesson. This is between the queen and me, and I am perfectly safe within the queen's chambers."

"You are never perfectly safe anywhere, Princess, especially not today. I felt something—"

"I know. But you don't answer. What? What did you feel?"

"I don't know. I already told you that. But it was magic, that much I do know."

I wanted to laugh at him for being so silly, but I managed to keep it serious. "Gwyn, it's attached to the cathedral. There's magic done all the time."

"Not like this."

"Not like what?"

"This! This time. It's—different. This had a sinister feel."

"Ooh, a sinister feel. Ruh roh, Raggie!" When he failed to ask about the relevant and humorous reference to Earth pop culture I'd just made, I blew it off and continued, "Look, the queen's lessons to me are private, confidential. I'll let you accompany me to the door of her chambers, but no farther, and that is that, okay?"

Conceding defeat, Gwyn nodded and then followed me from my own room down the long decorated hall to the door at the other end. I knocked.

"Something is wrong," Gwyn asserted, dropping his voice low and slow for dramatic effect. I stuck my tongue out at him.

"It's just another test." I pushed the door open, went on in, and closed it behind me, shutting myself off from the growl of frustration that came from my guardian.

He was just being silly, I told myself. I'd been to two lessons so far and had faced unexpectedly challenging tests both times. This was just a simple test of my assertiveness—as queen, I would have to make my own way in the world, to find that which I needed and sought.

Careful, Princess. I sense your better, smarter self worrying itself.

Hush, you.

I knocked politely, and after a few silent moments of waiting I opened the door leading from the antechamber into the queen's private area.

It took a moment to register what I was looking at. In the powerful presence of the queen, I'd never really looked at the inside of the queen's private chambers, for one thing. It was beautiful. White gossamer lace spun everywhere, backed by white linen festooned with pearls. What wasn't white was deep rich wood tone, and that was just the vertical support pieces. A beautiful clear crystal chandelier spun slowly, apparently under its own power, illuminating the room with a steady sequence of white flashes. The fragrance of lilac hung in the air, lending everything a tender, feminine touch.

Amid all the splendid beauty lay the still, pure white corpse of the queen, supine on the floor as though she'd just lain down to take a nap. But she wasn't napping. Her face was whiter than I'd ever seen it, and it didn't take a magic spell to tell that she wasn't breathing.

I yelled something, I can't recall what. Everything went numb, but I leaped to action in spite of it all. Suddenly I was leaning over the body, and despite her skin being white as a sheet, I felt for a pulse—nothing. I shook her once, then again, weirdly hoping that she would suddenly wake up, rise, laugh at the clever test she'd laid out for me.

Live! Live! I shouted at the corpse. *You've got too much left to teach me!*

I come.

NO! Stay away. You can't do anything here.

Strong hands yanked me onto my feet and away from the queen. As I watched, the Lady of the Bedchamber bent over her former boss. She gazed down into the beautiful, peaceful face, then she raised her face toward me. Our eyes locked, and I saw reflected in hers the same thing I was feeling—lost. Hopelessness. Fear.

I am above. Which roof do I need to tear through?

None, Kluzhka. I am in no danger. All is well.

You have a strange definition for well.

Go now.

More people crowded in. Some wore brown of priests, and their fingers wove blue nets of healing power, but I could tell without Draignerthol's help that it wasn't helping. Black clad people arrived. Gwyn's presence registered, and I could feel blue waves surrounding me from his own hands.

None of that mattered. It was surreal. The queen, normally such a vibrant and upbeat presence, just laid there, cold and silent.

Dead.

Someone, probably many people, were screaming things. I couldn't make any of it out. The whole room filled with hazy marshmallow paste, it seemed, and everything was stuck in slow motion against it.

Keion and the queen's daughters joined Meredydd at their mother's side. All three shot me looks of shocked fury, an anguished sob escaping one of their lips and a quiet "You...murderer" whispered by another, but their attention was focused too tightly on the corpse to register anything greater. I tried to yell that no, it wasn't me, I didn't do it, but found it impossible to yell as now four hands pulled me rapidly, impossibly so, out of the chambers and carted me down the hall.

The door to my room shut behind us, and the figure I recognized as Dad let go of one arm. He looked at Gwyn, who still held the other, and breathed, "Keep my daughter here. Keep her safe."

The king accelerated his nearly-seven-foot frame back toward the door and left the room at a sprint.

It all slowly crept over me in ever-increasing waves of horror. The queen was dead, murdered, and probably by the same sort of magical villainy that had taken Aerona's life. A murderer was alive in the castle. That murderer had now struck twice. And then...

Kiirajanna had no queen.

I was next in line, but I wasn't ready. There was no way I could be queen. None. And yet the land needed a queen.

Meanwhile, as a last layer of the ever-blackening horror settled in, I realized the implication in the fact that I'd been first to the queen's side, connecting it with the angry whisper I'd heard from one of her daughters. Everybody, at least the queen's kids, and likely many more people, were actively wondering how I'd done the deed, killed their queen.

Keep me safe? I wanted to laugh at the silliness in that. Nowhere in the castle was safe, truly. The queen's chamber had magical protection wards on the doors going in, I'd noticed once, and the queen herself had a guard force nearly as large and agile as the king's, and it could have responded in seconds to her call. None of that had mattered in the end. She'd been murdered in her own inner chamber.

It didn't make any sense, and that was what scared me the most.

Princess, come to me.

I come.

I unfolded Gwyn's arms from the supportive wrap he'd held, and wiped the tears that I hadn't realized till interrupted by Kluzhka that I was leaking. The world was colder, bleaker now, but there was still one ally I knew I could trust.

Two, maybe, but I wasn't quite ready for that right now.

"Let me go."

"Princess, your father—"

"I don't care. I'm warning you, let me go," I said through clenched teeth, right hand gripping Draignerthol as tightly as I could.

"Threaten or not, you know I can stop you," he said, and his eyes told me that he was certain of it. "You know that I should."

"Whatever. I know that you won't try. Kluzhka will rip you limb from limb."

"At least take me with you."

I thought about it for a minute. If I left him here in my room alone, he was sure to face a fiery king's wrath once the initial shock was done and over. That wouldn't be fair to poor Legolas, not at all.

I nodded. Then I turned and sprinted out the door and down the hall, taking the stairs two at a time. Finally I ran out onto the green expanse of lawn.

A shadow passed overhead. I know how big Kluzhka's wing-span is, but it still makes me gasp when confronted with the size of the shadow it casts. Chortling softly through the bond we shared, the wyvern wheeled and set down, walking sideways to turn about. Without a word, I leaped up onto her back, and then I helped Gwyn take a spot behind. I marveled for a minute at how good his strong arms felt wrapped around my torso, and then all thought of that ripped away along with my breath as she took off with a mighty leap.

Within the span of a breath or two we were up, flying above the trees, headed toward the clouds.

Where to?

I don't know right now. To be honest, I don't care. Somewhere far away from that damned castle.

Far away from that damned castle it is, then, Princess.

Kluzhka banked toward the high mountains in the east, earning a gasp from both of her riders at the same time. The wind whipped through my hair and across my skin, its pressure and briskness cleansing me of my presence at the queen's death. Soon the castle, and the scene it contained, was only a tiny speck as we soared up and away into the clean, cold air.

Mountains

Now that we're here, shall I go hunt you a nice, juicy deer to eat, Princess? Steak on the hoof, so to speak?

Mmm, raw meat. Sounds wonderful.

I shall be right back!

No! No, I was kidding. I don't want raw meat. It sounds disgusting.

Suit yourself, Princess.

Hush, you.

"That's weird."

"What's weird, Gwyn?"

"Now that we're here, by ourselves, without so much noise going on about us, I can actually tell when you and your familiar are talking. There's this weird buzz in the air at the same time as you mess your face up like this," he demonstrated a really weird expression, and then continued, "and then it dissipates. Then there's a different buzz, a louder one. Not—louder, really. Stronger, deeper. That wyvern is pretty powerful, you know."

"Yes, yes, I do. I know, I know. She tells me every chance she gets."

"She? Have you ever asked what a male wyvern is like compared to her? Are they stronger, or weaker? Faster, or slower?"

"Um, no. Why would I ask such a silly question?"

"It's not silly." Gwyn turned to hide his flush. We'd stood in the clearing on the side of the mountain for some time, Kluzhka flapping her wings to stretch the muscles out after the exertion of flying two elves up into a significant altitude while my protection mage and I stood face-to-face, neither of us willing to be the first to admit how nice it felt to not have our legs stretched out around a wyvern.

"We need to make a fire, if we're going to be here for a while," he continued, heading into the tree line. "It's cold already, and going to get colder. I'll find some wood; you prep the pit and try to find kindling."

Kluzhka acted according to my mental request and scraped out a fire pit with a single claw. I reached down and pushed my energies into the ground, connecting and communing with everything around. It wasn't the same as it had been down on the valley floor near the castle, but as I probed and sensed gently I realized that was just a shift, a quality change. Instead of massive oaks and elms, we were surrounded by tall pines. Evergreens are more individual than their deciduous cousins, it turns out, though that's really a strange thing to say, and not completely accurate. But while I'd been welcomed into a massive chorus of "us" down below, up on the mountain side it was a series of individual greetings I sensed, and many of those mere acknowledgments of my presence.

"We're going to need kindling sooner than later, Princess," Gwyn interrupted my grounding efforts as he tossed some chunks of dead wood by the fire pit.

"Nah." I walked over, tossed a few of the logs into the pit, and channeled fire through Draignerthol. Within moments we had a blazing fire going.

"We're going to have to talk about when it is proper to use Gaia's gift," Gwyn grumbled.

"Why? Look, I've been prohibited from using magic—Gaia's gift—since I got here and figured it out. And now the queen is dead, and people think I did it, and I'm on the run, and so are you, and hey, nobody's even calling me by my first name anymore, so who cares when I do or don't use magic?"

He thought for a moment, and then said,"You should. Look, Alyssa, it's like this—no, I can't even come up with a good analogy. There's positive, and there's negative, in the world, even taken entirely without our presence. What you do with your hands, with your intent, is positive. The flames catch slowly on smaller tinder pieces, and as they gain the energy they grow and can catch bigger pieces on fire, and as they do they consume larger pieces from the outside in. It's a natural growth. What you did was force yourself on them. You forced the flames to catch the whole piece, and that was...." His voice trailed off and he stared off into space, a pensive expression on his face.

"Negative?"

"Well, yes, that's where I was going, but now that I am there, I'm not sure I did the concept any justice."

"You didn't. I don't get it."

"It's—subtle. Difficult to understand. It took me a while once I was with Gaia's people. The bottom line is that when you can do something with your own hands, you should do it that way."

"Hmmph. Maybe." I wasn't ready to agree to anything like that; I'd just found myself with pretty much carte blanche approval to use magic whenever I felt like it.

I am hungry, whether you are or not. I will go hunt now.

Fine, Kluzhka. Go eat. Knock yourself out.

What a strange expression that is. The wyvern punctuated her statement by lifting her powerful body up off the ground and winging away at tree level.

Gwyn stopped lecturing me and went to gather more wood, leaving me alone to my thoughts and devices. Before long I got to watch Kluzhka through our strange mental link as she pounced on a fine young stag and drained the beast of its life blood. Then she meticulously pulled the skin away from the flesh and gently layered the choicest meat off of the carcass, sending me savory little mental notes the whole time. I could tell she relished the chance to tease me.

I turned my attention away from the mental link, shutting it off as thoroughly as I could. To stay busy I started hunting around for a possible shelter. There were plenty of upright trees around the clearing, and lots of fallen branches about. Some of the trees looked like they were about right for—*for a what?* I'd never made a shelter before, not by myself nor with anybody else, so I had to be honest with myself that I had no idea how to do it by hand.

…which, I realized, gave me an out. I didn't know how to do it by hand, and so I couldn't by definition do it with my own hands, which meant that Gwyn would have nothing to argue about if I did it by magic.

Pulling a force strong enough to move earth through my dragon pendant, I reached downward at the edge of the clearing. Up came a mound, and then the top separated and kept rising as the edges pulled downward and began looking like walls. Soon I had a three-wall manger-looking contraption made entirely of earth, and it looked sheltered enough to sleep in. I nodded, congratulated myself, and released my magic.

It collapsed.

"Not much of a structural wizard, are you?" Gwyn's voice sounded from the other side of the clearing. He approached, shaking his head. "Prin—Alyssa, you've got to learn not to leap in and start beating things apart with magical power, in spite of how powerful you really are. Let it be done naturally, and—" he waved my objection away before I could voice it, "if you do not know how, then ask."

The boy speaks truth.

Hush, you. Go back to your slaughter.

Oh, I am done. It was awfully tasty. In fact, it still is, with the warm blood sitting upon my taste buds like happy little spots.

Thanks for that mental image.

No problem, Princess. I shall bring you back something. You are hungry, even if you do not admit it.

Something I can cook, hopefully.

Your wish, my command.

"So..." Gwyn slid in once the link had gone silent for a few moments. "Your familiar was just now speaking of how she is likely to eat me for badgering you, yes?"

"Actually, she said you speak the truth. And I admit it. So I don't know how to build a shelter. How is that done?"

"Let's do it together. It's one of the first things I was taught by the people of the earth. It's really easy, actually. By hand, anyway, not by..." Gwyn made a show of waggling his fingers in the air to illustrate what was apparently supposed to be the magical method.

It was cute. I laughed.

Soon we'd worked up a sweat. He was pretty good at building, I had to admit. He showed me how to notch out some logs—with magic, he allowed, since we didn't have any cutting tools up to the task—and stack them carefully in a way that gravity held the notches together. Then he built two platforms, one about two feet above ground and the other double that at the front and sloping downward toward the back. We lined the lower platform with strong limbs—to support our weight, he explained—and the top platform with several layers of pine boughs. It didn't take long, and soon we had a shelter that looked fairly comfortable to me.

Here you go, Kluzhka announced, landing on her back legs while holding two rabbit corpses in her foreleg claws. Gwyn looked at my blanching face, chuckled, and got to the work of skinning the little beasts with his belt knife.

Before long he and I sat happily on one side of the blazing fire with Kluzhka curled into a large ball on the other side, eating rabbit off of hand-made skewers. It tasted delicious, especially with the appetite I'd worked up building the shelter.

"We can't stay here for long, you know."

I nodded. I'd already figured that out. The queen's placid corpse still haunted my vision, and as I granted it presence and voice it shouted the word "Duty!" at me.

I shuddered.

What, then, was my duty? I couldn't ask the queen any longer, so I had to figure it out for myself. It wasn't external. It couldn't be. It had to be based on my love—not for myself, or for anybody specifically, but for the people of Kiirajanna. The same people, a tiny voice inside my thoughts reminded me, who had rejected me as crown princess not long ago. The same people, it continued, who right now were full of fury at me because they assumed I killed the queen. But none of that mattered, or could matter, and I knew that with a cold certainty. The people might or might not be mine to rule, the crown possibly mine to take on, but it had to be worn by someone in the times ahead. That felt like far more of a negative burden than a positive one, if I had to use Gwyn's balance talk. Regardless, it appeared to be fully my burden, and mine alone, and I was forsaking my most important duty, to them, to Kiirajanna, and to the prophecy, by sitting here like a sulking little girl on the mountain side.

Nobody trusted me, though. Well, the elf and the wyvern with me did, but they were the only two who trusted me. But then I realized that wasn't correct either. Seph trusted me. Dad, who would be furious with me, would still trust me. Grigor would still trust me. I was pretty sure I could win the Lady of the Bedchamber over. The queen's kids were probably a lost cause, but then again I could only imagine how unbelievably angry, hurt, and utterly devastated they must be in losing their mother. I'd have to give them a wide berth, staying as far away from Prince Charming as possible for a while.

I really didn't want to go back. All that anger, all the rage I knew would be awaiting my return. Sternyface would be...sterny faced.

But Seph would be there, and I needed to be there for her. And who would look after L.T.? I had to go back.

I didn't want to, though. I let my mind linger in its imaginary moment of bliss, seeing me and my protection mage sidekick forge a lifestyle up here in the mountains free from the Cult, free from intrigue, free from Prince Charming and his sisters.... Free.

"Gaia's people are coming, and will be here soon," Gwyn broke my reverie and announced.

"How do you know that?"

"I know. A protection mage can sense presences, and sometimes actions, though the latter is not terribly clear for me yet. More importantly, I know my people. What you did in creating the pile of rubble over there will have been sensed for miles around. Such a forceful use of Gaia's gift would bring them running no matter what, but with the rumors you created of a dragon coming back to the realm, that will be their greatest fear. They will approach cautiously, but we should probably at least ask your wyvern to gain some distance from us, if we do not go, ourselves."

"They wouldn't mean us any harm, though, right?"

He broke a stick and fed it into the fire, both of us watching as the flames played along its bark. It was getting dark, I noticed.

"I am not certain, Alyssa. If they approached and saw a wyvern, they would very likely come in on offensive. Too many of our people have been taken down by her kind for her to receive any other reception. If they merely see us, two white-skinned elves seated about a fire, they will probably just hang close and watch. If at all they will come in curiously. Whether they attack or not will be a good question, but given the ferocity of the magic you have been working that they may want a more thorough investigation, and the people here will have no way of knowing it is you."

"So, yes, they would mean us harm, is what you're saying."

"Probably, yes."

"Why aren't they here already? They can teleport."

"They can, but as they can sense your magic, they must assume that you can sense theirs as well. Remember, never do anything by Gaia's gift that you could do by hand instead."

"Would you know whether there are any here yet?"

He guffawed and looked at me with a lift to his eyebrows. "Of course I would know if they are here. Protection mage, remember? You were the one who campaigned for your father to accept me based on that, weren't you?"

I sighed. He was right, but he didn't have to put it that way.

We are going to return, aren't we?

Yes, Kluzhka. It is my duty.

Yes. You are right. It has been good being up here in the clean air with you, though. That elf would make a good mate for you, you know.

Kluzhka!

What? He is smart, and strong. He is humble as well, though I can tell he carries a strong sense of self inside. He does not show us his private portions, though, and that is a good thing.

I giggled aloud and sent her a mental image that matched what she'd said.

Well, I did not mean that. But if your strange elf libido is strengthened by that, then so be it.

Hush, you.

Gwyn had watched the conversation between her and me go back and forth, clearly interested. "It is so strange. I can almost hear your tone rising and falling as the two of you pass messages back and forth. I had no idea such a thing was possible."

"It is, apparently. We were talking about you, by the way."

"Oh, really? About how handsome and capable I am?"

"Not quite. Well, she was. I mean, I—oh, never mind." I found myself twisted around backward on that conversation and had to hit the eject button. I didn't want him thinking I liked him, not that way, not while he had to be my protector in the little cubbyhole near me, but at the same time I didn't want him thinking I didn't like him, either.

I had to admit I was thoroughly confused as to where the romance part of my story was going, but I was certain that I had to get the queen part of it going down the right, dutiful path first.

"Let's go, Gwyn. They need me down there, whether they know it or not."

"Let's go, then."

Together we climbed up on Kluzhka's rough scales and launched into the evening sun, heading back west and south toward the castle.

That was a nice spot. I will have to return to hunt more.

Gwyn warned me that his people were on the way—

I can see them, remember?

She lowered her gaze and pressed her heat sense through the link to me. I had to whistle; we'd been surrounded by a few dozen elves.

Right. And they probably wouldn't like you much, so you should probably stay away for a while.

Advice taken, Princess.

Thanks.

YMGREINI

To prostrate yourself, to grovel
I wasn't about to do this.
But...how to heal the wounds?

Reconciliation

The castle was gloomier than I could have imagined it when we returned. The sun still glimmered on the western horizon, but its rays of warmth seemed to stop well before the castle walls began. Kluzhka let us off her back right at the front steps. I let Gwyn lead me up, forcing myself to step calmly ahead, while the wyvern winged back toward the security of the high peaks to the northwest.

The throne room door was shut. I approached tentatively, but I could hear voices from behind it. There wasn't much point in playing nice any longer, I figured, so I opened it and let myself in as all conversation ceased.

Six pairs of eyes bored into my soul from inside the room.

I shut the door firmly behind me in a deliberate motion. The encased silence felt like a tomb.

"Look, I—I must—I apologize for running away earlier. I had to clear my head. But I didn't do it."

I almost slapped myself in frustration. I'd rehearsed that speech all the way back but it still came out as a jumbled fluff of stupidity.

"We know that," Dad said from where he sat, slumped miserably in his throne. "We do," he corrected Keion, who had snorted in derision. The prince spun and stomped out of the room, slamming the door after himself.

"The prince is...." Sternyface, the only one standing straight still, started to explain, but she ran out of words too soon.

"Yes, I know. I can't even imagine what the prince and his sisters are feeling right now," I acknowledged. "To find their mother like that must have been horrifying. And it's easier to blame it on me than to leave it hanging out there, wondering who might have committed the murder. I do get all of that," I nodded at my father, who was suddenly starting to sit higher, appraising me with a little brighter expression. "It will take a long, long time to get past today, but I hope that we are able to eventually. In the meantime, though, we have a queen's death to investigate and avenge."

"Princess," Grigor said. He was standing back, hidden within the shadows, not broadcasting much of anything, feeling-wise. "I must advise that you should return to wherever you were, at the greatest urgency possible. This castle is clearly not safe for you any longer. I mean no offense, boy, but a single, young, self-styled protection mage cannot hope to stand against someone powerful enough to slip in and take the queen's life from her with the rest of the castle unaware. You are both in danger, as are you, Cadfael. You should leave, too, for that matter. Find a safe place to weather the storm while we investigate the crime. Just till it blows over."

"You advise me to run away? Never," Dad spat. He was getting some color back thanks to Grigor's suggestion, but the color he had scared me a little. "Besides, we have no reason to believe that this will blow over, as you say. Who will rule the land if we abdicate our thrones? No, I will not leave, and neither will my daughter. That is your stance, also, yes, Alyssa?"

"Oh, absolutely. I…" I started, hoping to come up with a stirring speech, something that would win the hearts and spirit of everyone in the room. I had seen recordings of great speeches before as part of class, and an inspiring, powerful orator was an incredible person to have around when the chips were down.

Apparently I wasn't one of those, though. That hit me like a wet towel to the back. I just couldn't find any inspiring words to say.

"I'm staying," I managed. Hey, it was the intent that mattered.

"She will be fine under my protection," Gwyn argued. "I have greater powers than you think, Master." I imagined Grigor's deeply obscured, hawk-like face screwing up in disapproval at the tone Gwyn put into the formal term, but he continued quickly, "Besides, there has to be a reason for the attacker to have targeted the queen and the princess's former bodyguard rather than going after her directly. Would you agree?"

"I would," Sternyface said, nodding. "That is part of the puzzle that we cannot work out, though, The queen is—was—indeed powerful, in her own right, but why her?"

Master Owain, who'd slouched silently in the opposite corner from Grigor till now, cleared his throat. "I have been thinking on that. It is possible that they were not the primary targets for their own sake. I think they might have been killed to send a message to the princess herself. Nobody hated the queen, nobody, especially not enough to want her dead. But anyone wishing to make Alyssa vacate the throne would see her as an excellent medium in which to mold a strong message. And, I should add, it has worked quite well so far, yes?"

"It has," I said, nodding. Then it hit me: "But where's Seph? She would make another excellent medium for a message, right? I—where—"

"Your cousin is fine. I have her under guard," Dad said. "We can go see her in a moment if you would like."

"I would, but you know what is most disturbing about our situation, I think?"

"Please, elaborate."

"That my cousin has to be under guard in the castle. That we have to be holed up here in this room together to have a conversation. That nobody feels safe in the castle right now, or at least I'd assume that is the case. The fear and gloom is palpable when you walk in the front doors, Dad. We have to do something."

"Do something, like...?" Dad asked, his hands going wide.

"I don't know. Investigate, maybe?"

"My priests have investigated the murder," Sternyface said. "And?"

"And nothing, unfortunately. She was killed through magic."

"Asphyxiated? Like Aerona?"

"No, not that we can tell. When people are choked, they die with fear in their eyes. She died peacefully. It is as though she saw something that pleased her, and then her candle was snuffed. It is—perplexing."

"May I go see the body?"

"Later, Alyssa." Dad said. "For now, you have a duty to perform. If it is as gloomy and fearful as you say outside that door, you are the only one who can lessen that. You ran away earlier. That is perfectly understandable to us within this room, but its impact upon the castle cannot be understated. You must be seen out and around in the castle. We must go see your cousin. We must laugh and play dice. Let Arianna's children mourn. They certainly deserve it. But for the rest of us, we must show our people that we are sad, yes, but that our spirit is not broken."

"Arianna?" I asked.

He nodded. "The queen's real name was Arianna, and a beautiful name it is. She set it aside when she took on the weight of the crown, with the promise of picking it up again once a new Talaith is named. And I must add, that is now you, Talaith."

"I'm…." I literally staggered under the weight of that pronouncement.

"The realm needs a queen," Sternyface said. "We can do no better than our current Crown Princess Alyssa, can we, Talaith?"

"I have to confess, I wasn't ready to hear myself called by that name."

Dad shrugged and said, "I doubt anyone ever is. You can be particularly forgiven. Most queens have peaceful transitions, with the elder queen stepping aside pleasantly amid a public ceremony, using time-honored phrases to bestow our most treasured and beautiful name upon her successor. That public ceremony at this time would be tacky, of course. Still, as far as I am concerned, my daughter, you must be our queen."

"I'm not really ready, though."

"No one ever is. You will do fine—or at least as well as anyone could be expected to, given the challenges you face."

"Thanks, I think. I somehow expected it to feel different. It doesn't, does it?"

"The world's problems do not go away due to elevation in status, Talaith," Sternyface intoned.

Suddenly Grigor walked out, his face angry. At least he didn't slam the door like Prince Charming had, but it still made me jump.

"He believes strongly in the position he has argued," Dad explained. "He simply feels as I do, that your safety is paramount. Unfortunately, what he believes that means is opposite to the remainder of us. He will be angry for a while, but he will come around."

"Well, I would like to see my cousin now, anyway. Can we go do that?"

"Of course. Lead the way, Talaith."

I waited for a moment for someone else to move, and then realized what had happened and allowed a self-conscious grin to peek over my lips.

"I don't think I'll ever get used to being called that."

"I believe that you will," Dad said with a gentle smile.

Seph was in her room, glaring angrily at the four guards standing there wearing the king's black livery. Her face lit up when I came in, though.

"Alyssa! I was so scared you wouldn't come back! I mean, I knew you would be okay, but—are you sure you're safe enough here?"

"I think so. Yes," I corrected myself, remembering Dad's comments. "I have Gwyn, who's at least as good as the squad guarding you."

"I can't say I doubt that," she said, giving the four of them a glare. "Your Majesty," she greeted my father, and then Sternyface as well. "Master Owain, what a delight to see you here!" she said, glowing, when the grizzled old ranger stepped through the door.

"She is Talaith now," Sternyface corrected Seph, who shot me a startled, confused look.

"Let's—not start that just yet, okay? I'm happy still just being Alyssa to you."

"You cannot," Sternyface objected, and my dad shook his head in emphasis. "The queen is the queen to all, not only to those she chooses. We need a queen, and you must be that queen, and to all. I—I am sorry, Talaith. This has all happened in such a backward, startling manner, and your head must be reeling much more than you are showing. That is to your credit, but please. Keep in mind that we all understand what you must be dealing with and will grant you as much time as you need. But we—Kiirajanna—need a Talaith."

"Thanks, High Priestess," I said, a little surprised to hear kind, if firm, words coming out of Sternyface's mouth for once.

"I am Naissa now," she corrected. "The queen need not use titles of respect for anyone."

"Thanks, Naissa," I parroted. "I am still not ready to be queen, I guess."

"You keep saying that. We all keep disagreeing with you. At some point we must move on from that topic," Dad said.

I took a deep breath; he was right. "Okay, fine. So what about these fun and games you said we need to be showing everyone to make them happy?"

"Let us take some dice down to the dining room. It is past time for food, in any event."

"Won't it be seen as...." I couldn't quite finish the sentence for all the negative words I wanted to put in.

"By a few, perhaps, who will in turn be advised by those who understand our intent."

I'd never played dice with my dad before. It was weird. He sat down beside me, with Seph and Master Owain across the table, and Sternyface took the seat on the end. Dad told the guards, who'd followed us from Seph's room, to grab us some food and then get some dice for themselves.

"Noise. We need to make some happy noise," he said.

We played for quite some time, never really getting up to making noise at the level that he was probably wanting us to. Still, it seemed to work. A crowd gathered slowly, many of them glancing fearfully my way. I noticed, but I knew that I couldn't show it. Instead, I forced my lips up into a huge elf grin, willing my eyes to shine with an intensity that I didn't feel at all.

"You are smiling too much," Dad whispered. "Remember, this is supposed to be a somber day of mourning."

"Like Aerona's?"

"No. Not like Aerona's. There is no tradition governing this, but to give the queen the same mourning as we gave Aerona would be unseemly. We will figure that out later. For now, smile, but not too much."

"Smile, but not too much. Gotcha, big guy."

If I'd expected a response to my sarcastic quip I would've been disappointed, but I didn't. He just kept playing as though nothing had happened.

He was right, though, so I put away the huge smile and instead nodded and grinned at all newcomers. They got over their fears, probably when they saw who all was playing dice with me, and slowly the dining room filled up with people eating dinner. A low rumble of voices finally reached out and filled the hall, and Dad smiled at all of us when it happened.

"I still wish to see the queen," I mused at one point. I wasn't really trying to make a huge point; I was just relaxing and speaking what was on my mind.

"Later," Dad whispered. "Do not think on or speak of such things now. Pleasant, remember?"

So we were pleasant. We went through and played several long games of dice, running through till one person lost all their pebbles and then redistributing to start anew. Before long Dad rose, walked into the throne room, and returned with an armload of bottles filled with dark liquid.

"Pass them around," he ordered, and his order was obeyed. Soon everyone held a cup containing a shot or two of the king's whiskey. He watched the progress patiently, waiting until the last cup was attended to.

He stood taller, raising his shoulders and his chin to tower above everyone. He raised his glass and said, "My friends, we have lost a great friend, a true leader, an exceptionally wise woman. We *will* find her murderer and avenge her death, I give my word to you this evening, but for this night, at least, let us celebrate all that her life was devoted to." A stream of tears belied his words, but he bravely wiped at them and raised his voice louder. "Tonight, we commune together. We share stories of her life."

"I would begin, Your Majesty," Keion's voice sounded from the stair landing just outside the dining hall, and all eyes swiveled to his tear-streaked face and those of his sisters standing a stair above. He stepped into the room and accepted a cup of the whiskey for each of his sisters, passing each behind, and then one for himself before nodding and continuing. "It was—shocking, devastatingly so, to lose our mother at such a young, beautiful time of her life, and we have all been beside ourselves with grief and anger. But Mother would not want her death to tear us one apart from another, and so my sisters and I have come, in spite of our grief, to join with you. If it is in your desire, King Cadfael? And yours, Queen Talaith?" With that, Keion bowed to me, and gasps filled the room.

Shocked, I glanced at Dad, whose eyes now misted over and face spread in understanding and relief for the prince's gesture of recognition. My father tilted his head in a quick, subtle, unmistakable gesture.

I took his cue and bowed in return to Keion—not as a peer, but with the delicate head dip I'd seen the queen—the former queen—use to formally recognize those slightly beneath her in rank. Keion saw, smiled sadly, and winked.

"It would be my greatest desire, Prince Keion," I heard my voice saying, and suddenly the room took in a collective sigh of relief.

Keion launched into tales of his mother's travels as I quaffed Dad's whiskey and poured a second. We had a huge battle ahead of us, but at least we faced it together.

TWP

pronounced "toop"
Dumb. Stupid. Ignorant

The word has nothing to do with
the amount of whiskey
that has been consumed.

To See The Queen

"I will accompany you to the queen's repose," Grigor said the next morning. He'd dropped by my room first thing and apologized profusely for his temper, and I'd declared it okay as elegantly as I could. Now, we were good. He'd been as upset as the rest of us, after all.

"Thank you. Gwyn, are you ready?"

"You should leave your guardian here, Talaith. The queen's repose is a sacred place, and a guardian coming along sends the wrong signals. Besides, I can protect you through the cathedral. He should accompany us to the hallway between the two, of course," Grigor added, attempting to placate Gwyn's glare. I still jumped a little when he called me Talaith; in spite of Dad's assurance that I'd get used to it, I wasn't even close to that yet.

Gwyn turned his glare toward me. "I disagree with the advisor, my queen. You are in no less danger anywhere, and while I respect his ability, he cannot—"

"No," I said, holding a firm gaze on my guardian. "No. He is right. It is important that we put up a show of being secure in our ability to move around the castle, and especially the cathedral. I would not want to anger High Priestess Naissa by moving into her area with an armed guard, either. No. I will be fine. I don't even believe you should accompany us to the hallway, to be honest. Appearances are crucial, Gwyn."

"As my queen orders," he said with a glare and a bow that was somewhere between regal and mocking.

I sighed. Some day, I hoped, I wouldn't have to worry about ticking off my favorite people in the name of pleasing my other favorite people. They were both right, though, or at least they both had really good points. But if I couldn't walk freely around the castle with Draignerthol at my breast, what good would I ever be, anywhere?

"Lead the way, Grigor."

He bowed and stepped out, and I followed, vaguely aware of another of L.T.'s fits in the little elm's corner. I managed to avoid rolling my eyes; that tree was more possessive than any puppy I'd ever heard of. And yet I had no idea—how, exactly, do you discipline a tree?

With that silly question lingering on my mind, I kept a straight face and followed Grigor as we quietly, solemnly, walked down the hall and then turned down the stairs.

Keion met us halfway, headed upward. Luckily he didn't do anything outwardly hostile, but as he passed I saw and felt the hot glare he shot at me. It made my heart skip a beat. I thought I had come to terms with the dueling facts that he would always be my strongest crush while at the same time he and I were never meant to be together, but it did not make his intense anger for me any easier to deal with.

"It shall pass, Talaith," Grigor muttered and continued without missing a step. I realized I'd stopped to let my emotions run their path, and stepped quicker to keep up with the man who was my father's secret uncle and closest ally.

At the bottom of the stairs one path led out the front doors of the castle while the other led back into and through the hill behind, doors branching off toward the grand ballroom and the grand dining room to either side. It was this path back that led to the grand cathedral of the elves, which was a little bit ironic now that I knew how, and why, the elves refused to have any sort of religion. Still, it was where I'd received my lessons starting on my first full day in Kiirajanna, and it was the location of Sternyface's office, where I'd been upbraided several times for—well, more than several things.

It was where I'd punched her in the face, but that's a different story.

It was also where the queen's body—former queen, technically, but I couldn't bring myself to accept that. Not yet, anyway, and I wondered if I'd ever be able to. But it was where her body lay in state.

We walked with a heavy bearing down the hall. It felt like a slow march, in fact, as though I were walking to a funeral. Which, I admit, we sort of were. I didn't really want to see the queen's corpse, to be honest. I had no desire to ever see it again. But I had to—my duty, more than anything else, required that I at least try to uncover the details and the cause of the queen's death. She had been a good queen, and a wonderful person, and her lessons were what had let me make it this far, so I owed at least that to her.

Grigor stopped at a door I must've walked by a hundred times but never seen opened. It was halfway down the hall, under what had to be the deepest part of the hill. The door itself was a simple piece with no engraving, which wasn't that surprising considering how few of the doors in the cathedral had any sort of ornamentation anyway. Still, if this was the door beyond which the queen's body lay in repose, then I would sort of expect more. Nothing outright or garish, of course, but I wondered why what was obviously a very special chamber wasn't better labeled at its entrance.

"The chamber rests halfway between the religious and the militant powers of Kiirajanna. It is considered a naturally balanced location for rulers to lie in state," he answered when I wondered aloud. I shrugged; it made sense when put that way. Elves were weird when it came to some of their—our—customs, I had to admit.

"Through here, Your Majesty," he said, holding the door open for me. I entered, and he followed, shutting the door behind. The hall we were in was about twelve feet long or so, and was also unornamented. Dust stirred from the floor as we stepped toward the only other door at the opposite end.

"How did they get the queen's body through here without disturbing the floor?"

"Oh! There is another entrance, Your Majesty, but it is only for use by members of the sacred brotherhood. Other visitors like us must come this way, and I suspect we are the first with the will to attempt viewing of the former queen's body."

"Okay, that is fine," I said, and opened the door at the opposite end. It opened into a small, square, chamber that was empty. "Where's the queen?"

"The exit is on the other side, leading directly to the chamber they have set the queen in," he said, pushing me gently into the room. "Can you see it yet?"

"No—ohhh," I said, peering so deeply into the gloom that I didn't stand a chance of noticing the attack from behind until it was done. I felt the dagger as it entered my back, sliding cleanly through the skin and then between my ribs. I actually felt it pierce my heart, felt the blood beating out of the wound as the dagger was pulled out and reinserted, this time puncturing my left lung. I also felt a strange tingling warmth spread through my limbs, numbing everything as it went.

I tried reaching for Draignerthol and, at the same time, my mind screamed for my body to spin around to face him. My feet didn't behave, though; it was like I stood in a vat of jelly. My arm blew me off, too. Draignerthol, meanwhile, hung lifeless against my chest. I could feel nothing through the ancient relic; there simply was no power there to connect to. Instead, the only thing I felt was my body falling, heavily, toward the floor. It hurt when I hit, but as I lay there I realized there was nothing to be done about it. I simply couldn't move.

Kluzhka! Kluzhka, I—need you.

Nothing. That line was severed, somehow. What had he done to her?

"Why?" I managed to gasp. It's surprisingly hard to ask silly questions when your chest has been run through multiple times.

"Why? Why now, finally, I have done my master's bidding, and will receive his reward when he enters this realm," I heard Grigor's voice rasp. "You probably deserve to know some things, daughter of my nephew, before you pass from this world into the next. You should know that I bear no ill will toward you, personally, but that I only do as my master commands. You should know that it was I who killed your stupid guard, who let me into your room so easily with you gone, and it was also I who ended the queen's life. Yes, dear, I am a mage, myself, and quite a powerful one, if I may brag a little. Oh, why wouldn't I be allowed to brag a little, yes? What are you going to do to stop me? But where was I—oh, yes, your predecessor. She was even easier to kill, trusting me as she did while I simply put her to sleep and then stopped her heart with a drug that none in this realm know of. It was— perfect. Flawless. Granted, she needed to go, but more important, I needed for you to have a reason to follow me into this chamber. And now I will see that you run away, blamed for her death. Do not waste your last efforts struggling. As you have probably already guessed this chamber is never visited by the High Priestess's order. Yes, I selected it well.

"Oh, I know that you are desperately clutching not only to life, but also toward the pendant you have relied upon as your sole source of strength. I took the time to shield this room, however, and so you cannot reach out. You cannot even call out to that ridiculous wyvern you call a familiar. Hopefully now she will return to my master's service in his preparation to enter Kiirajanna and bring a new peace to this realm. He will reward her. He might even allow her to be the one to feast upon your cousin's bones. But now, as you must have already found, your power, your special magic, is taken away, and so oh, too bad, my dear, you have nothing. You are nothing. You will die nothing. You are a simple little Mississippi girl, and you will die a simple, stupid, careless little Mississippi girl."

As his voice droned on it seemed to gain even more of a sneering quality. Maybe that's normal? I don't know; I hadn't been murdered before. It was getting harder to hear him, though; everything was darker, more muffled. Much as I wanted to fight against it ending this way, I knew I didn't have anything to battle this with. The outcome was given, but the one good thing would be I could stop listening to Grigor's truly annoying sneer soon.

"I see that the poison from my dagger is already doing its job. How does it feel to lay there helplessly, knowing that within moments your life will end, Princess? Oh, I am sorry—Queen. Talaith, yes? How did it feel when you got to be called by that exalted name? Did you preen with pride? Daddy's little girl, become somebody powerful? You were on top of the world, yet—oh, poor you. It was yours for less than a day. How sad is that, hmm? How...."

As the voice finally faded away, receding into the darkness that overtook me, I had one final, irreverent thought about how I'd always doubted that, in the end scene, the antagonist of all those stories actually delivered a standard, cliché monologue like that. Obviously I'd been wrong. It didn't matter much, though. Soon I was floating, disconnected entirely with my body.

Soon, I was nothing.

I was dead.

The queen of Kiirajanna, for the second time in two days, had been murdered. And this time, it was entirely my fault.

WYRTH

A miracle.

It's weird that, as with all Elf words,
the plural is hard to form.
But who needs more than one
miracle?

A New Dawn

"Alyssa, you must awaken. I can do so much, but only so much." The voice sounded in my head, through my head, and not through my ears, and that confused me. I knew I had one voice up in there, and had gotten sort of used to Kluzhka's temporary visits, but this was different. Two voices? How'd I get two voices up there?

"I—cannot."

"You must. Your people need you."

"But—but I am dead."

"No. You are not dead," the voice insisted.

"Yes. Yes, I'm pretty sure I am. I felt myself die."

"You did, yes, but.... No, you didn't. Not quite. You felt yourself come quite close to death, actually. Look, why are we arguing this matter? The poison from your assailant's dagger has run its course, and so now its paralyzing effect is gone. I managed to keep your brain going, barely. I can restart your heart now. It will be difficult restarting it without the holes being healed, but they cannot be healed without the heart beating blood, so—it is a—

what do you call it, a catch twenty-two? Oh, let us just say it will be difficult. Very, very difficult. But the good news—terrific news, in fact—is that I believe it can be done. I—"

"So what's your point? I am dead, remember?" I didn't think this conversation was going anywhere useful, and just wanted the voice to shut up, bless its – um, heart?

"So my point is that you do not have to be dead. The fact that you and I are going back and forth is proof enough of that. Regardless, I need for you to want to live, or else I cannot do anything, and you will truly die. When you do, then your people will die to Xlixi as he and his minions come to feast."

"Okay, fine. Want to live, need to save my people. Got it. So who are you?"

"Who am…. What? You do not recognize me?"

"Now isn't the time to get philosophical. No. Who are you?"

"I am Draignerthol."

"Oh. Well, that's a relief; I thought I was crazy there for a moment. Now I guess that I'm talking to a lifeless pendant, so I know I'm crazy."

"You're—"

"When is Dumbledore going to show up to tell me that what I do from here is my own decision?"

"Look, the time for sarcasm is the same as the time for philosophy, and neither exists in much quantity right now, Alyssa."

"But how—"

"No. Not now. Now, I need for you to rise. I can use the motion to move, jump start if you must, your heart, at least a little. But it will be enough.

"Enough? Next thing you'll tell me is 'this won't hurt a bit.'"

"Oh, no. It will hurt. More, it will take more effort than you have ever put toward anything, in your entire lifetime. It will feel as though you have no strength, because in truth you do not. Your muscles are entirely starved, dead as they can be, because they have not had blood. Your blood has not circulated in a long while. But if you can but bear through it, and get yourself to and through the door into the hallway, I believe you can call upon magic once again, as the spell feels fairly localized. But I need for you to do it now, not later. Your ability decays by the moment."

"The door is probably locked."

"Why would your assailant lock a dead person in?"

"I—"

"Shut up and go."

"How long was I—"

"Not now. Get up. Now."

The voice in my head was right about one thing; I had no strength at all. I willed my arms to move, to push upward from the floor, and they ignored me completely.

"I can't."

"You can. You must, or you will die."

"But I already died."

"We've been through this already. Stop it. Move."

"But—"

"Move. *Now.*"

"I—"

"*Move!*"

The voice echoed loudly inside my—my head? I wasn't even sure I had a head any more. But I knew I had a being. I knew I had me. I reasoned—no, I knew—I knew that I wasn't dead. Not yet, anyway. I should be, but somehow I wasn't. Summoning a will I didn't realize I owned, I forced my arms against their protests to push, press, move, do something. *Move!* I ordered them, and bit by bit, muscle fiber by fiber, they started to obey.

Eventually, through painful, dogged effort, I figured I had gotten halfway up, and that made me want to cheer. The accomplishment buoyed me further, and with that burst I made it up onto my hands and knees. I turned, slowly, deliberately.

My hand landed in something viscous, almost but not quite wet. It was mostly congealed—I had to assume that it was my own blood—and so I didn't slip and go back down onto the floor. I wasn't sure if I'd have made it back up. I pushed the revulsion back, though, and kept moving—first one hand, then a leg, then the other hand, then the other leg. Two inches, four inches, six inches at a time, I struggled and fought my way across the floor.

How far had I gone into the room? It was only a step or two, I thought, but it seemed like a full Greek marathon to get back out.

The top of my head hit something solid—the door! I thought—but maybe? Maybe not. But it had to be the door. Doubt washed over me; I realized in that moment that I had no idea what direction I'd been going with my head down and my eyes glued shut. The door might be the opposite direction, in fact. My spirit sank.

Carefully, I inched my hand forward, hoping against hope I'd find a gap between the solid vertical and the solid horizontal. I had to be there. Something had to go right.

There was a gap.

My spirit soared. I was there! Now all I had to do—*all!*—was to rise and open the door.

That part turned out to be even harder than it sounded. I was able to lever one arm up and find the door handle. My fingers resisted, but finally obeyed and grabbed, and then the even harder part came as I pulled with all my might, pushing my legs to lengthen at the same time. Slowly, inch by inch, I managed to rise to my feet. They were—dead. Literally, my legs were dead, with no feeling whatsoever. I commanded my muscles to lock, to hold me upright, but only my grip on the door handle kept me up there.

I finally settled myself against the wall beside the door and pulled the handle, looking forward desperately to being outside of the accursed shielded chamber.

It was locked.

I tried pulling again, not quite willing to believe the results from the first attempt.

Nope. Locked.

That realization crushed me. I wanted to cry, to give up, to just collapse into a heap and die. As hard, as diligently as I'd dragged myself across the floor, as difficult as it was to get up to the door handle, and as close as I was to getting out, I found myself blocked by a stupid door lock.

"Just a moment, Alyssa. Just...no. Stop. Heart! Do not give up yet," the voice sounded, and I felt—something. My chest buzzed, like a tiny bumblebee. No, not even that, just like a tiny moth. I wasn't breathing, was barely holding onto a tiny sliver of life, but I felt Draignerthol's vibration through my cold, gray skin, and sensed a tiny tendril of blue energy snake out from it toward the door handle.

I heard the lock click.

The door opened. I rolled, used the final microscopic shreds of energy to shove my torpid body in the direction of freedom, and collapsed through the portal into the hall beyond.

I was free of the room's magical spell.

It hit, and my entire body was energized. The pins and needles you feel when your foot wakes up were nothing compared to this. The imaginary angry ants covered my entire body, amplified a hundredfold or more.

It hurt.

It hurt a lot.

I screamed till my throat was raw, which didn't take long.

Alyssa! Where are you? A voice in my head demanded. It wasn't Draignerthol this time. I recognized Kluzhka's mental link reconnecting. She sounded different—frantic, intense, much more demanding than I'd ever heard her.

Halfway down the hall between the castle and the cathedral.

I feared you were dead!

I was.

The silence echoed through our connection for several long moments.

You—were? Dead, you mean?

It's a long story. Longer than I knew, I figured, and probably much longer than I wanted to tell, and then I wondered where Draignerthol's voice had gone off to. I had some questions for that pendant. But in the meantime, I had to get out, and to do that I had to be able to walk again.

"Use me. Heal yourself, silly," the voice returned.

"There you are. Where'd you go?"

"Look, we have all the time in the world for small talk. Later. Now, you have a lot of worried people looking for you. Heal yourself."

"How long was I out for?"

"I will answer that once you heal yourself. *Now!*"

I was still in a lot of pain. It was—disconnected now, though; I'd gone through the pain and somehow emerged on the other side, and it didn't seem real any longer. But it was still there, raging around and through my body. I reached through the relic and, this time, gleefully dove in to the pool of magic energy that I desperately sought. I turned it on myself, used it. I flooded my body with blue light, closing the multiple wounds on my back, ignoring the momentary shock as I realized how many times my uncle had stabbed me, and forcing my lungs and heart and brain to all speak to one another again. Soon I was rewarded to feel my heart beating at a regular pace. Then I set about numbing the pain. I wasn't quite as successful at that, since I had no idea how pain worked, but by pressing cool air against my skin and running the pressure up and down like a massager I was able to soothe it a bit.

I rose.

I was whole.

I was alive.

Then, I was angry.

Who can I eat?

You remember Grigor, my dad's uncle? I sent her a mental picture.

Him? Yes. He always seemed slimy to me.

Why didn't you say so?

He was your father's uncle, that's why.

Okay, whatever. Look, find him and bring him here if you can. He's a powerful mage, though, so be careful.

Ooh, a powerful mage. How scary. Look, Princess, I used to eat powerful elf mages for breakfast.

Queen, now.

Queen, Princess, whatever. If you weren't my familiar, you'd still be lunch.

I love you too.

Whatever. Quiet, so I can hunt.

Hush, you.

Whatever.

I had to get out, so I took a step. It was hard, but I managed. My anger served as fuel; I wanted to see Grigor run through. I had to live to see that, which meant I had to get out of the hallway. I pushed one foot forward and nearly toppled over as a result. Luckily the wall was close, and I used it to steady myself.

I took another step. I didn't fall that time, either, so I figured I was getting better.

Another step took me further toward the outside. I was getting there.

Another step, and the pins and needles, I noticed, were almost gone.

I smiled what was probably a feral, scary grin, and then I took another step.

Finally, after what seemed like hours, I pushed the door out into the main corridor and stepped out. My timing was perfect; the two priests walking toward me stopped and turned whiter than a pair of hospital sheets. They stammered, and I met their confusion with my best smile. I'm pretty sure it came across as a sneer, because both of them suddenly looked very scared, too.

"Your—Your Highness—Majesty—" one of them managed to connect. "You—you look—you look dead."

I stopped and looked down at myself. My clothes were soaked in dried blood. My hair felt matted to my head, probably similarly soaked and congealed. My skin was still whiter than theirs, and my veins were a deep blue.

I did look dead.

I had to work up enough spit to speak, but I was angry enough to manage.

"Well, I was. Dead, that is. I was dead. But now I am not," I announced, and then thought about the predicament I was in. There was simply no way I could find the strength to make it down the hall to the castle, much less up the stairs to my room for a bath.

"But I need your help. Can you help get me back to the castle?"

With that, both men sprang to action, each of them taking me by the arm and lifting me just enough to take the weight off of my feet. They walked, half running, still managing to appear solemn, down toward the castle, carrying me gently toward safety. One of them yelled something, his head turned backward, and suddenly four other priests darted past us, each looking at me with horrified eyes as they ran toward the castle doors.

The doors swung open, loud footsteps becoming clearer on the other side. Suddenly Dad was there, holding me, and Gwyn, Seph, and Master Owain stood by his side. Keion ran up, and his eyes filled with tears when he saw what I looked like.

"We—we thought you were gone," Dad finally got out. I realized that he was holding himself upright only through great effort. He was silently sobbing, tears rolling down his face.

"I was."

BRADWR

A traitor.

Manhunt

"What happened to you?" Dad asked urgently. His impatience was understandable, given the two hours I'd forced them to wait while I took a luxurious bath. I deserved it, I figured. Not only had I literally come back from the dead, I'd done so while covered in my own blood and slime. The mirror in the bathing chamber agreed with the priests; I really did look dead, still. My eyes were sunken, my skin pulled taut and whiter than a sheet. After the rush of tingling agony, regular feeling was slowly coming back all over, and I found the only way to sooth it was by soaking in a long, hot bath. I managed to scrub all the blood away, and by the time a lady showed up with my robe my fingers looked ridged and soaked. But I was happy, because the mirror confirmed that I'd regained a lot of color. My hair looked okay, too.

The bath didn't take the whole two hours, of course. Little Treebeard was beside himself and it took some time to calm the sapling down. He'd been unhappy that I hadn't spent any time with him recently, but when he'd sensed me go away—who knew a tree could sense that, right?—he'd been frantic. It took me a while to calm him down, singing quietly and softly, and only then was I able to slip behind the changing screen to put my clothes on.

So, finally, two hours later, we were back in the throne room. Dad insisted that I sit in the queen's throne, and Keion looked moody as always but nodded, accepting the fact that I was taking his mother's seat. Sternyface, instead of her typical perch behind and between the thrones, stood to my front and peered into my face, as though she could somehow unravel the whole mystery by reading it there. Gwyn, Master Owain, and Seph were there as well, and everybody looked like they were about ready to go rip somebody apart, starting with Grigor but probably not ending there. They were *mad*.

Meanwhile, I shoveled food into my face as rapidly as I could between comments. I felt completely, utterly starved, totally emp-ty inside, like my belly button had bounced off of my spine and then just kept bouncing. They'd refused to let me have "heavy food," but the cheese and apples and other fruit were delicious.

"Well, I believed Grigor when he told me I shouldn't take Gwyn with me to see the queen's body," I said, and then told the rest of the tale.

Sternyface shook her head at the part about the chamber. When I was done with the whole tale, she said, "That chamber has not been used in years. It was built to be our safe space, hon-estly—somewhere to make a final stand if we need to, my priests and any of the king's guards remaining, all back to back and de-fending the rulers, but there is no conceivable—well, there has been no conceivable situation when that could be important. Now, though, I wonder. So Grigor—"

Dad interrupted. "So Grigor admitted to killing Aerona and Arianna?"

"Yes, he did."

"And he has escaped the castle."

The statement wasn't really a question. Everybody present just shrugged, since nobody really knew the answer. But the best assumption was that yes, the Cult leader's job completed, he would have run away in fear of his own life once Dad got hold of him, and I said so.

"I will send a force—a strong force—out after him. He will not escape."

"Dad, be careful. I didn't see him work any magic directly, but he must be very powerful to have accomplished what he's done so far. You'll only be sending men out to their death. I've already got Kluzhka looking for him from the sky. Let's let her do her thing, since she brags so much about her particular ability in hunting elves."

"If Grigor knows the secrets of the other realm as you describe," Gwyn said, "then he will know how to avoid a wyvern's hunt, and he will also know to expect one. Unfortunately, I also do not believe your forces will be likely to find him, Your Majesty. Believe it or not, there are a great many ways to hide in the woods, some of them in plain sight. Gaia's people have been doing it for centuries, and so we would be better suited to hunt for the villain."

"I—no." Dad argued, but I shook my head.

"Father – Cadfael, Gwyn is correct. We need to bring the other elves into this. We need their help. They have powers that we do not even understand yet, thanks to our centuries-old taboo on practicing and learning magic. They are best suited to hunt Grigor down, and to face him when they find him. But," I waggled a finger at Gwyn, "they must know not to kill him, even if he tries to resist. *I* want to be the one to do that."

I admit, that was bluster. I'd killed men in battle, to be sure, but I doubted I could slay a guy who wasn't battling against me. Still, it felt good to say.

Keion saw right through it. "With all due respect, Alyssa—Talaith, I apologize. Your Majesty, I do not believe you have the darkness within your soul to run another elf through," he said. He shot me a wistful smile. His gesture was one of friendship, at least, and I nodded in return.

Still, I argued. "But this one has already run me though."

"Yes. Yes, he did. And—no, Talaith. I have seen you in action, and I have seen you in reaction. You are much too kind at heart—a wondrous thing, only not in this case—to be the one to punish Grigor, nor any other elf, for his sins."

"I suspect you may be correct, Keion, but still I demand the right to try it and find out. He will die, one way or another, for his crimes."

"That, I believe we all agree with. But on that matter, how goes your wyvern's hunt?"

"Let me check."

How's the hunt going?

Wonderfully, if by wonderfully I am really saying that this elf is obviously one slippery devil. He also got a very big head start, though.

How long was I out?

I lost contact with you early yesterday.

Yester.... A day! How—well, never mind. I will seek counsel with the priests later on the matter of life and bodies and so forth. You keep doing what you're doing, and remember not to kill the guy when you catch him.

That's the fun part, though. She sent me what I hoped was an imagined scene of her talons ripping an elf in two, the blood landing on her welcoming tongue.

Can I at least get an arm or a leg as a trophy?

No!

I had to ask.

I know. And I almost said yes, given what he's done. But don't do it. I just claimed that as my right as queen and—well, as the murdered one. Sort of murdered, anyway. Mostly murdered, let's say. Oh, and don't be too surprised if dark-skinned elves start helping you look.

I will not be surprised if they look for him also, but I would be very surprised if one of them ever tried to help me do anything.

Fair enough. Good hunting.

You, too.

"Your wyvern said something that shocked you?" Gwyn asked.

"Was I really out for a full day?"

"It appears you were out for a full day, plus some. Yes. But you said that—Draignerthol?—the voice you heard claimed it had to wait for the poison to leave. Have you heard any more from this voice?"

"No. I've tried. He's not answering me any more. I don't—it's not something I can understand yet."

Sternyface said, "None of us do. This is quite a strange story. But yes, you were apparently gone from us for more than a day, which tells me that I need to have your physical form looked over closely, Talaith. It is good to see you sitting here talking to us, but who knows what lingering effects await the coming days?"

"Fine," I said, nodding. I had no idea what being looked over closely would entail, but it couldn't be worse than that moment when every muscle and inch of my skin had awoken. "So, Gwyn, you'll get your people to look for him, and I'll keep Kluzhka on it, and Dad, your forces need to remain close by here in case we have any other—dangers."

"Agreed," Dad said, and beamed a smile my way. "Alyssa—Talaith—it is good...."

"Yes, it is," I interrupted. I needed sleep, and my father was the one person I felt comfortable, queen gig or no, being slightly rude to in order to make my point. "Sorry. Look, I need to finish this food, and then I need to get some rest. I'm about to collapse right here, to be honest. And then, tomorrow, I'll head out to get Glynis's support."

"You'll what?" several voices objected at the same time.

I glanced around into the sea of startled expressions, and then shrugged as I put another bite into my mouth. Figuring nobody would overcome their shock in the seconds it took me to chew, I luxuriated in the taste. Finally, I swallowed and nodded. "You heard me. I'm going to visit Glynis."

Everybody shook their heads, and several voices fought to register the firmest objection to my newly announced plan.

"She has responded so far by whipping—"

"She is firmly against you, specifically—"

"The south is as close to at war with us as it—"

"You can't risk the queen's crown once again in a—"

That's a really stupid idea, Kluzhka injected. *But bold. I like it. If you're going to go down, you might as well—*

Hush, you.

"I can risk, and I will risk. I must risk, in fact," I stated, raising my voice's volume to the grandest I could do right then. The room fell silent, faces expectant while everybody waited for me to explain myself and my clearly insane idea.

I breathed in deeply, then launched into the explanation. "So, she disagreed with me, right? Or did she? I believe, based on what I saw in her body language and her glances, that she was following Swadda. She's still following Swadda's lead, in fact. Have we received our emissary back from the great western clan?" I glared at Dad till he nodded. Yes, he explained we'd received an identical response. I nodded and continued, "So, we know there's a danger there, a dragon about to eat somebody else. We know that we have to bind together to face such a fearsome beast. Who better to deliver that message than me, considering all that has happened?"

"A company of your father's armed men, is who better than you. Highness. Majesty, rather," Keion inserted, his voice urgent. Keion's slip of the honorific didn't make me mad, but Dad's fervent nod did. "You have, indeed, faced death many times, more than any young ruler has a right to. You've died, in fact. The realm is just plain lucky, blessed beyond our belief, that you have returned alive. You have no right to risk yourself once again in a senseless manner."

I had to take a short breath to calm myself, but then plowed ahead in response. "I have every right, Prince. More than that, the last lesson your mother imparted to me was that of duty, and I have that duty in this case. Look, I didn't ask to be Dragon Queen, but that is the mantle I must wear. I didn't ask to be opposed by the elves of the east, the west, and the south, yet that is the reality I face. I didn't ask to be hunted, stalked by a creature from all of our worst nightmares, but the creature is there, and we must face him. Together, as one. East is gone, but—"

"Well, not entirely gone," Dad interrupted.

I turned and glared.

He held up his hands to ward off my anger. "There is more than one settlement to the east, just as with every clan. Nowhere had the same concentration of population, yet in your absence nearly ten thousand elves—refugees, now—have arrived and sworn allegiance anew. More arrive hourly. Your place is with me, helping settle these now-homeless clansmen in."

I nodded. "That is good news, and I agree that my place is here beside you. After I convince Glynis of the need to join us. No, Father," I quickly over-spoke his objection, "You know I am right. I can see it in your eyes that you do, that I am the best hope for convincing her, and once she is convinced, I believe Swadda will follow. We must bring our people back together, or we will all be eaten by a dragon. It is that simple."

"You're not going alone," Keion stated, arms crossed over his chest.

"I go too," Seph stated in a voice that allowed no counter.

"Of course, the trio shall ride again," I agreed.

"Trio?" Gwyn asked, his eyebrows arching. He shot a meaningful glare toward Keion.

"Um…quartet, then. Aerona never did forgive me for taking off for the library without her, and she'd haunt me if I did the same to you now."

If you gather too many, I may have trouble carrying you.

We'll ride horses.

Smelly beasts, and not very good to eat, either.

Hush, you.

Yeeesssss, "Your Majesty."

I ignored the insult and returned to the conversation to my front. Dad was still shaking his head, as was Sternyface.

"You know I have to do this."

He shrugged and finally let out a long, deep breath. "Fine. I also know that you will refuse the two thousand guards I would put at your back."

"Glynis won't even let me in to her city if I bring your guards along."

"The elves of the south do not have a city, at least, not one that would be recognized by that term," the Lady of the Bedchamber's voice broke in from the side. Keion and Seph jumped, but I was pleased to note that my spidey-senses had actually worked that time. She continued, "I see that Talaith and I have a fair amount of discussion ahead of us regarding the customs of our southern brethren, and if she and her—companions—are as intent to depart at first light as I suspect, we should begin soon. If Your Majesty agrees?"

Dad nodded, as did I, and the group broke up. I grabbed the plate in front of me, intending to continue eating on it in the sanctity of my room, but Meredydd hissed. She took it, instead, and handed it to a maid who suddenly appeared at her side, who nodded and darted away.

"Queen Talaith will find her plate awaits her in her room. She cannot be seen carrying a plate of food through the castle," she reprimanded me quietly once everyone else was out of earshot.

"Queen Talaith is starving and doesn't really give a darn—oh, whatever," I grumbled. It went against my basic constitution to be served, but I had to admit I probably couldn't successfully carry a plate up two flights of stairs in my present weakened condition anyway. I staggered off on legs that still weren't the steadiest.

LLUDDEDIG

Exhausted.

As in, 'I felt exhausted just learning that word.'

Second languages aren't fun, even when they're technically your first language.

In Search Of Allies

I rose the next day still feeling completely drained. The Lady's lessons had lasted well into the dark hours, and then L.T. didn't want me to leave him again, even just to go across the floor to the bed, at least not until we'd had some good—um, tree-to-human time. Was it one-on-one time? I'm not sure how we got there, but my times with L.T. had expanded greatly. He could—he can talk. What started so many months ago with me holding one-way sing-song conversations, mostly with myself, was now a full-on communing experience.

He couldn't talk, talk, of course.

Still, it felt almost as vivid. All I had to do was put my hand down onto the soil in his pot. Just as I had with the great trees of the forest, that physical connection allowed me to connect directly to my little elm friend. He couldn't directly commune with the forest outside, since his soil and their soil were not connected, but the group sense still somehow ran through, weaker though it was. After the first couple of awkward connections I'd been able to release myself into the trees' world of consciousness, a strange spiritual map of energy that Little Treebeard led me frolicking merri- ly through.

In that world he could speak, and I could reply. It wasn't vo- cal, but the thoughts were there.

Yes, I was talking to a tree.

After hours listening to the lady lecture, the exhausted me had let him drag me about the ragged woods that seemed an aw- ful lot like the northern region. It was more fun, he—well, he "said." After a while, though, I had to stop him and ask to be shown the south, with its huge rain forest and high canopy, and he obliged.

Every so often we'd run across an elf in the tree- consciousness. He explained that these were the rangers, the ten- ders of the forest, always busy connecting to and singing spots of soil and plants into shape and beauty. They were there, solid, but they never seemed to notice me.

I asked if we could explore the tree-consciousness to find where Grigor had escaped to, but he said no. Sort of, anyway; at least, there was a strong "no" feeling. I asked for an explanation and received a string of images showing that unless someone worked a particular type of magic spell, one that directly impact- ed nearby trees, their presence wouldn't register in the tree world at all. Ah, well; it would have been nice to pick him out and find him, but I let that manhunt, and the feral pleasure I knew it would bring, slip from my mind for the moment. Besides, I was sure Kluzhka and Dad's troops could find him quicker than I could, and I was also sure that Dad's troops would handle him much more humanely than I would when they found him.

Kluzhka, I wasn't sure about, but I knew she'd let me see when she found him, and I could guide her from there.

Well, probably.

As time crept along we frolicked among towering trees, L.T. showing me through a massive swath of rain forest to the south. I tried to ask how closely what we were seeing mirrored the real forest, but there wasn't any way to form that sort of question across the bond we used. Instead, I just relaxed and enjoyed the frolicking.

After a time—I have no idea how long—I realized how raggedly exhausted I was and begged to return to the physical world and my own bed. L.T. grudgingly agreed, but not before explaining to me that I could make the same connection from wherever I went. Further, he explained, he *hoped* I would make that same connection from wherever I went. In fact, he downright *expected* it, which is really strange to say of a tree no matter how enlivened that tree has become. Now that we could commune that way, he made me understand, he'd be content to sit, alone, in the room with me away on my dangerous mission.

But only if I agreed to visit him regularly in this way, he argued, and the little form that I saw as him in the strange not-place that we shared stamped its little foot petulantly. It was so cute.

I went to sleep that night giggling over the time Dad had to send a contingent of troops galloping northward to bring a thrashing L.T. to me so that peace would return to the upper halls of Cysegredig once again.

The next morning, I was both exhausted and more than a little afraid that the expedition I was setting off on would prove, at best, a wild goose chase, and at worst might get my friends and me killed. It's one thing, I realized, to think and speak of duty in the abstract, but when you're about to set off on a thousand mile journey that might end in your own death, and a second death at that, you—well, you pause a little. At least, I paused.

Breakfast was eaten silently. Dad and Sternyface both joined us in the pre-dawn quiet of the dining area, but other than occasional breaths there just weren't any noises. Even Booboo remained behind Seph, watching us all eat from his crouch on the floor.

I had no idea at that point how much I'd yearn, later, to return to that slightly grumpy version of silent communion.

A few minutes later, though, I gained a reason to start suspecting. As the party walked out the front doors of the castle and down the steps that represented the official start of our journey, we ran into a much-too-cheerful tower of female elf, and her cheerful dog, too.

"Hi, Gwenda!" Seph greeted her old childhood friend. I grumbled something in an attempt to cheerfully greet the strange girl, but Keion and Gwyn didn't even try.

"Princess! No, Your Majesty now, isn't it?" the tall one began warming up. "I'm so sorry to hear about your mother, Prince Keion, though I am honored to be in your presence now, and that of the newly named Talaith herself. Can you believe that I thought I was the Dragon Queen? All based on a silly birth mark that I thought I had. But I'm glad and honored to answer the call to accompany you—oopsie."

Her voice, so terribly bright and cheery in the comfortable morning gloom, trilled upward through an annoyingly pitched scale to break like a pixie's as she tumbled to the ground mid-curtsy.

"I don't—wait, accompany us?" I asked, realizing what I'd heard. "Why would you—"

"Who invited you to accompany us *anywhere*?" Keion cut me off, shooting directly for the target.

Seph finished helping her friend back to her feet, stepped back, and sighed.

"I, um—" Gwenda stammered. Keion's glare could throw off some powerful heat when he wanted it to, and even in the darkness we could all feel it.

"Who invited you?" he growled.

"The king did. Well, not him in person. His brother came by last night and asked if I would come. He said he had received a message. Oh, Your Majesty!" she called out, seeing my father's tall figure standing against the door frame. "Was that message wrong? Am I not wanted here?"

Dad chuckled, eliciting more early-morning glares from our party. He came down the stairs and raised his hands in supplication. "That message was not wrong. I did ask my brother to send someone he felt best to join the party."

"Why?" Keion asked, steel in his voice. I wasn't sure if it was the early morning hour or the recent demise of his mother that made the prince so bold as to verbally assault the king, but if Dad felt the same way, he didn't show it. He smiled opened his mouth to reply, but Sternyface followed him down the steps and finished the conversation in a voice that matched Keion's steel for steel.

"Because the prophecy says so, that is why."

"The prophecy says so...." Keion repeated. It was too dark to see, but I swear I could hear his eyes roll upward.

"Yes. It is the prophecy which has been guiding us this far," she retorted.

"Wait—you knew that the prophecy said we would be making this journey?"

The prince's tone was disrespectful, but Sternyface ignored it.

"We found reference after the conversation, and after some research and reflection determined that was what it meant."

"Research and...reflection. Fine. And that prophecy says we have to journey with her?"

"Not her, specifically, but where it speaks of a journey southward it has five companions, not four. I would have figured you might desire the highest chances of success."

Keion's darkened head swiveled my direction. "And you didn't know about this?"

I shrugged, his tone putting me on the defensive. "I haven't read the entirety of it yet."

"Why not? It's—about *you*."

"It's mostly about me, yes, but there are other parts. But it's also written in ancient Elvish, Keion. In high poetic meter, at that. When's the last time you had to read ancient Elvish poetry?"

"Fine. Can we not find anybody else?"

Seph turned to object, fists going to her hips, but I stepped in. "No. Keion, it's fine. Gwenda and I and Seph have all spent some time together, and so we have—familiarity. She is who my uncle picked, so it is she who will go with us."

Keion snorted and stormed away toward the horses that had been brought around for us, nearly walking directly into a large shaggy shadow in his anger.

"What—is this?" he demanded, the growl from the dire wolf making the answer to his question pretty obvious.

"Cuddles is my pet, Prince Keion. He is usually very well behaved. I will make him stop growling directly, I promise. But—"

"Cuddles is—your pet. A dire wolf. Your pet. A dire wolf as a *pet*. Ranger, did you know of this?"

"I did know of it, Prince," Seph replied, her voice halfway between defensive and humored. She was obviously enjoying Keion's discomfiture.

"I—it—urgh," the Prince said, the last coming out as a guttural growl as he spun around the massive canine and resumed the trip. "Just keep the thing out of my sights, okay?"

"Yes, Prince Keion!" Gwenda cheerfully replied, and then turned toward me. "Thank you so much for sticking up for me, Princess—Queen, that is. I am so sorry, I do not have the niceties of court down yet. I was given so little time to prepare. I just barely even had time to pack. I don't mean that as a complaint, of course! But what you see in this old leather bag is all I could bring for this journey, and—"

"Fine. Just shut up," I growled at her. I felt bad for saying it almost immediately, and added into the injured silence, "Please? Look, it's much too early in the morning to speak so much, after all. Let's just get ourselves onto horses and get going."

Getting ourselves onto horses proved difficult in her case. She was so tall that they had to work to find her a horse that fit. Once they did, the poor beast nearly bolted under Cuddles's vicious glare. Then there was the matter of her shoes; she was still wearing the strange red platforms that Seph once told me were her affectation at thinking she was the chosen Dragon Queen.

But I didn't ask. No, sirree, I wasn't going to go there.

Once we finally got mounted, with the sun starting to peek over the horizon, we set off to the south. This time there wasn't a company of king's men galloping alongside to see us off, like we'd had on our trip north. It wasn't a ceremonial trip; we all knew the mission and the stakes that lay ahead of us. Once we all managed to tune Gwenda's incessant chattering out, it was even sort of pleasant.

As usual, we ate lunch on horseback, stuffing cheese and sausage into our mouths as the horses plodded along at their slow, steady pace. We stopped to rest them briefly a few times, but none of us felt like we had much time to waste. Without a word each time—without any but Gwenda's words, I should say—we waited till the horses stopped sweating, picked ourselves back up, and took off once again.

As the sun dipped to the horizon we stopped at the first ranger cabin I'd seen in a while. As before, this one had a couple of comfortable beds and cots inside plus a wood stove and a table, all sturdy and only the slightest bit decorative if you looked at them in a rustic sort of way. Seph cooked a pot of what I'd taken to calling ranger stew, using the herbs she'd learned about from Master Owain, and everybody ate happily.

Mostly to stop Gwenda's line of banter, Keion and I started in on our best probable strategy against a dragon. Neither of us knew much about the topic, but he knew more than anybody else in the party about strategy and I knew more than anybody else in the party about dragons, so it was close.

"It's too bad we don't have machine guns," I mused after a particularly perplexing series of observations about more things that probably wouldn't work against Xlixi.

"I was just dreaming about that last night," Keion said with a nod. "Not about having machine guns to face the dragon; that's a bad idea for a couple of reasons. But something about the coming martial conflict made me recall what it felt like when I was studying tactics on Earth, learning to be a machine gunner and a rifleman because those are the foundation of the Earth-based military forces. Shooting a machine gun isn't at all like you probably think it is, you know."

I didn't know, but I didn't care much, either. Gwenda apparently did, though.

"No, Prince Keion, I did not know that. Why is it not like what we probably think it is?" she fawned, showing off by pantomiming rapid-fire from something—a bow, maybe, that looked nothing like a machine gun.

He shot me a glance of triumph before turning to his newest fan and explaining, "Well, when you watch a machine gun being shot, you see and hear only *thug-thug-thug-thug*, like that," he demonstrated with one of the fire sticks, holding it pointed toward an imaginary enemy and miming the repetitive recoil of the gun. Gwenda nodded and changed her own pantomime to match. "But when you're shooting it, you actually feel and hear the mechanisms within it working. First the cartridge is shoved into the chamber, and then the firing pin causes it to explode. The reaction to the bullet suddenly flying forward sends the bolt backward on its rails, and then it catches another bullet cartridge by the casing and shoves that one forward into the chamber. The constant movement inside, the back and forth, feels like it's coming alive."

"It sounds magical," Gwenda murmured, earning her a snort from Gwyn.

"It's not magical. Far from it," my elf protector said.

"No, not magical," Keion agreed. "But powerful. Too powerful, in fact."

"Too powerful? Is that why they would be a bad idea?" Gwenda asked.

Keion nodded solemnly. "That's part of it. That's a big part of it, in fact. With much of the magical weaponry we developed here in Kiirajanna in our war era, and most of what was developed entirely without magic across the ley gates on Earth, it is possible—easy, in fact—to kill an elf without ever having seen him."

"That's barbaric," Gwyn intoned.

Keion nodded agreement. "Barbaric, and worse. It leads to societal desensitization towards killing. Wars on Earth are no longer clashes between mighty foes, but rather people playing dispassionate games on video screens, destroying armies with no real care that what they're actually killing is real people."

"But even with it being barbaric," I argued, "this is a *dragon* that is attacking our people. My people. I don't care if it's barbaric if we save elf lives in doing so."

"But that's the other part of the problem. It wouldn't save elf lives. It wouldn't even do any good, I suspect," Keion said, then his face curled up into a satisfied expression when my cousin nodded agreement.

"Alyssa," she started, and then corrected herself. "Talaith—"

"Can we stick with Alyssa, please? At least when it's just us?"

She shook her head vigorously, and again she and the prince shocked me by agreeing on something. "No, we can't. You have already shattered enough traditions; why not follow this one for once? It's not like we are bowing and scraping, at least not here. But you are now queen, and that means that you are now Talaith."

I glared at them both for a long moment before shrugging. "Fine. Go on. The dragon?"

"We saw what you did with the shield around your wyvern friend, Aly—Talaith. You remember that, when you surrounded her with a magical sphere that projectiles, our arrows, could not enter?"

"Of course."

"So what is a machine gun bullet, except a faster projectile than the arrow?"

I thought for a moment and then nodded. "Good point."

"You've already admitted that we have no idea how powerful a dragon is or may be in the arcane, other than your wyvern's assurance that he is extremely powerful. I would imagine you could probably bring any number of guns, no matter how large, over from Earth and have no impact on the final battle."

"Well, that's terrific. So, arrows are out, whether fired from a bow or from a—machine—arrow—whatever. And you're probably going to have some trouble as a swordsman against a dragon, Keion. What's left in our tremendous arsenal? Big rocks, maybe? Do we need to go get some attack helicopters to fly through the ley gates?"

"My people," Gwyn observed quietly.

Keion surprised me yet again by nodding a slow, quiet agreement. "Yes," he breathed with a deep sigh of acquiescence. "I know it is uncomfortable for some to discuss such an option, but the magic of the dark elves is truly our best hope. A score of thousands of arrows do as little damage as a single against a monster that can shield such, but if the score of thousands of magic users join together, it might break down the shield."

"There aren't a score of thousands of us, though."

"How many are there?"

"I—I do not know."

"So, three thousand, four hundred, and thirty-two, to pick a round number out of the air. Plus Aly—Talaith, darn it, now you have me making the same error, Ranger—plus Talaith and her mighty magical relic. That's almost a score of thousands, you must admit."

"I must admit, yes," I muttered around a yawn, which everyone else took as cue to rise and work on bedding down for the night. Luckily there were three beds in the cabin, one long enough that Gwenda actually managed to curl up a little and fit into. The boys took a minute to figure out protective watches and spells and then headed out toward their pup tent.

SARFF

Serpent or wyrm. Not the same as neidr, or snake. Seems like I've pointed out this word before, but this particular wyrm keeps inserting himself into my story.

Face To Face

The next day started calmly enough. We rose, mostly cheerfully. Even Prince Charming, once he made it inside from the tent that he and Gwyn had shared, managed to smile a little over the steaming cups of coffee. Gwenda gave us what was becoming a normal dose of her incessant chatter, but nobody seemed to mind.

"The Fellowship of the Ring seems happy this morning," I observed, wishing in spite of my own cleverness that we actually had something resembling a hobbit along with us. It would have been cute, if nothing else.

"What?" Gwyn asked, his eyebrows knitting in confusion. Keion shot me the same look, though I noticed that the two vats of testosterone were still not making eye contact with one another. Unless they were talking about machine guns and other killing things, that is. It made me wonder what the night together in the fairly small tent had been like.

"Nothing. Earth reference."

"She makes those all the time," Seph confided.

He nodded.

"It is raining," Keion observed drily.

"It will rain throughout the day, and quite heavily," Seph added her own ranger twist to the cutting cheerfulness of the conversation.

Everyone else smiled, nodded their pleasure, and continued sipping.

The elves are—strange. In many ways, granted, but when you look at their reaction to rain, they're particularly strange. In Mississippi, such a forecast would have sent gloom around the table. I'm pretty sure it would have done the same in just about any other location on Earth. Rain! No, not rain! On Kiirajanna, though, rain was something to be cherished, to enjoy. For one thing, elves didn't dress in fancy fabric that could be ruined by getting wet. Elf clothing, particularly travel garb, was sturdy and actually a little more comfortable, not less, when damp. For another, it gave the rangers something extra to do as they tended to the surge in growth afterwards. A third reason was that elves pride themselves on moving through nature silently, and it's much easier to do that in rainy or even just wet conditions than in dry ones.

But mostly, the elves just liked the rain for the change it brought from the sunshine. It didn't rain very often, and so when it did they celebrated.

Maybe it was more accurate, I reasoned silently over my own coffee, to say that the humans are—strange. But that was too much philosophy for my poor head to ponder the first thing in the morning.

As we climbed into our saddles, in fact, the only one of us who didn't beam up into the rain was Booboo. The powerful wolverine hissed, glared up at Seph, shook its fur resolutely, and then trotted off into the woods, wolverine head held high if to say its point was well enough made. Seph grinned, shrugged, and followed her familiar.

In what was probably only an hour, though it seemed longer thanks to the incessant commentary by Gwenda, we reached the portal that led to the southern part of the continent.

We'd argued about the plans from there, a little. I knew that Xlixi could pervert the portals as he had during my hunhymgais. In fact, only the extent of his power was still up to question, not the fact that he had power by the bushel full. Kluzhka was solidly against us taking the portal; she knew her former master's power much better than we did. Still, it was easily a two week ride without, and since we didn't really have two weeks to spare we'd all agreed that we had to chance it.

Luckily it went off without a hitch. I followed Seph and Keion through, stepping into a wondrously tropical landscape. The dense forest I'd heard about was still up ahead by several long hours, but the ferns and the moss combined with an almost visibly shimmering heat told me all I needed to know about how far south we'd come.

It kind of reminded me of summer back home—in Mississippi, that is.

The wet, cheerful rain from the north was gone, but the air was full of water anyway. The humidity blanketed my shoulders and my chest, forcing me to actually think about the process of breathing for a little while.

Ugh, humidity.

I missed Mississippi, but not that much, it turned out.

We gathered, sent Booboo and Seph out ahead, and set off rapidly, grimly aware that we were already in what might be enemy lands and needed to get the mission done and over with one way or another.

We'd only made a few hundred yards when Kluzhka shrieked, her mental voice filling my head.

HE COMES!

I didn't need to ask who she meant; I could sense her terror through the link. There was only one being in the universe I could imagine her reacting that way to. I opened my mouth to warn the others, but a gigantic winged shadow blocked out the sun overhead and made the warning unnecessary.

A little more warning next time would be nice, I was able to send in spite of my own near-panic. I got a response from the wyvern, but it was all a strange freaking-out sort of mental gibberish. At that point even her regular snarkiness would've been better than the terrified senses that flew across our connection.

I suddenly found myself in the center of a tight circle—more of a triangle, honestly. The prince of the realm leapt in front, arrow nocked, and both Gwenda and Gwyn fell in tight behind. I felt Draignerthol buzz and recognized it as a sympathetic acknowledgment of whatever magical aura my protection mage had pulled about us.

I wondered where Seph was. She hadn't been gone long, so I figured she had to be just barely out of sight to our front.

"Guys...." There wasn't much I could tell them, though. I fought down the urge to chuckle at the antics, useless as they were. Keion's arrow couldn't even penetrate Kluzhka's skin, much less that of the massive dragon that was landing just ahead of us. I had no idea what Gwenda expected to accomplish with her long dagger, either. And while I couldn't tell what Gwyn was trying to do with magic, it was pretty obvious that nothing was coming of it.

I wanted to reach up to take Draignerthol. I also wanted to raise my own bow and take aim at the evil beast's heart. But I knew, deep in my core, that all I could accomplish in that activity would be just as useless as what my companions were doing. Instead, I just sat there waiting, calming myself and my horse as much as possible.

Xlixi settled his bulk onto the ground and folded gleaming red wings about a wide, muscled torso. He looked even bigger than I remembered from the last time I'd been face-to-snout with the monster. His long neck snaked toward us, his face somehow featuring a wicked smile in spite of all the scales.

"Keion, no," I warned the prince. I'd fought by his side for long enough that I recognized the subtle tightening of his neck and fingers leading up to his release of an arrow.

He heard, and he stopped, but he turned his head to glare at me.

I just shook my own head slightly. "No sense losing a perfectly good arrow."

"Ahhhhh," the dragon's deep, rolling voice filled the area. "Your Highness—no, Majesty, now, if my agent tells me the truth—has wisdom beyond her meager years. Oh, and I do apologize for that unfortunate poisoned dagger business. Killing you was never, has never been my intent, and my agent has been suitably punished for his disobedience."

"Grigor? Punished?" Keion demanded, his voice harsh and tight.

"Yessssss, Grigor was his name, wasn't it? He was—tasssssssty. Don't look so disappointed, my dear. All my subjects who go against my bidding must meet that fate. But my fair queen, I must suggest that you would do well to advise your underlings in how to address your overlord."

"Underlings!" Keion objected, his face flushing.

"Boo," the dragon said, and I sensed his magical power washing over us. Instantly Keion and his stallion tried to flee in two different directions. Luckily the horse feared the prince just a little more than it feared the dragon, because it only took a moment of struggle before it gave in to his command, wheeled to the right, and fled the scene.

Sounds from behind told me Gwyn wasn't as well off. His horse's hooves thundered one direction, while I could hear his footfalls sprinting away in terror in another.

I'd felt his terror spell before, and learned to resist it all on my own, so I just smiled at the beast. Then I noticed a flicker of surprise, the slightest raising of his armored brow, as he and I both noticed Gwenda step forward with a dagger in hand and a glare on her face.

Scared as I was even without the terror spell's effects, though, I couldn't keep the image of the rows of charred corpses out of my mind, or the memory of the smell either.

"Overlord? I have no overlord."

"Nooo, not yet. So, are you prepared to make that oath of fealty yet, my queen?" the dragon said, his voice smooth and inviting.

"No. You killed my people."

"Did I?" The beast actually managed to sound coy, which just made me angrier.

"Yes, you massive monster. I was there. I saw the rows of corpses. Men, women, and children. Don't you try to deny it."

"Deny it? As though your fleshy little approval means something to me? No, no, I admit, I was there. I was hungry, you see, and I wanted to eat, as all creatures do. Only, when I arrived, they did the unthinkable—they fought me. What a pity it was, burning all of those elves just to get one small morsel to eat. You know, my queen, you could have prevented that. One tiny oath, and you can rule as you wish. I will do no harm to you or to your companions. Your people will come to know me as the overlord and will not attack, and so I will have no need to burn so many. You could have prevented that disaster, and one oath now can prevent any—regretful mishaps—in the future."

"So you're saying it was my fault."

"Well, in a way, yes. Now that you mention it, I suppose that I am. How clever of you to reach that conclusion for yourself, I must say. And you can prevent further mistakes on your part, you know. All you need to do is swear fealty to me. It will take almost no time, and then you can be on your way. I promise I will spare your friend there, and her little dog, too."

A memory of when I'd heard that line in a movie flashed through my mind and I almost laughed over the mental image it brought. Forcing the image, and the associated and very out of place humor, out of my head, I shook my head. "No. I will not swear fealty to a monster like you."

"Such a pity. Is she one of your good friends, or just a member of your entourage?"

"Just go away," I ordered. It was useless, but there wasn't anything else I could think of to say that would have been less useless. I wasn't about to give Xlixi any knowledge he didn't already have, no matter whether he ate Gwenda or not.

"Mmmm," he said, clearly considering the idea. His long, hot tongue snaked out toward her, but it quickly recoiled with a slash across its tip, the dragon's blood dripping from her dagger.

The dragon took another moment to eye us both thoughtfully. He ignored the dire wolf and its low, angry growl; I doubted the mighty windbag would stoop to eat dog flesh anyway. Finally the massive head nodded.

"I—will do as you request. For now. In my absence, my queen, you would be wise to reconsider your stance. How many of your elf friends must die in dragon fire before you recognize the truth in my words, I wonder? Swear fealty to me, and I promise eons of peace and prosperity for this land."

"Punctuated by occasional dragon snacking on my people? No."

"It is nothing more than the circle of life. Do reconsider. I will give you—a while. But I will return, and expect your oath then."

"Go away."

Apparently my order was the funniest thing he'd heard in a while. As his wings whipped out and pulled his body into the air, a booming belly laugh filled the clearing. One mighty push sent him up, and another started him moving, and then he disappeared, taking his evil-sounding laugh with him.

"Well, that was—" Gwenda started.

"How did—" I started.

Prince Charming galloped in, long black locks streaming and furious expression set. Gwenda and I both stopped talking and looked, her with undisguised admiration over the swirlingly visible testosterone and me with a fair amount of concern over the inner turmoil I could read through his masked features.

Seph and Booboo raced across the clearing toward us, and Gwyn loped in on foot. He gave a short whistle, the sound amplified by a touch of magical energy, and within moments his horse cantered back toward the silent party as well.

"Well—"

"How did—"

"That was—"

I return.

Thanks. Coward.

Well, that stings. You wouldn't want the high king to control me into doing something bad, would you?

I'm kidding. We all survived.

I am not certain how. Your weapons are as feeble as your brains.

Hush, you.

Fine. I'll just be over here if you need me. Human.

"Is Kluzhka okay?" Keion asked. He'd been the only one to not launch into the tumultuous commentary moments before, and I could tell that his own personal anger still welled up inside him. He was dealing with it as he knew how, by trying to read me, to protect me.

His presence combined with the fiery countenance he presented cut through and quieted the other jabber.

"She is fine. Thank you for asking."

"She didn't come to your defense," he said, his voice making it into a question on the reason behind her apparent failure.

I explained what I knew of a dragon's ability to control a wyvern as easily as he caused fear in elves, but when the prince's face darkened at the mention of the fear I diverted the topic quickly.

"How did you fight down the magical terror, Gwenda?"

"I never felt any magical terror," she explained with a shrug.

"How?" three of us asked, and Seph added, "I even felt it to the point that I fled, too, and I wasn't anywhere near you. How did you not even feel that?"

"Interesting," Gwyn mused. He was the only one who hadn't asked her how, and now he edged closer to the girl. He reached toward her, fingertips brushing the air less than an inch from her body. "Forgive me, but stay still for a moment, please. I need to test something," he added. I could see the blue energy tendril reach out toward her—to tickle? To smack? But whatever his purpose, it failed. The blue energy just wouldn't come close to her. He moved his hand over, tried again, and repeated, "Interesting."

Gwenda watched Gwyn's hand closely, her eyes not appearing to see the blue tendril of power.

"What are you doing?" she asked. "What's interesting?"

"Your—body. It—repels...." Gwyn kept studying her, turning his attention to her clothes. "Are you wearing any jewelry?"

"Do I look like I am wearing any jewelry?" she asked, insulted. Elves outside of royalty didn't wear much jewelry in any case, and even royalty only wore bangles while in the castle.

Keion broke the mood. "Look, you two can figure that part out later. We just came in contact with a dragon, and now we need to get to Glynis to report that and also to finish our mission." He wheeled his horse back around and launched into a trot.

As we fell obediently in line behind the prince, Gwyn moved up beside me.

"How did you avoid the dragon's fear spell, Alyssa? Don't tell me you didn't sense it."

I shrugged. "I just did. The first time I came into audience with His Royal Halitosis he tried the fear spell trick on me. It hit hard but then I pushed through it. It doesn't seem to affect me now."

"Interesting. Did Draignerthol help?"

"I didn't have Draignerthol at the time. When they took me prisoner they confiscated it. It was in taking it back when I realized how much magic I could do, by myself."

"Fascinating. You must teach me how to 'push through it' as you have."

"I don't know if I can."

"You must. I fear there will come a time when the safety of all of Kiirajanna relies on our ability to defeat that spell."

I shrugged. "Let me think about it. I don't know if I have any idea how, but I'll come up with something."

Gwyn nodded and fell back to his spot behind me in line. The rest of the trip was made in silence, which should have seemed a blessing after Gwenda's incessant chattering.

Then we were captured.

Captured!

We were captured soon after, but there's a correction I have to make first before I tell that story.

The rest of the journey was mostly silent, I should say.

The tylwyth teg, the little faeries of the realm, had been absent the first day of our journey, a fact that surprised me when I noticed it since they'd made themselves known on every other journey I'd taken. It surprised me, also, that I hadn't noticed it yet. I'd been engrossed, I guess, in dealing with Gwenda's outright weirdness combined with the strange glances she and Keion had begun sharing.

After we launched again from our encounter with Big and Smelly, they appeared. It was suddenly, without any warning, as is their normal way. I sensed a little one flying overhead and turned my eyes upward to look at it. The eight inch tall faerie darted sideways and then back several times, apparently looking us over.

"Well, hello there, little folk," I said, and then turned to grin at Gwyn when I realized we'd both said the same thing at the same time.

He looked at me, smiled, and said, "We are blessed with visitors."

The smile was what did it, I suspect. An avalanche of faeries came at us then, each one trying to get closer to either Gwyn or me than the other faeries were. They were all chittering, too, and loudly, in their strange faerie language.

"They recognize you as their queen, though they're abjectly refusing to call you Talaith," Gwyn observed after a few minutes.

"How do you understand them?"

"Alyssa," he said, using my name instead of the queen's traditional one, and it seemed by the emphasis he used to be a matter of deference to the faeries. "My people, those elves you call dark-skinned, revere the tylwyth teg. We commune every chance we get. We speak together and hold council. You didn't know that?"

"I—probably should have guessed," I said, nodding to the deep connection to magic that his people—and, I would argue, my own now—shared. That was a very different attitude from that shared by the other elves, my father's folk, who looked down on the faeries as mischievous troublemakers to be shooed away.

At that moment, Keion reminded me of my father's folk's attitude when he turned around to see what we were talking about, huffed unpleasantly, and turned back to the trail ahead. I giggled, remembering when they'd taunted him by driving a moose directly across his track.

"What's so funny? What's going on?" Gwenda asked.

"The tylwyth teg are here. We're happy for it," I explained.

"The who?" she asked, a confused look spreading across her face.

I lifted my right hand from the reins gently, letting one curious little fellow land on the flattened palm. "These guys. Faeries. Don't you see them?"

"I—um—huh. Yes, my queen." Expression darkening, she spurred her horse ahead toward Keion's, gaining distance from which I barely heard a low-pitched comment about how the queen might have lost her sanity. Keion just shrugged.

"They are overjoyed to see you, now that you have survived your encounter with the great sky-beast," Gwyn interpreted. "But they warn that even greater danger lies ahead. You should dissolve into the woods, join with a clan of the earth people—my people—that resides nearby. Otherwise, they say, your future is dark."

"Any darker than my recent past?"

"I can't say, and neither can they. They're just particularly nervous about it. They're describing a very changed society in the elves of the south. It's much less free-spirited, and now much more warlike. They have armed everyone down there."

"Everyone? Like the elves of Cysegredig, everyone?"

"More so, it sounds, though you would be well advised that the faeries exaggerate nearly everything."

A few seemed to understand elf well enough to stick their tongues out and blow very wet raspberries at Gwyn, who erupted in a belly laugh as a result. Then a couple dozen actually flitted down to grab my horse's mane and bridle, pulling the mare off toward the right.

"Stop it!" I ordered, and they did, though they all pouted.

"I've never seen them so insistent," Gwyn whispered.

"I understand," I raised my voice, trying to reach any who understood our language. "But I have a duty to fulfill, and that duty lies ahead. I know there will be dangers, but as you already saw, I am not without my own abilities to meet those dangers head-on. Thank you—thank you very much indeed—for the warning, but though I will take note of them gratefully, we still must plunge ahead into the darkness, for all the realm's sake."

As one, the whole cloud of faeries physically deflated, shoulders sagging and wings dropping. They stayed aloft, apparently, through magic rather than any sort of aerodynamics, so it was actually fairly spooky when they all just stopped moving like that. As one, they sighed, their reedy-thin voices dropping to a middle key that was probably at the bass end of their range. Then they all vanished.

"Well, that was interesting," Gwyn said.

"I know. I've never seen them demonstrate like that."

"Oh, that was nothing. Regular. Tell one that he can't have a button and you'll get the same response. But they won't grab it and try to take it like they did to your horse. All that said," he continued in a whisper, "did you notice how not only couldn't Gwenda see them, but they apparently didn't notice her, either?"

"No, I—well, that is weird."

"Indeed. We selected a strange traveling companion, it seems."

"I think, technically, she selected us."

"Even stranger."

"Yup."

All conversation stalled and we rode on. An uncomfortably silent hour later we crested a ridge and peered down into a mass of trees, their upper leaves providing a canopy so thick we couldn't see the ground beneath.

"Welcome to the southern clan, Glynis's stronghold," Keion said.

"The way ahead is clear, if a little dark," Seph told us, having ridden back to meet us as we came into sight.

"One would expect darkness under such trees, ranger," Keion chided.

"Not that kind of darkness, Prince," she retorted.

"We didn't come this far to stand here and talk about the dark," I said, silencing them both. "Let's—let's ahead." Yes, it was a very poorly constructed order, grammatically, but I think everybody else was dreading it as much as I and so nobody seemed to notice. Without another word Seph and Keion wheeled their mounts and entered silently, grimly, the pair leading the way. I followed, and Gwyn and Gwenda fell in behind, the latter with her sharp dagger already bared.

Apparently I can queen well enough when I want to.

A hundred yards in, things abruptly changed. The silence of the deep, dark woods was pierced by shrieks and howls, mimicry of animal sounds crafted by elf throats and mouths. A dozen muscled bowmen dropped to the forest floor before us, arrows nocked and ready, and I could sense many more hitting the ground behind and to the sides. Keion and Seph took it stoically, the warrior prince calmly looking around to gauge the force that faced us.

I did what queens do. At least, I did what I guess queens do, there not being any instruction manuals for the job back at the castle to have referred to, and me not being there to refer to them if there were.

I rode forward, as calmly and bravely as I could manage on the outside in spite of the terror that threatened to make me lose the contents of my stomach. I stopped just ahead of the ranger and warrior, sat squarely in my saddle, and looked for an obvious leader. There wasn't one. Instead, I raised my voice and spoke to the group as a whole, praying that voice wouldn't crack out of fear.

"Noble warriors of the south, I come in peace with but a few companions. I seek an audience with Pennaeth Glynis."

They all laughed at that. I took the long moment to glance around and size them up. There wasn't any chance of a fight, and Keion probably already knew that. There were well over a hundred of them, each clearly ready to skewer us with one arrow after another from his full quiver. There really wasn't any chance of us living through it. Each of the closest elves had eyes focused on me, watching my hands closely. Either they'd been at the clearing that day or they'd heard the tales and knew to shoot me before I could reach up and touch Draignerthol. They probably didn't know that I didn't need to touch the relic, but the odds of my getting a shield up in time were pretty low regardless.

Besides, I reminded myself, I hadn't come to fight. War was already upon us; instead, we needed peace.

Somewhere, somehow, we had to have some peace.

"Look. Things have changed. Talaith has died. I am Talaith now. I must speak with Glynis to bring an end to this madness, this hatred. The days of elf versus elf must end. You must take me to speak with Glynis."

Finally, a woman stepped forward through the ranks of archers. It was hard to keep from gasping; she was breathtakingly beautiful with bronze skin covering long, muscled limbs and only a loincloth and some golden bracelets to cover that. She held a couple of handfuls of fabric up.

"We will take you, though where we take you is none of your concern. Be satisfied that we do not put arrows through you here and leave you atop the ridge for the scavengers to eat."

At her sharp gesture, two of the bowmen lowered their bows and took the fabric strips. The pair worked quickly, dismounting and disarming us and then binding our hands together behind with blindfolds over our eyes.

They pushed us ahead at a rapid clip. I couldn't see anything at all, though I was able to reach out and sense that my companions were being pushed along with me, and also that most of the force that had gathered to capture us melted away back into the forest once we were marching.

I lost track of time, though something spurred me to count strides. I had no idea what good it would do once we got wherever we were going, since there was no way to know whether we'd traveled along a straight or a curved line, but at least it gave my sensory-deprived brain something to do.

At eleven thousand, five hundred and thirty-two, we stopped. By that point I was hoping and praying to have the binding removed from my head. I was crushed when I felt a rope being tied around my chest instead.

"Do not raise your arms," was the command, and then the ropes pulled upward.

It's terrifying, dangling when you can't see how high you are or what you're dangling over, but I managed to remain calm. Hey, at least they tied the rope around my chest and not my neck. It hurt, a little, especially in the armpits, but fact was, I was glad I was still breathing.

Finally a hand grabbed my arm and pulled me sideways. The tension in the rope released, and then the rope itself was untied. My feet on a solid surface was a heavenly feeling.

Then we were pushed to march again, only now I couldn't sense anybody else. I could feel them, someone's hands on my shoulders, and I could hear the breathing and noises of movement nearby.

The comforting sensation of others being present was just plain gone. I knew they were there, logically, but something in that was missing. A whole branch of sensory input was no longer there.

Then the ground began moving, wiggling up and down, and I froze. That delighted my captors, who laughed loudly at my expense. I was able to fight down the anger, though, by focusing on what I could learn. It was one data point, at least, as I counted half a dozen different voices laughing.

Another strong push kept me moving. A few more steps and the noises of ropes creaking helped me realize that I was on one of those rope-hung board walks, the kind you see in the movies stretched out across a canyon or between two treetops, the kind that bounces up and down with every step and usually has that one special board the hero's leg crashes through at just the right, scariest, moment.

Luckily the bridge didn't have that one board. I guess, anyway. At least, I didn't step on one. I don't know what I would have done, blinded as I was, if it had, and besides, I wasn't that kind of hero. I didn't feel like any kind of hero at all, to be honest. But soon enough the terror ebbed and the jostling ended as we stepped onto what was obviously a platform.

With a whole lot less ceremony that I would have expected, the blindfolds were ripped away, our arms were untied, and our well-armed captors filed out and closed the cell door behind them, leaving a couple of wickedly-grinning guards outside. Each flexed massive chest and arm muscles at us in a nearly-naked display of bronze-skinned testosterone, and then each unsheathed and displayed long, sharp swords.

"I need to see Glynis," I ordered.

The two guards ignored my statement and continued their posturing. I repeated the command, and earned the same non-result, and then I joined my companions in taking stock of what we had.

We were weaponless. We were horseless. We were at least two hundred feet up in the air, housed in a cell with thick wooden floor and ceiling and iron bars that wrapped around a massive tree trunk. On the other hand, we had pillows and blankets, a table full of fruits, breads, and cheeses, and what was obviously intended to be porta-potty sort of buckets.

"All I need now is a few good books and a dragon to visit every other day, and I'll feel like I'm back at home," I mused.

Nobody seemed to find that funny, though, as everybody plopped down onto blankets and sat glumly.

Can you hear me?

Of course, Princess.

I'm queen, Kluzhka.

Whatever. You're still prey to my kind, so remember that next time you go poking around dangerous areas.

Yeah, yeah. That's me, just a-pokin' around everywhere. Hey, can you tell where I am?

More or less.

Where am I, then?

In a tree.

Well, that's helpful.

I suppose you will bless my heart now? I don't know how to give you any directional information that is more helpful. You are in a tree, high above the ground, deep in the forest.

Could you get to me if I needed you to?

Well—that's—it's complicated.

Complicated? It's just trees.

Have you ever seen what a tree limb can do to a wyvern's wing? There are thousands there, and I couldn't see where I'm going to safely teleport in, either. And how would I fight off all those other little prey-beasts while my wings are broken?

So—no. We're on our own.

Oh, I wouldn't say that. I can get to you, yes. It will be difficult and fraught with danger, but you know me—difficult and danger are my core being.

Smart aleck is your core being, Kluzhka.

I believe you are looking into a mirror, Princess.

Queen.

Whatever.

Hush, you.

"Is Kluzhka on her way?" Gwyn whispered. I came to, realizing he'd been watching my face closely again.

"It's—complicated, she says."

"We're on our own, then."

"Pretty much, exactly what I said. But I feel confident that we'll succeed."

"You don't lie very well, my queen."

"So what good news do you have, then?"

"If Kluzhka would have a hard time getting to us, so would the dragon."

"I suspect he'd just burn his way in."

"Oh. Well—no, then. I don't have any more good news than you do." He sat back and crossed his arms against his chest.

I looked around at the crew I'd brought. Everyone was withdrawn into themselves, faces brooding. Keion's countenance was as dark as I'd ever seen it, and Seph's matched. Even normally-cheerful Gwenda, who I'd heard utter muffled "oopsie!" comments over and over during the hooded walk, sat staring down at her own hands.

If there was anything to be gained by acting the part of queen at that moment, I didn't see it. Instead, I resolved myself to wait with my fellow prisoners.

An Audience

We didn't have to wait very long, which was a good thing considering Keion's angry temperament.

As the temperature dipped and the shadowy darkness under the thick canopy of the trees grew even more oppressive, the animal-like hoots and cries of the people suddenly started up again. We all rose. The two showboys, who'd settled into easy crouches outside the cell door, leaped up and started prancing and dancing again. This time, though, their show wasn't for us, but rather for the intensely beautiful woman striding down the bridge toward us.

It was Glynis, only I'd not seen her in her native garb. Amazonian came immediately to mind, but she eclipsed that. Like the four women with her, she wore only a waist wrap-around and sandals for clothing, her bare, bronzed breasts openly displayed. Also like the four women, she wore several golden bracelets around both wrists. Unlike the women, she wore a golden circlet woven into her dark, wavy hair.

A single horizontal black streak was painted on her left cheek. That, according to the Lady's briefing, wasn't necessarily a good thing, but it wasn't bad either. If she were coming to deliver a death sentence, both cheeks would be streaked. It was related to some sort of vision thing, but I couldn't for the life of me remember what I'd been told about it as the cell door opened and she and her four handmaidens stepped in.

I looked down at her right hand. It held a charcoal pen at the ready. Apparently I had but one moment, one attempt to win her over. If I failed, she would finish the paint job and end our journey in a way I didn't want to imagine.

The thought flashed through my mind that it might be all for show. She wouldn't, couldn't, dare to kill the queen, particularly when I'd come unarmed with a small and clearly non-hostile party of companions. It would result in all-out war, and thousands—tens or even hundreds of thousands—of elves would die. The alternative she must have thought of on her way here was to hear me out, at least talk to me, and if nothing else release me back to find my own way home.

Then again, considering her expression and those of her ladies in waiting, if it was a bluff, it was a good one.

Relax, I told myself. It was all an act. It had to be all an act. I had a crucial part to play, but it wasn't an impossible one. The Lady and I had rehearsed. The penalty of failure would very likely be death, but the reward for success was—well, it was just how it had to be, as Momma would've told me if she'd been there.

Besides, I reminded myself, I was, in fact, the queen.

I stepped forward, careful to act assertive enough to suggest my queen status, yet also careful to avoid displaying any challenge to her authority in her own home. Instead, I slowly walked over to her, eyes directly meeting eyes. I reached out with my right hand and saw no reaction in either her or her stoic followers. My hand came to rest on her bare chest, just above her heart, in what I'd been told they would recognize as a show of utmost respect and caring.

Somberly, with as much intensity as I could press into my own voice, I intoned, *"Gadewch i mi fwyta eich cachu."*

My own party reacted immediately. Seph and Gwyn both gasped, and in spite of all his martial discipline I actually heard a quiet *"eww"* from Keion. The loudest, a panicked gurgling sound, came from Gwenda's throat off behind to my left.

From Glynis's group, though, there was nothing. Not an eye muscle flickered as the sound of my voice trailed off along with those of my companions. The silence stretched, filling one long moment and then the next, as I waited to see whether success or death awaited me.

Finally Glynis herself broke the stillness, reaching back to hand the charcoal to one of her followers. She smiled then, a careful, measured smile, and inclined her head almost enough to be a fully respectful gesture.

She said one word.

"Frenhines."

I breathed for what seemed the first time in forever.

Frenhines.

Queen.

I'd done it.

The icy rigidity of the faces of the ladies with her melted slightly. None of them smiled, just as I did not dare to smile. But they relaxed, and the mood lightened.

Gwenda fainted, her super-tall frame tumbling to the cushion below with a muffled thud.

Glynis glanced over, and then returned her gaze to my face. "You should see to your people. I will have more food and drink brought. Then you and I, we need to speak. Privately. I will send someone to guide you, later."

She turned and left, women following single-file. The massive bronzed supermen at our door left, too, without bothering to close the door. Within a few minutes a couple of smaller, more adequately clothed men brought our weapons and laid them neatly on the floor, bowing deeply before they left.

Keion roused Gwenda fairly quickly. She smiled and whispered, "Oopsie."

"What in the heavens and earth above and below and the forest about was that?" Seph demanded, using an elf idiom I hadn't actually heard anybody use before, one that I'd heard was reserved for the most intense shock possible.

I shrugged, trying not to grin at her seething discomfort. "A greeting."

"No! No, it most certainly was not a greeting," Keion argued. "Greetings are cheerful 'hi, how are you,' or respectful 'hello' or even sometimes, more appropriately for this time, a somber 'it is good to see you even under these circumstances' sorts of things," he said, demonstrating the appropriate hand gestures for each of them. "That is what I recall my sisters and me teaching you not that long ago, is it not? I do recall, yes? And so *that*, what you said, was *not* a greeting. It was...."

"Vile," Gwyn finished when the prince seemed to run out of steam. "But then again, Prince Keion, none of us has ever been down in the south to know their ways."

"I have," the prince objected, but I shook my head.

"You were very young, were you not?"

He nodded, shrugging the point to me.

Gwyn accused, "You had some...prior discussions with Meredydd, didn't you, Talaith?"

I finally let the triumphant smile my success was due creep across my face. I nodded and admitted, "I did. She explained the greeting I must use in order to gain their trust and fellowship, and I used it. Of course, I have no desire to—"

"To eat her feces? No, I'd hope not," Keion, expression still disgusted and more than a little outraged, finished.

"It's just an idiom, Keion. A signal. Offering to eat someone's poop down here is a statement that you will do anything, no matter how disgusting, for that person."

"Nice job, but just be glad she didn't actually have any for you to test yourself with," Sephaline shot in, earning chuckles throughout and lightening the mood.

"Oh, I am. Though I'm not sure what I'm in for when she has me led to her private meeting chamber."

Gwyn stroked his chin and mused, "You have to admit, eating poop is still better than being skewered and hung to die."

"No," Keion objected. "No, mage, I have to admit no such thing."

I looked over at him, keeping the glance meaningfully sideways. "I wonder whether my father would admit such a thing. I'll have to ask him when we return."

Keion's face colored at the implication, and he sulked by turning his attention to rubbing Gwenda's bare feet, now that she'd taken them out of the ridiculous shoes she wore.

"Are you feeling better?" he asked gently.

"I am, thank you. Much better. The mental image—"

"Forget that. We're all right now, and we'll get home soon enough."

Seph and I exchanged glances. She seemed almost as disgusted by the prince's attitude as she'd been by my greeting. Luckily the moment was broken by the arrival of two more men with trays of food. I realized how empty my stomach was when they uncovered a hearty pork roast and vegetables that filled the cell we were in with delicious aromas.

We ate, a somber silence filling the cell. We'd succeeded, so far, but none of us knew what lay in our future.

Stomachs full, we sat quietly once again, each deeply immersed in a moody pool of our own thoughts.

Finally a younger, very bouncy elf girl walked to the entrance of our little prison-away-from-home. She looked like a maiden-in-waiting trainee, with a single white cloth wraparound that left her bosom bare, and a conspicuous lack of bracelets. Even her sandals were fairly plain, with only a single wrap instead of the long, winding wrapping that Glynis had worn up to her knees.

"Glynis would like to see you now, Talaith," she said informally. I waved off Keion's objection before it began. Meredydd had been very clear that the elves of the south didn't stand on any sort of formalities. While the clan that lived in the northern reaches of the continent embodied a patriarchy where strength and vitality, generally of men, was revered and elevated, in the south it was the exact opposite. Men, she'd explained, were just the line warriors—the massed archers we'd been taken prisoner by—always commanded by a woman. The women, meanwhile, were always highly trained in both hand-to-hand and sword fighting, and so while the south rarely if ever competed well in the summer games of strength, nobody else on the continent had ever or was likely to ever mess with them in a military battle.

Among the men, rank was a matter of brawn, and the two doing the Mister Universe show outside our cell earlier were just making it clear that they were fairly high ranking and thus deserving of guard duty over VIPs. Among the women, rank was worn in gold on the wrists and, in the supreme example, upon the brow.

I followed the girl, who would not have a name until she earned her first bracelet, silently down wooden rope bridge after wooden rope bridge. Platforms were interconnected in a dazzling array that stretched farther than my eyes, which had finally grown accustomed to the darkness under the canopy, could see. On some nearby trees I counted a dozen platforms, the first only ten feet or so from the ground and the topmost wedged into the highest branches. Most platforms contained residences with the same sort of gaily painted doors and window shutters I'd seen in ground-based villages around Cysegredig. There were others as well, though I couldn't say what most of those were used for.

A few elves walked the bridges out and about, but not nearly as many as I'd expect in such a large gathering of homes. I asked my guide where everyone was.

She simply shrugged and said, "Home."

We finally approached what was obviously Glynis's residence. It was the biggest one I'd seen, for one thing, and it was the structure in the precise middle of the tree. Meredydd had explained that the elves of the south liked to envision their city as a three dimensional project, which meant that the highest ranking would be right in the middle, not just in the cardinal directions but also vertically.

We entered through a rainbow-striped door. The first room looked like a more rustic version of Dad's throne room. My throne room, now, a jab of memory scolded me, but I managed to ignore it. Glynis's audience chamber was empty, though, and so I followed the little girl off to the left. She held back a curtain, and I walked in to see the leader of the southern clan seated at a round table.

"Thank you," she said simply, and the girl nodded and let the curtain fall. Footsteps told of her departure from the home.

"So, Talaith," the woman started, steepling her hands in a perplexed gesture. "What an interesting situation we now face. You seek my help. I seek yours. I am not certain the two are aligned, but I am willing to speak them over. Still, our situation calls for some...privacy."

I nodded. "Go on."

"You have shown great courage, and an equal amount of wisdom, for one so young. No, really, I mean that, Talaith. Now is not the time for false modesty or for—what is that Earth idiom? Buttering you up? Such a strange set of linguistic oddities you bring with you from that other world. But I begin to sound like Swadda, with her meandering words that writhe like the snakes she cherishes and yet never quite make it to the point. I am not Swadda, so let me get to it. Word has reached my people of the massacre of our cousins to the east. I assure you, we have our own defenses here, and strong ones, some of which you have already observed, but yet my people have become...scared. That fear...changes things. A little. None but I believed you earlier when you spoke of a dragon, and you faced revolt as a result, but now all believe, and all fear. All want you to bring about an end to that fear."

Something small she said caught my attention. "None but you? You believed?"

She nodded. "I did."

"You sure seemed averse to mentioning that back then."

She shrugged, so I pressed my objection.

"Were you afraid of the reaction?"

A snort was her first response, followed by, "Talaith, as I already spoke once, I deeply respect your courage and your wisdom. And yet I am nearly three times your age. Do not attempt to goad me with words when we are in such pressing need of peace."

I did the math and looked more closely at her body, which was boldly displayed. At nearly sixty, she was impressively well toned and preserved.

She caught my eyes and apparently read my thoughts from my face. She smiled. "Our priestesses are particularly strong in physical preservation healings. But I shall take your question at face value and respond directly. No, I was not afraid of the reaction. I am the leader of this clan, and were I to have told them my own knowledge in regards to dragon lore they would have followed me. They would have spoken of their own belief, even, though most would not likely have been entirely sincere in those assertions. The other clan leaders might or might not have followed me, as their own choices determined. But to maintain my own clan's standing among the others, I cannot speak of our secret."

"Your—your clan's secret. What—wait, no. I guess if you told me, it wouldn't be a secret, right?"

She shrugged. "The queen should know. Your predecessor did. It cheers me that, if she confided in Meredydd, that confidence was not then passed along to you, nearly as much as the shock at our traditional greeting in your companions' faces brought me joy. I saw, in that moment, that the south has a true ally in you."

"It would have been difficult to have prepared them for that, you have to admit."

"I do. I do indeed. Say, would you like some tea? Your predecessor had a taste, and even an intricate royal process, for it. Sad as I was to hear of her passing, that is one tradition that I should hope to see continued."

"Murdered," I stated as I watched her pour a cup of tea for my side of the table.

"Right. She was murdered. As, rumor holds, were you. Which is the other side of the point to which we must reach in this conversation, by the way. So, to get to it, I must start with pointing out that the secret of the southern clan is that our leader always comes from a select group of librarians."

"Librarians?" I let my shock show on my face, and she smiled broadly in response.

"So, that means.... There's a library here?"

"Yes. There is indeed. The platform just above this houses the collection, in fact. We are proud to host nearly as many works here as were contained in Alecsanddrha."

"That place," I said. The name of the library I'd burned down still stung.

"Was huge," she finished, missing my point in her desire to get the conversation moving along its desired path. "Yes, but we have nearly as many works, including some wonderful scholarly debate about the nature of the prophecy, as well as the nature of that pendant you brought back with you."

"Draignerthol."

"Yes, if we must state the obvious."

"So—you're a librarian, a sage, not a warrior."

"Yes, that is true."

"And that is why your status is a secret. The other, more war-like, clans would not respect you if they knew where you'd come from."

She sighed and tried to cover it with a belated sip of tea. "Yes. That is the truth. Our army is a match for any of theirs, I believe, and yet in a battle of leadership personality, we must maintain our own advantage."

"So why do you follow Swadda?"

"I do not follow Swadda." She looked like she wanted to throw her cup at me for suggesting it.

"Of course you do not," I said, squelching my immediate thought of direct apology. "I should not have suggested that."

She stared at me with an unreadable expression for several long moments. Then she allowed a grim smile and a mild chuckle. "You are wise, and quite smart, also, for one of your young age. And still you do not yet know what it is that you do not yet know. I could use one such as you as queen, if I desired. Others certainly do desire. But I—I do not. I had a desire, desires, once, but you should know that the arrival of the prophesied dragon changes that. Now, I truly only want you to be successful so that my people, and all of Kiirajanna, may live. We should drink to your success."

She moved to signal for something, probably a stronger, more adult beverage than tea, but I shook my head and held my hand out.

"Let's wait till we have that success, and then we can all drink to it."

She nodded. "Wisely and well spoken. Though I am certain that you can best the dragon, as you clearly did in that strange land of his. With, what did you call them, skyscrapers?"

I nodded. "It was a mock-up of my native world, actually. The dragon was trying to find a way to breed elves more efficiently, and realized there was no better model than New York City on Earth."

"Breed?" Glynis looked disgusted at the term.

"Pretty much. He and his massive entourage of wyverns needed to eat, and apparently they find elf flesh the tastiest. The one friend I made there seemed to fear 'public service' the most out of everything, to the point where she fled to live on the streets as what they call a 'zhopi,' or outcast. Then, when they picked us both up for 'public service,' they didn't bother hiding what that actually meant."

"And so that is what he wants to establish here? An elf city for breeding?"

"I think he's more interested in a hunting ground, honestly. His wyverns, particularly the one I bonded with, are bored with elves bred for them to eat. They cherish the hunt. The dragon goes out once a week or so, in fact, and does that in his own realm. Apparently he wants to extend his hunting grounds to encompass Kiirajanna as well."

"So why did he need your fealty? That was what you said he was after, right? Why not just eat you first among the elves?"

"To be honest, that's the central issue I have. I've been wondering that, as has Kluzhka."

"Kluzhka? That's her name? It sounds so—harsh. Guttural."

"Their whole language is. Luckily I had Draignerthol to translate, most of the time. But yes, wyverns are actually self-named, and quite intelligent creatures, to the point where she keeps insisting that I, not she, am the creature. She compares their love for elf meat with our enjoyment of the flesh of the pig."

"That's fair enough, I suppose. We've known, in our lore, that wyverns are incredibly intelligent, but they tend to avoid us as carefully as we avoid them. I wonder if, for the sake of knowledge, you'd let me communicate with your Kluzhka once the—the situation in front of us is resolved."

"Sure, I guess. I mean, I'm certain she'll have something to say on it, but I don't see why she'd have reason to object. We'll see."

She nodded. A curious expression crept across her face as though she were just thinking of something, and she asked, "By the way, where was Draignerthol when you were being held and questioned in this New York City skyscraper?"

"Taken from me."

"Taken? Against your will?" I saw her eyes narrow slightly, and I started wondering where the line of questioning was going.

"Not entirely. I didn't have much will at the time. They'd shot me up with a knockout drug, and when I woke up the pendant was gone."

"That is interesting," she mused, a little too thoughtfully for my security.

"Why is it interesting?"

Apparently I failed at keeping my suspicions from my face, because she quickly raised her hands in a peaceful, reassuring gesture. "No, I mean you no harm, and have already given you my word. You are my queen. I do not bend my knees to swear fealty except for the one public celebration that is tradition, but you have as much loyalty at this point as you ever will from me. It is just that—your pendant is treated in a manuscript in our library. In several, to be truthful, but one in particular goes into significant detail. It is not a major treatise, particularly since we all believed the relic lost, never to return. Now that it has returned, though, I am—curious."

She took a deep breath, then asked, "Has it ever—spoken to you?"

I sat back, wondering how much to reveal to the woman. She was presenting herself as an apparent ally, a vassal even, but I'd been lied to more than once already. It wasn't that long ago she'd been beside the others calling for my head. Still, I didn't see how the revelation could hurt, and besides, I hoped she might have something useful for me in return.

I nodded. "Yes. When I lay dying, a strange voice ordered me to get up and heal myself. It later revealed itself to be the voice of the pendant, though that is the only time I have interacted with it. What do you know of it?"

She shrugged. "Not much beyond what you have just said, unfortunately. But I wonder if further inference cannot be made. You said the dragon demanded your fealty. My rangers have given me to believe that the dragon visited you just to the north of our clan-home. If I may ask, my queen, what did he demand upon that visit?"

"The same as before. My fealty."

"Your fealty. Just yours," she said, the statement forming a question at its end.

"Yes, but I would presume he includes the remainder of the elves in that, as you all—wait, no. As far as his agents will have told him, none but the northern elves follow me. But no, he wouldn't have attacked the east without a motive to drive south and west into a mutual protection pact, much as you and I are discussing. Would he?"

"You were kept in a cell block in the skyscraper, yes?"

"Yes, with Xlixi at its top."

"You got Draignerthol back." This time her statement was just a statement.

"Yes. Well, no, I didn't just get the pendant back. I took it back, when we escaped."

"You took it back—from where?"

"The wall, behind the wyvern guard on the floor I was kept. It was hanging on a hook."

"On a hook, where you could see it and know where it was."

"Yes. I see what you are thinking. Yes, Kluzhka and I have already talked about it being a setup, several times. We just can't figure out why."

"May I—may I try something? A little test of a theory that may be forming in my head? Would you loan me Draignerthol for just a moment?"

"I—I guess—so?" I didn't want to. I hadn't been physically separated from the relic since the night I'd returned from Pazhbojanna. But I sort of wanted to trust her, I needed to trust her, and besides, I was pretty certain I could pull Draignerthol back magically if I needed to, Then I realized that if I couldn't pull the pendant back magically, there wasn't any point resisting anyway.

I removed the pendant's chain from my neck, laid it on the table, and pushed it toward her. With an expression of reverent awe, she reached out and pulled it the rest of the way.

"Now, to test my theory I need for you to mentally declare me an enemy, Talaith. Tell Draignerthol to resist me." She reached out with her own weak tendril of blue magical force, as I shaped my mind around the image she'd requested.

Draignerthol lay inert on the table. Even the eye socket gem refused to glow.

That wasn't the only surprising thing, though. Far from it. I was too busy holding my jaw in place where it needed to be to say much about the experiment at hand.

"You can do magic," I accused.

"I am a librarian, Talaith. All librarians are given special abilities to preserve books. You have successfully, I believe, argued that those abilities are the same as magic, and I have no desire to debate the matter tonight. But that power was actually what I was trying to use on the pendant: a simple anti-yellowing effort. He—refused."

"He?" She'd given it a personal pronoun, and that confused me more.

She nodded, pushing the ancient relic back toward me. "The one piece I had not yet told you, Talaith, is that in the lore it speaks of Draignerthol not as a pendant, but as the physical encapsulation of a sentient being. We do not know who, or what, or when, or for that matter why, but that is what is in the words."

"Oh. Oh, wow. A—oh. A sentient being, in a pendant?" The implications of that smashed all about me. Could I continue wearing it, using it—no, using him—knowing it was a being? How would he feel about it? Did I care? Should I?

Remembering who I was in front of, I shoved all that back in my head and physically straightened myself up. "So, that is the first I have considered the matter. I shall consider it further."

"That is not the point I was after, Talaith," she said, shaking her head but still smiling. "Draignerthol has a choice, an ability, of his own, and yet he has chosen to obey and, in a manner, to bind himself to you. Again, for what and how and why and how long we do not know, but it might be that the pendant answers only to one person, and that one person is you."

She waited for me to nod before continuing, "And so—were you to swear fealty to the dragon, what would your pendant do?"

"That's—that's what he's after, isn't it?"

She nodded, smiling gently and laying out her hands across the table. "Maybe. Probably. Yes. We cannot say for certain what mysteries lurk inside a dragon's mind, but I believe that we might have hit upon the core issue."

"So—but that doesn't help us defend against the dragon's next attack."

"Not directly, no. Still, it is said that understanding your enemy's motives are the first step toward his defeat."

"Who said that?"

She smiled, mysteriously this time. "That knowledge is to be found in the library, Talaith."

I shrugged. "I would love to spend some time researching that and other questions here, Glynis, but I think I need to go see Swadda soon."

She nodded. "Wise, and brave, you are, my young queen. Yes, I agree with your assessment of the need. Go with speed and safety, Talaith. I will send my own banner, and with it some of the south's top strategists, to join your council at Cysegredig in the morning."

I couldn't help the relieved sigh, but by her expression she understood.

"That is—wonderful news. Don't take the portals, though. We believe that Xlixi—the dragon—controls them, or at least knows when they are being used, and we don't—"

She nodded again. "Yes, that is of course how he managed to bring you to his skyscraper world, and I suspect that he revealed himself to you soon after you passed through the portal, yourself."

I nodded.

"We shall avoid their use, then. The dragon may guess as to the success of your visit, but there is no need to tell him directly."

"He has agents. My father's uncle was one, but only one. Beware of your own ranks."

"I shall."

I nodded and rose. "Thank you for your company and your conversation tonight, and for your warriors in the upcoming battle."

The little girl who had led me from the cell was waiting just outside the door, and she led me back to my companions. Keion was dozing, while Seph and Gwenda were chatting at the table.

Gwyn leaped up from his seat, but the strange tall girl we'd brought along beat him to greet me as I entered.

With a strange smile, Gwenda placed her hand on my chest. "I would like to eat your poop, Queen Talaith."

Her sincerity brought a huge smile to my face and a bark of laughter to my throat. "That—that won't be necessary, but thank you. And just to be completely open and honest, let's not use that greeting ever again, okay? Nobody needs to be eating anybody else's—well, you know."

Keion, Seph, and Gwyn, who'd all stopped and clapped their hands over their faces in horror, got over their revulsion quickly and joined me at the table, where I filled them in on everything I'd learned.

"Swadda next?" Keion asked, his face radiating displeasure at the idea.

"Nope. Actually, a good night's sleep next, and then we visit Swadda of the Serpent Veils after."

CACHU

Literally, poop, as in feces.

I'm sort of ashamed to put this into my story, but it does fit.

To The West

I got braver the next morning.

I'm not talking about combat bravery, or standing-nose-to-nose-with-a-dragon bravery either for that matter. I'm talking about doing-something-weird-in-front-of-friends bravery, which is, in my opinion, probably the bravest bravery of all.

I missed L.T. Since I'd figured out how to communicate with him through his tree friends, I could always connect. I'd managed to slip away the first night on the trail, in fact, and sidle up to a tree, reach out, and chat—or at least do what amounts to chatting—with my good buddy elm sapling. But I awoke the next morning, still up in our massive treehouse, tree cell, or whatever you wish to call it, missing him and wanting to chat. But I had two problems.

The first problem was that everybody else was already awake and up. The other problem was that I didn't know how to reach the ground to escape their vision.

And then it hit me—I had no need to care about their opinions. I was, after all, the queen, and if I wanted to communicate with my tree friend back home, well then by goodness I was just going to do it.

I walked to the middle and wrapped myself as far as my arms would stretch about the tree trunk. It wasn't far; even up here the trunk was about ten feet in diameter. If I remembered my math right, it would have taken about six and a half of me to stretch around the tree fully.

See? Who said we'd never use math in real life?

But it was a moot point. I didn't need to go all the way around. I just needed contact.

Everybody else was a little busy, anyway. Somehow Booboo had made it up during the night, carried no doubt by the southern elves as a gift to Seph, and she and Gwyn were discussing ranger magic and familiars. They'd brought the dire wolf as well, and that beast surprised me as it sat calmly beside the prince and nuzzled him. Keion and Gwenda had a weird conversation going that sounded like neither of them wanted to talk about anything important but both of them still wanted to keep talking. You know, the sort of conversation that has a "the leaves are beautiful up here," comment followed by "yes, I wonder how long it takes to reach the ground when they fall," and so on.

And then I hugged the tree, and talk stopped.

Keion gave me a weird look and a "What are you doing?" query that I ignored.

Gwenda just stared, joined in that by the ranger and mage.

As energy flowed from me into the tree and then down to the earth beneath, I heard Seph's intake of breath. She recognized what I was up to, of course; it was, after all, ranger magic. Gwyn, meanwhile, let out a meaningful hum and relaxed into his pillow.

Little Treebeard was, as usual, excited to hear from me. He was so excited, in fact, that he danced. That's strange to consider, a potted plant dancing, but in the thought-cloud, trees don't look like trees. L.T. looked like a little boy. I'm not certain whether he chose to mimic my blonde, spiky hair, or I created it for him in my own mind, but he ended up looking a lot like me regardless. And he played! He—his spirit, or his presence in the thought-cloud, or whatever it was—ran toward me when he sensed me calling out and leaped around me, jumping up and down and spinning one direction and then the other.

He finally calmed down, and I was glad to hear that he had very little to report. Dad hadn't visited like he'd promised me he would, but L.T. didn't really care one way or another as long as I showed up here. I told him about our success and he leaped and cavorted once again, picking up on my own happiness and joy. Then I told him about meeting the dragon again and he grew somber. I explained that we needed to head toward the west next, and that while I was going through the desert I wasn't certain I could find a tree to communicate. He told me that during his own travels through the thought-cloud he'd run across many from the west, mostly beings with wet centers and hard, spiny surfaces who were just a bit—slower—than the other trees. I laughed and explained those were cacti, and that the odds of me hugging one were pretty low due to the pain level involved. He seemed to understand, and we broke the connection gently.

"That was—wild," Gwyn said. "An entire conversation through the magic you pushed into the tree and received from it. I could tell, the same way I can tell when you're talking to Kluzhka, but it was—different. Wilder. Stronger. But that makes sense; these trees are amazingly massive."

Seph nodded, shook her head, and then nodded again, bewilderment stretched bleakly across her noggin. "I've never.... I mean, I know you have a familiar, Cousin, and a powerful one at that, but I've—well, I never really thought about you doing the same sorts of things I have spent years—I've been trained to—well, to do them. You—you were talking directly to that little elm, weren't you?"

"Yup," I agreed, proud of myself, and pleased that Seph, our ranger, had recognized why.

"You can talk to trees?" Gwenda asked, awestruck.

"Well, sure, but so can Seph," I argued, Gwenda's awe overwhelming me enough to bring out my usual modesty.

"Not like Talaith can," my cousin countered. "We're lucky to have her along, I'd say."

"Heh. Thanks, y'all. Gotta remind you that I'm the one who brought us in the first place, though. Speaking of, are we ready to go yet?"

"Breakfast?" Gwyn asked hopefully.

"Um," I said, turning toward the cell door, but apparently it had already been thought of. Two young girls, both clad modestly without gold adornment, trooped in and set out a feast of ham, sweet potatoes, and fruit.

As we were finishing, Glynis paid us a personal visit, every ounce as ceremonial as Meredydd had said it would be if we got that far. "Talaith," she said, speaking loudly and forcefully from the door, "I come to bid you farewell and fair journey. May your paths be sure and your missions well-ended." With that, she spun and left.

We left the same way we'd come in, only this time without the bindings and the bags. The warriors guiding us explained, mostly to Keion in that proud voice warriors always seem to adopt when discussing tactical stuff, that to become a warrior they had to learn how to raise and lower themselves via the ropes and pulleys that spaced out everywhere. It had to be that way so that they could map out a three dimensional battle front against any invaders. They didn't make us lower ourselves, though, a fact that pleased me to no end. Booboo got put into a safety cage to be lowered, a fact that pleased him not at all, but the dire wolf was — still — weirdly placid about it. Soon, we were on our way, our horses well cared for and watered and our bags replenished with supplies.

"That was fun," Seph mused as we stopped atop the ridge and looked back over the rainforest we'd just left.

"I want to go back." Keion said.

Gwenda nodded. "I want to dress like them," she said and started to take her top off. We all jumped in quickly, objecting to her plan to go topless into the west.

"You should wait till you get some golden bracelets. Otherwise you'll look like a novice," was Seph's winning comment. Gwenda accepted the logic with a nod and left her shirt on.

So I'm good enough to carry you now, huh, Princess? Kluzhka taunted. We'd discussed the trip, which was a week that we didn't have by horseback. None of us wanted to risk another meeting with Xlixi, though, so we all agreed to let the wyvern fly us. Even Gwenda agreed, once she'd made it clear that she was actually terrified of heights.

"You didn't say anything when we were hoisted onto the bridge," Seph objected.

"I was blindfolded."

"Surely you could feel yourself going up into the air."

"I was a little more scared of dying by arrow right then."

"You didn't object to being so high in the air on the platform."

"I was on a platform. Duh."

"You didn't—oh, never mind." Seph gave up trying to figure out her best friend's fear.

Kluzhka was strong, but she couldn't take us all at once. First she let the prince up onto her back, took off with a wide sweep of her powerful wings, and vanished. We waited a short while, and then with a pop she reappeared and dropped to the ground.

Next.

Did you leave the prince in a comfortable spot?

No, I left him atop a ring of cacti surrounded by a thousand angry elven warriors. What do you think? Yes, of course, and you're next.

She'd already flown Gwyn and me together once, and it made sense for my magical protector to go on the same trip as the one he was guarding, so he climbed onto her back using her rear knee as a step. He reached out his hand to pull me up, but I shook my head. I had a much better idea.

Going for the style of it, I gathered magical energy and then pressed air underneath my feet to levitate comfortably up to that level. Then I allowed him to guide me into a sitting position to his front.

I have to admit, I enjoyed the feeling as his arms shifted me around and then wrapped themselves tightly around my midsection.

Don't enjoy it too much, Princess.

Queen now.

Whatever.

Shut it, you, and stop reading my mind.

Your mind, your breathing, that little soft moan you let go of—not hiding much, there, girl.

Just—just get us there, okay?

As you wish.

Once again she propelled herself upward, the two bodies on her back seeming to make little difference, and with a pop the world vanished away. I felt the familiar lurch inside, and then almost immediately we were back – still? – flying over the world, only—it was a different world entirely. Gone were the grasses, the ferns, and the massive trees. In their place were all sorts of green spiny things, lots of green spiny things, with even more green spiny things in every direction. Some were shaped like barrels, and others like the cacti out of cartoons with arms shooting out and upward. Kluzhka flew down low so that we could get a closer look, her shadow growing huge as she descended. Soon we ripped across the ground, her legs just barely clearing the tops of the cacti.

It was still just late spring, and mid-morning at that, but I could already see heat waves rising from the land. The sun beat down on the top of my head, raising my temperature by what felt like dozens of degrees. It was hot, much hotter than I could remember ever feeling before.

Kluzhka's flight reached a cliff and banked to the left, sailing along and slowing till she reached an overhang area. Prince Charming glanced up from an already-established campfire where he sat polishing his sword.

The wyvern dropped us off without another word, or, more impressively, any more snarky comments, and then left again.

"Your wyvern—Kluzhka, right?—scouted around," the prince explained. "The city is just over there, around the base of this cliff, and will take us a couple of hours to get to once we start. But we're fairly safe here; she didn't even see so much as a snake in the immediate vicinity. I would recommend that we enjoy the shade here through the hottest part of the day, and journey on once the sun diminishes a bit."

"How do you know?"

"How do I know what?"

"That last bit. Can you talk to Kluzhka?"

"Since when do we have to talk in order to communicate?"

"I...guess we don't. It seemed silly, is all."

"Not as silly as us believing we're going to defeat a dragon."

"Ouch," I was stung by the surprise comment. "That's pretty negative, don't you think?"

"Just being realistic. Forget I said it." He turned his gloomy expression back to his blade.

I shrugged and settled down by the fire, staying far enough to not add that heat to the sweltering temperature of the day. Still, the flames were as hypnotic as bonfires always are, and I let my-self drift in thought to their unpredictable rhythms.

Kluzhka dropped off the horses next, carrying them in terri-fied pairs, only taking the time in each flight to send me a fairly disgusting mental image of what she'd prefer to do to the beasts instead of ferrying them across the continent. I replied, each time, with a mental image of elves celebrating a wyvern, which was as close to gratitude as I could manage.

The last flight brought Seph, backed by Gwenda, with a fero-ciously angry Booboo under one claw and a dire wolf under the other. It was funny, actually, to watch the wolverine's reaction once she dropped him to the ground, as the killer beast circled and spat and shrieked out a horrific war cry. Kluzhka, mean-while, landed a few feet away and made a point of ignoring the furball. While Seph and Gwenda climbed down from her back, she whuffed what passed for wyvern laughter.

"Oopsie!" came the predictable cry as Gwenda's feet didn't quite make it to the ground before the girl fell into a sprawling heap upon it. Keion shook his head, grinned, and went over to help her up while the rest of us just smirked.

We settled in to rest while the sun crested. It wasn't all that bad under the shelter of the rock, but I wasn't sure how hot it was getting in the direct sun. To check, I stepped out of the shadow to stand in the sizzling rays, rested for long enough to absorb the real heat of the day, and then skipped quickly back in under the outcropping. It was like going from Momma's skillet to her oven set on broil. I told my party that, and gratefully accepted another water skin that Glynis's crew had filled.

Mentioning Momma brought a knot to my stomach. So much had happened since Dad took me home last Christmas, just a few short months before. My whole outlook on life, on myself, on the crown that was now mine to wear: all changed. My relationship with Seph and Keion: changed. What I could do, with and without

Draignerthol's help, had grown immensely, and yet I was still the same terrified girl under the pendant. Momma, meanwhile, probably had no idea, and I realized that if I died out here in the desert, she'd never really know how or what I was thinking, or even that I was thinking about her.

I didn't have any paper, though. That hadn't seemed like a luxury I needed to pack along with me. Swadda would, probably, and if the pennaeth of the west didn't kill us on sight, I would ask her for some to write home with.

"There's no poop-eating offers to shock us with here, are there?" Seph asked, breaking in on my thoughts.

"Huh? No. That's a particular nuance in the south, and even there it's grown out of favor with all but the highest level interactions. No, for Swadda I brought this," I said, holding up a special water skin and a vial of oil.

"What, are you going to wash her feet?" Keion scoffed.

I glared over at him and responded in kind. "As a matter of fact, yes, I am. Or offer, anyway. How much do *you* know about the traditions of the elves of the west?"

He waved an apology. "Not meaning to insult. I just—I really don't know much about them, I suppose. I await your explanation so that I may learn more about those traditions, my dearest queen."

I shrugged, not sure how much sarcasm he'd intended. It didn't matter much, really. The heat was having an effect on us all. I took a breath to release the irritability that was settling across my own shoulders and set into an explanation. "So this one isn't just the top leadership. When any traveler is met by a leader from the west, the traveler offers to wash the leader's feet. It's like in my own hometown, where when you visit you bring a small gift, only in this case, the gift is water, which is the most precious resource out here. Feet-washing is a luxury and isn't done very often regardless, even in the act of bathing that they typically practice, and at the same time it's a gesture that says we will use our water before we use our host's."

"Well, that makes sense," he nodded. "What about the oil?"

"That's mostly just a gesture of esteem. The oil soaks into the dry skin and feels luxurious. I brought some from Cysegredig that Meredydd gave me, but Glynis provided this vial to use. It's a mixture of palm and coconut, which can only be found in her region, combined with the concentrated sap of a tree that only grows at the border of the west and the south. She explained that it has cleansing properties above and beyond any soaps we might use, and will leave Swadda feeling like her soul is uplifted. By using it, I will be demonstrating to Swadda the bond that Glynis and I now share, making a point that is stronger than the words might."

"Well, okay. Good ideas, then."

"Better than that, actually. When I offer to wash Swadda's feet, that sets off a decision she'll have to make. If she accepts the foot-washing, that is the same as accepting us as guests, in which case she'll be bound by tradition to wash my feet in return. Then the tradition states that no matter what, the guests cannot be harmed while under your roof. Thus, if she accepts my gesture, she'll be bound by tradition not to kill us. Which is pretty important."

"Important, sure. We'll see if it works that smoothly," Keion muttered, earning him dark glares from Seph and Gwyn, while Gwenda just nodded, wide-eyed. "Not that it matters much, I suppose."

"What do you mean by that?"

The prince laid a long, flat glare on me before finally apparently making up his mind to respond. "I mean I don't really think that it matters much, Alyssa. Talaith. Whatever. Whether we're killed by Swadda or eaten by the dragon, we're still dead and will have failed the mission. And I honestly don't see any way to avoid one or the other." Gwyn started to say something, but Keion silenced him with a challenge, "Don't tell me you think you can best that beast, mage. Even I sensed its power, and you must have also. We saw what it did to the elves of the eastern reaches. What sort of fools would we be to think we can defeat that even with the elves of the south, the north, the west, and even your dark brethren all on our sides?"

I let him wind down and then took a deep breath to reply. "Look, Keion, I am—"

They come.

Who comes?

The elves of the west. A caravan just left the city headed your direction.

How many?

More than enough to fill my belly well for weeks.

Kluzhka....

Only if they act violently toward you. I should land.

No, stay aloft. I have no doubt that you can land quickly enough if you need, and the approaching force probably understands that as well.

I would be more comfortable to be standing there when they arrive.

They would not, and that is the point. I am here to make peace, not war. You have to retool your thinking, Kluzhka. You were trained by a dragon. Now, though, you're so much more than a killing machine of a beast.

A beast, you said?

More than, I said.

Kluzhka broke off the connection. I looked up involuntarily, though I doubted I'd be able to see anything.

Keion caught my upturned gaze and interpreted it correctly. "Kluzhka sees something?"

I nodded and told them about the vision she'd relayed to me. "A hundred spears marching in a pretty tight formation. It's led by a—a—I do not know the word. Palanquin, in my native language. You know, a curtained box carried on two poles by four people."

"Swadda?"

"I don't know. Maybe. Probably. I don't imagine anybody else would want to be carried like that for the time it will take them to get here. It seems like good news, anyway."

"As in why would she come along if she were just sending troops to kill us?" Keion asked. "Maybe. Maybe not. She might wish to see you dead with her own eyes, Talaith."

"Thanks for the cheerful thought, Mister Negative."

"It is not my role to cheer you up. It is my role to stand by your side as we face these elves of the west. As such, I merely remind you that we should not let our guards down no matter who comes along."

"Point taken. And as I was about to say earlier when Kluzhka interrupted me, I am one of those fools who believes we can defeat the dragon. We have before."

"Hmmph," he grunted, face set and eyes peering into the distance toward the city.

"We will discuss it more, later. If we survive this encounter, of course." Truth be told, I didn't know what I was going to say to Keion. I felt the same way he did, at least a little. I'd knocked it out of the park with Glynis, but Swadda would be tougher to convince, and even then, I knew Xlixi was going to be nearly impossible to beat.

But I had to try.

There wasn't anybody else if I didn't.

Somebody had to, and that was me. And I needed Keion to be on my side.

We lapsed again into an uneasy silence, reminding me of the previous evening in Glynis's cell. Fate was on its way, and there wasn't anything I could do to influence the outcome until it got here.

That made me even grumpier.

We ate. It was hard to begin, with all the stress draped over us for the encounter that was headed our way, but once I settled down and started chewing it helped deal with the stress. I had something else to focus on, and that was nice. Glynis had sent us off with some cured pork and some boiled eggs, knowing that it would be okay to eat for a few hours if we kept it away from the hottest part of the day, and also that we would cherish something besides dried jerky, cheese, and bread.

It was good, actually. The eggs had been pickled in some sort of sweet-sour brine, and not only were they tasty, but it was also fun to watch Gwenda carefully taste one. She'd apparently never tried them before, and didn't know what to think about it till after her first bite. Then, she declared her love for the food and inhaled three more, Seph giving up her share with a grateful look on her face.

The temperature, meanwhile, continued to climb. I looked out across the desert floor wondering how anybody could possibly even exist there, much less choose to remain on purpose.

The waves of heat rising from the cracked, dry floor suddenly resolved into the caravan we'd been looking forward to meeting. They came rapidly, trotting along at a pace that amazed me given the harshness of the land. From the time I spotted them till they arrived was mere minutes.

They fanned out, a guard of the largest, meanest-looking soldiers forming a barrier to our front while the bearers set the palanquin down carefully. The others, a hundred in number each armed with long spears and long, curved swords at their sides, formed a semi-circle and set spears at the ready.

"There's no cavalry," Keion whispered to me. I was certain he meant something important by the observation, but I didn't have the time to ask for explanation. The men, dressed in flowing pantaloons and light, airy shirts, pulled light-colored veils up to cover their faces, leaving just their dark eyes exposed. With their heads wrapped in cloth, they looked like well-armed creatures from a mummy movie.

Silence draped across us. We all stood, them veiled, their ten-foot-long spears with sharply flared metal points lowered. Only the palanquin's bearers looked semi-relaxed, large arms folded across barrel chests. They wore the same cloths draped over their heads and the same loose-fitting pants and shirts as the warriors, but none was armed in any way that I could see.

A soft, murmured command slipped out of the palanquin, and one of the bearers—the biggest one, a brute that could have stood eye-to-eye with Padrig—stepped over. He drew aside the heavy curtain, and a long, slender leg slithered out. A matching leg followed, and then the rest of the heavily-veiled body rose from the cushioned seat. She strode toward us, her body moving sinuously, the serpent-scaled veils rustling with the movement.

She stopped beside her own front line, the dozen men holding ready their wicked swords instead of spears. She nodded.

"I understand you have come to beg for peace, or perhaps just for mercy," the voice, a clear, ringing woman's contralto, reached across the gulf her soldier's weapons and stances had created.

I nodded, both relieved and terrified.

Swadda had come.

To Wash, Or Not

"You come to my land, Talaith, knowing you are not welcome here. Why?"

So much for niceties, I figured. But Swadda had never been the nicest of the rulers, Meredydd had warned me. I remembered snorting a sardonic thanks. That was a warning I didn't need at all.

I stepped forward, putting up as brave a front as I had in me.

"I have come for many things, Swadda. I shall begin simply, with a humble offer of washing your feet." I held out the flask of water in one hand and the ointment in the other, its southern elf engravings clear. I was taking a risk, letting my hand away from the relic that was my source of power, but it had to be done.

Her chortle didn't sound promising.

"Wash my feet? That I allow you to remain breathing is a tremendous concession. It is the greatest I am willing to grant, at this point, as a matter of fact. I see from your companions' faces that you had expected me to be as quick to swoon as my neighbor to the south, but I shall grant you the favor of an insight, helpful as it may be: I am not as quickly impressed. Frankly, it would not do my relationship with my neighbor any honor for me to describe specifically how little her reaction means to me."

"Well, you haven't killed me yet, so it appears that there is at least a little room for discussion there."

"Do not tempt me. You have no idea how often I thought upon the joy of seeing you impaled by arrows on the march here."

"What is keeping you from it, then?" Since the feet-washing diplomacy hadn't worked, I figured the best approach involved strength and logic.

She nodded slightly, the veil shifting up and down with a hissing sound. "A fair question, so it shall receive a fair answer. I hope that you might know the answer to how my people might avoid becoming the next collection of dragon's prey. There is some—I shall just call it speculation—that you are the key to such things. You are, after all, the only one of us who has faced him and lived. The creature is a him, is it not?"

"It is. He is. Xlixi is his name—his short name. He once told me the entirety of his name but most of it cannot be pronounced by our mouths." We'd talked about his full name, I remembered. I couldn't recall whether he'd actually told it to me or just told me I couldn't pronounce it, but didn't figure that made much difference at the moment with arrows pointed at my chest. Better to keep her impressed. And talking, too.

"I see. You alone among us know his full name. That in itself makes you seem awfully—familiar—with the beast, does it not?"

She had a point. I had to remember to avoid over-sharing. But I still couldn't grant her that ground, so I shook my head. "Familiar? I was the beast's prisoner, standing in its lair one poorly-phrased response from adding to the piles of elf bones on the floor. He told me his name solely to provide another example of how his race is superior to ours, in his opinion."

"You—disagree with that opinion, I take it?"

I chose my next words even more carefully. "The dragon is a fearsome foe. Clearly he is capable of wiping out the entire eastern clan all by himself. He is both physically and magically stronger than any elf, and even than many large groups of elves. Some might call that superior, and in a way it is, but to me there are more important, more defining qualities than physical and magical strength."

"Such as?"

"Bravery. Kindness. Respect. Love. These things the elves know well, while the dragon has shown no evidence of any of them. They may, in fact, be the secret to defeating the powerful beast." I made the last part up, but it seemed as likely as anything else.

"So the dragon might be defeated by love," Swadda taunted, her guards chortling in response. I ignored them but I could feel Keion bristling.

"You have some strange logic, Talaith. Regardless, I must point out that there are some who say you are responsible for his attacks. That, without you, the dragon will go away as he has remained away for centuries."

I shrugged. That one was easy. "There are always some who say wrong things, as I am certain the exalted leader of the western clan knows. Those who say this thing are wrong. As he explained to me during my captivity, he has been building his own breeding ground for elves in his own world. He comes here now because it is the ancestral feeding ground for his kind, and because his own experiments with breeding in captivity have been— boring, for lack of a better term—and now he seeks wilder prey. It is, thus, not my specific appearance that brings his presence upon us, but merely the timing." As I spoke, I remembered what Glynis had told me about Draignerthol, and that started me thinking about the timing of the relic's reintroduction into Kiirajanna. Instantly, though, I decided to leave that part out of the high-stakes discussion at present.

Swadda seemed to consider for a moment, and then with a gesture ordered her troops to stand down. Gwyn actually exhaled slightly in relief, and I wanted to turn around and hit him for giving that chink away. Luckily the rest of my party was too disciplined to show it if they felt the same.

It hit me in a flash that not twelve months ago I would have been the one sighing in relief, to all the high-ranking elves' embarrassment.

Well, I'd learned quickly, so Gwyn would, too.

He'd have to.

Swadda's veils shifted in what hinted at disapproval, then she bowed her head very slightly, almost jerkily, toward me. "Young one, I shall grant you the honor of my hospitality, but only because I wish to hear more about these defining qualities you speak of and how they might be useful against a dragon. I will withhold judgment on the honorifics related to royalty for the time being, and I will certainly not accept your offer to wash my feet. You may, however, follow us back to my capital, where I will receive you into my tents. There I will grant you safety for as long as you remain present and welcome. Now, let us return to shelter."

With that, she turned and practically slithered back into her palanquin. As soon as the heavy curtains closed against the heat, the bearers heaved it up from the solid desert floor, spun it expertly, and headed back along the path they'd come. Her cavalry rushed to form up in lines around it, leaving my little party to stand and watch.

"You weren't expecting an invitation to ride with them, I hope," Keion's half-whisper, in English, rolled drily from where he was standing.

"Expecting? All I was just hoping for was to avoid getting all of us killed."

"Hmm. Positive thinking, the power of. Nice job."

"Thanks. I think. But I was really just trying to talk her into talking."

"Well, you did a good job of that."

"Thanks. I guess I can celebrate 'nobody killed.'"

"Hey, from what I've heard, some days when you're in charge, 'nobody killed' is a tremendous accomplishment."

"So far. The day isn't over yet, unfortunately."

"Well, there is that. So we should probably start moving if we're going to keep up with the convoy, which I assume is a chief requirement to stay in Swadda's good graces."

I jumped onto my own horse, and the rest of my party did the same and fell into stations around me. "If 'you're safe in my household until I decide to turn you out' is her good graces, I'd hate to see her bad side."

"The good news," Keion noted in a continued half-whisper in English, "is that I think her bad side is what you avoided seeing back there. That, and the sharp ends of several hundred arrows."

"Bless her heart."

"You—I haven't heard you bless anyone's heart in some time, Alyssa. Are you feeling well?" Keion shot me a sly grin along with his quip.

Hot as it was, I wasn't much in the mood for joking. "Guess I'm going native, slowly but surely, huh?"

We were silent through the rest of the trip, mostly out of the effort of pressing our mounts forward in the oppressive heat. Meredydd had warned me about this part; even though it was still only late spring, the heat of the desert ratcheted up faster than I could have imagined. As the sun rose higher it seemed to be purging every ounce of moisture from my lips, my throat, my eyeballs, the inside of my nose, anywhere that had ever been moist before. In place of the comforting moisture, the sun left scarring, searing heat.

The head scarves helped a little. Meredydd had insisted on us wearing them, an insistence Glynis echoed. It didn't make any sense how a simple piece of cloth draped over my head in the heat could make it seem less hot, when that same piece of cloth draped over my head in extreme cold would have made it feel less cold. It didn't make sense at all, but it worked as intended, and so I was happy for it anyway.

More than once, Kluzhka broke into my brooding thoughts in her desire to help.

I can fly you to the city quickly, so you won't have to suffer through the walk in the hottest part of the day.

No, Swadda and her warriors will react poorly to your presence.

I react poorly to them making my familiar suffer so.

I am not your—oh, never mind. No. Just—no, I must complete this journey on my own, Kluzhka, if I am to be queen of these people.

Suit yourself.

It was hot, though—hotter than the devil's sauna. Hotter than I'd ever felt before. Hotter than...well, it was hot.

Eventually I fell to concentrating on my horse putting one foot in front of the other, and then repeating, just to keep myself from curling up and dying in this tragically severe land.

More than once, also, Draignerthol warmed up against my chest. Each time I pressed back, resisting against its force, instead of my usual rejoicing and drawing it to me. Swadda hated me specifically for my use of magical powers, and to survive this walk through the help of the relic would do me no good in cultivating her favor.

It seemed like it would never end. We dropped off the horses and walked a couple of times to avoid risking death for the poor beasts. That was when we discovered the evil little barbed things that rested on the ground in a seemingly random pattern. I was wearing solid leather moccasins, and I made a point of avoiding anything plant-like on the desert floor, but those little puffs of cactusy spines still seemed to somehow reach out and snag me as I walked by. The first one grabbed and dragged at my skirt hem. I reached down to remove it, only to be stopped by hisses from Seph. She strode over and pulled out a comb from her belt, showing me how to use the tines to flick the ball of spikes away. I nodded thanks, unable by that point to wet my lips to speak. She turned her own dry lips up in a huge grin and spun about, continuing the trek.

Finally, somewhere right in between utter debilitating dehydration and certain death, we arrived. We were led through the stick-framed cloth gates that opened in the walls surrounding the settlement. On the way through I noticed that the walls themselves were nothing more than simple sheets of cloth. It all seemed strange and flimsy.

The city turned out to be built around an oasis full of the most beautiful, wettest water I'd ever seen. I thought about running straight over to it, and I could sense the same from most of my companions, but I was proud of all of our discipline in not breaking and sprinting to the water.

Swadda's palanquin and her cavalry, of course, had all made it back much sooner than the rest of us, but a huge elf with a wicked grin and an even more wicked pair of swords led our small party to a tiny, shallow lake that stood in the center of the open area around which a strange-looking desert city was built.

Elves love colors in general; I already knew that. Every town and village I'd ever been to was decorated in a way that Mississippians might consider overly colorful, even gawdily so, with bright cloths accenting brighter paint on doors and window sills, and none of it with an ounce of consideration toward establishing a matching set of hues.

Elf towns were virtual rainbows.

This one seemed even more so. I realized after a moment that it was the shocking regularity of the construction that caused the discord of coloring to stand out stronger. Every home was a replica of the dozens that stood beside it, all squat square whitewashed adobe things with whitewashed clay tile roofs. Each had one door and one window on the side facing the central lake, be it north or south, and nothing at all on the east and west sides. They were all the same sizes, too, a little wider east to west than they were deep from north to south.

The white walls met the white roofs and the white hard-packed sand to form an entirely uniform strip that the sun's horrific rays lit up like a giant, searing, incandescent light bulb. It would've been hard to look at if not for the addition of colors in the accents.

But oh, the colors! Each door, window sill, door mat, and even the thick curtains inside the windows blazed a different shade, each one trying to be brighter than its neighbors. Teal cloths draped around windows were adjacent to a door painted lemon yellow, and a bright orange door mat clashed vividly with the cherry red door on the next house down.

"Not much need for architectural ingenuity when their sole purpose is to keep the occupants from dying in the sun," Keion observed quietly in English as his massive war charger sloshed water around in its mouth.

"Yes, but there's no variance anywhere," Seph complained.

"From what I have been told, they are ordered to build the same size structures so that no one captures any more runoff water than their neighbors during the brief rainy season. They recognize that water is their key resource, and so they each collect what they can in cisterns underneath their homes. For one to capture more than any other would be unneighborly."

I shrugged. "I received the same information in the Lady's lecture. It does makes sense. You know what I miss, though? There's no tylwyth teg."

Keion snorted and shrugged, while Seph nodded. She'd noticed the lack, too. The little fairy creatures had been everywhere before, usually just out of direct sight. The gossamer flutters had been a strange thing to get used to in my vision's periphery, but get used to them I had. Now they were gone, and it was a stark contrast.

"The little beasts are only content in the safety of their forests. Out here they'd be baked in the sun, and their little wings would shrivel. Hey, maybe we should find a way to lure them all out here," Keion muttered.

I feigned outrage and then shook my head. "No, you beast. Their buzz was a constant reminder of where I was, and I miss it," I insisted.

"Your dinner awaits, young ones," the elf guard stated flatly. Keion and I should have been, and probably would have been, offended at the total lack of honorific or gesture, but we expected this sort of treatment from Swadda's clan. Honestly, that they would feed us at all wasn't something we had been certain of.

"My men will take care of your horses. Please follow me," he said after we'd glanced an acknowledgment his way. He turned and took off down the main road, beside which the trickle of water that fed the little oasis streamed along a rock-lined path. We followed, noticing a slight rise in the elevation as we headed toward the hills that bordered the town to the west.

I thought back to Ganolog, its sturdy log wall erect against the threats of the northern forests. Brown was the color there— brown mud, brown logs, brown thatched roofs. Brown there versus white here, a distinction due to the raw ingredients available for construction. Houses here were built with four walls, standing separated a couple of feet versus smushed together in rows, again due to the relative prevalence of raw materials, plus something Meredydd had told me about the additional walls holding out heat better. And then there was the log pole barrier wall itself, which did a fine job keeping bears and wolves out of town but would do nothing against the venomous snakes and scorpions that counted as dangers in the desert and thus was missing from Swadda's capital.

Other than those three differences—well, and the brutality of the sun's rays that beat down on us as we walked—the town visits felt way too similar. Both were eerily absent of elves doing typical elf things—children playing in the street, adults greeting us as we walked, or any other sort of personal contact.

But there was an explanation for that too.

In Ganolog, Padrig's people were too focused for frolicking. We'd arrived at the high point of their efforts to put up food and other supplies for the winter, so every ounce of energy they had was devoted to work.

Here, I guess they were just terrified of us.

The ones who didn't hate us were terrified of us, I should say. I had no idea how many were in either group, but the combination of the two seemed to be right at a hundred percent of the inhabitants of the city.

The avenue slowly narrowed as we approached the solid cliff face. The riverlet that wound by the path grew a little deeper, and the pain of the beating sun lessened ever so slightly as a light, airy mist enveloped us. We could just hear the gurgle of twin waterfalls as they fell around both sides of an inlet into the side of the hill, an area that would be shielded from the sun in all but the early morning hours. Both waterfalls gathered in pools, the runoffs snaking along and down to join where they formed the small brook we'd followed.

Inside the opening in the cliff face stood our destination. Instead of the squat adobe, that area was separated off by curtains, each fold of fabric displaying a set of colors woven in a pattern which made it unique among what had to be hundreds of them hung about in a house of cards effect.

A house of very colorful cards.

We took the diagonal split in the path toward the north, where a small footbridge passed over the precious water about halfway along the little flow's length. It was pretty, with little succulents and reedy grasses clustering close as they could to the life-giving water's edge in the shadow of the cliff.

I was surprised, though, to watch our surly guard pass right by the bridge and continue toward a side house.

He stopped, and two only slightly less burly guards stepped out of the building, the only one to not bear a swish of colors. Even the heavy window curtains were black.

"This will be your quarters while you are in Dwrsanct," he said, and then indicated the two sword-bearers behind him. "They will keep you safe while you are here. The pennaeth will send for you when the time is suitable to her needs, and until then you should take care to not be observed outside of this dwelling. Tensions are—high," he ended with a sneer. "Your supper is inside, and your saddle bags will be brought."

He stormed off, leaving the two silent guards beside the door.

"Well," I said, not sure how to follow the insolent statements with any sort of reaction that might be considered regal.

"Well," Keion agreed, in the same voice.

"Well," Gwenda mimicked awkwardly, and then the tall, lanky girl strode in. "I'm hungry."

Keion's eyes followed her in, then swiveled back to meet mine with a shadowed, helpless look. "Well," he repeated with a shrug, and then he entered second, followed by the rest of us in turn, Gwyn taking the final slot after a long, meaningful look around.

We were all hungry, I guess.

Gwenda stood over at the table in the center of the house looking down, her face wrinkled up in distaste.

"Eww," she said as our ears heard a bar slide into place outside.

A Dinner And A Show

I tried the door. It was, unsurprisingly, barred on the outside.

Keion didn't seem to believe me. He tried the door too, and then he did believe me.

Gwyn grimaced. "Want me to blast it open?" He gathered a blue shroud of energy around himself in preparation for the spell while Keion shocked and horrified me by actually nodding.

"No! No, what are you thinking? Did the heat get to your brains? Look. We were in a cell in the south, and that worked out fine. And…. We can't go blasting our way through things. If we do, we'll start fights, and elves will die, and even if we're fortunate and the dead elves aren't us, we'll still have the death of fellow elves on our hands at a time when we need to be coming together to defeat a far worse foe. Come on, you two. You think the thousands of elves who live here will ever follow me into battle even if we succeed in destroying their leadership?"

"They did just lock us into a cell, Alyssa," Keion observed.

"They said it was for our protection," I shot back, realizing how weak it sounded as it came out of my mouth. Gwyn and Keion both snorted, and then gave each other a surprised glance over the mutual agreement.

I growled in frustration and continued, "Whether truly for our protection or not, the fact is that there's no way Swadda is going to leave us to rot in here. If that was her plan, she would've just shot us out in the desert and left our bodies to rot. Right? I need you both to calm down, take things as they come. How about we get the window curtains open?"

"Can't," Seph replied. She'd been over there trying, and I could tell that there was something solid nailed behind them.

"Okay. Well. Lights, then?"

There were two oil lamps hanging from opposite ends of the main roof joist, and Gwyn and Glynda made short work of lighting those. That allowed me to see more clearly what what it was on the table that Glynda had been repulsed by.

Our dinner, apparently, was intended to be a combination of rat, scorpion, and worm.

At first I wasn't sure what sort of animal the little roasted bodies of beasts belonged to. Looking closer, though, I could make out the cone-shaped noses, tiny round ears, and chisel teeth that I recognized as members of the rodent family.

"*Llygota*," Keion said, his voice dripping with disgust.

"What's a llygota?" I asked. My elf language vocabulary had become fairly extensive in the months since I'd arrived, but it didn't include that. Granted, technically the word was formed as a plural, and I'd tossed it into the question like a singular, but I didn't have the energy to deal with grammar on top of everything else.

"Llygota," Keion repeated, pointing to the rat corpses and making his best "I'm so disgusted" face. Everybody else seemed to agree—everybody but Gwenda, who was holding up one of the skewered scorpions and examining it. She looked more fascinated than horrified, but I wasn't sure how long that would last.

"Oh. I got that. But unfortunately the word wasn't part of the priests' language training," I explained drily.

"What is this?" Gwenda asked.

"It's called a scorpion in my native language. I don't know the elf word for that one either. Look out for the curved tail; there's a stinger at the end that will hurt you if it still has venom, and we have to assume it does."

I wasn't as worried about scorpion or rat, honestly. Each place was set with a plate, a cup for what I hoped was water laid out in pitchers, a few skewers of scorpion, and a bowl. What was in the bowl presented the greatest challenge to my stomach as I watched the collection of grubs moving and...wriggling. I lifted one, in part hoping to get everybody's attention away from the rats. It was white and very fleshy, nearly two inches long and about as thick as my pinky.

"Oh, look, a cream-filled one," I muttered, mimicking a line I remembered from a cartoon movie back home. Keion and Seph, who understood the English, stared at me in horror. Everybody else followed their gaze and joined the two in horrified expressions as I screwed up my courage as much as I could, tossed the wriggling tube of repulsiveness into my mouth, ignored the imaginary screams of my horrified taste buds, chomped down firmly, twice to end the wriggles, and finally, forcefully, swallowed it down.

I stood there in silence for a moment, hoping for all I was worth that the grub wouldn't come right back up the same way it had just gone down.

"Is—is that food where you come from? This Missiwhoppi place?" Gwenda asked.

I poured a cup of clear liquid from the pitcher and took a mighty swig, washing every bit of the worm out of my mouth before I replied. "Well, not so much in Mississippi, particularly. At least, not that I know of. But there's a show on—the—" I took a break and pantomimed what I could of a TV before continuing, "where this guy goes out to remote areas and eats food that people in—in Mississippi—wouldn't normally eat. I've seen him eat—grubs—" I muttered the English word, having no idea how to even attempt any sort of elf translation, "and scorpions, and even what we call nutria. What they call nutria, anyway. Yes, it's a giant rat, but apparently people in the more primitive places on Earth—Africa, Louisiana, and so forth—eat them all the time."

"It is a rat." Keion argued, turning up his nose.

"Yes. Yes, it is. And I am looking forward to eating it no more than you are. But don't you see what she's doing? We're being tested, just as Glynis tested us, and the only way through is to do what we're clearly expected to do. I didn't see many cows or chickens on the way in. Did you? If they eat rat, then I, being their queen, must eat rat also. But I'd just as soon call it nutria instead," I spoke more quietly, admitting to myself that the whole idea really was disgusting.

Bravely I used one of the primitive forks provided and pulled a hunk off of thigh. I piled the meat into my mouth and chewed, slowly at first.

I was surprised. It was actually pretty tasty. Maybe I was just that starved, or maybe nutria was better than I imagined, but whatever...I swallowed.

"Mmm, it's good! It tastes like chicken!" I called and took another bite. It was a little lie, to be honest. It didn't taste much like chicken, but it really wasn't bad at all. A little dry and chewy, but that was in line with the assumption that it had been roasted on a spit over an open fire.

"So, what do we do with—these?" Gwenda asked, pointing a stick bearing a roasted scorpion in my face.

I shrugged. "Eat them."

"How?" She turned it back around toward her own face and sniffed. The impaled black armored body looked ferocious even in death, so I couldn't blame her.

"I don't know. I remember hearing that people on Earth eat those too, but I have no idea how. Here," I said, picking one up. Since I was being the brave one anyway, I figured I might as well try it. "I'll—" I crunched a pincer off, and it was like a thick over-done potato chip. It was salty, and it was enormously crunchy, and—well, that was about it. Nothing scary grabbed my mouth and tried to kill me, so—well, it was food.

"It's pretty good," I lied. "Just eat it, but be careful not to get it stuck in your teeth. And I'd still avoid that pointy end, because the poison may still be there, and it may have, oh, I don't know, psychedelic properties or something."

My example, followed by my lack of death, seemed to satisfy all but Keion. As everybody else took a place at the feasting table, he shook his head. "I will not eat rat."

I shrugged. "Suit yourself. There's also these tasty grubs here. Yummmm! And the—chips on a stick, I guess I'll call them. They're good too. Or you could, you know, starve yourself. I doubt your particular talents will come in incredibly useful in this mission, anyway."

His face darkened into a scowl. "You should not...." His voice trailed off as Gwenda shot him a smile between two bites of scorpion, her hand waving invitingly to the seat next to her. "I—I suppose you are right, Talaith. I should set aside my pride and eat what is provided."

"You have, after all, gleefully eaten my trail rations, my prince," Seph pointed out, probably by way of keeping me from passing out in shock. Who was this guy, and what had he done with our arrogant and self-assured Keion?

"Well, that is a—a good point," Keion answered, studying the rat closest to him and then plucking a few long strips of meat from the flank. "It is—not very much like chicken, Alyssa, but it is good for a long-traveled appetite nonetheless."

There are some very tasty goats up here in these mountains. Would you like me to drop one by your cabin and distract your captors long enough for you to cook it?"

No, Kluzhka. This meal that has been provided us will do.

It is a rat.

It is made of meat. We will survive, and I need to win Swadda's cooperation, not kill her in a pitched wyvern battle.

Okay. As your kind are so fond of saying, suit yourselves. I was just suggesting....

I know. Thank you.

Sarcasm?

No, honest. Thank you. Just – don't forget that offer when we're out of here, please.

Gwyn was staring at me as I disconnected from Kluzhka, so I told the table of her offer. Keion looked glum, maybe a little overly so, at my refusal, but everybody else snickered.

The laughter broke down any remaining misery, and we dug in. We were all hungrier than we'd realized, and once we got over our disgust at what we were eating, we ended up cleaning the table.

Just as we'd settled into the limited furniture to sit and let the feast digest—I still occasionally felt, or at least imagined I felt, a grub wiggling around in my stomach—the bar was thrown to the side and the door opened. A huge shape stood silhouetted against the darkness outside.

"Swadda will see you now," we heard, and I recognized the voice of the same guy who had led us so cheerfully to this little house in the first place.

I looked over at Keion, who looked more excited than he had in a while. We all leaped to our feet but his bellow stopped us.

"No! Her," he said, pointing at me. "Swadda will see her. The rest of you will remain here."

I waved both Keion and Gwyn down with a gesture and, as bravely as I could, followed Mister Big and Ugly off to see his clan leader.

When I exited the building I was glad to see that my internal time clock wasn't as far off as I'd feared. It hadn't actually become night yet, but the cliff blocked the sun's rays from reaching any of the homes on the higher level of ground around the leadership cluster. It was actually a little bit chilly. I glanced out over the little city and saw a clear demarcation between daytime and shadowy night, and wondered if the same distinct line existed between the brutally hot and the pleasant as well.

I didn't have much time to ponder that, though, as we rapidly crossed the foot bridge into the little complex that was Swadda's home. I was fascinated by the complete lack of walls. Instead, the entire floor plan was laid out and separated by tapestries hung from a grid of rods laid out above our heads. Most were opaque, and very beautiful, while others, which seemed to serve as doorways, were transparent gauzy things in a multitude of hues.

The halls weren't straight, either. I guess that's the advantage to having temporary walls like she did; you can put up another tapestry and just like that change the floor plan to have a hallway dart off at a right angle to the direction it had been going.

Other than the bright-colored tapestries and the right-angle turns we kept having to take, though, it was the same treatment we'd received upon arrival: silence. Nobody seemed to even be around. I could tell they were close by, of course. My senses, already on high alert, gave me a steady series of readings about elves spread around all over the place on the other side of all the fine tapestries. None seemed particularly hostile to me, either, but every one of them was just plain silent.

The inside of the tapestry maze was much larger than it had appeared from the outside, as far as I could tell from the number of times we had to turn right or left. Sometimes I wondered if the main hall led completely around a room or two, but I always seemed to lose track of where I was after the next turn.

Suddenly we came to an apparent end of the trip, as a solid tapestry hung to the left, to the right, and directly in front of our continued progress. The hangings to the sides continued the existing theme of colorful chaos, the left side bearing an orange, red, and yellow representation of a spectacular sunrise while the right side provided an eye-startling mess of fuchsia and magenta stripes. The clash was, I realized, what had kept my directional sense off-balance, as the reeling sensation finally slowed down and stalled as I took in the design to my front.

While every other tapestry in the place had been primarily warm colors—varieties of yellow, orange, red, and gold—this one was cool and almost soothing. Blue pools of water were surrounded by brown and green trees and sagebrush, and the whole scene looked completely inviting.

At least, it looked inviting until I drew up close enough to tell that every single design on it was actually created out of differently-colored snakes.

Snakes. The whole thing was an optical illusion. From far away, it was a beautiful picture of a landscape. From close, it was a teeming display of hundreds of varieties of serpents.

I wasn't given much chance to study it, though. As I approached even closer it was whisked aside to reveal a small reception room. At the other side sat Swadda, her regal pose enhanced by her carved mahogany throne.

The throne was the only furniture in the room, of course. Why should I, or any other visitor, expect any sort of deference from her?

She was far from the only inhabitant of the room, though. Human, yes, but…. All around, coiled across the entry and laying along the armrest of her throne and everywhere else, awaited huge, terrifying snakes. Dozens of snakes. There were big snakes and small snakes, striped ones and plain. Someone who cared about snakes could have told you all the different varieties in that room, but all I knew was that any snake was a bad snake.

We'd had a snake identification class in high school where I'd joined the majority in proclaiming them all "nope" snakes, as in "Nope, I'm not getting close enough for it to matter what species this snake is."

These were *all* nope snakes.

Hundreds of snake eyes, and two human eyes, stared at me expectantly.

I knew what I had to do, but that didn't make it any easier. I don't like snakes. Not at all. Not even when it was just a little green garter snake that Sarah's little brother wanted to impress me with back home. He was cute. The boy, I mean. The snake, not so much.

Yet if I was going to impress Swadda, apparently I had to literally walk into a literal pit of snakes.

I'm not sure, but I think I'd rather have faced Xlixi again.

That thought flashing across my mind actually brought me the courage I needed. Of course a mature dragon was a greater threat than these little vipers could ever be. I'd faced him down, right?

I stepped into the chamber, being careful to step over the three inch thick, yellow snake lounging along the door sill. One quick, decisive step, and I was in.

There, I thought. That didn't hurt so much. I stepped forward again.

And again.

After a few of these momentary movements of terror I came close enough to confront Swadda of the Serpent Veil. Or Veils. Whatever she wanted to call herself, I was there. And then I noticed, in thinking about her title, that her veils were actually not there. It was the first time I'd truly looked into her face.

To tell the truth, she had a beautiful face, with large almond-shaped brown eyes, long dark lashes, and a pair of elongated cheekbones that would have done any supermodel proud. I wondered how often others saw it as clearly as I did at that moment.

"You seem hesitant," she observed, her mouth rounding the words up into a sort of verbal grin.

"I don't like snakes very much," I said, figuring honesty was the best approach. I'd made it across, at any rate, so as far as I was concerned whether I liked it or not was irrelevant.

"I believe the feeling is mutual, my dear. See him?" she asked, pointing to a massive gold-colored python glaring at me from a couple of feet away. "He never narrows his eyelids like that unless he's contemplating eating something. Or…some*one*."

I took a moment to return the snake's narrow-lidded glare, then responded, "I've had much larger reptiles look at me that way, so he'll need to do something a little grander to intimidate me."

She actually chortled at that. "Well said. You are aware, I presume, that our serpent brethren are considered as people in my lands?"

"I noticed that they weren't on our well-stocked dinner table."

She chortled again. "I hope you and your companions enjoyed your meal?"

"It was different from what we were used to, but the sustenance was much appreciated. I would request, though, that whatever tests you have in mind for me, you not inflict upon my companions as well."

I could tell by the sudden drawing up of her eyebrows that I'd chosen the wrong tactic. "The tests inflicted upon your companions? That was actually an introduction to how my people have been eating for centuries. Are you interested in coming to know my way of life in any degree of detail, or are you somehow thinking that you can issue edicts from Cysegredig and get me to whimper and obey on bended knee like...some others?"

I was stuck, and we both knew it. An apology to someone who respected strength as much as she did would be just as offensive as not apologizing for my blunder at all. But the reality was that eating such strange, fairly disgusting creatures after her rough throw-off of the party earlier had put me in a foul mood, so of course I wasn't ready to compliment her choice of feasts.

Be up front with her, Kluzhka's advice came unbidden. Several snarky replies came to mind, but I had a much too important conversation going on. Kluzhka was right.

I gave Swadda a nod of acquiescence. "You have it right, I am interested in coming to know you and your people's way of life. And I do appreciate the feast you laid out before us. I had no way of knowing the tradition behind the food, but still, I did not mean to offend." I glanced around, started to attempt to lighten the mood by making a joke about snakes, but then thought better of it. "I suppose the animals you fed us, and the snakes here, would have been the only reliable source of meat, and since snakes are sacred, that narrowed your choices, yes?"

She raised an eyebrow and considered what I'd said for a long moment before responding. "Not sacred. Not...precisely, anyway. It is difficult to explain, but I shall try. The snakes are our brethren. Do you have any siblings back at home?"

"This is my home, now, but no, I have no siblings."

"I see. Well, could you imagine the fine young Prince Keion dining on one of the beautiful sisters he has?"

"No."

"That is it, then. As for the feast, neither the rat nor the grub are native to this land, but my people long ago discovered how to keep them, to raise them efficiently enough to feed ourselves. As I am certain you have noticed, we do not have the abundant forest and water resources you have in the capital, so raising larger mammals would be a ridiculous waste. But you did not come here to talk about our livestock practices, did you?"

I was shaken by the question from a disturbing memory of Xlixi using that phrase in telling me about his own livestock practices, farming the elves on Pazhbojanna. I shook my head. "No, I did not. I came—"

"Good. Tonight we shall introduce a new side of you to my people. Believe me when I tell you that I, personally, bear you no ill will, nor have I ever. Yes, yes I know," she said, raising her hands defensively at the expression that leaked its way onto my face, "I have spoken strongly against you, but that was merely doing my job as the leader. My people do not see you—do not see any of us as we are, to be honest, but you specifically are not you, but rather the subject, the agent of terrifying prophecy and legend. That is why I have ordered your party so carefully guarded as protection. Tonight I have called for a ceremony, a grand celebration if you will, and you will make your appearance and become one of us, one with us."

Something about the way she said it raised my hackles. "What does becoming one with you involve?"

"A short walk. It is simple, really."

"Over a bed of coals, of course."

She seemed surprised. "The mistress of the bedchamber told you of our ceremony?"

My heart sank. I was just being sarcastic.

"No, she didn't, bless her heart. Just a lucky guess."

"Well, you will not be alone in taking the walk of pride. We have several youth looking to become true members of the clan, and it is time that they will get their chance. *After* you, of course. If you are not too scared?"

I bristled, but stopped when I saw smug satisfaction spring to her face. I shook my head and steadied myself. "No. I am not scared."

"Good. I am certain you do not need this warning, but I must deliver it anyway. You must avoid the use of magic during the ceremony. Otherwise, I cannot be responsible for the reactions of the crowd."

"Of course," I said. I didn't believe her. By my reasoning, she was the clan chief, and a powerful one at that, so she could be responsible for the reactions of the crowd if she chose. Still, there were way too many snakes in the room to argue with their human.

"I will have my bodyguard return you to your quarters to prepare," she said, dismissing me abruptly and quite rudely, but I decided to let that go also, dumping it into the "there are more important things to worry about" category.

As the big burly guy led me back through the winding tapestry halls, I wondered how my companions would react to the latest news.

LLOGSI

Fire. Or burned.

What fun it is to be 'llogsi.'

A Firewalk

"You're going to what?" Gwyn asked, his voice incredulous.

Keion let out a loud guffaw, which was amplified by the tight space of the tiny cabin we were being "protected" in. We all looked his way, and he responded to the unspoken questions by snickering, shaking his head, and then pointing at Gwyn and at me in turn. "I was just struck by how often I have asked our darling Mississippi-bred princess—queen—that exact question, in quite the same tone. You do come up with some—interesting—ideas, you know that, right, Talaith?"

"Not my idea. Apparently Meredydd either didn't know this ritual, or chose not to tell me. Or maybe Swadda just made the whole thing up, but she seemed too smooth for that to be the case. And besides, she made a point to tell me that there's going to be kids following me doing it. Look, whatever the case, I have to walk across hot coals. Without using magic, too. Any suggestions?"

"My shoes?" Gwenda pulled her platforms out of her travel bag, which had apparently been brought during my time in the tapestry palace. I smiled; the bright red super-tall platform shoes were one of her many quirks, an affectation she used to make herself taller back when she believed she was the undiscovered dragon queen. She'd switched to more comfortable moccasins while traveling, and I hadn't even realized she still had them.

"I suspect they will object to those, even if Alyssa—Talaith—doesn't," Seph muttered darkly from the corner. Apparently, as she'd growled in explanation to me earlier, Booboo was having a rough time in the desert. The clan wouldn't let the wolverine in to the oasis, and the poor little killing machine wasn't used to waiting so long for a drink. In a state of rage the wolverine had made a mistake of facing off against a cobra, not really knowing what it was, and also not knowing that the things always traveled and fought in pairs. Luckily an angry wolverine can run faster than a cobra can slither, so Booboo managed to escape serious injury except to the little animal's pride. That injury flowed through the bond to Seph, though, and so my cousin was madder than a yellowjacket near a running lawnmower.

I'd asked Kluzhka across our bond to find another oasis for Booboo and Cuddles, after Seph relayed me the frustration she felt. The wyvern had sniffed, such work being beneath her pride, but she'd done it, and so now the two beasts were able to sate their thirst.

"Yes, probably. Thank you for the offer, though. I suspect I have to walk across them barefoot, like I've seen done on—shows—before."

Keion shot me a sharp look. "They do that on Earth? On purpose? How do they manage it?"

"I don't know. I've only seen it. It's practiced by the Buddhists, or the Hindus, or somebody, as a way of proving you can control matter with your mind, or something like that. I wish I could remember, or had some way to access Google here."

"Who is this Google?" Gwyn asked.

"A—um, a sage who knows everything. You have but to ask and you will find out."

"Can we go visit him?"

"Visit? No!"

"I meant, later, of course. The mighty sage couldn't help us now. We would have to finish this challenge and then make our way back to the ley gate. Your father could probably help us find the closest one to the sage's—what does he live in, a castle? A mountain cave somewh—"

"Just stop. No, we can't go visit Google. Google is—oh, never mind. Look, the only thing I remember is something about how the water on your feet evaporates and causes a barrier against the flame. I think. And I remember seeing the careful pace of the walkers; apparently if you go too fast your feet press too hard into the flaming coals. But that's it."

"Maybe you will get to go after the kids, so you can see what they do," Gwyn offered.

I shook my head. "No, Swadda specifically said I would be leading the ceremony off. I suppose it's an honor."

"Well, whatever happens, Draignerthol managed to bring you back from the edge of the afterlife before, so I'm sure the pendant can heal your feet after. But burns hurt, you know," Keion said. "You must prepare yourself mentally for an unbelievable amount of pain."

"Okay. So, how do I do that?"

"Well, you—you prepare yourself. Mentally."

"Well, gee, that's mighty helpful. Bless your heart for giving me such a wonderful tip."

"Just trying to be as helpful as I am able," the elf prince grumbled, crossing his arms over his chest, before adding petulantly, "my queen."

I sighed. "I know. I'm as grouchy as Sephaline is right now, I guess. I think I'll do what's best for us all and go sit in the corner and work on preparing myself. Mentally. Quietly."

I didn't have the chance for any mental preparation, though.

The door opened as I turned toward the corner. Swadda's bodyguard's massive body blocked the opening, grinning wickedly at me. "It is time," he said eagerly. "The rest of you may come quietly if you wish, though—for your protection—you should keep to yourselves and remain close to my men."

"We wish," Keion and Gwyn both grumbled, and the entire party rose to follow me toward my foot-incinerating fate.

We were led across the creek on a tiny bridge and down the bank opposite the one we walked in on. At its end, on the other side of the oasis, was a tall bonfire glowing orange and red in the darkness, flaming into the heavens alongside a flat patch of glowing red embers. The now-veiled figure of Swadda was illuminated by its light, standing in front of a few hundred of her people.

Everyone was silent, all eyes pointed our direction as we were led up to the fire. I ignored the glares in favor of getting a good look at the scene of my torture, though. The coal runway didn't seem too long, only ten or twelve feet and about half that in width. I calculated that I could be across it in five or six steps, but then I recalled seeing on the show where they took smaller steps to avoid the impact. I figured I would try it that way first, and if it was just too painful anyway I'd just skip like a mad woman and get across it, clumsily but unmagically. They wouldn't be scoring me on form, anyway.

Then I wondered—would they be scoring me on form?

It took me a minute to notice the other part of the challenge. To each side of the strip of glowing embers, and in front and behind, it looked like the flickering light of the fire made the ground seem to wiggle. As the scene resolved, I realized it wasn't firelight upon ground I was seeing at all, but rather a massive pit of vipers.

Apparently I had to start and end by making sure I didn't step on a two-foot-wide strip of snakes.

More snakes—just what I was hoping for.

One of the western elves, a short, slender woman whose face was lined from years of smiling or being in the sun, or maybe both, interrupted my blossoming horror by tugging on my arm. "This way, please." She motioned off into the darkness, where a couple of tiny huts stood alone.

I nodded and turned to follow, motioning Gwyn to stay put. He glared and crossed his arms. It was silly, security-wise, to leave him and go alone, but so much on this journey had already topped that silliness that it didn't seem to matter.

I followed.

She held the door open and I entered the darkness as bravely as I could manage. Before long I heard a lamp being lit, and then light sprung up to reveal nothing nearly as bad as the murderous torture chamber my imagination had worried me with, but a simple makeup studio instead.

"Take off your blouse and your shoes, sweetie," the woman cooed. I did as she asked, and then, seeing her reaction, quickly pulled Draignerthol's chain up and over my head. As soon as I removed the pendant, her horrified gaze turned back to the one a grandmother might wear. I tucked the pendant between the folds of my clothes, making mental note of exactly where it was, and then gave it a few side-eye glances.

I was already missing its power.

She went to work painting my face and upper chest with white, red, and green paint in long, thick strokes. There weren't any mirrors, so I had no idea what she was doing to me, but "go with it" seemed the best advice at the moment, so I did. She finished quickly and then moved down to my feet, where I got a white band around each ankle and a white painted strap running down the center of the top of each foot. She put a red line on each side of each white line, and then used the green to run a weird set of slashes sideways and around the toes.

After what had been only a few minutes, she stood and examined the work she'd done. She nodded once, firmly, obviously pleased, and then said, "Put your blouse back on. Only the boys do this topless."

I complied, then asked, "Any advice? I've never even seen this ceremony done."

She stood and watched me as I put my top back on, and then her hard expression melted slightly. "We tell all the children this, so... Make sure your feet are as wet as they can be. Don't step on the snakes. Don't run, but don't stop either. One foot in front of the other, delicately," she ended as she demonstrated the last tip. Then she opened the door. "You'll do fine. Oh, and don't use—that thing," she muttered, her eyes going to the folds that covered my magical relic.

"Wouldn't dream of it," I agreed and stepped out, carrying my stack of clothes back to the party. Wordlessly, I handed it to Seph to keep safe for me. She let her eyes track over whatever design the woman had painted on my face, and then nodded. The others in the party did the same, and so I turned and slowly, regally marched toward Swadda, trying to think about anything besides the ordeal I was about to put my feet through.

Three others joined me before the clan leader. The two boys were topless and had white, red, and green lines painted over their faces, necks, and chests, while the girl wore a blouse similar to my sturdy traveling shirt. While the boys had shaved their heads, the tops of which were covered in designs as well, the girl's painting, which I assumed must be similar to mine, was like what I'd seen on my feet: white outlines, red highlights, and green accents. It seemed tribal, in a bright and colorful way.

Swadda raised her voice to speak. "Tonight we have special visitors for our *cerdded tan* ceremony." I let my mind focus on the term briefly, hoping the linguistic effort would help me forget the pain that was ahead of me. Cerdded tan literally meant walking in fire. I was surprised that, given how expressive the western elves were known to be, they'd pick such a literal, unimaginative way to name such an important ceremony.

"So, like, let's have a ceremony for joining the tribe," I imagined an early westerner saying. "Let's make it walking across a bed of coals." "Brilliant! But what will we call it?" his fellow must have asked, and after a long, thoughtful silence, possibly a bit of brainstorming, whatever might have passed for a focus group or two back then, and some long sessions with strong alcohol, they all came up with "fire walk."

Or something.

The crowd booed slightly, bringing me back to present. It was me they were booing, it turned out. Swadda said a few more words about me, and they booed again in a very uncharacteristic way for elves. I met Swadda's eyes through the veil, which was remarkably easy to see through in the fire's brilliance. She actually looked a little bit sympathetic to me for the tiniest of moments before holding her hand up for silence.

"Alyssa was born on a different world, with different rules. She has come to us to learn our way of life. This is honorable, my friends. Tonight she proves her resolve in the same manner our youth do, facing the same test they and we have faced for generations. Should she succeed, we must grant her the honor she seeks."

There were a couple of discontented murmurs from behind, but nothing like the earlier boos. Swadda turned to address me directly, her voice raised to echo from the cliff wall. "Our high priestess has blessed you with the traditional marks of our people. Are you ready to face the fire's truth?"

311

"I am."

I didn't figure it was time for a speech, and even if it were, I didn't have one to give. I just wanted to get to the other side of the coals from where I stood.

"Then stand in the life-giving water, and step forward when you are ready. Should you stop you will be consumed. Should you race forward like a child you will live in dishonor. And do not step on our brethren, or else they will strike you. Go when you are ready."

I walked to where the clan's high priestess had laid a small flat dish of water right next to the snake pit. I almost couldn't feel it when I stepped in; the water was air temperature, and it was only a fraction of an inch deep. It was just enough to wet the bottoms of my feet, where I'd heard I needed it the most, while leaving the ceremonial paint job dry and undisturbed.

Six rakes, three from either side, appeared and shook the coals up into a brilliant blood red, ending my thoughts about trying to place my steps carefully into the darker, presumably cooler, spots. As the men pulled their rakes back to vertical they all grinned wickedly at me. I returned the gesture with what I hoped was a much less wicked grin, but given the stress of the moment I couldn't be certain.

I was as ready as I was ever going to be, so I stepped forward.

The first one was a doozy. I concentrated mostly on avoiding planting my foot in the pit full of hungry vipers, and then on making a longer than usual step without falling down, and in doing so I completely managed to forget the heat that awaited my sole on the other side. It didn't really burn; the water did its thing. I actually felt it creating little vapor pockets. It was very, very warm, though, and uncomfortably so, and in the moment of surprise I nearly lost my balance. I tottered for a moment, exquisitely mindful of what would happen if I planted my tuckass right in the snake pit I'd just stepped over, and that tottering cost me some of the vapor barrier. That hurt, but worse, I could smell the skin starting to burn.

I moved, not really having much other choice. Just as I'd been instructed, I placed my right foot a few inches in front of the left one and took the weight off the now-abused member. As good as it felt to pull that foot off the coals, though, I knew I had to keep moving, keep walking, so I gritted my teeth and placed the left one down in front once again.

Each step hurt more than the previous one. The singed spots grew as the protective vapor dissipated. I knew I had very little time left, but I didn't dare run. The burn hit a critical point, and I escaped. Oh, I kept walking, step after step. But mentally I managed to disconnect from the pain. Turned out, it wasn't even that hard. I didn't do anything specific, honestly. I just stopped caring. I was going to make it to the other side, regardless.

And I did.

At the same time, it felt as though it had taken an eternity while it also seemed to take no time at all, if that makes any sense whatsoever. Soon enough, I found myself lifting one crispy-charred foot, and then the other, across the far snake-filled chasm and stepping to safety.

I kept myself disconnected, though, not sure how bad the pain would be if I didn't.

Immediately I was grabbed and whisked away by two burly guys. Back in the little hut, I slowly allowed my attention to come back to my feet as I watched the old woman vigorously rub a salve into their fleshy bottoms. She worked quickly, but effectively, and within moments she stood looking down, appraising my feet and me at the same time.

"You did well, my queen," she said quietly and then slipped out of the room, leaving me to wonder if I'd just heard what I thought I heard.

Wondering if Swadda would react the same, I left the comforting shelter of the hut and returned to my group, grabbing my shoes and pendant while we watched the next kid, the other girl, make what I'd just done look easy.

The boys followed, each passing the test with vigor. Apparently watching somebody else do it makes it easier to be brave when it's your turn. The last kid even turned around twice, walking backward for a couple of steps before spinning again and continuing with a great big arrogant grin, bless his young little heart. Several in the crowd muttered and snorted; apparently they didn't appreciate the gesture any more than I did.

Each was whisked away by the men, and each returned with greasy, salved feet after a few minutes with the high priestess. Swadda said a few fairly generic, meaningless words, and the ceremony ended. The crowd dissipated without any further emotion, positive or negative, directed my way, and I was glad for the silence.

"So how did it feel?" Gwyn asked as we settled in to our cabin for the night, each of us claiming one of the bunks that had been brought in during the ceremony. Apparently, I thought, Swadda hadn't figured we would stay the night until after I had faced her little challenge.

"I really don't want to talk about it. I almost didn't make it across."

"Let me see those feet," Gwyn demanded. I held them up for inspection, already knowing that he wouldn't find anything to heal.

"The salve that the high priestess used on the burns was very nearly magical itself," I explained in response to his quizzical look. "But the magic she used, herself, to heal them was actually quite magical."

"Hmmph," Keion muttered. "They're using magic and condemning you for using magic at the same time."

"At least she's not denying it like Sternyface did at first." We shared a look, though neither one of us had the courage to voice our thoughts in a small, confined room. She gets it, and I think I she wanted me to know by her expression and gaze that more of the others get it than we'd hoped. I think it's going to smooth out and maybe work itself out."

"Well, we'll see," the prince said, shrugging into his long nightshirt and using the cover to remove his pants. "For now, I need sleep."

We all turned in, though I had a hard time getting my brain to settle in and rest. I was way too concerned about what my next meetings with Swadda would bring.

DDEWR

Brave

That whole double d thing is fascinating.
Keion is 'dewr,' with a hard d sound.
Because I'm a woman, I get the double d
soft sound.
Love our gender specifics, right?

Surprising Support

"Well. You certainly are a brave and determined young woman, at least by your demonstration last night," Swadda started off the next morning once I'd been led down her maze of tapestries. It had seemed a little different from the day before, but I couldn't tell for certain, and it didn't seem like the time to ask if she moved her walls overnight.

"You are clearly your father's daughter."

"I prefer to think that I'm my mother's daughter, and if you were to meet her you might agree."

She studied me for a moment, stroking her long chin thoughtfully. "Perhaps. This Mississippi must be a wild and wondrous place, to have given rearing to one such as you. Tell me, before we get down to business, one thing you recall from your childhood home that is different from anything I might have seen here."

"Okra," I said simply, and then realized I probably didn't have the energy or the time to explain okra to her. "Better thing, kudzu. Where I was raised, they had brought a vine for food from a more damp, forested climate, much like the southern elves inhabit, long ago, but they didn't tend it like elf rangers do here. It

317

was allowed to grow, and it ended up taking over vast swaths of forest. So if you imagine the forest around Cysegredig, then add massive random areas that are almost too thickly vined to walk through, that's what our forests are like back–in the world I grew up in."

"Interesting. Is this vine dangerous to you?"

"Not really, no. It slowly kills the trees it grows over, I'm told, but it doesn't harm people. It's actually edible."

"Hmm. An interesting thing to recall. So, what about the people? Are they very different?"

I thought about that for a minute, and then shook my head. "No, not really. Archery isn't as big a deal there. Though, I guess it is if you exchange the bow for a gun and arrows for bullets–same thing, just more powerful. But the people shooting them are pretty much the same. But speaking of that, I can't help but wonder if guns from Earth might help defeat the dragon."

She shook her head gravely. "I can't imagine these bullets, if they operate the same as arrows, would have any better effect against a grown dragon, but I appreciate the thought as much as I appreciate your bringing the topic around to what is important. I must admit that I am at a loss as to how best to proceed, though please keep that between us. Good faith between rulers, yes?" She sighed as I nodded, and then she continued, "Your predecessor, Talaith, had some–challenges–walking the fire path, but she succeeded as you just did and then spent a few months here learning and coming to respect my people's way of life as only first-hand experience will allow. You did very well last night, winning the support of many of my people, including the high priestess herself. So the next obvious step is to have you spend a few months here as well; we might send your party back to more comfortable existence at Cysegredig, or they might stay here, or–well, no, before you object to either option, please allow me to continue. The challenge with either option is that I doubt Xlixi–that is the dragon's name you gave us, yes?—I doubt he will give you the opportunity to properly induct yourself into our hearts. To assume he has not infiltrated my people with his agents, when all the other clans have suffered the presence of his spies, would be foolish. I fear I must grant you my—premature, perhaps, but vital nonetheless—approval so that we may come together and marshal our forces as the people of Kiirajanna. To do otherwise would be...imprudent."

I was in shock, hearing all that. She'd shown me nothing but derision and insult, and yet now the story had changed. I wanted to find out why, but one thing bothered me about her statement.

"I should say, now, before we go any further, Swadda, that I was not going to object to the idea of remaining here to learn your way of life. Far from it; under different circumstances it would be an absolute pleasure." I might have been lying a little about the degree of pleasure, but it didn't matter. "I was objecting to the relative comfort you were implying in Cysegredig. I am pretty certain that I and my companions can find ways to be just as comfortable here in the sanctity of your city."

"I suspect your cousin would disagree, at least as her wolverine familiar is in question. We did allow the beast as well as that other mongrel to slip in to the oasis last night after the ceremony, by the way. Now that you are accepted here, my rangers suggest that your cousin might consider recalling him to her side for his own—protection. The desert can be a brutal place even for a powerful fighting beast. And speaking of beasts, how is your pet wyvern doing?"

Kluzhka, how's it going? You watched me walk across fire last night without a single snarky comment. Are you okay?

I am fine. Since I am not your pet wyvern, I chose to return to my mountain hideaway. Do you need me to teleport to your location to drop on that wicked woman's head?

No, thank you. I think we are reconciling nicely.

I silenced the connection as quickly as I could, fearing that somehow Kluzhka had heard the pet comment and might seek to prove the opposite. I saw Swadda nod, slightly, to herself.

"You saw that conversation happen, didn't you? You're a ranger, yourself. Or, at least I should say, you have ranger powers."

To answer, Swadda inclined her head and started communicating. I watched in amazement as I recognized what Gwyn had said he'd seen in me. Only, Swadda wasn't talking to one serpent; she was talking to them all. As a large, slithery group, they all moved across the floor to face me in a single line, all except the big one draped across the back of her throne with its head by her hand. That one just nodded in a weird, creepy sort of way.

"I thought—how—you have dozens of familiars!"

"I do. Thousands, in truth. It is—hereditary, just as Glynis's clan leadership falls upon the best librarian. Not that I am supposed to know that, but—well, you see, the ability to communicate with every serpent in the realm has its benefits. Your predecessor, just as every Talaith before her, managed to keep those abilities secret, and I trust you will manage the same."

"I will manage, yes. My world is just a lot more complex than I'd ever thought it might be."

"You must learn to get used to that, Talaith. My world becomes more complex nearly every single day, and I have many days on you at this point."

"I—yes," I stammered a little, struck by the fact that she'd just, finally, referred to me by the queen's traditional name. She'd implied it already in the conversation, but this was a direct statement just as clear as bending a knee might have been. "That has, I admit, been one of my greatest challenges to get used to. I thought Mississippi was a challenge, but even that level of complexity pales in comparison with what I am learning of Kiirajanna. And—thank you."

She nodded. "Now, Talaith, perhaps you and I could spend some time discussing how we might go about defeating our common and incredibly powerful enemy, the dragon?"

I had a brief thought that I could play this one off, bluff my way through it. She was uncannily good at detecting bluffs, though, from what Meredydd told me. I decided it wasn't worth it to try.

"I don't know. I honestly don't. As you know, I have faced the dragon, personally. I have smelled its fetid breath. I have been touched by its disgusting tongue. More important, I have seen and felt the enormity of its power. It is a creature every bit as powerful as the legends would have us believe, Swadda, and I have no idea how to challenge it, much less defeat it."

She actually smiled at me. "And so you expect me to believe that you came all the way here to the desert, bringing along with you some of those you hold dearest, all while believing that we stood no chance against the beast that wishes to make us his feast? You secured the fealty of both Padrig, who I actually respect far more than my public displays would suggest, and Glynis, while having no idea how to proceed? I would not call you a liar, Talaith, yet I have a difficult time believing your claim."

"And yet, you have called me a liar before."

"I called Princess Alyssa a liar. Talaith, I would not. You are new to the crown, but you must understand and keep the difference in mind."

"Ah. Okay, well, I wish I had something better to say, but I am being honest when I admit to not knowing how the dragon will be defeated. I know it will happen; it must, because it has been prophesied, yes? And it has happened in the past. Then, the battle was won through bringing all our forces together and maximizing our use of arcane powers."

"There, see? That is how we shall defeat the dragon this time."

I shook my head, temporarily silenced and dumbfounded. I finally found voice enough to reply, "No, we have no arcane powers to speak of."

"Sure we do. I am led to understand that one of your companions has a fairly impressive amount of power, and there are the dark elves—is it true that you have been successful at bridging that divide? I see in your face that it is. So there, we have it."

"That is not a plan."

She smiled and shrugged. "Have you ever studied the art of planning for battle?"

"No, I have not. That's Keion's area."

"Well, then, ask the young prince how specificity in battle plans most often works out. In the meanwhile, though, please accept my suggestion that the people need to hear their queen speak with certainty, even when she herself does not feel it. It is the strength in your eyes and the courage in your words that have the power to inflame our warriors' hearts as they charge into battle, particularly against a dragon. Always remember that."

"I will, thank you," I said. It was hard putting the right inflection into the words. She was talking down to me. But she meant it for the good, bless her heart, so I didn't want to come off as sarcastic. At the same time, though, I knew better than to be too thankful or too anything else that might give her an upper hand in the future.

"So," I decided to push it a little. "I have your fealty, then? Will you swear publicly?"

She snorted. It had a ring of good-natured humor to it, so it wasn't a completely bad thing. "Let's take a little time, shall we? You have my promise to join your side against the dragon, should he choose to attack us or our brethren directly. Once this is over, I would ask you to come visit with us for a longer period of time, after which I *may* swear that oath you seek. Right now, though, there is too much division among my own people on what we are to do about a queen who relishes the use of magic. I would rather not inflame the passions when they may be needed—elsewhere."

"I see."

"Good. You are young—very, very young for one in your position—but you are wise. Now, what of the dark elves?"

"It is good to hear someone else speak openly of them."

"You do enjoy squishing our favorite traditions, do you not? But there are no dark elves in the west. Surely your protector has told you that?" I let the question go unanswered—he hadn't, but it hadn't come up because there hadn't been a reason for it—and she continued, "So yes, it is something we speak openly of. It seems that their powers would be extremely useful against a dragon."

I wanted to gloat. Oh, how I wanted to gloat, bless Swadda's blackened heart. She'd been hammering on me, calling for my exile, even, for no other reason than the fact that I saw magic as the only way out of the situation we were in. Now, she was calling for magic as, if not the only way, at least an extremely useful way.

But I didn't.

"Yes. Yes, I agree that their powers will be extremely useful. I have already been in contact with them, as you are aware. They will come when needed."

"How will you communicate to them that they are needed?"

"Well, Gwyn can communicate directly." I wasn't absolutely certain that was true, but it sounded right. "On a similar note, though, how will I communicate to you that your forces are needed?"

"You have a wyvern horde at your back and call, do you not? I would think that communication with me would be simple."

"Can you speak with the wyverns?"

"No, but they can." She indicated the reptiles that surrounded us.

You can speak with snakes.

I can, yes. I prefer not to, though.

Why?

Low creatures with even lower aspirations. I can only talk to some, anyway. The common snakes are not sufficiently developed. But those near where you are, I can communicate with just fine. Why do you ask?

Swadda just brought it up as a way to communicate if the dragon shows up.

Oh. Did you know that dragons can communicate with snakes as well, little one?

That stands to reason. It would also make sense that dragons could control snakes just as they do wyverns, right?

You learn quickly. Go you, oh smart one!

Hush, you.

"Your pet wyvern gave you bad news?" Swadda guessed, and I quickly put away my sour expression.

"She agreed that she can speak with snakes," I said, leaving out the judgmental part. "She also pointed out that it is very likely that a dragon can also, and if the dragon can communicate, he can likely control the snakes too. That is what concerns me."

"I take it from your comment that dragons can seize control of wyverns. Which is why you're not counting on your winged army in battle against him, yes? Interesting."

"I've asked her to avoid being around when he is, yes. My concern right now, though, is you, considering where you're seated and the fact that neither you nor your companions can instantly evacuate as a wyvern can."

"Ah. Thank you for your concern. If the matter comes to a head, I suppose we shall see which of us can exert the tightest control over my friends' attention." She didn't seem nervous, which sort of unnerved me. What was this woman capable of? Or was she just bluffing?

"In the meantime, while you are certainly welcome in my charming city for as long as you choose to stay, I presume that you will consider your mission complete and return quickly to your pressing duties at Cysegredig."

"So? What did you learn?" Keion asked when I returned to our cozy little cabin, looking up from where he'd obviously been showing Gwenda how to sharpen a sword. I glanced away; if nobody else was bothered by how closely the two were seated, then I guessed it was just petty for me to be.

"Wyverns and dragons can talk to snakes."

"That's—not surprising," Gwyn pointed out from his seat at the table, where he was working at sharpening a dagger. "The implications are dangerous, though."

He caught on quickly, too.

"That was all you learned?" Keion pressed, either not catching the danger or electing to ignore it.

"She has agreed to an alliance for now. Later, once the dragon issue is taken care of, I can return for a while and learn their culture, earning her oath just like your mother did. But she—suggested—that we should return to Cysegredig secure in the knowledge that our mission is complete."

"You didn't wash her feet, did you?" Gwenda asked.

"No, it didn't come up."

"I thought that was a major part of our mission."

Seph sighed and then spoke up, "No, the mission was to earn Swadda's allegiance. Washing her feet would have just guaranteed our safety, which was pretty much already done. Which is why Talaith forgot about it, right?"

"There were—a lot of snakes in the way."

Seph shrugged. "That, too. Well, we're packed. Let's get back to civilized terrain."

"Is that Booboo talking, or Seph?" I asked, trying to make a joke.

She didn't think it was very funny, apparently, growling, "Both," in response.

We departed quickly. We had plans to make.

Needless

"I am—amazed. Wonderful job," Dad said. I tried not to let my chest puff out too much; the high accolades coming from one who rarely gave them, no matter how well I figured I deserved it, needed to be shared among my team. I started to voice that opinion, but he cut me off. "One of your strengths is your overbearing humility, my daughter, but please take a moment to consider that you and your companions were given up for dead several days ago when you set off to somehow win over a couple of clan chieftains who had called for your head. Now, you stand here with success written across your shoulders. Our odds of success against the dragon, I believe, have increased substantially."

I let a smile creep to my face, but that was it. In spite of the congratulatory mood Dad's words attempted to buoy, the somberness of the empty throne to his left still hung heavy on everyone. I could sense the same from everyone in my group, particularly Keion, who stood beside me with his eyes locked on the golden chair back that his mother's frame used to block. I was queen, I supposed. I had been recognized as such by both of the clan chieftains I'd won over, though not in terribly strong language by the most recent one.

People even called me Talaith, the customary name the queen took on.

I needed to quit, I realized, with the "I supposed" nonsense. I was the queen, for all intents and purposes. No, not even that qualifier fit. I was the queen, period. I knew, in my head, that I'd earned it. That was my throne now, much as I hated its former occupant's not being there. My throne, my crown, my....

So why didn't I feel like it?

Fact was, I wasn't ready for the throne yet, and I had to assume that everybody in the room, including me, knew it. I might have earned it, but no matter my accomplishments so far, I still had a long way to go before I could realistically hope to fill Keion's mother's shoes, or her golden seat, or the void that her murder had left behind.

If I were honest with myself, I wasn't certain I'd ever fill any of those suitably.

Still, I had to try. The elves needed a queen.

It was my duty.

"So Grigor made his way back to Xlixi's lair, then?" Owain asked, his eyebrows up since I'd made that part of the report. I was sure the grizzled old ranger was insulted that the dragon's agent managed to slip through his tracking.

"So the dragon said. I—wouldn't give him complete credibility, though," I said.

"He has not lied to you yet, I believe," Dad interjected.

Kluzhka?

Yes, my familiar?

Um.... I decided to let that go for once. Can dragons tell a lie?

Those rats you ate back in the desert looked awfully tasty to me. I wish I could have eaten one too.

Huh? Where did that come from?

*I just told a lie, silly. If I can do it, you can probably safely
bet that so can Xlixi.*

Oh. Right.

"I suspect, whether he is as overwhelmingly advanced in
power compared to us as he believes himself to be, or not, the
fact that he appears to believe the encounter all but won might
be evidence enough that he is telling the truth. Why would
someone lie needfully?" Sternyface pointed out.

"Were this an elf, I would agree, High Priestess," I said, using the title deferentially even though technically I didn't need
to. It was a weird reversal; before when I'd been expected to
show formal signs of respect to her I had never really wanted
to. Now that it was not expected, it felt right.

She looked at me quizzically, so I explained, "A dragon's
entire operation is foreign to us. His way of thinking is not the
same. He is, I believe, purely evil. Purely malevolent, purely
arcane, and very, very long-lived. We should not expect him to
behave as we would under similar circumstances. Though I did
just confirm with my wyvern that a dragon can tell a lie."

"Well said, and thank you for the confirmation, Talaith,"
she granted me a minor victory that, given our shared history,
felt like a major win.

I didn't have time to celebrate, though. "We are still a little
bit short in the battle planning department. Which reminds
me—Keion, Swadda told me that detailed battle plans are a
waste of time and suggested I ask—seek your advisement in
the matter since you have made a history of studying that topic
in detail. What are your thoughts on plans in general and in
our case, specifically?"

I was in the throne room with a whole lot of doers, including Padrig and my father, and I half-expected somebody to try
to overstep my question with a suggestion on doing something.

Nobody did, though. If anything, Padrig, Owain, and my father actually looked interested in the prince's answer.

Keion cleared his throat and stepped forward to stand in the middle. "I will try to make my response brief, though it is interesting that you ask a question that is often in the center of military experts' debates. It was an ancient Earth war historian who coined the term *rhyfelniwl.*" Keion paused to let the term's literal meaning sink in: war-fog. Considering just the couple of battles I'd been part of, I could see where it might be a good choice of words. Dad and Padrig nodded approval, but Seph, Gwenda, and others looked confused, so the prince continued, "In his writings he explained how uncertainty takes over the battlefield more often than not. Sometimes there is literally a fog present, and so neither allies nor foes can determine how the battle is progressing. Even without a literal fog, terrain or other things get in the way of a commander's knowledge and thus his, or her, ability to lead. On top of that, no matter how much any group of soldiers speaks of the honor of valor in battle, there comes a moment when a soldier's death is clearly a real possibility, even a probability, and it is at that moment that the fog of the mind becomes a problem as some soldiers follow through with appropriate military actions while others—many—most, perhaps—make more—selfish decisions. That may not be the kindest term, to be honest. All of us are concerned with self-preservation, though, yes? So there is within all of us the person who, seeing the reality of an enemy's sword, arrow, or burst of magical flame, would choose to turn and run rather than die in place. You have faced it; am I wrong?"

"Not at all," Dad said, pointing his affirmation at those in the room who looked skeptical. The high priestess, surprisingly considering her age and her position and what I assumed of her background, was one of those, but she seemed swayed by my father's response.

"So," Keion commanded our attention once more. "Given the fact that both sides of a conflict have soldiers who go in fully expecting to win, and others fully expecting to lose, and those in between who are not certain whether to wet themselves, and also given the fact that warfare is essentially an elf affair, won or lost less by tactics and more by hordes of elves who make key advances or retreats in the moment, there is a substantial uncertainty in the whole thing. Uncertainly in spite of, and occasionally because of, the level of planning. This is the fog. Many leaders, Swadda apparently being a member of this group, think that the uncertainty implies a lack of need for real planning, since the fog will happen whether we plan thoroughly or not. Others, though, and I am of this group, believe that the stronger, and better disseminated, the plan going in, the more chance that the fog will not disrupt it. The logic is simple: if those doing the fighting know the plan exists, and know what it is, they are far more likely to focus on it than on the immediate danger of the battle to their front. Victory is never a given, but with thorough planning—and communication of that plan—it is far more likely."

"Well said, Prince," Padrig said, his hearty approval booming in the throne room.

"Yes! Very well said!" Gwenda chimed in a little too exuberantly, causing an immediate awkwardness to hover in the air. Keion's face flushed, and he stepped back quietly to resume his place beside me.

For my part, I nearly laughed out loud. Bless their hearts, I should be annoyed at the display, but it was so—cute.

Keion chose the moment to mutter darkly about how this was a dragon we were facing and that nobody could really expect to live no matter how much planning we did. For once, the prince's voice was ignored, pointedly so by the older folks in attendance.

"So, now we are convinced of the need for a plan," my father's voice cut in, and I could tell by the hint of an expression on his face that he was thinking the same thing I was. "Do we happen to have any solid candidates for the rigorous development of one?"

He looked at me, giving me the distinct impression he was now thinking the exact opposite of what I was. I didn't care how *frenhenis* I was feeling lately, a Mississippi girl wasn't the one to plan how to face a foe that even Keion obviously still felt was undefeatable.

Everybody else stared uncomfortably at the floor, the ceilings, and the thick curtains that made the walls for several long, heavy moments. Finally I decided that I couldn't take any more silence.

"I'll go. Here's one, or at least a plan towards a plan. Look, this isn't just a Cysegredig threat, this is a threat to the entire realm. This realm has some very smart people in it, not all of whom are in this room. We're missing Glynis, for one thing— did you know she is a librarian by trade?" Sternyface nodded as though it was old news. Angrily I sent her a mental *thanks for the heads-up jab*, even though I was certain she couldn't receive it, and continued, "And the dark elves. No, Dad, listen. Thanks in part to our decision to shut down the practice of magic, the dark elves are left with the only solid group lore regarding the battling of dragons. We should—we must include them."

"Not here in the castle."

I sighed, but held back my retort. Not only was it not the time to call out my dad once again on being a racist, but it didn't do any good; the term rolled off his back anyway. He didn't come from the same culture, with the same cultural memories, that I did, and that just had to be that.

Bless his racist heart. I didn't have time to deal with it, but I knew I had to cross that bridge sometime.

"Fine. Neutral ground, just as we agreed to with—the other clans," I said, stopping short of naming the chieftain of the eastern clan. His death was still too recent, and elf customs are elf customs, after all.

"Can you set it up?" I asked Gwyn, who nodded. "Fine. We'll assemble at the same knoll, as soon as we can all get there given the uncertainty and its related urgency. I will ask Kluzhka to bring both Glynis and Swadda as quickly as she can wing them, and as quickly as they will come. She will, of course, need to take messengers from the Crown with her, because her language skills are a little bit lacking."

My language skills are not lacking, she objected when I relayed the message.

I have never heard you speak the elf language out loud.

That does not mean that I cannot. How do you think I gave direction to the elves on my shifts back at the growing factory?

That was in that guttural draconic language, though.

Doesn't matter. I can speak your language too.

Oh. Well. Right. I will cancel the request for messengers to travel with you.

Please do.

"Can you get an invitation to Masu?" I asked Gwyn.

He nodded. "Of course."

I turned back to the company, excited for the chance to be doing something other than just standing around talking about doing something. "It is settled then. Let us ride!"

"Beloved Daughter," Dad addressed me in a tone that bridged between adoration and condescension, "please give me, oh, I do not know, an hour or two, perhaps, to gather my soldiers and prepare them to ride with us?"

"But all those troops might—" I started to object.

"Be needed should the dragon appear," he cut me off. I couldn't argue with that wisdom. Not that I was certain the king's vanguard could do anything against Xlixi, truly, but the force might be important. I nodded, and he continued, "I will not have the entirety of our senior leadership gather in one spot unprotected."

And so it was decreed, in spite of my misgivings that the black-clad soldiers would just be a tasty appetizer for the dragon if he did actually show up. Dad set off to prepare his army for movement, and Gwyn set off the other direction to get word to the dark elf leadership. Meanwhile Seph and Master Owain set out to get word to the rangers to meet us there, and the high priestess did the same for her head scholars.

Me? I had nothing better to do, so I treated myself to a bath to wash off the desert grime. Meredydd joined me, soaking in all the news I gave her and asking all sorts of detailed questions. The tapestry maze in Swadda's was a fascination, apparently; while my predecessor had been allowed in there also, Meredydd, who accompanied her long ago, had not. She was thrilled to hear of the success of the southern elf customary greeting, also.

"You couldn't tell me about the firewalking ritual ahead of time?" I chided gently.

"I confess, I did not think of it. It did not occur to me that you might have the opportunity to practice it."

"You didn't think I would make it that far, did you?"

"Well, I—I had fears. But more to the point, I believed that if you did make it that far, the firewalking would be deemed unnecessary given the gravity of the situation at hand."

Before long I was nice and clean, Gwyn was back, and everybody was formed up. Seph and Master Owain took the lead as the ceremonial scouts, while the other several dozen rangers fanned out around us. Dad rode in front, me on his right and

Keion on his left. Behind Keion, of course, rode Gwenda. Sternyface and her gaggle of priests rode in a separate knot, back behind us a bit. Kluzhka and a team of wyverns had already deposited Glynis and Swadda, with their associated retinues, on the spot where they were already setting up a meeting area.

My spirits crested with the sun.

Since we were passing through extremely familiar territory, both Owain and Seph dropped back to ride with the royal group.

"Has this path been scouted for Grigor's passing?" Dad asked, his voice casual as though the question had just presented itself.

"It has, Your Majesty," Owain replied formally. "He did pass this way, it is believed."

"It is—believed? By whom? Generally your pronouncements bear more certainty, my friend."

Owain's face darkened. "It is difficult to explain. Generally we can track the passage of any elf, or even the smallest beetle upon the grass. But on Grigor's trail, a darkness lays, obscuring the passage. It is similar to, though much deeper, darker, and more poisonous, than the blight, as though the dragon's magic stretches across the land to protect his agent."

"Not your—people's work, correct, Gwyn?"

If my new sidekick was put off by my father's question, as I would have been, he did a good job hiding it. "No, it was not, Your Majesty. As Master Owain said, this is deeper and darker than I have seen."

"Will it impact the land itself?" Dad turned back to Owain.

"I do not believe so. The magic serves, it seems, merely to obscure a passage. Its power is what surprises me."

"Well, at least it is not destructive."

I wished I could share my father's positivity in that. I knew how destructive Xlixi could be, and he did also. Plus, I had actually seen the blight at the library – crossed it, even – and I'd flown over it too.

"Given the darkness of the magic, though, we should take more care. Alyssa—darn, I keep forgetting—Talaith, you should ride behind the soldiers for your protection."

"I will not. I am as good with a bow as any of them, and I have a protection mage beside me and a group of stalwart friends surrounding me here," I said. Dad rewarded my stubborn pronouncement with half of a pleased grin and a nod.

The column moved slowly, at a pace so wretchedly sluggish it made me want to scream in frustration. I understood, of course; the ranger skills needed time to work. At one point I saw Seph and Master Owain break into what I called their ranger dance up ahead of us, weaving and moving from side to side across the trail to pick up on every possible threat. Neither was actually doing anything that might be considered dancing, but the way their bodies moved in tandem was as striking as any actual dance I'd ever seen. The two of them exchanged occasional glances, and once or twice a seemingly meaningful gesture passed between them. Neither brought anything back to us, though, which I took as good news.

Still, I just wanted to get there, to get the parley over with.

Before too long we could see the opening in the trees that signaled our destination. I was finally able to breathe, as I hadn't enjoyed the slow pace at all. I watched as Dad halted the advance of the warriors and sent Owain and Seph on ahead to scout out the area.

Suddenly, a visible, tangible shiver passed through our ranks as blackness swept over us. The horses Dad's men rode on screamed, bucked, and broke away, galloping back toward the castle. Most of the warriors, excellent riders that they were,

were hauled along, though a couple of the younger ones were tossed unpleasantly to the ground.

A terrible fear gripped my heart, a sensation I recognized immediately. I beat it down and looked around. I watched Gwyn struggle and finally resist it, squaring his shoulders and meeting my eyes in a glare of fierce determination. Well, that was one ally, at least, and for that I felt ecstatic.

The High Priestess stood, peering up into the darkness; I couldn't tell whether she was still with us or not, but at least she hadn't run away screaming like her priests. Dad and Keion both gripped their reins in a white-knuckled struggle, their faces blank as they fought an internal battle with the dragon's magic. A glance backward confirmed my earlier wonder, though. Gwenda—sweet, quirky Gwenda—sat calmly, immune, looking around for the source of the sudden darkness and apparently not feeling the dragon-terror at all.

A loud, sinister laughter boomed over the clearing.

"Where, oh where, are your vaunted troops running to, oh mighty elf king?" the magically magnified voice taunted from above.

I stepped forward, rage filling me with an insatiable desire to face the tyrant, to find a way to rip his throat out through his well-armored neck. He had teased me and my party. He had decimated the elves of the east. He'd sent someone to murder Aerona, and the queen, and me. Yet here he was on my turf, near Cysegredig itself.

I come.

You can't—

I must.

Nooooo—you know what may happen.

Yes, I do. You may be ripped to shreds. I must come.

Okay, but only if you think you can resist.

You resisted. I am stronger than you. I can resist too.

"Xlixi, quit hiding like a terrified child and get down here where we can see you!" I cajoled, pushing my own voice outward using the same magic spell, and then, as the wings swooped out of the sky, I realized how dumb the taunt might have been. The mighty wyrm came in hot, roaring to a stop right in front of me, the ground heaving to accommodate the force of the touchdown. As the dust settled a long, wet tongue snaked out and licked my face, teasing me again.

"Why, Princess, it is terribly good to see you still alive. I worried that the traitors to the west might do away with you. Your fear still tastes just as delicious, I must say. So tell me, how are you doing these days?"

"You have murdered too many of my people, Xlixi."

"Oh, we have already visited this topic, Princess. It bores me. I have only just begun. A dragon, you see, has a very large appetite, and your indelicate term is an awkward reference to my need to sate it. So, speaking of that hunger, are you ready to swear my oath?"

"I won't swear any oath to you, now or forever, you fiend. Get out of my land, get away from my people!"

"Oh, my. How feisty you are. I will have it eventually, one way or another." His tongue snaked out toward me once again. "In the meanwhile, your terror is quite delicious, I must say."

"Leave," I said, putting as much force into the word as I could. It earned me a deep, throaty laugh.

I am here.

"Oh, my little one! How long she has been missed from her home in Pazhbojanna! You brought her to me. How sweet of you!" the dragon cried. I wasn't sure whether he was congratulating me or the wyvern, but either way it sounded menacing. "You, my dearest little relative, should return to my side, shouldn't you? You've been gone so, so long."

I felt Kluzhka's control ripped away from her. The link was still there, but one moment it was a smart-aleck wyvern, and the next a dragon-controlled beast. She screamed a booming primal rage, and I screamed too.

"Sssoooo, that is the cousin I have heard so much about, is it not?" Xlixi said, snaking his neck to the side to peer at Seph, who was finally shaking herself out of the fear spell after rushing back to come to our aid. "Little Kluzhka, I would like to dine on her entrails. Please bring those to me."

Seph trembled as the wyvern, no longer mine to talk to, dove toward her. I raised Draignerthol to shield her, but Xlixi's power batted my spell away like a gnat. The dragon snickered evilly, and then, suddenly, Kluzhka was on the ground in front of Seph. She raised her terrible talons.

Master Owain stepped in between them. "No!" he cried, staring fiercely into Kluzhka's eyes.

Through two sets of eyes I watched in impotent horror as Kluzhka's six-inch, razor-lined claws sliced down, tearing three deep parallel gashes through the ancient ranger's torso from neck to groin.

Seph screamed. So did I, I think, and so did Kluzhka, who apparently felt my horror through the link as strongly as I did. In that moment I felt my horror fueling hers, which in turn fueled mine, and both continued to echo back and forth. In an escalating explosion of emotion our mutual rage bubbled and broke out.

It was enough.

Suddenly Kluzhka was back in herself. She spun toward Xlixi, a savage hiss erupting from her mouth. Through her eyes I saw fury tinge everything to a deeper shade of red. Her defensive crouch in front of my cousin was one of the most dangerous stances I'd ever seen.

"Oh. Oh, oh, oh, well, now, isn't that something? It is, yes? Cute, I would say," the dragon purred as his head swiveled back to regard me. "Yes, it is cute how she fights against me now that the deed is done. So tell me, how many of your friends, your lesser beings will I, personally or through agents, need to kill before you finally bow your knee to me, Princess?"

The cavalry arrived at the perfect moment, only they weren't actually cavalry, because none were riding horses. I could sense the arrival, but luckily for us Xlixi was celebrating in the ranger's death too deeply to notice. It was—weird. Amazingly powerful, but weird. A giant blue sphere of energy flew out of the trees behind, turning white with cold as it sailed along, and then the magical ball of ice slammed forcefully into the dragon's rear haunch. Its team of casters stepped out of the tree line and started forming another sphere even before the first one landed while their ground troops raced around them.

Set off balance, the massive beast lurched and roared and then turned to face his new foe.

I cheered in spite of the situation. I couldn't help it; it filled me with joy to see hundreds of dark-skinned elves pouring from the tree line, running full-tilt to take on their ancient foe. The old woman was right with them, though at her age I marveled that she kept up. Teeri, the younger warrior, led a sprinting phalanx directly toward the dragon while swirls of blue magic formed overhead. Before long, the swirls resolved themselves into offensive spells, and ice ball followed fireball which in turn followed bolt of electrical energy in pummeling the dragon.

"Shoot it! Its shields are down!" the old woman bellowed, and I remembered my own bow at my side. Seph had three arrows sailing at it before I had two, and Keion matched her draw for draw. All but one of the projectiles bounced off his well-armored hide, but Seph's third arrow lodged itself between two plates on the dragon's front shoulder.

Xlixi gurgled and then let out a menacing laugh. He turned leisurely toward me in spite of the arrows I was sending his direction, and then suddenly his arcane defenses rose, shattering the arrows mid-flight. I watched him spread out his magnificent azure power once more, and the charging mass of dark elves slowed in fear, briefly coming under his control before somehow popping back out and resuming their rush.

The dragon took a moment for one more smile before saying, this time with a hint of hurry in his voice, "Well, Princess, it seems you have some unexpected allies. I will see you again, I promise. For now—oomph—I shall take my leave. Enjoy your corpse. It looks—delicious."

With a loud pop, the dragon disappeared, taking with him nearly a dozen arrows lodged in various places on his huge body. The dark elves slowed to a stop and stood, chests heaving, swords out and ready for battle.

I leapt off my horse and sprinted over to Seph, who was collapsed over her mentor's lifeless body. I held her and rocked her as she sobbed into my shoulder.

"Seph, I—I.... I'm so sorry, Seph. Kluzhka—sorry. I should not have allowed her to come."

"No," she said, shaking her head. She brushed a stream of tears off her cheek and turned a determined, brave face up toward mine. "It was his time. I really believe that, Alyssa. Look, do not blame Kluzhka. If she hadn't been here, Master Owain would have sacrificed himself to the dragon directly. Do not blame your familiar. Never blame your familiar, Alyssa. She is a part of you as you are part of her."

"I—well, I—okay—but—I am—sorry," I stammered, the shock over the needless death, the sacrifice that didn't have to be, settling in, and at the same time I was completely floored at my cousin's inner strength.

I did notice Seph, when she mentioned Kluzhka, glance apprehensively around searching for the wyvern. I followed suit and saw that the wyvern was gone.

Where are you?

Gone.

I can see that. Gone where?

Gone away, to the mountain hideaway you created. I do not belong there with your friends.

Nonsense. You are my friend.

She severed the link forcefully, and after a moment I gave up and turned back to Seph. There was plenty of grief right there to worry about, anyway, and it was best, I figured, to let the wyvern be alone to deal with everything in her own head.

Meanwhile, we had some planning to do. With a groan, I rose and turned back toward the clearing.

A Discussion

An uneasy quiet settled over the gathered elves as I strode into the middle of the clearing. I was closely followed by the prince, the king, and the high priestess, and then by Seph, Gwyn, and Gwenda, by way of rounding out my little traveling fellowship. All of us shambled somberly, having just watched one of our legends die a heroic, if gruesome, death.

The receiving party greeted us just as somberly. Swadda and Glynis had both apparently set off fairly quickly, each with only a handful of soldiers. Padrig looked furious, embarrassed, and exhausted all at the same time, alternately sending glowers at his own soldiers and sheepish apologetic glances our way. I didn't need to ask; I could see it in his troops' faces that they, the mighty northern warriors who'd been sent ahead to secure the meeting site, had met the same dragonfear as my father's black-clad horsemen.

Glynis stepped over to Seph as we moved under the awning to join them. "Ranger, I am sorry for what you are going through. The loss of Master Owain is painful for all of us, but you must be in particular agony over the loss of your mentor."

Seph's neutral expression was impressive. I doubted if I could have kept such a straight face if I'd just watched a mentor, a guy that Seph respected and cared for nearly as much as her own father, be disemboweled. Yet she did, and in a flat, quiet voice, replied, "He died doing what he loved doing, protecting his fellow elf."

"Indeed," Glynis agreed and returned to her spot. She and everyone else pointedly ignored Sternyface, who shocked me the other direction by allowing a tear to run down her face. If anyone deserved it, though, it was her. Once her priests finally regained control over their dragonfear, they'd taken over the gruesome effort of collecting Master Owain's corpse, including all the pieces they could find, and arranging to transport him in state back to Cysegredig. She'd held tight to the stern in her face while overseeing the whole ordeal, but that must have been difficult even for her. A tear now that it was all over—maybe even a small stream of them, since that was what it looked like—was understandable.

"We must remove this to the palace to prevent another visit," Dad observed.

"No," I said, then corrected myself to spare my father's glare, "I mean, yes, you are right that we should, but can we talk here for just a moment first? I think Xlixi went away at least a little bit embarrassed, and it's not like he has any allies to call to his aid, so he's not likely to come right back. I—I really want to talk a little, now, without waiting for yet another movement of troops and horses."

"He has his wyverns back in his other world," Sternyface interjected. "That is what you said you saw, is it not?"

"It is what I said. I saw hundreds of them through my own eyes and through Kluzhka's, but I can't imagine he'd bring them here. For one thing, they're probably as likely as Kluzhka is to enjoy this landscape more than the city and so leave his side. For another, I doubt his pride would let him risk another defeat in front of his minions."

"That makes sense," Dad agreed. "So now, allow me to address the tylwyth teg in the fire directly."

The euphemism was the same as our "elephant in the room" back in Mississippi, but was far more energetic of a vision since a member of the faerie folk caught in a fire would be very, very angry and therefore very, very dangerous.

"The dragon's breath weapon is mighty, and both his armor and his magical shield are strong. Clearly, his claws are to be feared as well. But I believe we have just seen that we could beat all of those if we could just maintain our forces on the field en masse. How do we keep from running away in fear whenever he wishes us to?"

"How do you not feel the need to run?" Sternyface turned and asked Gwenda directly.

The girl pursed her lips and shrugged. "What need to run?"

"The fear, the all-encompassing terror that gripped my heart and forced my priests to turn and run as they'd never run before," Sternyface responded, a bit icily. "*That* need to run."

"You didn't run, either," I said. "Nor did the king or the prince."

"There is a difference, I believe, between not running because I was so busy fighting off the fear that I was incapacitated, and not running because she did not feel the fear at all," Dad said, shaking his head. "I am curious, also."

She shook her head. "I—I am sorry, Your Majesty. I can't answer the question. I—I felt fear when I met the dragon, both times, but I think it was just a normal bout of worry over possibly dying. In neither case did I have any deep desire to run."

"Both times?" Dad asked, turning a glare my direction. "Did you not tell me something I would find useful to know?"

I shrugged. "He accosted us as we neared the southern forest as well. He seems really intent on getting my oath. It makes me wonder why he doesn't just eat me."

"I believe the answer to that may be the key to the whole matter," Glynis spoke up. "Though my people do not yet have the answer to that, it is a question we have been working on. We have a couple of theories going. But that calls for longer discussion, which might be better and safer in the walls of Cysegredig."

"All this theory is fine, but how do we keep our men from turning and running?" Keion demanded. "I am not trying to be argumentative for argument's sake, but if we turn and run, or even merely sit our steeds fighting off the terror, it makes no difference why the dragon has not yet eaten Talaith. We must find a way to defeat him militarily, which means we must solve that piece of the puzzle."

"The prince is correct," Glynis agreed. "I think we need to solve both pieces of this puzzle, and quickly."

I looked around at the drawn faces under the awning and realized the conversation wasn't going very much farther. My father's face contained something I'd never imagined seeing there: defeat. I couldn't let it stay there, though; I knew that much. "So, we've established that we need to figure two things out. Great. Is there any way to protect the elves around Cysegredig and those in the south, west, and north, while we research?"

Teeri stepped forward from the shadow he'd allowed to consume his form. "That is where my people come in."

My eyes sought Dad's face curiously, and I was relieved to see his immediate negative reaction melt away into an expression of acceptance.

"Your people probably saved many lives today," Sternyface intoned, saving my father from what would obviously have been a similar uncomfortable statement. "But can there be enough of you to guard so many?"

Teeri scoffed, and the older woman to his side snorted. "We are like ants on the soil, moving, working, always hidden from your view. Until we are needed, of course, and then you realize the true magnitude of our number."

"What do you demand in return?" Swadda asked.

Teeri's face hardened, and he stepped back. The older dark elf stepped forward, accosting Swadda with her eyes as she did. She held the pennaeth's gaze in an expression that would have frozen a waterfall for several long, uncomfortable moments before replying. "We demand nothing," she spat, letting each word ring before beginning the next. "To voice the phrase insults us. We join our brethren against the wyrm just as we would hope they would join us. Whether we all recognize the folly of that second statement is beside the point, at least to us."

Dad caught up to the conversation and stepped in. "We— honor your words and desires and beliefs. It is just that those who came before us—wronged you, it appears. How can—what do you expect as a means of atoning for that debt?"

She snorted. "You owe me no debt, elf king. What has come before us died in its time as was proper, and what will be will live. If we allow the weight of the burden of history to bear on our words, our tactics will mire in the mud while the wyrm makes dinner of us all."

"Well said," Sternyface intoned, and most of the other heads in the circle nodded.

The group movement drew attention to the single exception: Keion, who was shaking his head.

"What is wrong, Keion?" Dad asked, shooting a worried look at me and several others.

"What's wrong? Your Majesty, I just stood by and watched Master Owain disemboweled by a creature who had no control over its own power. I heard Talaith shriek her own furious impotence while she watched it, too. We all watched as our arrows

347

bounced off its hide once it got over its surprise—an advantage we will not enjoy again. What is wrong is that I am certain that this time we are outmatched, outclassed. Defeated."

Padrig stepped in with a harrumph. "Are you someone besides the prince in disguise? Those are not the words of the daring Prince Keion who stood stalwartly beside me as we faced down the traitors in Ganolog, young man."

I nodded, joining in. "You charged into the blight, going up against innumerable dark creatures and even a wyvern," I accused. "You can't quit now."

"I have no intention of quitting, Alyssa. I just cannot shake the feeling that this is an unwinnable battle."

I ignored the use of my old name, hoping everyone else would do the same. Keion's negativity needed addressing instead.

"Oh brave prince, what have your studies of history shown you about the honor and odds of charging dauntlessly into unwinnable battles?" Dad asked, and I saw by the light slowly turning back on in Keion's eyes that he had it.

"What about the battle of the three hundred soldiers at Troy?" Dad pressed after a few moments of silence.

"It was Thermopylae, Your Majesty, and I am certain that you are aware that all three hundred soldiers lost the pass and died that day, yes?"

"But they held it with honor and, in doing so, allowed their forces to retreat to live and fight another day. As I recall my own lessons, their sacrifice and their valor are what ultimately saved the Greeks from Persian domination. And what of the battle of Cyelin?"

"Another case of the few holding off the many," Keion agreed.

"You are suggesting we fight a delaying action against the dragon?" It was Swadda's turn to sound skeptical.

"I am suggesting that we hold our heads up and fight as the proud warriors our heritage grants us. Our ancient foe learned from his wounds today, but so did we. We are stronger, more united, for it, and I ask our prince to join me in facing the future with our chests held high."

"You have that, Your Majesty," Keion answered, and I could tell by the light in his eyes that he was pretty well convinced.

"Certainly there are more closely-related battles to study?" Swadda asked.

"The literature of the age of dragons was—purged—at the beginning of the current age," Sternyface admitted, her emphasis on the word purged making her disdain clear. "We could not entertain the study of magic that those works contained."

"My library still has some of it," Glynis said, prompting some surprised looks. "What? We were less—directly involved. In, um, everything."

We all caught the implications of her word choice, and the silence hung over us.

I looked around and started laughing in spite of the desperation. Here we were, a surprisingly disparate and fractured society of elves, suddenly united against a common foe.

I was rewarded as first Keion, then my father, and then the rest joined me in laughter.

I couldn't help but think back to my arrival not quite a year before in what seemed like a flawless, beautiful elf society—the trees trimmed just so, the grass manicured seemingly on its own efforts, every face smiling warmly up at a beloved king.

Things sure had changed.

"We have come as far as we can with this discussion here," Sternyface finally said, bringing the last chortles to a close. "I believe we all have things to discuss and research. Glynis, may I send some of my scholars with you back to your library?"

"Of course."

"We should bend our heads together to discuss tactics the next time the dragon makes his appearance," Swadda said, and used her eyes to include Teeri in with Padrig, the prince, and my father. "It would appear that our resistance to the use of magic has lost its meaning when the alternative is our slaughter." The dark elves nodded.

"I will try to calm down a wyvern, and if I'm able to do that I would like to join your librarians," I said to Glynis. She smiled warmly and bowed.

"I—have matters to attend to," Seph said slowly, and we all nodded our understanding.

The group separated, leaving my father and me alone. He placed his hand on my arm as a signal, so I stood and watched the departures. I waved Gwyn off for privacy, and my protector nodded and moved away to the tree line.

"You have not yet learned to school your expressions," he accused in a gentle voice.

"I'm—kinda learning on my own now, Dad."

"Yes, and no one, including me, will fault you for it. But I saw what passed across your face. Are you regretting your decision to come with me last year?"

"Regretting? No. Not that, not at all. I was just thinking how much this land has changed since I arrived, and not just in my perceptions."

He nodded and allowed himself a sigh. "You show much wisdom for one who has not yet reached her nineteenth birthday."

"Not many nineteen-year-olds have been poisoned by librarians, shot at by archers, captured by a dragon, and murdered by a great uncle. It's kinda been forced on me, bless their foul little hearts."

"Indeed it has."

I looked around at the now-empty clearing. "I just can't help thinking about how many times I've ridden through clearings like this one, marveling at the beauty of the land, the manicure of the plants, the pleasant peacefulness of the people who live here, and how much they loved their king and queen. It's.... Now, there's blood and claw marks just over there, the land is at war, and we've had people looking daggers at you—drawing swords on you, even, and the queen has actually been murdered. Twice, I have to add. Nothing is the same, nothing at all. I was enchanted by the tylwyth teg pretty much everywhere when I arrived, but now they're nowhere to be seen. The whole place has gone upside down since I arrived, and the only thing that was added is me."

"Blaming yourself, my daughter?"

"Well, who should I blame, otherwise?"

"Do you believe that the speaker of prophecy was joking when he uttered his words about the coming of the dragon queen?"

"No. Maybe. I don't know. It begs the question, though, of how much in control of our own lives we are when a book written thousands of years ago says I'm gonna burn down a library, and then I go burn down a library. Doesn't it? And how do you know the prophet was a man, anyway?"

He snorted. "We do not even know the prophet was one person of any gender. It is just assumed, and it makes relatively little difference. As to the rest, philosophers in both worlds have debated that for millennia. As long as prophecy exists to guide us, there will always be a question of how much control we have over our actions and our worlds. But that is not ours to answer, at least not now. Let us focus on questions we can answer instead."

"Like how do elves with bows and arrows possibly beat a dragon?"

"You are not afflicted by Keion's doubts, are you?"

"Nope. I'm afflicted by my own doubts. I've seen what Xlixi can do. So have you. Honestly, Dad, how do we stand a chance against him?"

He shook his head gravely and then smiled ruefully. "I cannot know, Alyssa. Talaith, though you will always be my little Alyssa to me. I am many things to many people, and I have many strengths and an equivalent, perhaps even greater, number of weaknesses. You are seeing me at my weakest, and—perhaps that is for the best, my daughter, because wise as you are, you are the same. We are—I am merely mortal, and as such I am certain of only one thing. I am certain that there is an answer to your question somewhere out there for us to discover. Our people have beaten dragons in the past, and we are as strong as we have ever been, and so we will lay this one low in our future. Of that, I have no doubt, and you must have no doubt. I and you and all the other leaders must display no doubt for the benefit of the courage of our people."

"Our people hate me. I'm not doubting the decision to come, but I can't help but think that they would be better off if I'd stayed in Mississippi."

"Perhaps they would have. Do not look at me that way; I merely agree with your statement. It is, in fact, a possibility, a path we did not journey down. We have no way of knowing what might have happened. If not for you, perhaps the Cult of the Wyrm would have managed a more thorough infiltration of the palace. Perhaps the queen, and I, and all three of her children would be murdered with the Cult sitting in our thrones. Perhaps the dragon would not have bothered trying to obtain your oath of fealty, and instead the beast might have merely flown right in and started dining on our flesh. You must agree that all those are equally likely situations had you decided the other direction."

"But they—the people loved you so much. Now they just seem to look at you in fear."

Dad allowed himself another sigh and looked out into the distance before answering quietly, "It is, I would guess, a consequence of being a people at war. In the past we had the luxury of being beloved monarchs in a lovely era of peace. Now war is upon us, and we must be leaders, and leaders are not always beloved."

"I'm not sure I see the difference."

"You will. You have already learned so much, and there is still so much more ahead of you. But we both have matters to attend to that are much more urgent than these philosophical questions."

The elf king walked away silently, his proud frame unbowed. Several black-liveried guard members, who'd all been hovering just out of earshot, sprang to action and helped him into his war charger's saddle and rode off with him, the banner bearing the stag and the raven flapping proudly behind. I watched him depart, leaving the central meeting pavilion to me and Gwyn, and then I turned my attention back to my familiar.

ARFWYDD

Difficult, Obstinant.

Like a wyvern familiar, in other words

Kluzhka

Kluzhka.

Kluzhka.

Kluzhka.
What do you want?
Kluzhka, come to me.
No.
Please?
Your request becomes no less dangerous when you give it a pleading sound.

Xlixi is not around, so there's no danger.

You are aware that dragons can teleport just as quickly as I can, yes?

Yes. Yes, I am. But I am also aware that if Xlixi wanted me dead he would have killed me on any one of several occasions. He is not going to make you hurt me. Please, come to me so we can speak.

We can speak just fine this way.

I am in desperate need of your rapid transport to the south.

I believe those soft squishy things you call feet work just fine.

Bless your heart.

My heart does not need blessing.

Get. Over. Here. Now.

pop

I looked over at the wyvern. I could read the dejection and self-loathing written across the very essence of her being. I could also still see blood on her talons. It almost brought me to tears, so I did the only thing I could think of and walked over to her, throwing both arms around the beast's scaly neck.

What are you doing?

It's called a hug in my language. What's it called in your draconic tongue?

There is no word for this in my language, because we do not bother ourselves with such silliness.

You haven't asked me to stop, though.

Why should I? It is neither painful nor uncomfortable. It is just—strange.

Okay, then. I pulled away and stepped back to look her in the face. It had felt pretty strange to me, too; her armor plating was really sharp around the edges.

I need to go to the library in the south.

Just you, or you and that boy over there?

I doubt that I will be able to keep him from coming along.

Xlixi would relish making me kill him, you know.

That is the reason I need to go to the library—to find a way to keep Xlixi from being able to control you.

It is not possible.

Everything is possible.

You're cute when you're like that.

Like what?

Working so hard to remind me how naive, stupid, and tasty elves are.

Hush, you.

I was being perfectly quiet, but you insisted....

"Gwyn, Kluzhka is able to fly us to the south. Let's get going."

Able, yes. When did I say I was willing?

Are you not?

What if I said no?

"You two are sounding very childish, you know."

Kluzhka's surprise matched my own as I turned around to face Gwyn. "How long have you been able to eavesdrop on our conversation?"

He shook his head. "I—not long. I think I just figured it out. We've—my people—have been able to eavesdrop, if you wish to call it that, on rangers' conversations with their familiars for some time, though those conversations are far less complex than anything you two discuss. Seph and Booboo, for example, send images and occasional sensory information across their link, and that's fairly complex for what it is. But by attuning that a little higher I was able to hear the words in your conversation. I will be glad to respect your privacy going forward if you desire, of course, but I hope you permit that it was a fascinating discovery. Especially since—I wonder if it's possible—it must be. I must investigate further."

"Investigate what further?"

"Well, in listening in on the conversations, we can also determine, with a certain amount of inaccuracy, the location of both the ranger and the familiar. Kluzhka, your kind communicate through a mental link, right?" When she nodded, he continued, "I wonder if that means I can determine the location of wyverns—or, better, a dragon."

You can determine where Xlixi is, can't you? You did, once, when you gave warning that he was coming.

When he is nearby, yes.

That might be useful.

We really should go. If your boyfriend can hear our conversation and track us that way, I would not be surprised if Xlixi does not possess the same ability.

He's not—oh, forget it. Let's go.

Kluzhka allowed me and then Gwyn to climb up onto her back. I couldn't help but notice that this time Gwyn seemed—hesitant—hesitant, and very careful—and maybe a little bit jerky—about where he put his arms to hold onto me for the flight.

Oh, shut it, I sent through the link to the smug wyvern, but soon forgot the argument as the wind rushed through my hair and we soared high above the trees.

I don't feel like teleporting right now, she answered the question I didn't ask. Instead, she spread her long, thin wings and just sailed, letting her magic take over and power our flight directly south.

I realized I'd dozed off when Gwyn's arms shook me. "Alyssa," he shouted over the wind, "you need to see this."

We were flying over the blight that surrounded what had been the library. Only, it was much bigger. When Keion, Seph, and I had begun our charge across we could see the building from the edge of the forest. Now, though, I could only barely make it out from the air.

As Kluzhka's shadow cut across the darkened earth below, we saw all sorts of dire beasts scurrying to escape the wyvern above. I remembered the dire wolves and the ravens from our trip, but now they all seemed—bigger. There were more of them, too. And—was that a bunch of darkened bears, too?

Why is it growing, and not healing?

Do you not sense the magical taint across the land?

You mean the oily taste I have in the back of my mouth? Is that what that is?

The taste of elf flesh that has sat too long in the hot sun, yes. The land cannot heal itself.

"No, it cannot. Once the dragon problem is taken care of, my people will, with your help, turn our attention to this. Sorry, I hope it was okay of me to eavesdrop again. It seemed important."

"We're going to have to figure out some boundaries."

"And yet you have no problem hearing her speak of eating elf flesh."

"What did you expect wyverns to eat?"

I felt him shrug in response, which seemed fair enough. Between the wind and the foul taste in my mouth, which must have been replicated in his also, verbal conversation was difficult. Besides, my answer was weak enough not to deserve much response. What did he expect wyverns to eat, really?

I agreed with him, though. The nasty taste in the back of my mouth joined with a nasty, uneasy feeling in my core, nearly bringing tears to my eyes. It felt horrible. It was horrible.

Soon enough the sick flavor eased and we passed over the blight's southern edge and headed into open air over more beautiful forest. I had no way of telling speed, but Kluzhka must have been flying awfully fast. We'd made a three-day ride into a short flight.

The rest of the flight was actually even faster, and far less—oily-flavored.

The reception we received from Glynis's clan proved significantly different this time. Amid cheers and shouts of recognition, we were hoisted up into the towering tree limbs and escorted directly to the library, where the clan leader had already arranged for us to be set up with one reading area and two librarian assistants each. It was a good thing they were there. Unlike the squat edifices I was used to seeing, this library was contained in circular row after row built into the inside of a hollow tree. Circular stairways connected the dozens of floors, which my chief assistant, who was also the head librarian after Glynis, explained varied in size from what would be a regular apartment at the bottom to just a few square feet with narrow vertical pockets for rare scrolls up at the tippy-top.

I would've spent more time running up and down stairs than actually researching if not for the help.

We both dove into it quickly. Gwyn, it turned out, had been taught to read texts on magic by his new dark elf family, so he was actually faster at running down the elf scrawl on each page than I was. Still, I held my own, and by the time the head librarian cleared her throat to alert me to the presence of supper I had several likely sources piled up.

I grabbed the bowl of soup and picked it up, my feet already turning back toward the table stacked with reading materials.

She clucked.

"I—just," I stammered, realizing that it had been hours since I'd moved my head, much less licked my lips.

She understood where I was going with it, though, and shook her head. "No, *Frenhines,* the work will still be there once you have sated yourself. Take time away before your eyes become glued to the paper." When I made to object, she smiled and gave me what sounded like the real reason, "Besides, after the destruction of—the other library—it would not do to get soup stains on the irreplaceable works of our forebears, would it?"

The less-than-gentle reminder that I'd destroyed a library almost overrode the feeling of awe that warmed me at her calling me *Frenhines.*

"I will keep the soup away from the works, I promise. I just fear that we may not have enough time to do the research we desperately need."

"We all fear that, Your Majesty. Yet there is little to be done but progress. You and your consort must take care of yourselves, as you two are our only real hope of defeating the dragon." The matron gave me a motherly smile and then left me alone with Gwyn to eat.

"Good soup," he observed simply.

"Yeah." I was so distracted I hadn't even tasted the bite I'd put in my mouth, so I had no idea. "Did you see the look in the eyes of the elves who led us here? The head librarian wasn't kidding when she said everyone was afraid."

"I did. She's right, though. There's nothing that we can do except keep looking for answers."

"Speaking of which, have you found any?"

"Oh. Yeah, there's a big book she brought me that had the title of 'Answers.' The table of contents asks what you're looking for an answer to, and the eighteenth chapter is about dragons."

I gave him the sort of glare southern girls are famous for, but it didn't do much good. He was paying more attention to his soup than to me, so I decided I couldn't be too irritated at him for using the same line I would've used, and then pondered quietly, "I wonder whether it has anything to do with the resistance that Gwenda has to magic."

He nodded. "I suspect it does. I have the book of prophecy that contains the bit about her at my station, and was about ready to dive in when this welcome interruption arrived. What have you been discovering?"

It was really mostly small things that I'd been reading about, since I'd already read through most all of the primary work of prophecy. I told him about it, and we spent a little while in more or less comfortable small talk.

Before long we were back at it. The library staff wouldn't even allow us to bus our own dishes, grabbing them out of our hands and pointing us back toward the tables with gentle smiles warming their faces and fear lighting up their eyes.

We probably would have kept going all night, too, if the librarians hadn't broken our concentration by dimming the lights.

A glance over my shoulder told me that they'd erected a privacy screen and two cots entirely without us noticing.

"You need rest," the head librarian silenced my objection. "Both of you. Your studies will be in vain if you work yourself into a stunned coma."

We chatted about what we'd learned as we both slipped into the pajamas they'd brought. I laughed at the modesty of the ankle-to-throat coverings, especially in a land where most warriors, male and female, went topless or nearly so, but my dutiful young attendant primly explained that I was the queen, and that was simply that.

The Library

"Wake up, lazyhead."

I gave Gwyn the best single-eyed glare I could. It wasn't effective at all, so I sat up out of what had been an extraordinarily comfortable bed for the night. Giving him the double-eyed version seemed like too much effort, so I just grimaced instead.

"Fine. What time is it?" I noticed he was already completely dressed.

"Who cares? We have research to do."

"I care." I stamped into the tiny privacy area and relieved myself, and was met on the way out by a feisty little girl I hadn't noticed. She swept around me, snagged the bucket much too cheerfully, and took it out of the room.

"I wonder where they take that."

"Neither one of us probably wants to know. But living in the trees, it's not like they don't have plenty of ground area to dig waste pits."

"I know. It's just weird sometimes. Back in Mississippi we had running water, and there's even plumbing at Cysegredig. I can get used to what I used to consider camping activities when we're on the trail—you know, actually camping—but here it's just weird."

We both smiled silently as the attendant returned with an empty bucket. I noticed her sort of fade back into a corner this time, and was struck by how I didn't manage to see her there before.

"Talaith has a question," Gwyn started, but I shushed him.

"No, no. I do not have a question. None at all. We need to get back to research."

The girl looked at him, and then at me, curiously. When no further explanation was offered, she quickly returned to a neutral, waiting expression.

"And now, back to the joy of 'The Magic of the Third Age of the Elven Kingdoms,' and what a pleasant reading experience that is," Gwyn muttered and turned back to the table and the large tome that still lay open on it.

"The answer's got to be here somewhere," I said, trying to toss something bright into the conversation as I went back to my own current research target that was something along the lines of magical animal husbandry.

"No," he said, fixing my gaze across the table. "No, the answer doesn't. We need to face that potential reality. I'm hopeful as you are that we'll find it, but there's no guarantees. Do we need to set a time to give up if we haven't found it yet?"

"Thanks for being mister negative, bless your little heart. No, we don't need to do that yet. What we need to do is put our noses into the books we have and read."

"As you wish."

Silence stretched till breakfast arrived. It was a simple collection of ham and eggs, obviously the production of the penned animals we'd seen on the forest floor. By that point I'd moved through animal husbandry and agronomy and was stuck in a weirdly technical book about how lighting systems of old used to work. I recognized some of it as an attempt to emulate the power grid on Earth, using copper wire and other materials brought over through the ley gates. And there was an actual chapter on how electricity ought to work, only the chapter admitted they apparently got it very wrong with their lemons connected to potatoes.

Part of me wished I'd paid more attention to the topic on Earth. Part of me just wanted to eat breakfast.

"Where'd you learn to read ancient elf?" I asked as we munched on food that was, once again, placed a careful distance from any of the works that were sheltered in the southern library.

"I used to think my parents wanted me to read, since they were the ones who brought me the books they'd found. But later on, after I'd run away, Teeri laughed and said his people had brought them, snuck them to the house, wrapped and by the front door, with my name on them. My parents hadn't ever had any idea where they were from. Then, later, the clan of the earth taught me how to apply my reading ability to the more ancient scripts. You have to admit, it's not very hard if even a Mississippian can do it."

"Yeah, well, at least we have nukes to kill dragons with."

"What is a nuke?"

I explained the little I knew of them, and finished with a terrified young man across the table from me.

"How can any people be—so destructive?"

"Well, it's a matter of whether you'd rather all surrender and die, or use the big one to kill the ones who seek to kill you."

"At the cost of decades of blight like the one we flew over?"

"Well, I don't know if it's decades or not. I—I think they're living in Nagasaki again."

He shook his head. "I would rather go down, with our descendants remembering that we died protecting each other and our land, too."

"Suit yourself, dragon fodder."

"I—no, Talaith, you are our queen. You must recognize the moral depravity of such a solution."

"I used to, until all the people – my people, now – were at risk." I took another bite of ham and chewed slowly to stifle the flow of current conversation.

The rest of the morning disappeared between the pages of several of the dullest books I have ever read. One was the theoretical treatise that apparently spurred the rangers to manage the forests to their current manicured state, and another was an accounting of ranger forces around the start of the current age—which was kind of interesting in its total tally that would have blown Seph's mind at how large it was. I made a point to pass that along when I saw her next.

Lunch was delivered—a nice thick stew. It smelled incredible. I rose, my legs carrying me all on their own toward the meal, my stomach protesting at how hungry it suddenly remembered being. It had been several hours since our breakfast, I had to admit, but it didn't seem that long. Still, the stew smelled very, very good.

Gwyn moved even faster than I managed, so I had to pause to let him get settled. As I did, I noticed how odd it was that the room was extremely crowded. In addition to the woman who was spooning hot stew into two bowls, a woman with an awful lot of bracelets for a servant, three brawny guys stood against the wall.

"Mmm," Gwyn said. "You've got to taste this stew."

I turned to glare at him but my eyes landed on the woman and stuck there. I knew her from somewhere. I stared for a few long moments, long enough to let Gwyn get a good lead on me in shoveling lunch in, and then it came to me.

"You're—I didn't get your name."

She smiled the same pretty smile I saw when she'd accompanied Glynis to our cage the first evening we arrived. I wondered for just a moment why one of Glynis's chief ladies would bring us lunch, and then she interrupted me.

"You should eat, Talaith. You must be starving."

She was right. I was starving. But as I turned to the table to eat I saw Gwyn clutch at his throat, his face rapidly taking on a blue sheen and his lips turning white. Stuck in a moment of horror I watched her leap across the table, slip a dagger out of somewhere behind her, and slash down the side of his throat in a single, smooth motion, then turn for me.

Meanwhile pairs of rough hands grabbed my lower arms from behind, forcing them down to my sides and away from Draignerthol.

The blue pendant was glowing for all it was worth. The woman's eyes locked on it as she readied her dagger to strike.

They were good, my attackers. They'd struck quickly and paralyzed me initially with shock. Luckily for me there's something about being grabbed so roughly that shook me right out of it. They'd managed to pin my arms so I couldn't physically reach the source of my power, but they apparently didn't know I'd been practicing without it.

The woman was the dangerous one, so I hit her in the face with a conjured column of air. It pushed her back, staggering, and I knew I'd have to do more to her. But it gave me time to deal with the burly guys behind. I'd already been stabbed in the back once and knew how much it hurt. I didn't want to give them time for that. But as I gathered the energy for another lightning bolt I remembered the books all around us. I'd burned one library down and didn't want to be responsible for doing the same to the other one.

Instead, I switched lightning to heat and applied it near my arms, causing the men to yelp, release me, and stagger backward. That was what I needed as I spun, grabbed Draignerthol to connect to the greater power, and tried out a spell I'd seen in the dragon's book.

An arrow of air formed along my arm as I drew back an imaginary bow. Clunky, it was, especially in a small space, but it was the weapon I knew. Besides, I was essentially just guiding air with my mind, so it didn't matter what the make-believe bow looked like. I loosed three shafts, piercing the men's torsos to great effect, blood spurting out of heart wounds and everything. As the three still-jerking corpses fell I twisted around to face the better-armed attacker of the group.

Unfortunately the woman had already recovered and was in mid-flight across the table once again, this time with her dagger in the lead. I ducked, but still caught the slash of steel across the back of my shoulder.

Poison. Of course, it was poisoned. The wound instantly erupted in searing pain. It felt like the dagger had packed lava into the wound it had opened.

I raised a hand toward her as she uncoiled from landing. She glared at my palm, a snarl stretching itself across her face.

"You will—" she started, but I was done with it.

What happened next is something I'm not particularly proud of, but I'll still probably remember it forever. Anger does funny things to magic. By funny I don't mean humorous, either.

What I intended was to wrap her in air, maybe tie it off, and keep her bundled up while I did something about my protection mage who was bleeding out at the table. But the thought of Gwyn roused my already high level of adrenalin, and I grabbed the wrong element.

Instead of air, I wrapped the woman in fire and squeezed.

She didn't last long. Half a scream, and that was it. By the time her body hit the floor it was blackened and charred, almost non-human.

I didn't give it any time for thought, though. Attackers down, I spun to the table, praying it wasn't too late to help Gwyn.

It wasn't. He was almost dead, but not quite. Long ago in the first library-based debacle I'd learned how to cure poison, though whatever was in the stew this time was far more potent than what they'd served then. Still, it could be cleansed if I could only get his blood to stay in his body.

Luckily I knew the spell for that. After getting stuck in the back by a poisoned dagger, myself, I'd made sure to poke into the forbidden section of the library at Cysegredig to find a healing book. It's actually one of the easier heals to do. Two of them, technically, I should say—first you close the wound, and then you coax the body to spring to action to make more blood. The mechanism is already there, you just have to magically goose it.

I did.

There were lingering problems, of course, even once I got Gwyn's blood pumping again. He wasn't breathing, but that was simple enough to fix with a couple of magical whacks to his chest. Whatever poison was on the dagger was still in his throat, and was probably hurting him as much as my shoulder hurt me, but after getting the more lethal part of it out I had to set it aside and deal with my own injury.

By that point I had help. A little too much help, in fact.

"I'm fine," I argued with the librarian who wanted me to lay down to deal with my shoulder.

"You are not fine," a familiar voice rolled from behind me, its steely anger not even a little bit disguised.

"Hiya Glynis. Welcome back."

"Some welcome. We must discuss this, my queen, but first you and your companion must be treated."

You have got to stop getting yourself attacked in places I cannot go.

Hush, you.

I am serious. You would not believe how difficult it is to watch such a battle, even knowing that you had your assailants at a significant disadvantage.

It's even more difficult to fight it.

That—can be debated.

"Is your wyvern all right?" Glynis's tone made it clear that she didn't really care about the answer to the actual question.

"She's—fine. She's admonishing me for getting myself attacked under your tree cover, is all. Your area is well-selected for protection against wyvern attacks. How is Gwyn?"

Protected against our attacks only so long as we do not wish to burn it to the ground, you should say.

Hush, you. You can't breathe fire, anyway. Can you?

I didn't have much time to ponder what Kluzhka's stony silence meant as Glynis's healer leaned into the rapid-fire prognosis of Gwyn's injuries. My healing had saved his life but he had a while to go before he was well enough to continue his work, was the gist. And, apparently, so did I.

I shook my head.

"There's too much at stake for us to rest and recuperate, and you know it. I've healed myself and others from poison before, and I can do it again."

It was her turn to shake her head.

"I mean no disrespect, Talaith, but we have never seen the like of the poison Gwyn ingested. His organs—he is alive, but only barely so. And—"

"It is not an option." I knew the old woman meant well, but I did my best to infuse my tone with my own sincere meaning.

I might not have convinced her, but I did manage to shut her up. She bowed stiffly.

"As you wish."

I turned a gesture to the smoking corpse on the floor. "Glynis, I—intended to keep her alive. For questioning."

"I would hate to see anyone you intended to kill, Your Majesty."

I sighed, barely able to hide the grin I got from her wry response. It wasn't a funny situation, not at all. I could have died, and Gwyn almost did meet his maker, and it wasn't funny at all, dang it—so why did I feel like busting out in full-chested laughter in spite of the searing pain in my shoulder?

"So," I blurted once I finally got the urge under control, "I did recognize her. She was—"

"I know who she was. I recognize her clothing and jewelry. She is—was—in my inner circle. I cannot adequately describe the betrayal I am feeling, and I am not the one who was physically attacked and wounded. My honor is yours to—"

"Glynis, right now I—maybe it's the adrenalin, I'm not sure. But I don't care about whose honor is whose. I only want to bring the betrayal to light to consider whether it's the only one. Are you safe in your own household?"

She nodded slowly. "I was not willing to bring that up so openly, but your question is a good one. The wyrm's agents are opportunistic, that much seems clear. I shall do what I can to discover all truths," she paused to glance around meaningfully, "and in the meanwhile I will have a healing bed stationed down here. You will wish to continue searching for your own truths, I believe?"

I nodded, glancing back at Gwyn where he lay on the floor. He was alive, it was clear, but his breathing was ragged and his hold on life seemed tenuous at best.

"We'll—continue," was all I could say.

LWCUS

Lucky.

We were lucky to survive that one.

The Possible

"I've got to get better at detecting poison," Gwyn's voice croaked.

I nearly cried in relief.

"How much of the thanks that I am still alive do I owe your healing magic?" he asked. It was difficult to hear his weakened voice from the bed in the corner, so I moved over and sat on its edge.

"Most of it," I said. We didn't have the time for false modesty, or for any modesty at all, really. He needed to know. "The poison—Glynis's people examined the soup and figured out what it was, but I don't remember much—was a combination, one used to dull a person's access to magic, and another rare but deadly concoction that makes scrambled mush out of a person's organs. I stopped it, but it was already too late with all the damage that had been done, so I had to reverse it all."

"How?"

"Her librarian found me a book on internal medicine of the second age. It gave me an idea what was in there, and Draignerthol helped me probe and knit things back together. Turns out my pendant knows something about our anatomy."

"No real surprise. The thing did piece you back together entirely without your help."

"True enough. How are you feeling?"

"Stupid. I let a basic trick with poison take me down."

"Physically, I mean."

"Oh. Terrific. Never been better."

"No, really."

"How do you expect me to feel? You died once too, remember? But just like you, I don't have time to wallow in pity over how much I ache. Help me up and over to the desk."

"You need to rest."

"How long have I been resting already?"

"Like, half of the afternoon. You need more rest."

"I don't get more rest. You said so yourself. We have a dragon to beat and research to do in order to make it happen. Help me up."

"No, I think—"

"Help me up, Alyssa."

"Talaith."

"Whatever. Help. Me. Up."

I thought about being indignant, very, very briefly. But he was right, and I couldn't deny it no matter how much I cared about his health. There was a dragon about to eat us all.

"Thank you," he muttered as I helped lower him into his seat at the desk.

Then he passed out.

"What...what happened?" his voice, still weak and reedy, sang again from his sick bed in the corner, several hours later.

"You passed out. Duh."

"You carried me back over here?"

"I had help. And that help threatened to kick us both off of the tree if I help you back over here."

"Well, I—"

"And Kluzhka said she wouldn't catch us."

"Well, what am I supposed to do?"

I pointed to a steaming teapot by his bed. "Drink that. You need healing."

"The dragon's not going to beat himself."

I couldn't help snorting at the quasi-sexual meaning of the way the phrase would be translated into English, but then I shrugged. "It doesn't matter."

"What do you mean, it doesn't matter? We came all the way here to—"

"I think I found it."

"...to—what?" His tirade ran out of steam just like that.

I pointed once again to the teapot. "Drink. I'll tell you once you've drained that."

He rose to an elbow and reached, but the little girl in the corner was faster. She poured him a cup of the steaming broth-tea combination.

He sniffed at it. "It smells vile."

I shrugged. "It probably tastes vile too."

"Thanks for the encouragement."

"You're welcome. Doesn't matter how it tastes. You need to drink it. Unless you're too much of a wimp?"

"Goading like that won't work on me, and you know it. Still...." He sipped tentatively. "It's not that bad, really. A hint of ginger, some spice. And—bacon?"

The young attendant nodded, and I shrugged. "Close enough, I guess. At least, she agrees. Don't analyze it, drink it."

"Mmm, yum. It's hot, though."

"Drink it. Chug, chug, chug. Come on."

A few large gulps and the concoction was down, followed by the other half of the small pot. The attendant who'd brought it curtsied and skipped out with the tray.

"Now, what—" Gwyn said, attempting to sit up and then stopping with a wince before collapsing back onto his side.

"I'll bring it over there."

"Some protection mage I am."

"So, about that. You did uncover the plot. If I'd eaten the stew there wouldn't have been anybody to put your insides back together, you know. Your sacrifice saved us all."

"And here I am, broken, an anchor on our efforts."

"They say if you just let yourself rest, you might be ready to travel by tomorrow. Kluzhka promises to fly gently and get you back to Cysegredig."

I do not.

Hush, you.

"She doesn't, does she?"

I sighed. "You promised not to eavesdrop."

"When it's my own safety on the line, I can't really help it. But come on, show me what you found."

I laid the book down, open to the start of the chapter on a quirky theory on resistance to magic flow. Rising to an elbow, he read a few pages, then flipped back to the beginning and re-read what he'd already been through. His brow furrowed as he continued.

"Is it—what language is this written in?"

"Ours." I let my own brow furrow to match his. "Can't you read it?"

"I can. Sure, I can. It doesn't make any sense, though."

I looked at him, confused. I was more than a little worried that he'd lost his mind in the struggle. I pointed to the first line. "Here, it says 'Magic powers flow through currents in the air, much as—'"

"Stop it," he growled at me, using his free arm to pull the book out of my hands. "I can read it, I said. I know what every single word says. They just don't make a lot of sense when they're put together like that."

"I don't understand what you don't understand." I looked him square in the eyes, then continued. "It's simple...um...I don't know the word. The study of the world."

"You studied everything in Mississippi?" he looked disbelieving.

"No, not that. I just—there was one class, on—on what made things work." I stopped, pondering. How do you explain physics to someone who's never seen it? Especially after only one class, senior year. But then again, I thought, the elves didn't have much electricity either.

"So have you ever wondered how magic flows from one place to another?"

"No. Why would I wonder that?"

"Because that's the key to this chapter. If you understand how magic flows, it's like a magnetic force field. Only, there are things that keep magnetic force out. And that's what this is all about. That's the key. Do you understand?"

He thought for a long minute, forehead scrunching up in effort, and then gave up with a shrug. "No. But that's not important. You understand, and that's enough. Can you explain it to your father and to—what do you call her? Meanface?"

"Sternyface. And I really ought to stop calling her that."

"Why? You are queen now."

"Just because I can, doesn't mean I—" I caught myself about to give an old, tired English saying in elf, which didn't make it any less old or tired. Switching gears, I continued, "It seems like I owe the elf people—my people—a duty to be—to behave in certain ways."

"Duty? What is that?"

"It's...it's difficult to explain."

"It's not like we don't have some time to try."

"We need to get back, though. Or rather, I need to get back. You—no, stay there! You need to stay here and recover."

"Over my dead body. I mean that literally. You accepted my service—"

"And you performed that service well, taking a big one so that we both lived. You should rest—"

"I'll rest once the dragon is dead."

"He'd kill you by laughing at you, weak as you are right now. The magic-numbing poison hasn't even worn off yet. And now I know it better, thanks to this book, I know it's like a battery—you have to let the forces recharge. Slowly. You won't do either of us any good—"

"Lying here in bed. I'm coming with you."

"No, you are not."

"I hate to intrude..." a voice startled us both from behind me. I jumped and whirled in spite of recognizing the words as belonging to Glynis. "A very nice argument you are having, in fact. I didn't mean to eavesdrop, but I heard that you have a possible solution, Talaith?"

"I do. It's from this book. I'm trying to figure out how to memorize the whole chapter, or if I can successfully just steal it from your library. No offense, of course."

"None taken," she said with a smile, then nodded.

"So I need to get back to Cysegredig with the news. But Gwyn isn't nearly well enough to travel. And that is causing a problem."

"If I may be so bold as to suggest a compromise, then. And no, I am not saying that I wish to see noble Gwyn gone. But he is correct when he says that you have both accepted his guardianship, Talaith, and that is something that I take seriously. It is night outside, regardless, and so you should take the opportunity to rest, yourself. After all, you did not escape the attack unscathed, yourself. By the time you have gotten a good night's rest, Gwyn will likely be ready to travel also. Am I correct?" The last question was directed away from me.

Gwyn nodded, smiled, and settled into his pillow without a word.

"Fine," I grumbled. "Not sure how I'm going to sleep with this news on my mind."

"That, I can help with." Glynis stepped aside and let a serving girl in unadorned white robes serve us tea. "This is a mild sedative and should help you sleep soundly."

She was right.

GWYDDONIAETH

Science.

Who needs simple words when you have words like "gwyddoniaeth" for basic stuff I learned in school?

The Plan

"What is this about magnets and fields? I do not understand a single thing you are saying."

Dad's forehead matched Naissa's in its folds of consternation. Neither was getting what I was trying to explain, in spite of me trying it for the third time already. I sighed.

Dad took the opportunity to look over at a sickly Gwyn, who I could tell was doing his best to stand up in a strong show for His Majesty. He was failing utterly at looking strong, but I didn't have the guts to tell him that. Neither did Dad, which was good. I'd told the king all about the attack on his daughter, the queen, and how Gwyn had taken one for the team. Oh, I might have embellished it a little; Dad didn't need to know that the whole debacle started with Gwyn's racing me to lunch. But it was good to see Dad finally accepting Gwyn as someone who could guard his daughter, misled as he might have been about the incident in question.

Gwyn answered the unspoken question with a shrug. "I don't understand it either, Your Majesty. I trust her when she says she's found the answer, of course, but I have no idea what she's talking about when she tries to explain."

"And yet you thoroughly understand magic," Sternyface stated drily, earning her nickname yet again.

"But not physics," I insisted. I'd quizzed the head librarian immediately on arrival to find out how to say it in the elf language. She'd had to look it up, and what she'd found didn't make me feel any better about the odds of their understanding. It sounds like you're trying to say "physics" by drawing the first *fff* sound out and cutting the last syllable off halfway through. To be honest, it sounds more like an iguana has a head cold than a human—or elf—trying to describe how the world works.

Bless their hears, they hadn't studied it for millennia. And here I was, with one high school course in it, having to teach it. Granted, I didn't really understand it myself. Some teacher I was, I had to admit. But somebody had to figure it out.

The dragon wasn't going to beat himself, that was for certain.

Gwyn slumped a little farther, a tiny motion that Dad, Sternyface, and I all noticed. We shared a look that bordered on exasperation, or crossed over that border a bit in my case.

Dad took his cue from my expression. "Gwyn, we all appreciate your strength and courage. We will need to call upon it again, I am certain, in the near future. That is why we must insist that you seek respite in a bed of healing, either at your post upstairs or with High Priestess Naissa's healers in the temple. No, do not argue," he said to forestall Gwyn's obvious ramping up, "you have two choices, young man. You can go willingly, or..."

Spread hands and a slight leer made Dad's meaning clear on the second choice.

Gwyn looked from one face to another, searching for allies in his silly desire to stay with us. Finding none, he let his head sag. "I will go willingly, Your Majesty."

"Good. Rest well."

Gwyn stood and nearly toppled over before he steadied himself, grinned self-consciously at me, and shambled out of the throne room.

"He is not doing very well," Naissa observed, her tone making the understatement even more poignant.

"He died. The poison he ingested started ripping his insides apart, and I was only able to put him back together with Draignerthol's help. The whole flight back I sat behind him, my strength all that kept him from sliding off of Kluzhka's back."

I would've caught him, she interjected defensively.

And eaten him, probably.

Not when he's sick like that. Eww.

Hush, you.

"I will have healing tea forced down his throat if needed," Sternyface said. "Now, what about the resistance to magic? That is—unheard of."

I shrugged and tried explaining it again.

I failed again, obviously, judging by the expressions of those in the room.

Dad sighed once the silence had settled in sufficiently. "I believe there is a certain amount of irony here. Perhaps that is not the best word, but I can think of no better. It was not that long ago that we were convinced—not that magic did not exist, precisely, but that we would never be willing to give voice to its existence. Now that has flipped, and I am not certain why it surprises anyone that we may be struggling to understand what seems to be a core concept."

"But I need you all to understand."

"Why?"

"Because..." I paused. He had me there.

"I see. So let us move forward. What is the practical application of this knowledge? How do we use it to defeat the dragon?"

"Well, if we can keep him from gaining control over our fears, we can fight him directly."

Dad nodded, his face displaying a deliberately overplayed sense of patience. "Right. Yes. That is true. But the question is more specific than that. How do we keep him from gaining control over our fears, precisely?"

"Well, according to what I read in the ancient book, it's got to do with our magnetic field. Some, a very few, like Gwenda, have the field naturally, and these people are basically forbidden from ever touching magic. But for the rest of us, we can alter it. Change it. It's a—"

Dad interrupted with a nod and am impatient gesture. "I can tell you are excited about this, my daughter, but we do not have time for the lesson in how fields work. How do we change our fields, if that is what you are describing, to keep the dragon from being able to command us to flee the field?"

"Well, it—it requires magic."

He nodded. "Yes, I assumed it would, as did, I believe, everyone else here. We are well beyond the point where we can afford to be put off by that. So what must we do?"

"Find a way to invert the magical field weaves."

"Was that in English?"

"No," I answered tentatively. I was pretty certain I'd used the same ancient elven terms that I'd read, and the words didn't even sound like English ones. Most of them didn't, anyway, but—why was he asking?

"Oh. It sounded—foreign. So. Okay. So we must invert—magical field weaves. Well, if that is all, then what are we waiting on?" He glanced around at the others in the room, most of whom looked as bewildered as he did.

I stepped back involuntarily. "Dad, was that—sarcasm? From you?"

He scrubbed his face with both hands, then looked back up, eyes boring into me. "Alyssa—Talaith—I am sorry. We are here to discuss the defense of our lives and our people, and I am—weary. What you are speaking of is over my head. You and Naissa should discuss the technical parts of our defense plan between the only two of us here who can understand it, and then let us know when a practical application may be administered."

He started to rise but was stalled by the high priestess's hand.

"Your Majesty, I believe I understand what Talaith is describing, so a private conference is unnecessary. But to reverse the weaves, one must know what those weaves are. Do you know how to work that spell?"

I nodded. I'd found it in a book in the library down south, and started to tell her about it.

She held up her hand. "I don't need to know the spell. I probably wouldn't even be any good at it. It is enough that you know it. The main question is, can you counter it?"

"I can. Once I'd read about reversing the weaves I saw exactly what that meant."

"We must test this," Dad said, gripping the chair arms worriedly.

"I already have. The library attendant agreed to serve as my test subject, and it worked. She reported no sense of fear, even though I pushed the spell through Draignerthol as forcefully as I could."

"So, allow me to make certain that I have the plan straight in my mind. You are suggesting that you cast this reverse fear spell on all of my soldiers and all of the priestess's as well as the legions of...dark elves? How long will it take you to work this feat?"

"That would be difficult, and would probably take a while. But I believe that the high priestess has a trinket, a relic, that might help."

He swiveled his gaze to her wizened face, and she grudgingly nodded.

"Does this relic have a bold name like the one our queen wears?" he asked.

"Not that we know. It was not created by anyone with such elevated stature. Still, it is both powerful and useful. We use it for storing healing energies. We carried it to the eastern elves, in fact, hoping that it would do much more good than we were in time for. It…" her voice faltered, and I could see the memories of that death site in her eyes before she swept it away with an involuntary shudder and then continued. "There is no reason to believe it could not hold a counter spell as you suggest, but it has not been tested."

"So let us test it."

She nodded. "We shall, Your Majesty. Immediately, if we may be excused."

I glanced over; something had to be bothering her. She'd never seemed so deferential toward Dad before.

"Yes, but before you go—how do we propose to bring the dragon to where we are all gathered and prepared to meet it?"

I shrugged. My answer for that wasn't great, but it was all I had. "I think…I believe that I can call him through Draignerthol. No, really. There seems to be a connection that draws the dragon to the pendant. We've already had him visit more than once. I believe that, if I tell the pendant that I am ready to swear allegiance, it will bring the dragon."

"You would lie?"

"To save our people and kill the evil one, you're dang right!" I stopped and translated the English I'd slipped into back to elf.

Derisive laughter sounded in my head, echoing before fading into a voice I recognized.

My dear, lying to me is rather impossible. You should know that.

Conversation came to a halt as I pondered what to do next. Dad watched my faraway stare for a long moment and then broke the silence, "Is your wyvern telling you otherwise?"

I could. And I would. And, probably, I should.

Stop it! I can't handle both of you in my head at once.

We're always in your head, my dear. Both of us. At once. That you are challenged by it now is just proof that you are trying to take both of us seriously. That is a credit to you, certainly, but...where would we go? Your head is our little playground, so to speak.

Great.

You sound sarcastic, but who else has two wise counselors so readily available?

I was just about to say that.

I am sure you were. You are quite wise for being such a young wyvern.

Thank—

STOP IT!

...as you wish.

...ditto.

I looked at my dad and tried to wipe the glare from my face. It probably didn't work; I could feel the glare radiating, but he didn't deserve it. I tried shrugging it away. "Apparently I now have the benefit of two voices in my head. Back—in Mississippi," I paused. I'd been about to say "back home" but that would have sounded bad coming from the queen that I needed to be. I sighed, bringing another look of concern from my father, and pushed on, "This state of having voices in my head would qualify me for the crazy house, and probably some good drugs to boot. Here, though, they're telling me how good it is for me that they're here. Which they probably would back in Mississippi too, come to think of it. Dad, how do you know that you're not crazy?"

Dad's expression shifted rapidly from concerned to amused, and he physically deflected the question to Sternyface with a jerk of his noggin. "I wonder that all the time," he responded, "but that is our high priestess's area of expertise."

"There will be plenty of time for consideration of the queen's mental acuity once we have led the troops through the defeat of the dragon," she muttered drily, lancing both of us with a glare. "For now I am satisfied to assume the voices are both real and wise. What did the voices tell you about your proposed plan?"

"That I can't convince a voice already in my head of an untruth."

"Ah. Good. I suggest we file that in the rest of the facts that should go without saying. Did either of the voices suggest an alternative?"

I relayed the question, and after some indignant mutters received a reply that satisfied me.

"That is—not a good plan," Dad muttered when I relayed it to him.

"No," Sternyface agreed with him. "It is not, but in the space between 'no plan' and 'a perfect plan' it is nice to at least have a plan."

"But what if..." Dad started, and then laid out several strong objections. With Kluzhka's help I was able to answer them, and finally he sat back and took in a deep breath.

"Well, then, it appears we have a plan, or as much of one as we will be able to form. Go, then, and inform me when you know of the results of your test." Dad rose and glumly let himself into the private chamber behind the throne room, pointedly not inviting me to join him. It stung a little, even though as queen, now, I had my own private chamber to adjourn to. I still didn't feel qualified to step in there, though, and so I shrugged it off and left through the main door to return to my own room to check on Gwyn and start testing my ability to reverse-weave magical flows.

A Hero's Final Charge

"Talaith," Keion's urgent voice stopped me. I turned to see the young warrior's face open, blank, needy.

"Yes?"

"I need to speak with you. Alone." He glanced toward Gwyn, his face actually pleading rather than stern.

"I'll be there in a minute," I reassured my bodyguard, who glowered at me and then at the prince. "Go."

Gwyn nodded reluctantly and headed toward the door to the castle. I watched him step away and then led Keion into the throne room, closing the door behind us.

"Talaith," he started, and then stopped. His eyes were pleading; he was obviously lost in what he wanted to say.

"Alyssa, Keion. Talaith will always, to me, and I suspect to you also, be your mother."

He sighed, looking down. "That is—that is what I wished to speak to you about, actually. When I met you in the hall that day, I was—"

"Enraged, lost, overwhelmed in grief, rudderless, and the most logical place for that anger and emotion was me, right?"

"Yes, that is pretty well the crux of it."

"Keion, you and I both know that you and I are like one of those Hallmark Channel movies. Never mind, you wouldn't get the reference even if I explained it. But we've had a hard time of it, and I saw the real you back in New York City what seems like so long ago as you stepped up to defend me. You have fought by my side ever since we met. I know you love me. Not in a romantic – just, look, I know how you feel. I know you love – loved – still do love your mother, too. It's tough, and trust me, I can't imagine what you're feeling since your mother was taken from us. I loved and respected her, too, but nowhere near as much as you and your sisters did."

"So can you forgive me?"

I allowed myself a chortle, challenging though it was in a queen's tight-fitting battle armor. "There's nothing to forgive. You did what you did because it was what had to be done, and that is that. Neither of us has been in control of our destinies for any real length of time recently, and – well, hopefully some day that will change. Some day I hope to be Talaith, and you my Cadfael, and my father will be safely back on Earth with my mother making those silly goo-goo eyes at each other like they do all the time, remember?" He chortled at that, and I continued, "I just wish your sisters would come around to like me, or at the very least not hate me."

"They are already. They have been respecting their mourning period, as it right and traditionally required, but I have spoken with them. They know it was not you who took our mother from us."

"Well, that's a relief."

"So...Alyssa?"

"Yes?" His tone worried me.

"If we—if I do not make it through this battle, will you re-member me?"

I allowed myself one dumbfounded moment, and then tried to crush the topic with a pleasant grin. "Hush, you. We will make it through this battle."

"My own studies of martial activities prove that that is never something to assume for certain, but even so, how do you know your defenses will be successful against the dragon's spells?"

"I—" This was completely new ground, me reassuring the proud elf warrior. He wasn't, generally, a guy who needed reassurance at anything – sort of the opposite, really. Worse, the truth was that I didn't know it. We'd tested it as much as possible, with priests and priestesses and then adding warriors and even the king, with me loading up the relic with the reverse weave and then pushing fear through Draignerthol. It was remarkably effective; when I didn't have a shield spell up even my own father turned and ran from me, but with it, nobody moved. Still, I had to admit that I had no way of knowing whether the dragon could just press right through it on the battlefield.

I'd never faced an actual dragon before, at least not on an actual battlefield with actual fellow elves to worry about.

The controlling spell tests hadn't worked as well. Kluzhka's hackles were raised the moment I suggested that I try to control her as the dragon did. I finally talked her into it, and my reverse weave worked well enough, but the fact was that with my regular spell I couldn't quite take control of her, counter-weave or no.

And that was, she told me, quite all right.

"None of us has any guarantees, Keion. You, more than anyone else, know how randomly the battleground must play out. What was that death due to weird friendly fire you told me of, that – Stonewall Johnson?"

"Jackson," he corrected.

"Right. Stonewall Jackson. Random luck in battle. It happens. But we need to get out there and face it. All the clans are already gathering out there on the field, awaiting their commanders. I happen to be one of those—you know, elf queen riding into battle and all—so please know that I will certainly remember you forever if you somehow fall, but meanwhile, if you are done asking questions to which there are no good answers....?"

Keion relaxed and smiled, filling my own breast with a surprising amount of confidence.

Prince Charming was with us again.

He held the door open for me as we marched out to the front doors of the castle.

The armor of the elf queen was spectacular, I had to admit. It was a full suit of formed leather from head to toe, wrapped and formed so tightly that I had no fear of much of anything. Except, perhaps, a big sneeze. Or a dragon's talon, but I didn't want to think about that. Miraculously, though – or, technically, magically – for all its protection it didn't hinder my motion at all. And it was bright red, a color that the queen's ladies said would help me be recognized and followed on the battlefield.

...and hide blood, I hadn't added, because that just wasn't something a queen was supposed to say. At least, I didn't think it would add anything useful to the conversation.

Keion's armor was every bit as spectacular. He and my father both wore matching black leather, my father's purple cape against the prince's vibrant green being the main difference. The three of us created a commanding – and colorful, as usual – vision, to be certain.

Our horses had been brought around already, and Dad swung his leg over his tall black charger and took off without a glance toward either of us. Keion grinned and whooped, nudging his stallion into a gallop beside, and I urged Awel, my beautiful chestnut mare, into a gallop as well. Before long we were flying along the ground, three elf royals prepared to take on the evil foe.

We were prepared to take on the evil foe, with a lot of support at our backs, I should add. Ranging about the clearing in quarters of a circle were the four clans, each with a festooned elf at the lead. Everyone except the king's guard wore bright colors, and the black leather armor of Dad's highly trained battalion of soldiers cut an amazing image as they passed between Padrig's burly warriors and what remained of the eastern clan to take up a place in the middle.

The three of us—king, queen, and royal prince—followed, with Gwyn, Seph, and Gwenda close behind. Soon we were gathered in a massive clearing, just waiting on the dragon to appear. I looked back at Gwyn, who gave me a huge thumbs up—his people were ready. They hid off in the distance, deep inside the tree line, using their ranger powers to camouflage their presence from all scrying. All elf scrying, I reminded myself warily—I wondered if their magic would prove sufficient to hide them from the dragon.

I was conflicted, my negative thoughts bringing me down a little. I'd been told to never underestimate my enemy. Still, the fact was that my negative thoughts didn't make much of a difference. The dragon would attack on cue, or not. The dark elves, our new allies from millennia ago, would attack on call, whether Xlixi knew of them or not. Probably, anyway. I hoped they would attack; if they did not, all was pretty much lost. If they did, they might be enough to sway the battle, or – not.

And at the end of it all, the plan I was setting in motion might save us, or it might cost the lives of my father, the prince, everyone else I had come to love and respect, and even my own.

There really just wasn't anything to be done about all the maybes, though.

I looked around at the warriors—tens of thousands of elves in all. Some bore swords already drawn, and others had arrows nocked, while still others wore the brown robes of the priesthood. They were all ready to die, if needed. Not for me, nor for my father, but for the land they loved and for the people back in their homes who relied on them.

They were scared. Many were terrified, I could tell. But they were all, each and every elf, resolute.

My heart soared at that realization.

"It is, I believe, your place to make a speech," Dad whispered. "You are the elf queen now. The magnificence of the title becomes you."

"I don't have one ready," I objected.

"No one ever does in these crucial moments. Wing it. Tell it from the heart. You will do fine, my daughter."

I looked around at the huge force we'd gathered. "I don't think I can get my voice loud enough."

Gwyn spoke up from close behind, "Your Majesty, if I may interject, thanks in large part to your efforts, it has become permissible to use magic for what cannot be done by hand. Some of— most of—the people may yet fear your magic, but they will fear the dragon more, and many will in fact appreciate the present reminder that you are indeed both powerful and resolute in its use."

I nodded. Gwyn was right. This was a bridge we'd already crossed. Reaching in to grab energy through Draignerthol, I projected my voice: "Warriors! Warriors of the West, of the South, of the East, and of the North. Warriors of the king's guard. Warriors of the priesthood. Warriors of the ranger path. Today we come together on the battlefield. Today we stand and fight. Today we face a mighty foe, a fabled foe that some of you still may believe to be myth. The dragon is not a myth. It is a terrible foe, one who will eat you and enjoy it immensely while sucking the marrow from your bones, if we let him. Today, that shall not happen. We stand, united, against the dragon, and we *will* send him down to the depths from which he came!"

A cheer erupted from the ranks, nearly startling me off of my horse. I mean, a cheer—a real, honest to goodness, loud verbal cheer, apparently based on my speech. I wondered, briefly, what

Miss Staley, my old smiley speech teacher back in Mississippi, would've said. She'd had a time of it with me in her class, that was for sure.

"A very nice job," Dad whispered.

"Thanks."

"Indeed, a nice job," Padrig huffed as the leaders rode up to meet us. "So, Talaith, now what?"

"Now my wyvern calls the dragon."

"Calls the dragon?" Swadda asked, disbelief in her voice. "How, exactly, does one call a dragon? 'Here, dragony dragony dragony! Be a good boy and come to us now!'"

We all laughed, and I smiled. It was good to see everybody armed and blustering toward an external foe rather than each other. Most of the leaders gathered hadn't been around for the first plan, me lying to the pendant, but teasing the dragon to us was probably the best plan we'd come to.

"No, she appeals to its ego. Calls it certain things that no dragon can resist answering. You know, insults its – um, dragon-hood. And then, if all goes to plan, she scoots out before he can take control of her mind."

"Wait—we've already played that one out, and it didn't go well," Keion said.

"We have, but we're pretty certain that since she's broken a dragon's mental control once, she can do so again. That's if he even has time. The archers are watching and will pelt him as soon as he arrives to take his mind off of the wyvern, and besides, she's not his primary target. I am."

"Well, the day isn't getting any earlier," Swadda grumbled. "Let us begin."

I sent out the signal. *We're ready.*

Here, dragony dragony dragony.

The other voice laid in with some derisive laughter of its own.

Oh, come on.

Hey, that was funny.

I— I started to retort, but her bugle call cut me off as it rang both physically and mentally. She was blasting, hoping to catch the dragon, wherever he was in time and space, and anger it. She proceeded to say things about his dragonhood that weren't polite at all, and ended with a jest that was pretty well guaranteed to get her ripped into shreds if he caught her.

It went silent.

I was pretty certain it wasn't going to work as the seconds ticked away into minutes. I started wondering how I would keep the throne with the clan leaders wanting to see me deposed. I started wondering how it would feel to lie to Draignerthol as Plan B.

It was going to be a rough ride back if the monster didn't show up.

"Talaith," Dad said, and then the sky erupted in violence. A gigantic winged form materialized and swept its head back and forth, fire hotter than anything I'd ever experienced spewing from its open maw, covering the entire clearing from one side to the other.

I managed to shield all of us from the withering breath of fire, but only barely in time. Our horses bucked a little, but I felt the little brown trinket in my pocket warm up as it countered and negated the fear spell.

The mood shifted and I heard gasps from the clan leaders around us. They were looking up at the massive red body of the mightiest of creatures as he settled his bulk down to the earth.

I didn't have a long pause, I was certain, but the dragon's landing gave me just enough time to check in with Kluzhka.

Where are you?

Somewhere.

I don't have time to be coy. Where are you?

I really have no idea. When I felt him coming, I teleported, and then I teleported again, and then I teleported again. I am probably on the opposite side of the world from you by now.

Good. Stay there.

I believe your kind would respond—well, duh.

Hush, you.

Alyssa? Seriously, good luck, and stay safe. Win this one.

I will. I have no choice.

The link snapped shut with every bit of urgency and finality we'd planned. We all knew that Xlixi could try to grab control over her if she were present, but the wyvern and I had worried privately that neither of us knew if he could grab hold of the link between us to reach through and control her remotely.

The dragon's deep laughter rang out across the field as he surveyed all the elves who weren't running in terror. Apparently my pause was over. "So, my little elf queen, you have discovered the secret to spell negation. How wonderful for you." As his words rolled out another blast of magic came with them, and this time the elves did turn and start to run.

Good old Gwenda loosed an arrow. It flew wide, which wasn't surprising. She wasn't much of an archer, but she was the only one besides me who was unaffected—me because I'd built up an immunity somehow, and her because she had one naturally.

Still, it shocked the dragon just enough to stagger the flow of his magic. Elves stopped and turned as one. It wasn't a huge break, but it was enough for me to catch up with my own work.

He'd flipped the weaves, I saw. Not a lot, but enough that it was no longer perfectly matched by my counter-spell. That was okay. Now that I knew how to do it, I could flip them back. I did, and used Draignerthol to pour the new energy into the trinket and then fling it across the field.

The assembled elves took up a cheer once again.

The dragon, obviously frustrated, opened his mouth and bathed us in fire. It hit my blue wall and stopped, at least for the moment. I saw that Gwyn was also pushing magic into the shield, and together we held as the dark-skinned elves took the cheer as their signal and closed in. Soon the four clans and the outsiders all converged on the middle.

It was a fool's charge, it turned out. The dragon wasn't dumb, and so this time he had come in fully shielded and ready. The offensive spells cast by the dark elves bounced harmlessly off his side, while the elves from the four clans could do nothing but hack away at nothing, their swords and poles and axes and hammers not even getting close to the dragon's flesh, while he reached out time and again with long swipes of his claws that left bloody heaps of dying elves in their wake. His wings even proved themselves capable weapons, blasting backward and knocking the charging southern and western elves onto their butts. Then with a turn of his head and exhalation of fire he reduced those who'd stepped away from my shield to ashes.

It was hard to not scream in frustration. We were doing everything we could, everything we'd planned. It still wasn't enough.

Doubt crept in. Should I surrender? Tell the dragon "okay, you win"? He would eat a lot of my fellow elves, but it looked like a certainty that they were all going to die anyway.

Why not save us all the anguish of further battle?

I had to at least float the idea. Did Gwyn see the futility too, or was it just my own doubts surfacing?

I cleared my throat and said, over the roar of the battle, "Gwyn, we're—"

"Shut up," he growled. "We're going to win this thing, but I need your help, not talking."

A little shocked over the abrupt way he'd addressed me, I glanced his way, and that was what changed my attitude. In his fiercely calm, resolute face I found the strength I needed. Buoyed,

I bent my will into the magic even stronger than before, pushing the shield strength for all I was worth.

It wasn't worth much, really. But it was worth something. It had to be.

Keion and Seph joined the rest of the king's men in loosing arrows as fast as they could, but they merely bounced off the dragon's shield. Our hope had been that he would tire enough with all of the attacks that his shield might crumble, yet it still held as strongly as it ever had.

Meanwhile Gwyn and I held our shield tight in spite of the barrage of arcane attacks the dragon sent our way. Xlixi pounded us with everything he had, from fear spells to dark clouds to ice to torrents of lava. Each time he shifted the weaves, I shifted the counter-weaves, feeling myself getting more adept each time I did it under pressure. I noticed before long that I was actually anticipating his shifts, changing my own weaves simultaneously to the dragon's attacks.

The dark-skinned elves drew up close, their own shields firmly fixed, and then they split up into circles of ten to twelve in order to combine their magic. I watched it, and the dragon saw it too. Xlixi spun about, taking his attention from us for a moment to address the new threat. He raked their lines with fire once, and then twice, and I watched helplessly as their protective spells failed in spots and people under those spots roasted.

The dark elves started retreating, their numbers diminishing much too quickly. The clans didn't look like they were up for much more, either. The smell of roasted elf flesh spread across the battlefield and made me want to retch.

Desperate was an understatement.

Keion turned to me, dropping his bow and picking up his sword. He bowed. Through the tumult, I could still hear his voice clearly. "Queen Talaith. Alyssa. Please know that I have always and will always love and respect you. Please tell my sisters how I met the end with a noble charge, and ensure that my name is sung with that of the heroes of Kiirajanna."

"No!" I yelled, but it was too late. Prince Charming had already spun about and was charging, full-tilt, at the dragon, who was still turned about doing his best to roast, impale, or bite dark elves.

"Gwyn, help," I called, and gathered as much energy as I could. The books had warned of going overboard; apparently all the fantasy fiction I'd read about burning a sorcerer out had some truth behind it. None of that mattered to me then, there.

Something about watching someone run to their death brings certain realizations to life in your breast. In that moment, I realized what I'd always known: I loved Keion.

Not in the storybook romantic way, to be sure. We'd tried the kissy-face thing and it didn't work out for either of us. But his fate and mine, his heart and mine, he and I, would obviously be forever linked.

And now both his physical body and the very future of the elf people were hurtling toward their mutual doom if I didn't do something.

Something. I had to do something. Just as quickly as the realization had come upon me, so did a plan. I reached into Draignerthol yet again, pushing a wave of blue to and through Keion's charging form.

Gwyn expertly read what I was doing and wrapped his flows into mine, crafting a much stronger spell than either of us were capable of alone, in the same way braided cord is stronger than any of its strands. It might or might not be enough, but it was powerful. Together we wrapped the prince's body in a bright blue shield while we pushed vigorous strength into his limbs.

The prince made good use of the extra strength to leap, not attacking from the ground but instead taking a perch upon the dragon's back. Xlixi realized he had a gap in his shield, but it was too late. The prince plunged his sword between two scales. Gwyn and I adding our combined powers, pressing our full wills behind the prince's muscular arms, forcing his steel deep through the dragon's hide and into the beast's flesh.

It sank in to the hilt.

Xlixi screamed, the dragon's scream blood-curdling. The massive head snaked around, the neck curling back into an S shape. He struck, snapping at the prince, but Keion saw it coming and had already leaped away. The dragon's long, limber tail caught the prince in midair, though, and Keion's body flew over and past the line of attackers.

"Attack! Shoot! Now!" I screamed and pulled out my own bow. My mare hadn't gone very far, and so I leaped up onto her back and pressed her into a gallop. Not at the dragon, of course; instead, I circled, wanting all the elves to see me up, fighting, firing my bow, hopefully cutting a vision of the fabled Rhiannon of old come back to fight with and for them, my gleaming red armor shining for all to see.

It worked. The retreat stopped, the lines reformed, and the elves once again advanced on the heavily injured dragon, the arcane-master beast's shields wobbling and slowly beginning to fail. I hit it in one eye, a perfect shot between the armored plates, and to my relief – and a fair bit of disbelief too – the arrow sank in deeply. Xlixi screamed again, and his agony spurred new hope in the elves, both dark and light. Together we all pressed the attack, seeking to put the monster down.

The dragon swung around and turned its attention directly toward me, as I was now apparently its main threat. It hadn't directly attacked me yet, but that shifted suddenly as it pelted a series of spells my way. The brown relic in my pocket grew hot as I pushed counter-spell after counter-spell into it, fending off the mighty beast's attacks while allowing my arms to fire arrows on auto-pilot, appreciating Keion's expert tutelage over the many

months in the archery practice field while wondering, idly, hopefully, whether the prince still breathed wherever his crumpled
form lay.

There! I saw it, a chink opened in the dragon's chest shield.
Xlixi was so busy trying to fight through his pain and rage that
he didn't notice the opening as I did, and so I started drawing the
energy through Draignerthol for one final, hopefully mortal, blow.

Then...Draignerthol went blank, dead.

Suddenly I could pull my own energy, but the nearly godlike
power I'd enjoyed was no longer there. It just – didn't exist. Gone.
There was a huge hole where power had been. I felt lost. I struck
anyway, arrow and ice spell simultaneously striking the dragon
in the chest and causing it to roar once again. Xlixi roared in pain
and rage, over and over, thrashing and spasming. I struck again.
I reached deep into myself for another blow, one I hoped would
end the battle forever, and then the dragon blinked out of sight.

Silence spread across the field. Elves stood, disbelieving, in
the sudden emptiness, the peaceful stillness, of the clearing.

Everyone stood, shocked, spells and swords and bows still
held in striking pose.

And then, slowly, almost as one, they relaxed their weapons.

Then, they cheered.

A throng grew around, surrounding me, touching me and the
mare I still straddled, everyone smiling upward to me in those
weirdly authentic, full-faced elf smiles of radiant joy.

Gwyn reached me somehow. He, too, was cheering, tears
streaming down his face. "We did it! We did it, Talaith!"

"We—wait—no, we didn't—but he—" I stuttered, and then
Dad was there, too, still up and on his black charger somehow. He
reached across the distance between the horses and beamed.

"No, my daughter," he chided in a voice just barely audible
over the chants of the crowd. "Not now. We did it. The dragon
may have lived to fight another day, but on this day, on this field,

we were victorious, and we and the dragon all know it. We must celebrate."

I take it you won, somehow.

Somehow? Ye of little --

Well, I don't know how to tell you this, but I wasn't putting a lot of faith in the "here, dragony dragony" plan to begin with.

It worked, though.

Somehow.

So, thffffphphpht to you too. It was hard to blow a good raspberry across the mental link but I managed, our relationship having matured, I think, to that level.

Yes, apparently it did work. You should celebrate, long and heartily.

Well, yes. Sort of. Xlixi disappeared.

I saw. The link can only be blurred, it seems, not broken entirely, by the way. I watched the whole thing, as though through muddy pond water. He probably went back to Pazhbojanna. I could tell you were hitting him, injuring him pretty severely. Why did you hold back on the final blow? He seemed weakened enough that a single solid strike would have ended his days.

I...I don't know. I didn't mean to hold back. Draignerthol broke.

Broke? Into pieces?

No, it's still there. It's just—dead.

Oh. That's—not a good thing. Still, you are alive this day, as are most of your people. So at least you won.

For now.

Now is all that matters, Alyssa.

MARW

Dead.
Just...dead.

A Love Story

"I thought you loved Prince Keion."

"Me, too."

"Are you so unsure of your emotions, Talaith?"

"Alyssa, to you, please, at least when we're in private." My protection mage and I sat together in my old room next to my father's, waiting on my move into the queen's chambers, so we were about as private as we could get. "No, Gwyn. I mean – yes, I suppose so. I mean – I don't know. Back on Earth we have lots of examples for how girls my age are brimming with emotion, so unsure of the world that awaits us, so unclear on our own emotions and desires and…well, so on. I used to despise that stereotype, but I suppose that I've now proven it."

"No difference here, Alyssa. I suppose it's a little different since ours includes us boys also, but it's sort of an old joke about how young elves don't have any idea what they really will want to do, or be able to do, as old elves."

"Yes, well, it's confusing. During the battle, I did realize that I do in fact love Prince Charm—er, Keion. But it's not that kind of love. We used to flirt, used to cast steamy glances at one another, but that seems like a whole different lifetime now. Have I told you that we tried kissing once?"

"Just once?"

"Yes – well, no. We kissed after I'd arrived, and it seemed like a big deal. Then, much later on, we tried a real, long kiss out in the woods by ourselves, where we might have actually – proceeded with it. It just didn't – well, it didn't go anywhere. The first kiss was exciting, scary, bold – I was kissing a member of the elf royalty, after all – while the second one was just – I was kissing a brother, is how it felt. Does that – does it make any sense?"

Gwyn nodded, a pensive look on his face. "You've kissed other boys, yes?"

"Well, sure! Of course, I've…. I mean, there was Steve, at senior prom last year. Or, um, maybe two years ago now."

"I see. How did that compare to kissing an elf prince?"

"About the same, I guess. Nine-tenths saliva, and one-tenth wishing for more. I mean – you know, if I'm being perfect honest, and to be honest I'm not sure why I'm being perfectly honest, but I feel like I should right now, so – I've actually kissed Keion twice. Once was the night we celebrated my arrival, out in the darkness on the front porch of the castle, and – I guess I thought I felt something. Maybe I did? I was new here, and still just a girl from Mississippi, and still intimidated as heck by the whole elven royalty and castle thing. He was part of that whole mystique, and I think I kissed that more than any actual person, and so I felt – things – going off. By the time he and I tried kissing in the woods, all that mystique had worn off, though, and so it was – different. I don't really know how to explain it."

"I don't think you need to, though you did tell me about it twice just now."

"Oh. Thanks." Why did he have to point it out like that?

The silence stretched out, with even L.T. giving us the chance to share the moment. Finally he asked, his voice tentative, "So is it? Does kissing boys make you excited still, or are you – uninterested?"

"Oh, I'm interested. But now I'm also the elf queen, and that bears – a duty."

"Duty? What kind of duty?"

"Well, you know, duty is when you – "

"I know what duty is. You mentioned a specific duty without going into detail, and I was wondering how it counters the desire to kiss a boy."

"It – um – it means I have to weigh it against what's good for the people of Kiirajanna."

"You're making stuff up."

He had a point. "I – I guess I am. I just really don't know. People are calling me Talaith and dressing me in the fancy queen's battle armor, and tomorrow I get officially crowned, so I guess – ready or not, queen I am. But how does that work with the fact that I'm still just – a girl? I need romance, just as you do, just as my father does, just as we all do, right? I deserve all that, right? As long as it doesn't interfere with my obligations, I guess I should add."

"So what would the Talaith who came before you tell you?"

I thought about that for a long time, and luckily he let the silence draw itself out as I did. Finally I sighed. "I guess she would tell me – no, I'm pretty sure I can hear her voice actually saying this – that I need to be fulfilled as a person before I can be fulfilled as a queen, and that I need to be fulfilled as a queen before I can be fulfilled as a person. Not sure if that makes any sense at all to you, but she was pretty clear on how the two parts fit together."

He nodded. "So, then. Where does my queen wish to take this part of herself? Stow it away for a while and adjust to rulership, or explore it further? There are many young elves in the realm who, I am sure, would enjoy an opportunity to explore it with you."

I looked over at him critically. He was being coy, I could tell. I thought back to the night we'd met, dancing and cavorting in the village green where he'd grown up. I'd nicknamed him Legolas back then because oh, my goodness he was hot. He had high cheekbones, lovely and smooth alabaster skin, and eyes that twinkled in the candle light. His long blonde hair was almost a perfect match for my own, and the opposite of Keion's dark mane that the prince was so well known for flipping so sensually around his cranium.

As Gwyn/Legolas was physically light, Keion/Charming was dark. Yet when exiled for the practice of magic, Gwyn had turned to the dark elves, while Keion clung to the light skinned ones.

I'd fought for my life beside both of them. Keion had gone from making my knees weak to being a beloved brother-at-arms. What, though, had Gwyn become?

It was time to test that, I figured.

Well, it's about time.

Get out of my head, Kluzhka.

Just – observing. When wyverns decide to mate, we just mate. You elves are – weird. You make it really – complicated. But seriously, you deserve happiness, Alyssa. Step off the edge and see where you land.

That's an interesting metaphor, but thanks. I shall.

"Chatting with your wyvern?"

"I've got to get better at hiding it, don't I?"

He shrugged. "My queen, I am your mage. Yours, and yours alone. You will probably never be able to hide it from me."

I shrugged too, and then continued staring at his features, letting the awkward silence grow into minutes. I wasn't, after all, experienced at this. At this point I was pretty good at fireballs, at shield spells, and so many other things, but – this?

He broke the silence. "So what was her advice?"

"How do you know she gave me advice?"

"She's a wyvern. She considers herself the superior being. She gave you advice."

I tried glaring his smug smile down but eventually had to shrug and nod. "She did. You're right. She said something about leaping off a precipice and hoping to not die at the bottom."

His smile crept up slightly, not quite to the full-on beam that a happy elf radiates, but rather into a self-satisfied, knowing expression. "Do you remember the night we met, my queen?"

I sighed deeply, the memories flooding once again. "Of – of course I do. You were – you were – you were a true joy to dance around the bonfire with."

He nodded and changed the topic slightly. "Why do you call me 'Legolas'?"

"Um – how did you know?"

He shrugged. "I can't recall where I heard it, but I have. Who is this Legolas person?"

I explained the part from the Lord of the Rings trilogy, both in the books and in the movies, and how much he looked like the actor who'd played that character, both in physical features and in attitude.

He smiled, a toying twinkle in his eyes and a weird sensual uptick on the corners of his lips. "I'd hoped it was a positive reference."

I sighed and moved closer to where he lounged, relaxed, at the head of my bed. I was tired of the verbal jousting. I was tired in general, come to think of it, and that made my interest in games much lower.

"Shut up and kiss me," I growled.

"My queen, I –" he tried being coy again, but I cut him off.

"Not your queen. Not tonight. Not right now. Just Alyssa. Alyssa, the Mississippi girl you met so many months ago. Someone who thinks you are one of the most handsome boys in the entire realm – two realms, for that matter. No, shut up. Kiss me, please, and don't you dare make me beg more than once."

He brought our faces close, looked me in the eyes, and breathed, "Yes, my queen." Then his lips embraced mine. Our lips opened as our tongues tasted each other.

Fireworks actually did go off in my head. It was the exact opposite of my second kiss with Keion – emotions came alive and longing struck and suddenly I couldn't think of being anywhere else but in Gwyn's arms.

He stopped. "Was that – did you...?"

"I did," I said, and pulled him back into another embrace.

Coronation

I sat patiently, at least as patiently as I'd ever been before—which isn't saying a lot, I admit. But I did sit patiently while the queen's ladies—I...I guess my ladies, now, in practice, and officially mine very soon—primped and cut and curled my hair and dressed me up.

Coronation day was supposed to be fun, I'd been told. It was everybody's party. As in the whole, great big, entire realm. One huge party. All I had to do, really, was walk in, let them put a crown on my head, and then say "let's party" in a sort of official way, and that would launch a week or so of nothing but frantic joy.

Who could complain, right?

I wasn't complaining. I just—wanted a little more patience. Bless their hearts, it was taking a long time to get the curls to...curl.

I tried to deal with the frustrations of the styling torture by recounting how long and weird the path had been to get there.

411

The battle had sort of ended and everybody had cheered and celebrated, and then the dead and wounded lying around the clearing had suddenly mattered once again. Sternyface's priests went to work, and they had a ton of patching up to do on wounded elves. The dead had to be dealt with, too, and I was horrified to learn that over two thousand had perished in spite of the best protective spells I and Gwyn and the dark elves could cast.

It was a heavy price to pay.

Over the objections of nearly everybody else, I pitched in to arranging the dead, the other leaders grudgingly joining me. As I worked, the little elf girl from the eastern clan popped back in to my mind. I still hadn't learned her name. I resolved to do that, now that at least a temporary peace was won. Strangely, her face now stood for all of the turmoil, all the death we'd seen. The image needed— it *deserved* a name.

Meanwhile, Keion was the worst. Physically he was okay, with just a few broken ribs, a split collarbone, and a series of very dark bruises to nurse. Sternyface herself healed his injuries, leaving soreness and a few bruises as well as an arm that would probably stay in a sling for a while, but no real threats to his future health. But his charge was already the subject of bardds' clamoring tales, and elves everywhere swooned as he approached. Prince Charming's head didn't really need the ego boost, but he certainly got it. I—I worked through my own issues and kept smiling, pleasantly and benignly, toward and about him.

The matter of what to do about the dark elves required some serious diplomacy efforts. I really wanted them to join their brethren in equality as a recognized clan of their own, a discussion my father recused himself from on the basis of our earlier debates about racism. But Gwyn, Keion, and Padrig all advised me that neither the dark-skinned elves nor their paler brethren would be all that keen for the people of the soil to do away with a centuries-long way of life to find homes within the castle or its surrounding villages.

They were right, too. I listened to their advice and then approached the dark elders with what I hoped would be received as a suggestion rather than a request. Immediately, without giving it much thought at all, they unanimously and somewhat rudely turned the idea down. They would be happy, they explained, to join me in the revelry of my coronation, but there was no way they would lower themselves to our standard of living.

At least, they agreed to open communications going forward. No more hiding from our rangers, that meant. It also meant that I could learn from their magic wielders, and vice versa, and that wouldn't be a bad thing at all.

At the end of the discussions, I think I was the one who walked away with the greatest benefit. I had come to understand that the dark elves wanted recognition and equality, but not cultural incorporation. To ask them to move to "light elf" towns was, they had gently explained and I had finally understood, the same as asking them to give up everything that was important to them, culturally. They were who they were because of who they had always been, and that was very important to them.

As queen, I would need to teach my own lighter skinned brethren what I had learned in the process. Later, that is. We had some partying to do.

Finally, the ladies were done. I stood, solemnly thanked them for their efforts, and left the queen's antechamber—my antechamber, now, weird as that felt to admit—to process down the hall. Gwyn immediately took his place to my right. Keion, his right arm in a sling but otherwise holding himself up as every inch of Prince Charming, stepped in to my left side.

"You look lovely, Talaith," both said at the same time. I grinned a sheepish thanks and continued silently as ladies of the queen's chambers filled in the ranks behind.

I passed Seren and Meriel in the hallway. My heart still hurt for the queen's daughters. I knew they had to be missing their mother greatly. Still, I was overjoyed to see them look up, meet my eyes, and smile. Seren even nodded, gave me a slight bow of her head and the hand gesture of respect, and then grinned brilliantly, her expression filling me with both joy and hope for a peaceful future.

I made a point of smiling back and returning Seren's gesture, even though it was technically inappropriate from a queen to — well, whatever status they had. We'd figure it out, I knew, but I didn't care about technical levels of respect at the moment. I wanted them to consider me a sister, and I supposed that returning what I saw from them now was a great start.

My father was next. He stood at the bottom of the stairs, resplendent in his black velvet robes and vibrant purple sash. A wide grin lit his face from ear to ear.

As I hit the middle stair, he stepped aside with a grand flourish, and I gasped aloud.

"Momma!"

I blinked, disbelieving, trying to keep up a stately march down the treacherous steps while my eyes filled up with the happiest collection of tears ever.

Momma beamed proudly from the landing.

"How—?" I started to ask, but Dad cut me off, bounding up to process beside me down the stairs, whispering in my ear as he did.

"Now is not the time for explanations. I see that a brief note is in order, though, so it turns out that your thoughts regarding her likeness to Rhiannon were as close to the truth as we can determine. Your mother bears royal elf blood from an ancient and proud lineage."

"So—she can—"

"Yes, she can come across the portal also."

"So...." Meaning flooded my mind as I tried to focus on descending the main staircase without falling down it into a heap. "So you two are going to live here instead of in Mississippi?" I knew the answer as it was tumbling out, but I finished the question anyway.

It was too much to hope for, really, having Momma by my side, and I could tell from her expression that it was an empty hope anyway.

"No," Dad explained, drawing it out with an obviously fake wistful sigh. "I will be retired very soon, and I plan to live out my retirement well away from dragons and faeries and the like."

I halted us briefly on the landing beside Momma. "Has he told you?" I asked, keeping the question short because people were already acting antsy about the delay.

"Some. I look forward to the full story," she said, and then kissed me on the cheeks and reached up with a corner of her ever-present sleeve to wipe the moisture from my eyes. "You, my daughter, are stunningly resplendent in that gown Now, let's get this over with."

She smiled, and suddenly I realized what I should've seen sooner – her smile contained the same full-face brilliance that I'd come to expect in elves' smiles. I'd grown up with it my entire life, my momma's smile more vibrant than anybody else's I knew, and hadn't recognized it till now.

The clan chieftains were already spaced about the room. Each had already privately visited with me, and each had apologized for what had happened from their own viewpoints. Padrig, of course, had nothing personally to apologize for, but he still felt responsible for Grigor's treason. The rest were, of course, terribly saddened for what public pressure had forced them to do, and were ecstatic that I would be their queen, and were willing to forever swear fealty to me, and blah, blah, blah blah blah. I listened and, as Meredydd had instructed, avoided rolling my eyes at all the sycophantic baloney spewed forth.

They wanted forgiveness, so fine. I forgave them.

I would never forget.

They probably, hopefully, wouldn't either.

But, this day, it didn't really matter. I sent a warm smile around, and they returned it back to me.

Sternyface said something—I forget what—it doesn't matter, anyway, right?—and slipped a crown on my head. It was heavy, but not nearly as much as what I'd been through already, and that proved at least one old adage about leadership. I smiled at everybody, and then I said something—I forget what—it doesn't matter, anyway, right?—and then I simply asked everybody to party.

And then, we partied.

It was an amazing party. I'd never seen Momma let her hair down, so to speak; she had chaperoned a few of our high school dances, of course, but none of those were anywhere near as intense as that night. She and my father remained locked arm in arm, twirling the night away together. I've never seen, never imagined seeing, two people so deeply, obviously, visibly in love.

As I lay, exhausted, in my bed, sometime before sunrise but not by much, Draignerthol suddenly came back on.

It was just a blip, and then a hum that only I could hear. Then the eye flashed blue once again.

Hello, Alyssa. Talaith, now, formally, yes?

Yes, that is accurate, I tried answering as acerbically as was possible to a voice in my own head. *So, um, hi. Bless your heart, but where have ya been?*

I had to take a break.

How does a piece of jewelry take a break?

I showed you.

Okay, right, you did, so I was being sarcastic. Why in the ever-loving world would you take a BREAK? I mean, anytime, but especially right then, at that moment? I mean, victory was RIGHT THERE. If you'd stayed another moment, I would have been able to rid the universe of Xlixi once and for all.

That is why I had to take a break.

What? I sputtered mentally for a moment, then managed to continue. *Why? You didn't want me to kill Xlixi?*

It has nothing to do with what I want, Alyssa. I am, as you point out, merely a piece of jewelry. But I cannot kill, or even assist in the killing of, the only other dragon in the universe, for if I do, then I cease to exist, myself.

Cannot...other—wait. Other dragon? My sleep-addled mind was really taking its time, it seemed, coming to grips, but the outcome was weird no matter what grips it came to.

Yes.

So, wait. I'm sorry, but I'm not following you. What exactly does yes mean?

Alyssa. You are wise, wiser than many who have come before you. I am surprised, honestly, that you have not realized this before. I was created, millennia ago, from the essence of dragons, Alyssa. I was so named, Draignerthol, remember? It isn't just a pretty shape or a powerful name. I am, for all intents and purposes, a dragon-kind, or a—I guess I can explain myself more accurately as a quasi-living shade of dragon-kind. In any event, I am much closer to dragon-kind than to elf-kind. More to the point at hand, I can only exist as long as dragon-kind exists.

Xlixi knew that, didn't he?

Of course. He must have, yes.

Realization finally dawned on me, belatedly but powerfully.

So when I guessed that he didn't really want anything to do with me, he only wanted you, I was correct.

Overly simplified, but a bit over half correct.

Explain.

Xlixi could do nothing with me, directly, that he couldn't already accomplish through his own power. What he wanted—what he needed, to be honest—was you, bearing me. Had you sworn allegiance to him, since I am by all rights your relic to command, he would have held dominion over me in a way that was forbidden to him directly. It would have opened me and my amplifying power up to his own magic. And believe me, a dragon passing arcane power through a dragon's essence is powerful indeed.

I believe you. It's probably evil as well.

You really have no idea.

Tell me.

First, the dragon king tried to control me. Then, he tried to control you through me. When neither worked, he allowed us to escape with Kluzhka. Then he started journeying across the bridge, killing elves. Your definition of evil seems to be rooted in this image of using your kind as a breeding herd, and he would have done that in the most orderly, uncaring, efficient—you could say darkly evil—manner possible. He would happily have eaten you, in fact, if that would have accomplished his mission, believe me.

You keep saying believe me. Why?

You are an elf.

So?

Elves are skeptical. It is one of your most endearing qualities, but not when trying to have a conversation. Then, you are just annoying.

Thanks.

You are welcome.

I suppose you can't see my sarcasm face, so...question...can you tell when a dragon is lying?

Under normal circumstances I might deny that, but I will offer you this truth in return for my vanishing like that. Yes, I can.

So, when Xlixi said he'd eaten my father's uncle, was he lying?

Why do you care, queen?

It seems such a useless, trite ending for a guy who killed my guardian and the queen, and then attempted to kill me.

You would have preferred to torture him first?

I...I don't know. Yes? I would have preferred better closure, anyway. It seems...cheap.

I can understand that. No, Xlixi was not lying. Cheap closure it must be, then. The villain who killed your guardian and the queen did die in the dragon's maw.

Did he suffer, bless his dark, blackened heart?

Um – probably.

I suppose that's...a good enough ending for such a bad guy. But – question – so you're saying that dragons cannot lie to one another?

I am not saying that. We are much harder to fool than elves, is what I'm saying.

That's – that's enough.

So.... Now what?

Now what, for me, or now what, for you?

For us, I think. Unless you're planning on leaving.

No, I don't believe that would be appropriate.

That response got me wondering, but I let the pendant continue. *Go on.*

You have a lot of healing work to be done. I recall you saying something about working to heal the blight, and that is important. You should also look at healing your people, who've been through a couple of thousand years in a plastic bubble, effectively. I get the sense that lifespans are much shorter now than when I was created, as there seems to now be a sense of mortality that I can feel.

Sternyface talked about that.

I'm not one to advise, of course, but perhaps the queen should stop calling her high priestess by childish nicknames.

You're not one to advise, but you're going to advise? I'll take that under advisement.

Hmm. I believe this is when you might say "bless your heart," yes?

Bless your heart, yes.

Yes. So. You have plenty to accomplish now, queen of the elves, and I am and will ever be your loyal jewelry.

Not just jewelry. Pretty much a part of who I am. You are everything to me.

Agreed, Talaith. Good night.

With that, Draignerthol fell silent.

Sternyface—High Priestess Naissa—invited me to her office for a secret meeting the next day. The cozy feeling of her austere chamber, just the two of us sitting there, reminded me of when I'd arrived in Kiirajanna, though the topic was completely different.

My father, the dragon-fighting hero, was eager to abdicate the throne and return to "that simple, backwards area" of Mississippi with Momma. Thus, we desperately needed to select a new king to replace him.

"Keion," I stated.

"Well, of course it's Keion, but we have to at least pretend to fully consider the matter."

"He's been chosen pretty much since birth."

She sighed. "So, Queen Talaith, I take it that you are in agreement that Prince Keion should be crowned the new king?"

"Of course. There's—it seems a foregone conclusion. But—hey, wait. I remember when I arrived, you told me that the king was selected by a committee."

"Yes. He is. You are seeing that committee in action."

"But when I asked, you said the committee included the outgoing king."

"Yes. Your father has made his preference clear."

"Clear, that he wants to be replaced by Keion, or clear, that he really doesn't care as long as he rides into the sunset with Momma?"

A wide smile broke across her face, lighting up her expression for a rare moment of pleasure. "Both."

"I—I figured. At least, I'm not surprised."

"So, now that Prince Keion—Prince Charming, as I believe *some* in the court refer to him—now that he has been selected, I will ensure that it is what he wishes and then go about the task of ensuring a proper transition for the high priestess role as well."

"Ensure that it is what he wishes—you mean he doesn't get much of a choice."

"Of course he does not."

"And the girl he's been promised to since childhood?"

"Will be disappointed, but such is the price we all must pay for leadership and continuity."

"What about Gwenda?"

She shrugged, a wry smile on her face. "The king must father the next queen by a woman from Earth. There is no requirement that he must love the woman from Earth. Your father, in fact, was—is—rare—in that regard."

I nodded, finally starting to understand what had come before me. "So, for the high priestess role, that transition is some time in the future, right?"

The high priestess gave me a strangely sardonic expression. "Some time, yes. But you, Talaith. You, Alyssa, who stands as a version of Talaith, in an evolution we have not seen in many eons—I do not believe you will require my services for nearly as long as—as others have. I would beg of you that I might transition sooner, not later, in your case."

"Others? Plural? How—how old are you?"

"I am—old. The collective is—ancient. Naissa is very nearly as old as the pendant you wear and the spirit that inhabits it. I speak of a role, not a person, a persona, not a collection of flesh and fluids. She who shall replace me will become me, and add to our age. It is—complicated, my queen."

"You will guide me through the transition, at least, yes?"

She allowed herself a single snort, one that contained mostly humor tinged with the slightest bit of derision. "Of course. You will succeed as all Elf Queens of Kiirajanna have succeeded, Talaith. Of that, have no doubt. I and all my predecessors as well as my successors stand as surety to that claim."

I sat silently as a moment slipped into several others, the weight of the breadth of time evident in her pronouncement sinking in slowly.

"Thank you," I said, simply, once the moments had passed and the weight of her revelations had fully materialized.

"You are very welcome. Your right hook still needs some work, though."

I laughed at the memory of our first few days, my punching the high priestess of the land in the face when she insulted my Momma, and then, as we both let our laughter turn to chuckles, I spun about to return to the castle and take my place, for better or for worse, in the long line of elven queens.

in Kiirajanna at the time of this story.

Epilogue (The Final One)

I sat in the queen's throne, a lot more comfortably now. Keion, now Cadfael, was sitting beside me in the throne my father had warmed for so many years, and Sternyface – Naissa, whatever – stood ceremoniously between us. I reflected for a moment on how weird it was, sitting on this side of the throne room while my father, the former Cadfael, stood across from us where I used to stand.

He beamed. Momma, standing beside him, also beamed. Both of their faces lit up with a joy I'd never seen before. I'd dreamed of Momma's face so happy before, but only dreamed, and here it was in reality, and his happiness and Momma's seemed to multiply together to fill the entire room with euphoria.

I guess they had good reason to be happy. In just a couple of months in Cysegredig, they'd had a chance to see their daughter crowned elf queen, and then a few weeks after hand-fasted in the elf custom to the love of her life, Legolas – er, Gwyn.

Keion had moved in to Dad's old rooms, Gwenda joining him in sort of awkward timings that the rest of the castle just seemed to – overlook. His sisters had, weirdly enough, settled in to my old room once I was in the queen's chambers, and of course the queen's consort had taken up residence right where he belonged, beside me at all times.

Now that imminent death wasn't part of our daily lives, Gwyn's inspiring intellect and infectious sense of humor were even more captivating. I tried to remember every day to thank whatever strange luck brought me to the camp of the dark elves that night to reconnect with my Legolas.

Yet now, Momma and Dad were actually petitioning us to go "home" to Mississippi.

I wasn't sure how I felt about that. Growing up there, we were taught to be proud of our heritage, but we were never really sure what that meant. And while I was proud – oh, I was! – of a heritage of kudzu and okra, Kiirajanna had wyverns, and unicorns, and actual fairies, and manicured forests, and – well, and so on. How on earth was that something to leave?

Cadfael – the new one, not my dad – Keion, the names are just way too confusing sometimes – had pulled us into his private chamber behind the throne room to talk at one point. I suppose I'd gotten a little overly emotional, wondering why Momma would want to go back, and he'd stopped it with a request to continue the discussion behind closed curtains.

As it turned out, the new Cadfael preferred gin, just as I'd decreed my own private chamber stocked with whiskey in honor of what my father had shown me, so that was what he kept for himself. My father still had some great whiskey around, though, and he planned to leave it for me – after all, when he retired to Mississippi he would have a fairly massive wealth to draw upon – so he, Momma, and I sipped on what would be a fairly expensive bourbon while Keion sipped on his botanical stuff and listened.

Mississippi, it turned out, was what my mother had always known. She'd traveled with my father, of course, even raising me in the weirdly formal ways of Welsh castle life, but there was something about the gentle, slow Southern life that she loved and longed for. My father, meanwhile, couldn't bear the thought of being without his beloved any longer than he'd already had to (this, through tear-filled eyes) and, to be perfectly honest, he longed for the non-magical, really truly regular, life of okra and tomatoes in the garden rather than tylwyth teg flitting overhead.

Besides, all three reminded me several times, I could, as Elf Queen, cross the bridge and visit them any time I wished.

"I'll have a lot to do," I objected.

"Your predecessor said that too, yet she still managed to visit her family often in London in our early years," Dad answered.

"Momma – I – I don't know how to be queen."

"Of course you do. You've already proven yourself over and over. I've heard the stories, dear, and you have already proven yourself plenty wise, and plenty powerful. I – I and your father – are so extremely proud of you, everything you've done so far. We know you can face the future and be the best queen that Kirra-janna has ever seen."

And as I remembered that conversation, a couple of tears dripped from my eyes. They were leaving, returning to a simpler, slower life. I was coming into my own power. Yet I had allies, friends. Friends who were allies, allies who were friends, and weirdest of all was the overlap and difference between the two groups.

For the first time, I was certain I could stand up to the challenges I faced. I had every confidence in Keion's abilities as Cadfael, our king.

Gwyn, my true love, my heart and soul, and I were a bonded pair, unbreakable.

And my parents? They deserved happiness, whatever that meant to them.

About the Author

Dean by day and writer by night, Stephen H. King grew up being asked whether he was "that Stephen King." "Not the author," he'd say until his writing addiction took hold and made that into a lie. Now he writes and reads and blogs as The Other Stephen King--you know, the one who writes fantasy and science fiction. When he's not writing, he enjoys thinking about writing while going on hikes or long road trips. When he's not thinking about writing, it's usually because he's fishing.

Find other Stephen H. King works at:
http://TheOtherStephenKing.com

Read his ongoing thoughts about writing, authorpreneurship, and other key parts of life at his blog:
http://TheOtherStephenKingOnWriting.blogspot.com

STEPHEN H. KING